THAT MOMENT WOUL~~~~ ~~~~
HER LIFE

The sky began to glow w~~~~ ~~~~
and a gleaming mist flo~~~~ ~~~~
watched, the haze thinne~~~~ ~~~~
mountains in the distance. ~~~~ ~~~~ ~~~~led
and then grew brighter, glo~~~~ with shades of orange,
rose, violet and gold. Slowly the sun rose, stealing color
from the sky and burning away the mist.

"How beautiful," Rhiannon whispered. "It's as if the
world were beginning again."

"It's not a sight you can see from anywhere in Britain
but here," Maelgwn answered. "The sea, the mountains,
the misty air—that is the magic of this land. It speaks
of ancient mysteries, forgotten gods, barely remembered
dreams." He sighed softly. "When I was young, I loved
the highlands best. I once thought never to leave them.
Now, I find the sea calls me, too. I love to watch the waves
breaking and breaking, forever and ever. It reminds me
how short and insignificant life is, that a man should never
measure himself against the eternity of the sea."

Rhiannon looked up at her husband, watching him stare
out at the water. The morning light made his hair seem
lighter and softened the fine lines in his face. All at once,
she was able to stop thinking of him as a king and see him
as a man. She recognized the haunted look, the wistful
sadness in his eyes. Like her, he sought something far
beyond this place. But this man—perhaps Maelgwn the
Great was strong enough and brave enough to find it.

It was the moment she fell in love!

Praise for Dragon's Dream:

"Creative and compelling, *Dragon's Dream* provides fasci-
nating insights into an ancient time of mystery and magic.
Mary Gillgannon's writing is both lyrical and evocative."

—Kathleen Morgan

DRAGON'S DREAM

MARY GILLGANNON

PINNACLE BOOKS
KENSINGTON PUBLISHING CORP.

PINNACLE BOOKS are published by

Kensington Publishing Corp.
850 Third Avenue
New York, NY 10022

Pinnacle and the P logo Reg. U.S. Pat. & TM Off.

First Pinnacle Books Printing: March, 1996

Printed in the United States of America

10 9 8 7 6 5 4 3 2 1

To the memory of James Douglas Morrison
A Celtic bard and magician of my own time

May you and your red-haired consort
find peace on the Other Side.

Prologue

Llandudno Priory, Wales, A.D. 517

"He'll see you now."

Balyn ap Rhodderch raised himself stiffly from the stone bench in the priory garden, grimacing as his leg muscles protested the exertion. The monk waiting for him gave him a contemptuous look, then turned and walked away through the rows of sweetly scented flowers and herbs. Balyn hastened after him, stumbling slightly.

They entered a low, timber building. Inside, the stifling hot air reeked of unwashed flesh. Sweat poured from Balyn's skin as they entered the narrow corridor. His breathing grew labored as he followed the brother's rapid steps, and a squeezing tightness built in his chest. The place reminded him of a tomb—dark, airless, confining.

Some distance ahead of him, his escort paused at a small, rough-hewn door. "Maelgwn the Great," he said in a voice emphatic with sarcasm. The monk scowled briefly at Balyn, then disappeared down the hall.

Balyn glanced after him uneasily, wondering how he would ever find his way out of the mazelike dwelling. Slowly, he approached the doorway. For a moment he stared at the pattern in the wood. Then he took a deep breath, lifted a meaty fist and knocked.

"Enter."

The door swung open at his touch, and Balyn ducked into the small room. Sunlight slanting in from one narrow window struck a crucifix hung on the wall and made it gleam with brilliance. Balyn blinked, his eyes adjusting to the dazzling light which touched the dust motes in the air and turned them to a golden mist. He gradually made out a narrow, palletlike bed, covered with a familiar faded purple blanket. He blinked again and recognized the figure seated on the bed. The man's hair was dark, almost black, and it reached to his shoulders. A full beard covered most of his face.

"So, my friend, we meet again," the man said softly. As he smiled, his teeth flashed in his dark countenance.

"My lord," Balyn answered, bowing slightly. The man waited, watching him expectantly. Finally, Balyn spoke. "Abelgirth is dead."

The man sighed slightly and stood up. Balyn scrutinized his body, draped in a coarse robe. Maelgwn was thinner—the muscles had wasted some—but there was still power there, and the deadly, catlike grace that had once made the king such a formidable foe in battle. The tiny room seemed much too small for him.

"No doubt he died thinking I was a coward," Maelgwn said bitterly.

Balyn looked away. There had been a time when the coastal overlord, Abelgirth, had joined the other chieftains in mocking Maelgwn for his piety and his devotion to his dead wife. But at the end, when he knew he was dying, Abelgirth had called Balyn to him and begged him to seek out Maelgwn, to convince him to leave the priory and rule again.

"Abelgirth sent me here," Balyn answered. He hesitated, feeling the crushing anxiety start in his chest. So much depended upon him, on his words, and he had never been a man comfortable with words, at least serious ones. Give him a joke or ribald story, aye, he could do justice to it. But this . . . how could he persuade a man to climb out of his grave and live again?

"While Abelgirth lived, your kingdom was safe, but now the future of Gwynedd is threatened," he continued. "You must take up the kingship again. There is no one else."

"There is Elwyn . . . and Maelgrith . . . and Rhodderi."

Balyn shook his head. "They are not strong enough. The other chieftains will not rally around any of them. If you do not return . . . Gwynedd is lost."

Maelgwn sighed, his whole body heaving as if a great weight rested on his shoulders. "It is lost to me already. I buried my dreams with Aurora . . . and Evrawc . . . and . . ." he spoke very softly, ". . . my son."

"But we need you," Balyn said in a hoarse voice. "You are being selfish, Maelgwn. Think of the people who depend on you, who fought for you. How can you tell *them* you don't care anymore?"

The scolding tone of his own words worried Balyn, but he could not help himself. He did not know how to be persuasive enough, but perhaps he could shame Maelgwn, make him so angry that he would climb out of this trough of self-pity and fight back. He held his breath as he saw the vivid glow of rage in Maelgwn's blue eyes. The king was famous for his violent temper; more than one man had perished before it.

The flash of flame vanished, as if it had been quenched. Maelgwn laughed, and Balyn noted that his teeth were strong and white. The king remained healthy, despite the meager diet and inactivity of life at the priory.

"Selfish, am I?" Maelgwn chortled. "It seems it is my burden to have all manner of insults hurled at me. The brothers assure me that I am sinful and evil, filled with base thoughts of worldly treasures and the false glory of power. Aye, I am a sinful, sinful man." His face twisted in scorn. "I don't believe any mortal man can meet the priests' demands, only grovel and destroy himself, tormenting his pathetic flesh for the glory of God."

"Then why not leave? You don't belong here anyway. You are a warrior, a king. How can you deny the blood of Cunedag which flows in your veins?"

"It is accursed blood!" The tiny room echoed with Maelgwn's deep voice. "The rest of my family died fighting each other, obsessed with power. I thought I could escape the curse, but there is no escape. Look what became of my sister, Esylt. She betrayed me, she betrayed her own people, and all for a pathetic chance to be queen." Maelgwn's voice trailed off, almost into a sob. "When my son died, I took it as a sign that my line is meant to die out, to perish forever."

Balyn shifted his weight from one foot to another. Dear God, how was he to fight this, to overcome the darkness that seemed to fill the room? Seven years had passed since Maelgwn's wife, Aurora, had died in childbed and the boy child had perished as well. Why did the wound never heal? Could Maelgwn be right? Was his family cursed?

No, Balyn thought resolutely, he would not give in to this invisible enemy which had nearly defeated Maelgwn. He could still fight for his king and win. If only he could find the right weapon, the right words . . .

His eyes swept Maelgwn. The king was yet a handsome man, not much different from the charming, spirited prince he had befriended so many years ago. Always quick to anger, Maelgwn had been just as quick to toss off a friendly jest in the grimmest situation. Merely a boy in the beginning, he had bested them all with his bravery and courage. Tears filled Balyn's eyes. He loved this man more than anyone he had ever known. He reached out and put a soothing hand on Maelgwn's shoulder.

"Let it go. Try . . . please try to be king again. We need you."

In the silence, they could both hear the rustling sounds of the outside world, the coo of ringdoves that nested in the roof.

Maelgwn sighed with resignation. Aye, he did owe Balyn. For most of his life, this big, honest warrior had been his loyal friend. They had fought countless battles together, shared confidences, jokes, even women in their younger days. The bond between them ran deeper than blood. If he looked closely at Balyn's upper arm, he could see his own death written in his friend's flesh. Years ago Balyn had jerked Maelgwn out of the way of an arrow and caught the deadly barb himself. The old warriors believed that if a man saved your life, he had a claim upon you. Whatever he asked, you could not refuse. Balyn, in all those years, had never asked him for anything.

Balyn waited. His brown eyes glistened with tears that made Maelgwn look away.

Gazing up at the crucifix on the wall, Maelgwn's lips moved in silent prayer. Then he turned back to Balyn. "Go and tell the prior I am leaving."

"God be praised," Balyn whispered and then smiled, his face bright with joy. "I will tell them—pious fools. If they dare speak ill of you, I will remind them how lucky they have been. The shores have remained quiet for years, but someday the Irish raiders will be back. Then the holy brothers will be glad you are a king, fighting for their lives outside these walls, rather than praying for their souls within them."

Maelgwn laughed. It was a faint, tentative sound. Balyn knew he had never heard anything so beautiful.

Chapter 1

Narana tapped her foot impatiently at the doorway to the lodge. "Come, come. I don't have all day to wait for you!"

Hurrying to put away her sewing, Rhiannon followed after her stepmother, dodging dogs and children among the hide tents and roughly fashioned wood huts of the Brigantes' summer camp. By the time they reached the lodge of her father, King Ferdic, Rhiannon was sweaty and breathing hard.

Narana went in to announce her. Rhiannon waited outside, her stomach a bundle of knots. Her father seldom noticed she was alive, let alone requested her presence in his lodge. This summons was completely unexpected.

After a moment, Narana came out and nodded. Rhiannon entered and found Ferdic seated on a fur rug at the end of the room, his hands restlessly testing a new bow. Beside him lay a pile of weapons and armor. His lean, powerful body was draped in a brightly patterned tunic threaded with strands of deep green and blood red, his neck and wrists ringed with the enameled bronze jewelry of a warrior. With his long mane of brilliant red hair and his finely chiseled features, he looked every inch a king.

Rhiannon approached her father cautiously. She bowed. "My lord."

Ferdic stood up. "Rhiannon. Come closer."

She stepped to within easy reach of her father's jeweled fingers. Her head lowered, she gazed demurely at his dusty, leather-clad feet. After a moment, Ferdic reached out to grasp one of Rhiannon's long red braids, running his hand along it as a man might test a finely honed blade.

"I had not noticed before what a comely little thing you've grown to be." Ferdic's eyes swept over her, taking in every inch of Rhiannon's slim body. "You may well have a pleasing shape too, but one can hardly tell in that drab garment." He gestured at her plain, loose gown in disapproval. "Surely you have something finer to wear. You are a princess; you should try and dress like one."

Rhiannon kept her head bowed, hoping her father would not see the resentment firing her cheeks. Did he not know that her stepmother begrudged her any new clothes? Had he paid so little attention to his household that he failed to notice that Narana hated her?

There was silence between them. Ferdic slipped his hand beneath Rhiannon's chin, lifting her face so he could gaze upon it. For one brief moment Rhiannon met his eyes. Ferdic's beautiful blue-green eyes gleamed, cold and calculating.

Rhiannon looked away, struggling to hide her unease. As much as she hungered for her father's attention, this sudden keen regard did not gratify her, but made her nervous.

Ferdic removed his hand and leaned away from her. "Are you still afraid of men, Rhiannon?"

His voice was gentle, even kind. Rhiannon licked her dry lips and forced herself to answer. "Nay, my lord."

Her father nodded. "Esylt promised me she would deal with the matter."

Ferdic's mention of Esylt made Rhiannon's mind crowd with memories. The tall, dark-haired woman had been much more of a stepmother to her than ill-tempered Narana. Although Esylt had never lived with the Brigantes, she had often come to visit, or asked for Rhiannon to be sent to her. Esylt had loved Rhiannon and protected her; most important, she had been there to comfort her after that awful night two years ago when Llewenon had hurt her.

"It is good you no longer fear a man's touch, Rhiannon. You are a woman now. It's time you were wed."

Rhiannon's thoughts jerked back to the present, and she realized with a shock why her father had asked for her. Esylt had always warned Rhiannon that Ferdic would marry her off as soon as he found a husband wealthy and powerful enough. Apparently that time had come.

"I have thought upon your future husband a great deal," Ferdic said. "I have decided it is not enough that you marry a prince of our tribe. You are my only daughter, and the Brigantes recognize inheritance through the mother's line. It may well be that one of your sons could grow up to be a king."

Rhiannon gazed at her father in puzzlement. No one had ever suggested she might have more to offer her people than a generous bride price to enrich Ferdic's treasury. Was her father plotting something, using her marriage as a scheme to set up his future grandson as king over another territory?

Ferdic moved away and began to pace the room with a restless, feline stride. "I have made up my mind on a match for you. His enemies have discounted him as weak. They say his time is over. But I know better. He is a great commander and a shrewd man. If anyone can unite the Cymry tribes, it will be the man they call the Dragon of the Island.

I have sent a delegation to his new fortress, proposing an alliance between our people. In a few days I expect to know the Dragon's answer.''

Ferdic paused and regarded Rhiannon; his keen eyes pierced her relentlessly. ''I thought you should know what your future holds, Rhiannon. If it matters, Maelgwn the Great is said to be handsome, and not unkind to women. His devotion to his first wife was extraordinary. Her death so grieved him that he even renounced his kingdom for a time.''

Rhiannon scarcely heard Ferdic's last words; her thoughts focused on the name he mentioned. ''Maelgwn the Great?'' she breathed. ''Esylt's brother?''

''Aye. Much alike they were too, both in looks and temperment.''

Rhiannon's mind reeled. Esylt had spoken often of her brother, how handsome he was, how tall and kingly, what a brave and brilliant warrior.

''Nay, I could not,'' Rhiannon said faintly. ''I could not marry such a man.''

''You would defy me?''

Ferdic spoke softly, but his voice was full of threat. Rhiannon backed away a step, shaking her head. ''Nay, I mean . . . I . . . I don't see why he would want to marry me.''

Her father's expression relaxed. ''I'm going to offer him a dowry he can't resist. Maelgwn is fighting to regain his lands. He needs soldiers. He'll not refuse my offer of Brigante warriors.''

Rhiannon stared at Ferdic in dismay. The gods help her! Her father was bribing this man to marry her. Maelgwn might not want her, but he would be forced to take her as part of the bargain.

''Rhiannon.'' Ferdic sounded frustrated, almost angry. ''I thought you would be pleased. I know you were fond of Esylt. Your grief at her death was amazing. I had not imagined the old bitch so loved by anyone. Maelgwn is Esylt's closest kin. It should not be hard for you to bind yourself to such a man.''

Harsh, choking pain filled Rhiannon. Esylt's death had left a deep emptiness inside her, and her father's cruel way of speaking of her loss made it more difficult to bear. He had told her the news almost casually last spring, as if Esylt's passing was no more than interesting gossip. When Rhiannon broke down and cried in front of him, he only shrugged and told her it was nothing to weep over. Esylt was getting old, he said, and losing her looks. He hoped *he* died before he grew old and lost the respect of his men.

Rhiannon looked up. Her father watched her, as if waiting for her to say something. What *could* she say? She did not want a husband, especially one who had been forced into marrying her. But there was no point telling her father that. Ferdic had already extended the offer to Maelgwn, and he obviously did not care whether she was willing. He expected her to be grateful.

Rhiannon forced her lips into a wan smile. "I would be pleased to marry Maelgwn the Great.''

Ferdic smiled back at her, a grin so warm and dazzling that Rhiannon wondered if it weren't worth lying only for that, to see her father look pleased with her for once in her life.

The smile was gone quickly, and with it the mood. Ferdic lifted his hand in a dismissing gesture.

"Tell Narana to have a new gown made for you,'' he called out as she left the room. "Something that better shows off your charms.''

No one stopped Rhiannon as she hurried through the busy summer camp. She grabbed her cloak from her step-mother's lodge and set off rapidly for the cool, green refuge of the forest. She could not face anyone now, certainly not Narana, with her mocking voice, nor Bouda, who used to be Rhiannon's friend but was now too busy flirting with the young warriors to spend any time with her.

Rhiannon hastened through the trees, heedless of the brambles that caught at her clothes and the rough ground which threatened to trip her up. As the foliage grew thicker, she gathered up the skirt of her gown and crept forward on the moss-covered pathway. She squeezed through a dense thicket and came out near a large tree with a hollow trunk. Bending down, she wriggled into the small space.

Once inside, she began to relax. Here she felt safe, snug as a squirrel in its nest. She leaned against the inside of the tree. The sweat was itchy on her brow; her hair damp against her cheeks. She reached up and brushed it away and felt her pounding heart slow. Then she closed her eyes and concentrated. She willed herself to become part of the tree, to vanish into the forest forever. The rains would drip down her face; the snow frost over her eyes. She would become still, soundless, peaceful.

Rhiannon opened her eyes and sighed. Every creature, every plant was part of the same life force; there must be some way to change one thing into another. If only she knew the magic. Llewenon had promised to teach her how to shapeshift, but of course, that was only more of the magician's lies. She doubted he really knew how to turn himself into a tree or an animal, or visit the spirit world either. His magic was a lie, a way to trick other people into thinking he was important. Perhaps all magic was like that, she thought sadly. Perhaps there was nothing more than this heartache called life.

How often had she wished she had been born an animal instead of a human—a fox or a deer, or even a squirrel or mouse. Everything for them was simple. They were born, grew to maturity, gave birth to their young and died in a few short years. Although death in the forest was often brutal, it was usually quick as well. Animals did not seem to suffer as much as people did.

Animals also did not deliberately cause each other pain, as Llewenon had done to her. That had been the most horrifying thing, that he enjoyed making her suffer. If he had only wanted to bed her, she might have gone willingly. She had heard that sex magic was very powerful, and she was not afraid to try new things. But Llewenon deliberately tricked her. He lured her off alone and took her while her body was unready and unwilling. It hurt terribly, and he had taken delight in her fear and pain. His lust fed on her suffering; his awful thrusting inside her had grown more frantic as she cried out.

Rhiannon clenched her teeth in bitterness. Llewenon's treatment of her was unjust and cruel, no matter what anyone said. Narana implied that if Rhiannon had been an obedient daughter, Llewenon would never have had a chance to hurt her. Her stepmother insisted it was her stubborn solitary ways and her quest for magic which had led her into trouble. That was unfair. In the face of Ferdic's indifference and Narana's hostility, what choice had Rhiannon had except to retreat to the forest and her daydreams?

For years she had felt as if she existed in two worlds, the harsh loneliness of her stepmother's lodge, and the vivid enchantment of her private reveries. The two worlds seldom met. Occasionally, as she painstakingly embroidered dragons and serpents and wolves on her father's ceremonial clothes, she caught a glimpse of a way she could recreate the magic world that existed in her mind. As a child, she had discovered the cleverness of her fingers, and she had worked at needlework until even Narana grudgingly recognized her skill. Through her weaving and embroidery, she was able to find a sense of accomplishment and satisfaction which eluded her in the rest of her life.

Her other escape was the woods. As long as she could remember, she had felt a special connection to the misty, secret world beneath the boughs. Other children feared the beasts and spirits of the forest, but she was at home there. She spent long hours alone among the green and growing things, listening to the birds and spinning her dreams. Her favorite fantasy was that she could shapeshift and turn herself into bird or animal. As a wild creature, she would at last be free of the melancholy and frustration which bound her spirit.

Llewenon had discovered her interest in magic and shapeshifting and coaxed her to be his apprentice. He had taught her some things; she knew which plants eased fevers and stomach ailments and helped bones knit and other treatments. But he had not shared his real knowledge. Llewenon insisted that she was not ready. Then, one night he had come to her and promised to show her magic if she would go off into the woods alone with him.

Rhiannon shuddered at the memory, then wrapped her arms tightly around her knees, rocking herself in the cramped space. She must forget. It was over. Llewenon had been banished forever. Esylt called Ferdic a coward because he did not have Llewenon put to death, only sent him away, but Rhiannon could not blame her father. Llewenon was a bard, a priest, a healer. Many of the Brigantes believed the Learned Ones had the power to invoke a curse that could bring about painful death or shrivel a warrior's manhood. Rhiannon could not condemn Ferdic for failing to take such a risk.

She sighed. Llewenon was gone, but his evil still lingered. Even on the brightest, sunniest days, a shadow sometimes fell across her path, chilling her spirit. No matter what she was doing or how many people were around, the sweat would ooze from her skin, and her heart would race. The strange panic took hours to fade, and even then the sense of dread haunted her for days afterwards.

But her fear was not all that obsessed her. Sometimes her anger overwhelmed her. She wished then that Llewenon would come back and try to hurt her again. This time she would have a knife, and she would make him suffer. She would not stop until she had slashed off his testicles and thrown the bleeding mess far into the forest.

Such vengeful thoughts were foolish, Rhiannon reminded herself. Llewenon was gone; he could not hurt her again. And she'd best get over her anger toward men. She was going to be married soon—married to a king named Maelgwn the Great.

A sense of awe stirred Rhiannon as she recalled the name. Had there ever been a time when Esylt had not told her stories of the ill-fated southern overking known as the Dragon? Esylt always began her tales as the bards did, making it seem that she was speaking of a long-ago time when heroes and magic were common.

There was once a great king, she would begin. He ruled strongly and well for many years, until he married an evil woman. This woman was beautiful, but selfish. She turned the king against everyone who cared for him; she plotted for his downfall. Finally she died, but even in dying, she worked her wicked spell. She stole the king's spirit. He was too weak to rule, too weak to care about his people. His kingdom was shattered, and hunger and fear swept the land.

But there would be a happy ending to the tale, Esylt promised. Someday the king would marry again. His new queen would be kind and good, and she would win the king's love and restore his will to rule. With her at his side, the king would regain all that he had lost, and more. Someday he would rule all of Britain, and the whole island would prosper.

It was an enchanted story, told to a small child who was

eager to believe there could be happy endings. It was only later that Esylt gave the king a name, and later still when she told Rhiannon that the unfortunate king was her own kin, her youngest brother.

Rhiannon shook her head. She was surely not meant to be this great man's queen. She was small, shy, and—as Narana kept reminding her—plain. Most of the Brigante women stood almost a head taller than her, and their full breasts and hips were far more enticing than Rhiannon's slender body. Maelgwn the Great would likely be disappointed when he saw her. He might even demand that Ferdic lower her bride price or provide additional warriors. Her father would be angry, and he would blame her.

The thought distressed Rhiannon, but also made her resentful. She had grown up here in the woods of the north, and she had a place among her father's tribe. As Ferdic's only daughter, a princess, her people accorded her certain freedoms. As long as she did nothing to provoke her stepmother's wrath or draw her father's dispproving notice, she could live her life as she pleased.

Now, she was to be torn from her homeland and wed to a foreigner. She would have to leave behind the familiar landscape of dense forests and rocky pastureland. Her life would change forever. Rhiannon knew from experience that wives had fewer rights than unmarried women. They belonged to their husbands, and were almost completely subject to their will. Would her new husband allow her to explore the woods, to heal her spirit among the solitude of the trees?

A tremor of foreboding racked Rhiannon's body. A small bird chirped nearby, and she shifted her position so she could gaze out of the tree trunk. She spied a finch on a branch not far above her. Its song was sweet and joyful, a warble of delight for the warm spring day.

"Why?" she asked, gazing up at it. "Why must life be so unfair? Why can I never be free?"

The bird continued to sing. Rhiannon leaned back against the soft, rotting wood. How much better to be a bird than a woman, she thought, a woman trapped in the web of her father's ambitious plans?

Chapter 2

"Riders approaching!" the slender boy shouted as he ran toward the warriors drilling on the practice field. He paused before a dark-haired man who towered over the rest, then bowed and took a gulp of air before continuing. "There's three of them, my lord. Eleri said they looked like foreigners."

The tall man raised his brows. "Foreigners? That's all Eleri said?"

The boy took a swipe at the sweat trickling down his dirty cheek. "I saw them myself, coming down the coast road. Three men, all with red hair and bright garments. Irishmen, do you think?"

Maelgwn the Great looked down at the anxious youth and shook his head. "The Irish come by sea, not on horse-back." His gaze left the boy and met that of the bulky, broad-shouldered warrior beside him. "What do you make of it, Balyn?"

"Sounds like Brigantes," Balyn answered. A frown creased his pleasant face and his brown eyes were troubled.

"But what could they want? There's been no contact between our peoples in years."

The two men shared a thoughtful look, then Maelgwn turned back to the youthful messenger. "Return to Degannwy and tell Eleri to greet the visitors, but to delay letting them into the fortress. I want to know their intent before I welcome them to my hearth."

The boy gave a jerky nod and hurried off. Maelgwn motioned to the men gathered round him. They quickly donned their tunics and collected their weapons to return to the fortress.

At the gates of the timber hill-fort, three riders awaited them. Their horses were of the old Roman blood, rising a half-dozen hands higher than the native Cymry ponies, and sturdy enough to carry the tall, strongly built warriors. Two of the men had hair of a rich russet color, like a fox's pelt. The other's tresses were a shade between red and gold.

The man with lighter hair dismounted and moved to greet them. Maelgwn's earlier suspicions were confirmed as he recognized the vivid hues of the man's plaid garments. Crimson and green—the royal colors of Ferdic ap Cunneda, overking of the Brigantes. Years ago, Ferdic had been part of a plot to usurp Maelgwn. There had been bad blood between them ever since.

"Welcome." Maelgwn extended his hand to show he carried no weapons. "As visitors to our land, we invite you to dine with us and enjoy our hospitality. If I'm not mistaken, you are of the Brigante tribe. What brings you to Gwynedd?"

The man smiled, strong white teeth gleaming in his red-gold mustache. "We accept your gracious hospitality, Prince Maelgwn. Your eyes are sharp, for we do indeed come from Manau Gotodin, the land of the Brigantes. My name is Achlen." He gestured to the two men dismounting behind him. "My companions are called Urien and Brychon. We bring greetings from King Ferdic."

"What does Ferdic wish with me?" Maelgwn asked abruptly. With the formalized gestures of greeting over, he no longer felt he had to hide his misgivings.

"If you will show us into your meeting hall, we will gladly share Ferdic's message."

Maelgwn surveyed the visitors with narrowed eyes. He disliked the idea of an unexpected announcement before a hall full of servants, women and slaves. Ferdic was a tricky man. There was no telling what devious scheme he planned. Better to meet with these messengers in private.

"After we share food and refreshment, we'll gather in my council room. You can give me your message there," Maelgwn replied.

The Brigante man nodded politely. If he caught the subtle change in plans, he refrained from protesting.

Maelgwn and his men joined the visitors in the great hall for a hearty supper of salmon, boiled eels and mutton. The two groups exchanged information about neutral topics such as the weather, food supplies and their common enemies—the Picts and Irish—but made no mention of the reason for the visit. After the meal, Maelgwn led the three Brigantes and his four closest officers to another building. He closed the newly hewn oak door and gestured for the men to seat themselves around the massive table. "So," he began as he took a seat on one of the benches. "What does Ferdic want with me after all these years?"

Achlen, the obvious leader of the envoy, cleared his throat. "King Ferdic wishes to set aside the differences between the two of you and renew the ties between the Brigantes and the Cymry."

For a moment, Maelgwn was too startled to respond. He had anticipated some wheedling proposition from the northern chieftain, but nothing so brazen as this. A man he had hated and mistrusted for years apparently sought to become his ally. Had Ferdic lost his reason?

Maelgwn answered with all the disdain the ridiculous proposal was due. "What Ferdic wishes is not possible. Your leader has shown himself to be a traitor and a liar. I don't ally myself with such men."

Around the table, Maelgwn's men shifted restlessly, clearly uneasy with their leader's bluntness. Only Achlen appeared unaffected by Maelgwn's retort. His amiable expression did not waver, and his voice remained smooth and unruffled.

"Ferdic believes there is much to be gained for both peoples in such an alliance, but in truth, he did not expect you to be eager to renew the friendship. He is willing to sweeten the offer and show his good faith by sending you some of his best soldiers to aid you in your battle to regain control of Gwynedd."

This remark drew an audible gasp from the Cymry, and Maelgwn guessed immediately at the thought going through his officers' minds. The Brigantes were famed warriors. With such men fighting beside them, Gwynedd might well be united in one quick campaign rather than through years of fighting. It was like an answer to their prayers.

Maelgwn gritted his teeth. How like Ferdic to offer such a sly inducement. It did not matter; he would never accept anything from a man he despised. He made his response quickly, his voice taut with distaste. "I don't need Brigante mercenaries to fight for me. You may go back to your king and tell him I'm not interested in his bribe."

A wave of disappointment passed through the room, and some of the Cymry glanced nervously at the messengers. Maelgwn resisted the urge to tell the Brigantes even more graphically what they might do with their offer of an alliance.

Achlen's face showed no anger, and his voice remained

as reasonable as ever. "It's not meant as a bribe, Prince Maelgwn." He reached out a large, wind-reddened hand to the cup of mead before him and lifted it to his lips. Swallowing easily, he added, "If I were you, I would not reject this offer so quickly. Give yourself time to think on it. Or, better yet, come to Manau Gotodin yourself and meet with Ferdic."

Balyn, seated on Maelgwn's right, cleared his throat. "Perhaps we should examine Ferdic's offer in more depth. Rhys and I could make the trip north to talk to Ferdic and see what he has in mind."

Maelgwn turned, dreading the pleading look he knew he would find in his chief officer's eyes.

"Ferdic was a very young man when the troubles between the two of you occurred," Balyn continued. "Perhaps he has matured and sincerely wants to right things with you."

"It doesn't hurt to listen," a slender, hazel-eyed warrior named Elwyn put in from across the table. "You can't dwell on the past forever."

Maelgwn gave Elwyn a cold look, then glanced around the table at the rest of his men. They watched him uncomfortably, waiting for his response. He could read the hope in their eyes. They wanted him to agree to this alliance. How could he blame them? It had been two years since he left the priory and began his quest to renew his kingship. Loyal soldiers all, they had joined in his struggle to reunite a country now splintered among a dozen petty chieftains. There were still too few of them to launch an all-out campaign, and Maelgwn had been forced to put his meager troops to work building the new fortress at Degannwy and planting crops so his people might eat. But these men were warriors, not builders and farmers, and their blood bubbled every day with the urge to be off fighting. If he refused this offer of aid, how long would it be before even their fierce allegiance soured?

Sickened by the trap he saw himself in, Maelgwn turned

to Achlen and met the Brigante's expectant gaze. "Very well. Some of my men will return with you to Manau Gotodin and hear Ferdic out. But I have the final say in this matter. If Ferdic can't convince me of his sincerity, that he's truly changed his ways, there will be no alliance."

With that, Maelgwn stood and left the room.

The men left behind remained seated, exchanging troubled glances. Balyn splayed his huge meaty hands on the table and fixed the three Brigante men with a threatening look. "I warn you, if there is any trickery in Ferdic's plan, we will discover it and advise Maelgwn against you."

"There is no trickery," Achlen said. The faint lines around his eyes crinkled as he smiled entreatingly. "Ferdic is indeed sincere. Ever since last year when he heard that the Dragon was back, that he had built a new fortress and was fighting to win back his lands, Ferdic has planned this offer." He shifted his gaze over the men in the room. "There is another aspect to the alliance which I did not have an opportunity to mention to Maelgwn. Ferdic would like to see the agreement sealed by a marriage between his daughter and Maelgwn. He believes the alliance must be sealed by blood to be a lasting one."

There was silence. Glancing around at his fellow officers, Balyn guessed what they were thinking. Maelgwn hated Ferdic, and he would be appalled at the idea of marrying his enemy's daughter.

"What is it?" Achlen asked, obviously puzzled by their uneasy looks. "I'm offering Maelgwn the Great exactly what he needs to regain control of Gwynedd. Why should he hesitate over the minor matter of a marriage? Does Maelgwn have some other plan to secure his kingdom? Is Ferdic's proposal ill-timed?"

Balyn shook his head and sighed. "Nay, Ferdic's offer is not ill-timed at all. Maelgwn needs the men. He knows what an army of Brigante soldiers would mean for our cause. We could accomplish in one season what otherwise might take years."

"Then why does he hesitate?" Achlen's voice was low, slightly conspiratorial. "I was led to believe that Maelgwn the Great was a shrewd man. If his situation is as you say, he'd be a fool to reject this offer."

"Maelgwn's no fool!" Elwyn answered hotly.

"No, he's not," Balyn agreed. "But he does have certain blind spots, as does any man." He met Achlen's gaze coldly. "Perhaps your king failed to tell you about his past dealings with Maelgwn. Perhaps you are unaware that Ferdic once conspired with Maelgwn's sister, Esylt, to see Maelgwn destroyed."

"I have not heard the story," Achlen answered calmly. "But I'm certain there must be some confusion over Ferdic's intent. What would he have gained by plotting against Maelgwn?"

Balyn sighed. His stomach clenched at the remembrance of that wretched time. "Ferdic's goal wasn't to take Maelgwn's lands, but to usurp his own father, Cunneda, one of Maelgwn's allies. While Esylt plotted with an eastern chieftain named Gywrtheyrn to wrest Gwynedd from Maelgwn, Ferdic used Maelgwn's situation as a means to divert Cunneda from his own treachery." He shook his head slowly. "Maelgwn will always equate Ferdic with the vicious intrigue Esylt used against him. If she had succeeded, Maelgwn would undoubtedly have lost his life, as well as his kingdom. It's little wonder he finds it hard to trust your leader."

The younger of the two auburn-haired Brigante messengers spoke for the first time. "I never knew there was bad blood between Maelgwn and his sister. Esylt always boasted of her relationship to the Dragon when she visited our camp."

"Did she now?" Balyn tried to keep the shock from his voice. Why, after all these years, should anything Esylt did surprise him? "That is odd indeed. I doubt any of us in this room can forget Esylt's betrayal of her brother."

"But these events are many years in the past." Achlen waved his hand dismissingly. "We're talking about the future, Maelgwn's future as ruler of Gwynedd."

"So we are." A small, dark Cymry warrior named Rhys spoke up boldly. "And I, for one, think Maelgwn has dwelt in the past too long. I'm tired of waiting to begin our fight for Gwynedd. If I have to dig any more holes or spend all summer hauling rocks and timber, I'll go mad. I want to go to war. What can it hurt to have these Brigantes fight with us? I think Maelgwn is letting his personal grudges interfere with his judgment."

The Cymry men exchanged glances. Balyn could only meet their eyes pleadingly.

Solemn Gareth broke the silence with his quiet, thoughtful voice. "Despite the troubles in the past, I think Maelgwn will come around eventually. Except for the marriage plans. I'm not sure the king will ever agree to wed again."

"But it's time," Rhys insisted. "Maelgwn can't mourn Aurora forever."

"Ferdic's daughter, Rhiannon, is more than passing fair," Achlen put in. "Indeed, I believe she would be an uncommon beauty if she gave more care to her appearance."

"Enough!" Balyn stood abruptly, determined to end the conversation before the dissension among Maelgwn's men became any more obvious to their visitors. "Maelgwn has decreed that Rhys and I will travel north and talk to Ferdic. If we are satisfied with his intentions, we will come back and do our best to persuade the king to consider Ferdic's proposal more carefully. For now," he scowled at the group gathered, "it's inappropriate for us to second-guess our leader's wishes."

* * *

"It's difficult to fight the tide, isn't it?"

Balyn did not answer immediately. He merely watched Maelgwn stare out at the spectacular sunset from where they stood on the watchtower above the gate of the fortress. He had been reluctant to seek out the king after his abrupt departure from the council, but somehow he could not stay away. If Maelgwn wanted to talk about the unexpected message from Ferdic, he intended to be there to listen.

"What do you mean, Maelgwn?"

"If it turns out Ferdic's offer is an honest one, I will not be able to refuse."

"Of course you have a choice. If you think allying yourself with Ferdic is unwise . . ."

Maelgwn laughed harshly and turned, his features etched with bitterness. "Unwise, Balyn? Of course, it's unwise. But it's also likely the only hope I'll ever have of winning back my country. I've resigned myself to that. Still, it doesn't make my decision any easier. I'll never trust Ferdic. His sly, smug face will always remind me of . . ."

"Esylt." Balyn lowered his voice, thinking the very word distasteful to utter. He edged closer to Maelgwn. Did he dare probe his friend's painful thoughts? Would discussing things ease Maelgwn's suffering or worsen it?

"One of the Brigantes said an odd thing, after you left the room," Balyn began. "He said Esylt always spoke of you with high regard; he implied she even bragged of her relationship to you."

Maelgwn looked grimly into the gathering dusk. "How like her to play the devoted sister. I swear, I've never known another soul as incapable of honesty as Esylt. It seems to be her very nature to twist the truth. Every time she opens her mouth, some absurd mockery issues forth."

"Unless she meant her words," Balyn suggested hesitantly. "What if Esylt finally regrets her treachery? Mayhap over the years she's come to realize her betrayal of you was a mistake."

"Don't be absurd." Maelgwn's voice was raw, edged with a tremor of anguish. "Esylt never makes mistakes. She always knows exactly what she wants and does whatever she has to do to get it. It would be utterly unlike her to look back and regret anything."

"Perhaps you are right." Balyn took a step back. He had been a fool to think Maelgwn could ever forget . . . or heal. "She always was a cold-hearted creature, concerned with her own pleasure and no one else's."

"I've never known a more unnatural woman," Maelgwn said. "Every time she got with child, she used some vile herb to kill it in her womb. A woman who cares no more for her own flesh and blood than that surely couldn't love anyone."

"I suspect she had good reasons for aborting her get— she likely never knew who the fathers were. I always remarked that the woman was like a bitch in heat. She's close to two score years now; I wonder who she gets to service her these days."

Maelgwn made a disgusted sound. "I'm sure she still has the wiles to lure some spineless fool to her bed. Over the years, Esylt has entrapped dozens of men in her wicked schemes, not the least of whom was myself in my younger years. I doubt time has stolen all of her venomous charm."

Balyn held his breath, then asked the question which had nagged at him for years. "Do you still regret you didn't have her put to death when you had the chance?"

"Aye. That would have ended things, and perhaps I could have gone on with my life more easily. As it is, I'm never free of her. Even now, she comes back to haunt me—through Ferdic."

Balyn shrank from the suffering in Maelgwn's voice. He had meant to tell Maelgwn about Ferdic's insistence that a royal marriage be part of the bargain, but he dared not broach the subject now. It would be like rubbing salt in Maelgwn's wounds to inform him he must bind himself to Ferdic's daughter in exchange for the warriors he so desperately needed. There would be time to tell Maelgwn about this condition of the alliance later, after the journey to Manau Gotodin. By then, Balyn would have seen the girl for himself. He would have a better feeling for whether Maelgwn might accept her.

Balyn moved toward the watchtower exit. "I must be informing my wife about my journey north."

"I presume you'll be leaving in the morning?"

"Aye. We're all anxious to have this matter settled."

Maelgwn nodded and looked away.

Balyn climbed down the ladder to the ground. He paused for a moment and watched his king, standing on the tower, his tall form silhouetted against the eerie purple twilight.

Chapter 3

Maelgwn twirled a quill pen impatiently as he waited in his council room. Balyn and Rhys had just returned from Manau Gotodin, and he was anxious to hear their report. Recent events made the alliance with the Brigantes take on new urgency. Rhodderi, a rival chieftain whose lands lay to the west, had killed two of Maelgwn's men during a raid. The loss reminded Maelgwn painfully of the vulnerability of his meager forces, the futility of his plans unless he could recruit more men.

A report from Londinium, a settlement far to the southeast, also disturbed him. It was said the yellow fever had returned to Britain, the same plague that had ravaged the land a few years ago. If the pestilence reached Gwynedd, it would threaten his goal of uniting the country. He had little hope of ruling a country disordered by disease and death.

Balyn and Rhys finally filed in, and Maelgwn suppressed a sigh of relief. "Well, then," he began. "Who will speak?"

Balyn gestured to Rhys. "Tell him," he said firmly. "**You** understand the Brigante dialect better than me. Tell him what Ferdic proposed."

Rhys shrugged. "It's as Achlen said. Ferdic wants our people to be allies again, to restore the agreement you made with them when his father was alive. He says he will provide soldiers to help you win back your lands in exchange for an agreement to support him and come to his aid if he requests it."

Maelgwn quirked a brow skeptically. "Those are his terms?"

"That's not all."

"What else?"

Balyn and Rhys exchanged wary looks. Balyn finally spoke. "Ferdic wants you to marry his daughter."

"What?"

"He wants to seal the alliance with blood, yours and that of his daughter."

Maelgwn stiffened. He had not expected this. There must be some way to avoid this condition of the agreement.

"The girl?" he asked sharply. "Have you seen her? Is she of marriageable age?"

"Well, she looks very young," Balyn answered.

"But old enough," Rhys added quickly. "I thought her quite sweet and well-favored. It's not as though Ferdic is offering you an undesirable wench."

Maelgwn's head swam at the improbability of it all. Ferdic was not even as old as he. How could the northern chieftain possibly have a grown daughter? "Are you sure she's of Ferdic's blood?" he asked.

"The girl has passed seventeen winters; Ferdic a score and twelve." Rhys spoke quickly, his voice crisp with the authority of a man used to repeating messages word-for-word. "He would have been fifteen when he sired her. What matters is that Ferdic claims her. I kept my ears alert, lest anyone slip and say otherwise, but it seems the girl has lived with Ferdic for some time. Her mother is dead, but Ferdic says the woman was of noble blood."

Maelgwn leaned back heavily in his high-backed Roman chair. He had expected Ferdic to come up with some clever twist to his proposal, but nothing like this. His men would never forgive him if he refused this chance to win back his kingship simply because he was squeamish about wedding again.

"I must think on it," he announced tersely. "You are free to go."

Rhys stood and quickly left the room, but Balyn remained seated, watching him.

"What do you want? I said I would think on it."

Balyn shrugged. "I thought a friendly ear might help your thoughts run smoother."

Maelgwn sighed. "Perhaps. Perhaps I do need to talk about it." He stood abruptly. "Ferdic has me cornered. It's as if he knew what I dread most and has deliberately made me agree to it."

"Do you dislike the thought of marrying that much?"

"Aye, I do."

"Why? I know it was hard losing Aurora, but you must put the past aside sometime. You need an heir, Maelgwn. You care too much about Gwynedd to leave it unprotected after your death."

"You're right, but it doesn't change how I feel. The matter of the marriage isn't all of it. I don't trust Ferdic. What does he have to gain? If he asked for my help, I would have few men to send him. Right now, I need Ferdic more than he needs me. He's not a man to put himself at a disadvantage."

"He spoke of a kinship between the Cymry and the Brigantes. I suspect he hopes to gain a toehold of power here in the south. He may imagine a grandson of his blood ruling west Britain someday. He seemed sincere about regretting the rift between the two of you."

"You think he laments his part in Esylt's wicked plot? I doubt it. His only regret is they didn't succeed."

Balyn hesitated, then blurted out, "Maelgwn, you should know. Esylt is dead. She died of a lung fever last winter."

Maelgwn leaned forward over the chair. He knew his face had lost color, and he did not want Balyn to mistake his shock for grief. It was a surprise, that was all. This sick feeling in his stomach did not mean he mourned Esylt's passing.

"Are you all right?"

"Of course." Maelgwn straightened quickly.

"Perhaps this will help you let go of your anger, to begin again with this new alliance." Balyn spoke in his familiar, cheerful voice. "Esylt's dead, and there's no point dwelling on the unfortunate past. Perhaps Ferdic feels the same. Perhaps he seeks to put the past behind him and start over again."

Maelgwn shook himself. He was a fool to feel anything but relief. Struggling to respond to Balyn's words, he said, "Ferdic hasn't changed. The whoreson was always a schemer. Don't forget he plotted to have his own father killed."

"I'll concede Ferdic is unscrupulous. Still, we need his warriors. We can't wait much longer to make our bid for Gwynedd. We're so well-nigh desperate, we have nothing to lose."

Nothing to lose, Maelgwn thought grimly. Esylt had brought him to this state of desperation. If it had not been for her treachery, he would never have lost Gwynedd.

He forced his thoughts back to the decision at hand. "The girl . . . you say she is fair to look upon? What is she like?"

"She has red hair, which you would expect in Ferdic's daughter. She is also small, which you would not."

"Small?"

"Aye, a mere slip of a girl she is."

"And her face? What color are her eyes?"

"Some shade of blue, less green than Ferdic's. She does not favor him, except for her hair. Her features are small but regular, her teeth white." Balyn shrugged. "What more can I say? I thought her comely, but who knows what makes a woman pleasing to another man."

Maelgwn inhaled sharply, recalling another decision, another bride. "That's true," he murmured. "None of you—Evrawc, Rhys, Gareth—none of you would have chosen Aurora that day I selected my wife from among Constantine's three daughters. Yet, she was the one I wanted, the one who made my blood run hot."

"But when you wedded Aurora, you were the conqueror," Balyn reminded him. "Now you cannot afford to be so choosy. This Princess Rhiannon is passing fair. You could do much worse."

Maelgwn felt another jolt, another stab of remembered pain. "Rhiannon? Her name is Rhiannon?"

"Aye, I forgot to mention it. It's a Cymry name, is it not?"

Maelgwn nodded. "After the Goddess. It was also my mother's name."

Balyn shrugged. "Odd . . . but . . . plenty of children are named after one of the traditional deities. Some think it makes the child lucky."

"Rhiannon." Maelgwn shivered as he spoke the name. "My mother was small as well. I stood taller than her by the age of ten."

Maelgwn followed the track along the edge of the high cliffs above the breaking surf. The sea was only a short walk from the hills surrounding Degannwy, and he often came here to clear his head and think. The sound of the waves usually soothed him, but today his thoughts ran as wild and restless as the roiling gray sea. It was late afternoon. Soon he would have to return to the fort and announce his decision.

He turned to look inland. The sun shone through the misty air, bathing the distant mountains in a soft, rosy light. The purple-crowned peak of Yr Wyddfa seemed to float in the distance, a faraway jewel, beckoning. An ancient longing washed over him. So many years ago he had been a boy roaming free in those magnificent highlands. So many years . . .

A sharp pang of regret pierced him. Esylt was dead. He was surprised how strongly the news disturbed him. He had never been able to fathom what went on in his sister's devious mind. Now he would never know. What had made her so cold and evil? She had not been like that when she was young, but as she grew older, her ambition seemed to eat away her soul.

Or had she been born evil, and he was too young to know it? He wondered. There were those who thought evil was passed on from generation to generation, like blue eyes or swarthy skin. Certainly their mother, Rhiannon, had been evil. She had hardly waited for his father's corpse to grow cold before she set her sons at each other's throats like a pack of voracious wolf cubs after a choice piece of meat. It was sickening how little she had cared for his father's dream and how much for her own power. Aye, his mother had been a heartless, wicked woman. Why had the curse not been passed on to him? Or had it? Perhaps his own evil was more subtle, more difficult to detect.

He looked again at the highlands, watching them grow dark as the sun faded. For years he believed he had escaped the curse of his family. As the youngest, he was not drawn into the fighting until he was almost a man. He had time to grow up, to temper his ambition with compassion for his people. Childhood had been easier for him than for his brothers. Esylt was always there to look after him.

A dull ache started inside him. Odd to remember how

much he had loved and depended upon Esylt then. That was years ago, long before she turned into the greedy, jealous monster she became. Why had she changed? What had made her willing to betray him and her own people for the sake of . . . of what? That had always puzzled him. Why *had* Esylt betrayed him? At the time, he assumed she did it for the power, but she must have known how little she could ever hope to gain with allies like Ferdic and Gwyrtheyrn. That left only one motivation—her hatred of Aurora.

Rage filled him, blotting out his grief. Nay, he could not forgive her, even in death. She had cost him too much. Not only his kingdom and the men who died in the war with Gywrtheyrn, but those precious months with Aurora. If Esylt had not caused so much trouble between them, perhaps he would have realized sooner how much he loved Aurora. They would have known happiness earlier in their marriage.

But that had always been Esylt's purpose in life, to make sure no one else was happy. At least she had not lived to see him suffer the humiliation of being allied to one of his oldest enemies. It would have amused her greatly to watch him marry Ferdic's daughter.

Good God, he despised Ferdic! How could he care for the man's daughter? What if she had her sire's clever face and bright greedy eyes? How would he endure looking at her? He could only hope she was not as sly and manipulative as her father. He had already known more than his share of clever women in his life—Esylt, his she-cat of a mother, even Aurora in her loving way. He did not want another female plotting behind his back. Nor could he endure a loveless marriage such as his parents had had. Surely it was better never to marry at all than to live with a woman who waited for you to die so her sons could come to power.

Maelgwn shuddered slightly. His father had been a fool

to marry his mother, but perhaps Cadwallon had believed he had no choice. His bride had also brought him a valuable dowry, not warriors or land, but peace. By marrying a highland princess, Cadwallon had finally achieved an alliance between the coastal people and the mountain dwellers and ended decades of war. No matter what his feelings for the woman—and Maelgwn's mother had been an extraordinary beauty—it seemed likely Cadwallon had found the marriage a good bargain.

There was a lesson there, Maelgwn admitted. Kings married for the sake of their people's future. Wedding this foreign princess was necessary. If only it was not so hard, if only it did not feel like a betrayal of everything he had known with Aurora.

He gazed again at the distant horizon, feeling the filmy twilight cover him like a mantle. Aurora. Even now he could see her. Her face exotic and elegant, the proud lines echoing some haughty Roman ancestor. Her hair a swirl of dusky, silken waves, so soft and thick a man could drown in it. Her body lush and alive in his arms. She defied him and fought him, but when she lay beneath him, she was warm and yielding. She was brave, nearly fearless, she had even risked her life for him. But when she whispered his name in the darkness, she aroused something tender in him, something desperate and hungry and wanting, something only she could fulfill.

After she died, he had felt broken, empty, cursed. It took years to forget, to heal. He had been twenty-five winters when Aurora died, twenty-nine when he entered Colwyn, thirty-one when Balyn appeared at the priory gate and begged to see him.

Thank God for Balyn. If his loyal friend had not asked him to return to the world, to embrace light and life and feeling again, he might still be in the priory, wallowing in the pain. Balyn had reminded him of who he was—a king, a leader. All the prayers and deprivation of the priory could not blot out the knowledge of his destiny. Gwynedd remained his birthright, his soul. It was why he stood here now, watching the fading light over the hills.

This land was his, and he would not fail it. He would do whatever his kingship called him to do. He would marry this foreign princess, endure the bedding, get sons on her. He would try to bear her no malice for being Ferdic's daughter, but he could not hope to love her. There had been a time for that, when he was young and whole, before the scars of the years had formed a shield over his heart, and he knew that Gwynedd was the only mate left to him.

He started back to the fortress. It grew late; his men waited impatiently for his decision.

A mist had settled over the coast, and even though it was summer, Maelgwn felt a chill in the air. As he neared the fortress, the fog drifted and thinned and then grew dense again. For a moment, he sensed some vast pattern swirling around him. The forces of destiny reached out, pulling him in. The mist swirled and shrieked with silence, then parted to reveal the raw timber walls of the fortress.

Chapter 4

It was nearly dusk when the sentry announced a large traveling party approaching. At the guard's alert, Maelgwn climbed up to the gate tower. In the growing dark, he could make out no more than a mass of men and horses along the coast road. Their late arrival made him nervous, and he hesitated a moment before giving the order to open the gates. He could not help thinking that this would be perfect opportunity for an ambush. But he had trusted Ferdic so far, he realized, and he must trust him a while longer. He ordered the Brigantes welcomed into the fortress.

Even by torchlight, Maelgwn recognized Ferdic immediately. He had changed little since their last meeting nearly eight years before. The Brigante king's long red hair was still bright, his arrogant features still handsome, and the gloating grin he wore still irritated Maelgwn as he walked to meet him.

"Greetings, Ferdic, overking of the Brigantes. I welcome you to Degannwy and invite you to share food with us and celebrate in peace."

"We accept your hospitality," Ferdic answered, continuing to smile in his annoying way. "We will eat with you and renew the friendship between our peoples."

The rest of the Brigante escort began to dismount, and Maelgwn's servants came forward to take their horses and help their slaves with the baggage. Maelgwn could not help glancing behind Ferdic, trying to catch a glimpse of his future wife. She must be there somewhere, he thought uneasily.

Ferdic seemed to guess his thoughts, for he gestured to the back of the caravan and asked Maelgwn if he would like to meet the princess. Maelgwn followed Ferdic to where a small shape sat upon a shaggy gray pony. The girl had her hood pulled close to her face against the night dampness, and Maelgwn could see little more than her silhouette and her hands holding the horse's reins.

"King Maelgwn, I present to you my daughter, Princess Rhiannon of the Brigantes."

Maelgwn bowed, then reached up to help the woman off her horse. She was as light and dainty as a child, he thought as he lifted her down. Standing, her head came only to his chest. He looked down at her expectantly and waited for her to remove her hood so he could see her face. To his surprise, she did nothing. After a moment, his curiosity got the better of his manners, and he reached out and pulled back the loose cloak.

Balyn was right, she was a beauty—pale, delicate face, straight, freckle-sprinkled nose, small mouth, huge, luminous eyes. But despite her obvious youth, the Princess Rhiannon did not look girlish or naive. Her wary eyes gazed at him with the still watchfulness of an animal. She held his glance a moment, then her long lashes fluttered downwards. He studied the narrow face, searching for some resemblance to Ferdic. With relief, he saw none. And yet, she reminded him of someone.

Without thinking, Maelgwn moved his eyes to examine

the girl's body, hidden in the heavy cloak. Ferdic saw his probing look and laughed. "I had not fancied you such an eager bridegroom." He nodded to his daughter. "Remove your cloak, Rhiannon. Let King Maelgwn see what he has purchased with our agreement."

Rhiannon seemed to grow paler still, but she moved quickly to obey her father.

"No!" Maelgwn responded harshly. "That will not be necessary. I'm sure I will be satisfied."

Ferdic nodded. "Let us go to your feasting hall. It's time to eat and talk."

One of the women led Princess Rhiannon away, and Maelgwn escorted Ferdic to the great hall. As the two men walked side by side, Maelgwn felt his body grow taut as a bowstring. Years ago, when he first met Ferdic, he had badly underestimated him. He thought Ferdic very young then, barely even a warrior. But within months, he had stolen half his father's army and was fighting for the Brigante kingship. This time the man would not lull him into false complacency. Guest and ally or not, Ferdic was dangerous.

The meal was quiet. Ferdic's party was small; the rest of the Brigantes made camp outside the fortress. Ferdic and Maelgwn sat next to each other and discussed the details of the alliance, the exact number of archers, infantry and officers who would stay behind to serve Maelgwn and who would be giving orders to whom. Maelgwn's smithy would provide armor and many of the weapons for the combined army. It was agreed that the Brigantes would take a portion of the arms with them when they went home in the fall.

The other negotiations completed, Ferdic turned to the subject of Maelgwn's marriage to his daughter. "Are you pleased with Rhiannon?" he asked, his blue-green eyes glittering from the mead.

"I am."

Ferdic leaned over to speak into Maelgwn's ear. "It's

well you find her appealing, for there is something you should know before you exchange vows with her. The girl is not a virgin.''

Maelgwn turned and looked Ferdic full in the face, startled. A dozen questions came to mind, but he held them back. "Why are you telling me this now?" he finally asked. "Have you changed your mind about my wedding your daughter?"

"Of course not." Ferdic flashed his smooth smile. "I merely thought you should know. Does it matter that her maidenhead is already lost?"

Maelgwn shook his head. Once he might have cared about such things. Now it seemed meaningless. "Nay, it does not matter. As long as she does not carry another man's babe in her belly, I see no reason why I should not wed her as agreed."

"Good!" Ferdic said heartily. "I told you only as a matter of honor between us. Then, too, if you do not wish to wait to bed her until after the wedding . . ." He gave Maelgwn a leering grin. ". . . there will be no harm done."

"I will wait," Maelgwn said in a withering tone. "But I do wish to speak to her alone."

Ferdic took another gulp of mead. "Are you concerned she comes to this marriage unwillingly?"

"The thought had occurred to me. You treat your daughter more like a slave girl put up in a game of dice than as princess of your tribe."

Ferdic laughed. "Question her freely. Despite her meekness, you will find Rhiannon quite pleased to wed you. She thinks you are a great king; I believe she told me you were 'magnificent.'"

"What could she possibly know of me?"

Ferdic shrugged. "She must have overheard something among the women. Truly, your story is touching, a king so bereaved by the death of his wife that he forsakes his kingdom and enters a priory. It's a tale sure to capture the heart of a starry-eyed maiden."

Maelgwn went rigid with fury. This arrogant, conceited man was mocking him! It was almost too much to be borne. "Never mention Aurora's death again! Never!" he threatened.

To Maelgwn's satisfaction, Ferdic flinched. Then he shrugged again and smiled his silly smile. "I meant no harm. It's best if we forget the past. You are welcome to question Rhiannon. Whether she wished to marry you or not, she would obey me. Indeed, obedience will be one of her virtues as a wife."

Maelgwn considered Ferdic's boasting words. The Brigante king was the sort of man who paid little attention to women, and that made him a poor judge of their true natures. Maelgwn would meet with the Princess Rhiannon alone and satisfy his curiosity, and his doubts, for himself.

It took awhile for him to get away, and by the time the meal and the obligatory toasting ended, he feared the young princess was already asleep. He ran into Gwenaseth, Elwyn's young wife, outside the feasting hall and surprised her with his request to meet with his bride.

Gwenaseth smoothed her pale reddish hair away from her face and regarded Maelgwn dubiously. "It's been quite a while since I showed her to your bedchamber."

"*My* bedchamber?"

Gwenaseth met Maelgwn's startled glance with an irritated look. "Where did you expect me to put her? The guest rooms are filled with Ferdic and his men, and she deserves a soft bed after the journey she's undertaken. I thought you could sleep in your council room, as you usually do anyway."

Maelgwn ignored Gwenaseth's sarcasm. In the absence of a queen, she served as the unofficial mistress of Maelgwn's household. Although she was not much bigger than the Princess Rhiannon, Gwenaseth ruled Degannwy with a crisp authority even he was reluctant to defy.

"I want to speak to her tonight. It's important. You'll have to wake her if she's asleep."

"All right." Gwenaseth wrinkled her freckled brow in thought. "But where will you meet with her? It's not fitting for you to be alone with her in your bedchamber before the wedding."

"Have her brought to the council room."

"Too cold. The fire is seldom lit there. You must see her someplace comfortable. Use the weaving room—I was there a moment ago with the brazier lit. It will still be warm and cozy."

"The weaving room," Maelgwn agreed. "Bring her there."

Maelgwn looked around the small room, taking note of the place for the first time. This was women's domain and he seldom entered it. He walked about, touching objects casually: a big loom and two smaller ones, a spinning wheel, pots for dying wool, scraps of fabric, fluffy bits of yarn. As Gwenaseth said, the cluttered room was cozy. Perhaps his young bride would feel at home amid these feminine trappings.

Maelgwn began to pace. Surely Gwenaseth would not bother fixing Rhiannon's hair or have her put on jewelry. He rather liked the idea of having his bride come to him unadorned and sleepy. It would increase the intimacy between them. So far she was a stranger.

He frowned, recalling Ferdic's strange disclosure regarding Rhiannon's virginity. As hard as he tried to dismiss the matter as unimportant, he could not help being curious about Rhiannon's past. Had she lost her maidenhead at some religious festival? Entered into an illicit relationship with some young warrior? Remembering her demure, almost timid manner, both situations seemed unlikely. Princess Rhiannon's extreme shyness made him think of a beautiful wild thing, a fawn or a vixen.

There was a slight rustling sound behind him, and he turned to see Rhiannon waiting in the shadows by the doorway. Again, the very petiteness of his future wife startled him. He searched his mind, trying to recall if he had ever bedded a woman so tiny. Would it be even more awkward than first times usually were?

"Rhiannon, thank you for coming." He advanced toward her. The torch on the wall flickered and smoked, casting deep shadows over both of them. Despite the darkness, he immediately sensed her unease. He felt guilty for waking her, for confronting her tonight when she must be near exhaustion from her journey.

"I'm sorry if I had to wake you," he apologized. "I felt this could not wait until morning."

He took her hand and pulled her into the light. Her face was pale and drawn, and deep shadows beneath her eyes showed her need for sleep. He must finish this conversation quickly and let her return to bed.

"I want you to know," he began in a voice that he hoped was soft and soothing. "You don't have to marry me. I won't insist on it, and I will settle things with Ferdic somehow."

She stared at him; the expression on her face reminded him of a trapped animal.

"Rhiannon, please, tell me what you wish."

The girl's voice was impossibly soft, as frail and light as one of the fluffy bits of wool upon the floor. "I . . . I am willing."

Her words did not convince him. He could never remember seeing anyone so frightened with him, except perhaps an opponent in battle or a man he had condemned to death. It unnerved him.

Abruptly, he reached out and grasped Rhiannon around the waist. A jolt of energy seemed to pass between them.

Maelgwn could feel her trembling and almost hear the rapid thud of her heart.

"Why do you fear me, Rhiannon?" he whispered. "Is it your father?"

She shook her head.

"What then?"

It took her a moment to compose herself and form the words. She spoke in that light, airy voice again. "I don't know."

His eyes searched her face. Her fear was a shield he could not see beyond. He glanced down at her slight figure. The question was repulsive, but he had to ask. "Is there a babe, Rhiannon? Could you be carrying another man's child?"

Her eyes widened in horror, and she pulled away. "Nay!" she said. "Nay!"

Maelgwn clenched his hands into fists. He could not endure any more of this either. Rhiannon was a mystery, but beyond doing his duty to safeguard that her firstborn was of his blood, he had no desire to know his future wife's secrets. He had asked his questions, and she had answered. He would not press her further.

He smiled, trying to reassure her. "I'm sorry I disturbed you so late. Go back to bed. You have a long day ahead of you tomorrow."

He stared at his future wife for a moment, admiring her exquisite face and the long, flowing line of her unbound hair as it shielded her body enticingly. Impulsively, he leaned over and kissed her. Her lips felt cool and dry, her body rigid.

He released her with a sigh. "Wait here. I'll send Gwenaseth to take you back to bed."

Rhiannon shifted restlessly on the great, soft bed. Despite her exhaustion, she could not sleep. Her conversa-

tion with Maelgwn in the weaving room kept running over
and over in her mind. He had asked her, nay, near-begged
her to refuse the marriage. Why? Was she so unsatisfactory
a bride?

Recalling his probing look when they met, she moved
her hand down to her small breasts, then her flat belly
and narrow hips. Narana had always called her a mere
morsel of a woman, much too thin and slight to please a
man. Was that it? Had Maelgwn been repulsed by her small
size?

She shook her head slightly. It did not seem likely
Maelgwn would be particular about the woman he took
to wife. After all, she brought him a splendid dowry, and
she was not deformed or ugly. Even if he misliked her
looks, any reasonable man would marry her anyway, then
bed her only enough to beget an heir. It had to be something else, some other matter which troubled the Cymry
king.

Perhaps it was her lack of a maidenhead which distressed
him. Maelgwn had asked her about a babe—which meant
Ferdic had told him she was no longer a virgin. It was very
common for a Brigante girl to lose her maidenhead long
before she wed, but perhaps things were different among
the Cymry. Did Maelgwn think her devalued because she
had known another man?

The thought made her angry. She had not given her
maidenhead willingly; Llewenon had taken it. Maelgwn
had no right to judge her. He knew nothing about her!

Rhiannon struggled to suppress her anger. Maelgwn
would have to accept her past. If only she were not so
eager for him to like her. Why did she care? she wondered.
Why did it matter if this foreign king found her pleasing?

Mayhap it was because he was so beautiful, so compelling
himself. Remembering her first look at her future husband,
Rhiannon's breath caught. Esylt had not exaggerated; her
brother was a man to inspire legends. Extraordinarily tall,

with massive shoulders and long lean limbs, Maelgwn made other men, even Ferdic, seem insignificant by comparison. He had Esylt's striking coloring—thick, wavy hair the color of earth, tanned skin, dark blue eyes set under brooding black brows. His features were strong, but finely molded. Any woman would envy his straight nose, his sensual mouth and prominent cheekbones. But there was nothing soft or weak about Maelgwn. There was a fierceness to his strong jaw, a supreme masculinity about his broad, powerful neck. This was a man meant to rule, to command other men.

Rhiannon shivered, recalling his kiss. She could still feel his strong hands around her waist, the pressure of his lips. The kiss had been gentle, but, even so, it aroused her fear. How could she not be afraid of a man so big, so powerful?

Still, for all his accomplishments, Maelgwn the Great did not appear to be a happy man. She recalled the permanent crease marring the skin between his brows, as if his worries never left him; and the haunted look she had glimpsed in the depths of his piercing eyes. What had made him so grim and cheerless? Did he still mourn his wife, the Roman British princess who had died in childbirth?

Pity filled Rhiannon. She knew what it was like to lose the one you loved—she still mourned Esylt. But Maelgwn was a man, a warrior. It was hard to fathom her father grieving for anyone longer than a week, and certainly not a woman. Maelgwn was very unusual to have loved his wife so dearly.

Esylt had talked often about her brother, but now, meeting Maelgwn for the first time, it seemed to Rhiannon that Esylt's tales had little to do with the flesh and blood man. Maelgwn the Great looked awe-inspiring, aye, but he was not a godlike hero or magical king. She sensed darkness and despair in him, a deep grief afflicting his spirit.

Rhiannon sighed. Whatever reason Maelgwn did not want to wed her, it was too late now. On the morrow they would be joined as man and wife. Perhaps he would ignore her most of the time, as Ferdic did with his women. Neglect, Rhiannon knew she could deal with. If Maelgwn left her alone, she would be free to do the things she had always done—to sew, to daydream and wander in the woods.

Rhiannon turned over restlessly. Already she was desperate to get away and walk outside the fortress. After only a few hours at Degannwy, she felt trapped, suffocated. The dwellings inside the fortress were of an unnatural design. The walls met at sharp angles, and only a few openings let in air and light. She would never feel at home here, despite the obvious comfort and luxury of the place.

A wave of homesickness brought tears to her eyes. She missed the cozy clutter of her father's camp. She was used to bedding down on a small pallet of sheepskins in a lodge crowded with people and dogs and lit by the flickering glow of a hearth fire. This bedchamber was foreign, desolate, forbidding. Exactly like the man it belonged to.

She shivered again. She must try to sleep, to put aside her worries. Squeezing her eyes shut, Rhiannon curled up on the bed. She took a deep breath, then another. She pretended she was in her hiding place in the woods . . . safe, content, at peace.

Chapter 5

Rhiannon woke to a knock on the door. She had slept deeply at last, exhausted by her long journey and her worries of the night before. Opening her eyes with effort, she glanced around the luxurious room. The knock sounded again.

"Come in," she called out.

The door opened, admitting a small woman with tawny gold hair and greenish eyes. Rhiannon recognized her as Lady Gwenaseth, the woman who had helped her to bed the night before.

"Good morrow. I've come to prepare you for the wedding. Where are your things?"

Rhiannon motioned to the bundle she had brought from Manau Gotodin. Gwenaseth began to go through the small pile of clothes and jewelry. After a moment, she faced the bed. "This is everything? Your women did not make you a bridal gown?"

Rhiannon shook her head. Narana had begrudged her even the little finery she brought.

"Well, then." Gwenaseth's manner was crisp. "We'll

have to see what we can find for you to wear. You're near my size, or at least the size I was at your age. I must have something tucked away that would fit you."

Gwenaseth wrinkled her brow in thought, and Rhiannon tried to guess her age. Lady Gwenaseth was still very pretty, but her plump body revealed the slight slackness that came from frequent childbearing, and faint lines etched the fair skin beneath her eyes.

"Of course!" Gwenaseth exclaimed. "Green would flatter you, and it's nearly new. Wait here, Rhiannon. I'll be right back."

Rhiannon stared at Gwenaseth's retreating form. It surprised her that another woman would be so eager to help her look her best. The women of the Brigante were fiercely competitive. Rhiannon could not imagine them being so kind to a stranger.

In a few moments, Gwenaseth reappeared bearing a gown the color of spring foliage. She held it up for Rhiannon's inspection. "I scarcely wore it before I outgrew it as a maiden. The style is plain, but embellished with flowers and jewels, it will serve nicely. Here, slip it on."

Rhiannon stood up uneasily, feeling nearly naked in the thin shift she had worn to bed. She dutifully pulled the gown over her head. The fine, soft wool felt surprisingly comfortable against her skin. The design was different than any she had ever seen before; it fitted snugly in the arms and shoulders but was looser in the waist.

Gwenaseth frowned, wrinkling her forehead again. "It's too long and a trifle too big, but I think we can make it fit."

Skillfully, she gathered up the fabric on either side of Rhiannon's waist and eyed the result. "You *are* tiny. I'm small myself, and I wore this gown when I was even younger than you. There ... I will have Cordelia take it in and shorten it and have it ready in no time."

She helped Rhiannon pull the gown over her head. "Now, it's time to bathe you and fix your hair."

Rhiannon stripped off her shift and allowed Gwenaseth to help her into a tub which a slave had fetched and filled with steaming water. After washing Rhiannon's hair and body, Gwenaseth and the slave rinsed her with buckets of cooler water and helped her dry off. Still slightly damp, Rhiannon lay naked on a blanket as the two women used a pumice stone to polish her skin smooth and hairless. Although she was normally self-conscious about her body, Gwenaseth's brisk, matter-of-fact manner put Rhiannon at ease. When the slave girl brought an amphora of perfumed oil and began to rub it on Rhiannon's legs, she found herself relaxing like a contented cat.

The slave expertly stroked the muscles in her back and shoulders, then moved her fingers to Rhiannon's buttocks. As the slave's fingers smoothed the perfumed oil along the cleft of her bottom, Rhiannon tensed. Her body was being prepared for King Maelgwn's pleasure. The thought of him touching her so familiarly filled her with dread. Rhiannon's enjoyment of the massage disappeared. She lay stiff and uncomfortable as the slave finished the intimate task, smoothing the oil over her breasts until the nipples were pink and glistening.

Gwenaseth returned with the gown, now miraculously shorter and snugger. Rhiannon dressed quickly, and the two women waiting upon her turned their attention to her hair.

"It's so thick," Gwenaseth said in admiration, fingering Rhiannon's still damp tresses. "And such a gorgeous color. It would be a shame for you to wear it braided. I think I'll only plait a few strands at the crown and leave the rest long and loose. Maelgwn will like it that way, and wearing it unbound is most appropriate for a virgin bride."

Rhiannon stiffened. Virginity was apparently highly

prized among the Cymry. Perhaps her lack of it was truly the reason for Maelgwn's discontent.

The two women plaited flowers into Rhiannon's hair and combed it satiny smooth, then Rhiannon fastened her sandals and put on her simple bronze and enamel jewelry. The women stood back to scrutinize their work. "You look beautiful," Gwenaseth said with a warm smile. "Maelgwn will be very pleased."

Rhiannon started to shake her head, then stopped herself. It would be rude to reject Gwenaseth's compliment. The people of Degannwy would find out soon enough how Maelgwn really felt about his bride.

The women left Rhiannon alone, to eat and relax for a few moments before the wedding. Afraid to muss her gown by sitting, she ate standing up, nibbling on some cheese and barley bread. She reached for the urn of water, poured a small amount into an elaborate cup, then drank it. The wine, she ignored. The way her hands were trembling, she would be sure to spill it on her gown.

After eating, she wandered around the room, touching things in awe. Maelgwn's bedchamber was nothing like the bright, casual disarray of a Brigante lodge. The rich, elegant furnishings were arranged with a cold formality that made Rhiannon uneasy, but the room did not lack comfort. Indeed, it was the cleanest, most comfortable room she had ever been in. Woven mats covered the paving stones of the floor, and heavy embroidered cloths draped nearly every inch of the walls, except for the windows, which were open to the summer air. Examining the workmanship of one banner, Rhiannon's eye was drawn by the fierce gold dragon set upon the dark red cloth. This was surely Maelgwn's battle device.

Next, Rhiannon studied the ornately carved wooden bed. No wonder it felt so comfortable. The straw mattress rested on leather supports strung across the frame. Piled high with sheepskins and bedclothes of the finest wool and linen, it yielded to the sleeper's body, evoking the sensation of lying on a cloud.

In addition to the bed, there was a stool by the fire, two chairs and a small table in the corner. Rhiannon's father owned several rough-hewn tables and benches, but nothing like this. The furniture here appeared so graceful and delicate, Rhiannon feared to touch it. But it was obviously meant to be used; the chairs even had pieces attached to the seats to rest the body against. Such luxury goods were no longer available in Britain. Maelgwn had likely obtained them through trade with Brittany or Gaul.

Rhiannon frowned. The beautiful room lacked something. It almost seemed as if these beautiful things were meant to be looked at but were never really used. She glanced around again, searching for some hint of her future husband among the room's furnishings. Sweet scents masked any odors a man might leave, and the bedding had been freshly washed. The absence of any weapons, armor or men's clothing made Rhiannon wonder if King Maelgwn slept in his own bedchamber.

Noticing a bronze-banded chest pushed back into a corner, Rhiannon slowly walked towards it, her curiosity growing.

She turned to glance nervously at the door, then opened the chest. On top, she found neatly folded men's clothing. With trembling fingers, she dug deeper. Among a pile of heavy gold jewelry, she uncovered a cross studded with rubies. She pulled out the Christian symbol and stared at it. Had Maelgwn worn this when he lived in the house of holy men?

Beneath Maelgwn's things, Rhiannon's searching fingers discovered another layer. She tentatively touched some bright blue-green fabric and pulled out a gown as fine and gossamer as a spider's web. Below the gown, she found a carefully wrapped bundle; inside was an amber necklace, a beautiful bronze comb and several bronze and silver jars. Rhiannon opened one of the jars and sniffed, inhaling the faint fragrance of perfume.

She closed the jar quickly. A chill ran through her. These must be Maelgwn's dead wife's things. Rhiannon reminded herself how scornfully Esylt had spoken of Maelgwn's first wife. Esylt had called Lady Aurora a haughty, cruel and evil woman. She said Maelgwn was a fool to have married her.

Rhiannon sighed. It did not matter what kind of woman Aurora had been. Maelgwn had loved her. He had never stopped grieving for her.

Hastily, Rhiannon replaced the contents of the chest. Her heart pounded, and she looked anxiously toward the door to reassure herself that she was alone. Then she stood and walked to the window.

Her nagging worries from the night before returned, harsh and agonizing. She was certain now that Maelgwn did not want to wed her. He had agreed only because he needed her dowry.

Despite her attempts to will it away, a deep ache filled Rhiannon.

At least the wedding ceremony was over, Maelgwn thought with relief as he observed the revelry in the great hall. The day had gone smoothly. The Brigantes seemed impressed with the Christian wedding rituals, and they certainly enjoyed the wine and entertainment of the wedding feast.

Watching the lusty warriors who filled his hall, as they were dancing and making merry, Maelgwn could not help comparing Rhiannon to her kinfolk. She was so solemn, so quiet. She had scarcely said a word all evening.

Puzzled, Maelgwn let his eyes linger on his new bride. Her coloring was unusual, but very pleasing—blazing hair, pale but slightly rosy skin, eyes as soft and blue as wood violets. Her features were both graceful and provocative, and her body, beneath the heavy gown and masses of flowers and jewelry, appeared to be well formed and graceful. It seemed to him that Rhiannon should be surrounded by men, like a lush flower drawing bees. But she was not. The Brigante men more than kept their distance; they ignored her. It was strange, Maelgwn decided. Somehow it made him uneasy.

A movement in the crowd caught his eye, and he realized that the women had come to take away the bride. They would help her undress and then lay her in the flower-strewn bed to wait for him. Gwenaseth reached their table first; she took Rhiannon's hand and gently lifted her up to lead her away. For a moment Rhiannon's impassive expression faltered, and Maelgwn saw fear in her huge, lovely eyes. Then she regained control and went off quietly with the group of women.

As he watched her go, Maelgwn faced his own nervousness. It was his wedding night, but like Rhiannon, he had little enthusiasm for what lay ahead. He inwardly cringed as he saw the lewdly grinning Ferdic and a group of Brigante men coming toward him, their faces flushed with wine. The ritual of putting the bride and groom to bed together could be crude and insulting. The man was stripped and half-dragged to the bedchamber, with comments about his size and sexual prowess burning in his ears all the way there. Once in the bedchamber, the men might stay there half the night, drinking and joking coarsely. Maelgwn did not think Rhiannon was up to such rude merriment. For that matter, neither was he. He stood as Ferdic approached him, and his hand instinctively reached for the place his sword would be if he were armed.

"What's this?" Ferdic sniggered. "Our host seeks his weapon? Nay, Maelgwn, your sword will not serve tonight. You'll not satisfy my daughter with that lance. Let's see your other."

"Nay." Maelgwn's cold voice sent a hush around the room. "I have agreed to everything else you have requested, Ferdic, but I won't sacrifice my pride and Rhiannon's modesty for your amusement. There will be no bedding ceremonies."

Ferdic met his eyes challengingly. Balyn and Gareth moved quickly to flank Maelgwn. They wore no swords either, but the deadly determination in their faces brooked no argument.

Ferdic shrugged. "As you wish, Maelgwn. All those years in the priory made you as prim and sour-minded as a priest. You and Rhiannon are well matched. She's a humorless little thing, as unlikely to get a jest as any woman I've known. I wish you years of happiness." His mouth curled derisively as he moved aside so Maelgwn could pass.

Leaving the hall, Maelgwn walked alone to his bedchamber. He paused a moment before the door. It was a relief to be away from Ferdic and the others, but he could not shake the queasiness in his belly. He was not used to thinking of lovemaking as a task, but tonight that thought weighed on his mind. He had agreed to marry this woman, to bind her blood to his own, to take her body with his body, to plant his sons within her womb. Duty had brought him here, duty to his countrymen, his father's dream, the soldiers who followed him.

But duty made a poor aphrodisiac. He remained flaccid and unaroused, with no real appetite for what lay ahead. Still, he dared not hesitate. Like going into battle, if you waited too long, you lost your edge, your instinct. He must get on with it.

He entered the bedchamber and stood by the door for a moment, until his eyes adjusted to the darkened room. The lamp had not been lit, but moonlight shone in through the windows and Maelgwn could make out a small, motionless figure in the bed. He undressed quickly. The cool night air from the windows chilled the sweat glazing his skin. He crossed the room and got into the bed.

His fingers touched the smooth skin of Rhiannon's arm. She did not move as he caressed her. He shifted so he leaned over her, then pushed away the silken hair that hid the small, flowerlike face. He brought his lips to hers and kissed her. Rhiannon's mouth was still, her body rigid beneath his. Maelgwn felt his own tension increase.

With studied expertise, he licked the small, dry lips, and gently forced his tongue into Rhiannon's mouth. She tasted good, warm and sweet and young. Gradually, the thrill of other kisses came back to him. He recalled the delight of exploring a woman's mouth for the first time, the soft, satin splendor, the yielding, wet mystery.

Perhaps he imagined it, but he thought Rhiannon had relaxed slightly. He reached into the blankets, searching for her fragile, slender body. Rhiannon's skin was cool and dry, almost powdery, and it seemed to Maelgwn he could feel the milky paleness of it, like star flowers beneath the moonlight. He stroked her shoulders gently, then explored her delicate breasts. They were soft and beautifully shaped, with hard little nipples he longed to suck. He closed his eyes and began to enjoy himself. The flame in his loins kindled and caught, smoldering with steady, insistent warmth.

She had not expected him to be so gentle, Rhiannon thought with surprise. Despite his big fingers, Maelgwn was touching her with a deftness that quite took her breath away. Even his kisses were tender, and she actually enjoyed the feeling of his tongue in her mouth.

But in the back of her mind, the fear lurked. Soon he would want more than to hold her and kiss her. Soon he would want to be inside her, hurting her. His hand moved down her body, and Rhiannon felt her blood turn to ice in her veins.

How smooth and lean her stomach was. Maelgwn's fingers glided lower, seeking the triangle of springy curls between her thighs. Her hair would be brighter there, he knew, a deeper, more vivid red. Suddenly, he wished the room was better lit. He would enjoy seeing the contrast between her flaming hair and pale skin.

Tantalized by the thought, he moved his hand between Rhiannon's slim thighs. She went dead still. He wondered if she even breathed. Frustration nagged at him. Rhiannon had not resisted him in any way, but she did not welcome him either. She was dry and tight and clearly unready. He must arouse her somehow, make her relax and accept him. Otherwise, penetration would be painful for her.

Rhiannon felt as if she could not breathe. He tried to push his finger inside her. It hurt; it would only get worse. She wanted to run away, to scream. Thank the gods Maelgwn lay half on top of her so she could not pull away and shame herself. But how would she endure it? How?

His frustration increased. He stroked her as gently and tenderly as he could, kissed her as skillfully as he knew how. But even nibbling on her neck and earlobes did not seem to arouse her; the woman was not responding. He could feel the tension in her body, hear her harsh, rapid breathing. He could not remember ever having to work so hard with a woman. What was wrong? Was it him? Or did she simply dislike lovemaking? The other women he took to bed appeared to enjoy it, but they were mostly whores and serving girls. He was not so sure about high-born women. The only princess he had ever had before was Aurora, and she was certainly passionate enough.

He forced the thought away. There was no point comparing his two wives. Rhiannon was obviously very different from Aurora. Still, as a princess, Rhiannon should know he was duty-bound to consummate the marriage. The agreement with Ferdic would not be valid until he came inside her body.

She had not relaxed. He had the sense that if his tongue

were not in her mouth, she would be gritting her teeth. His desire dribbled away. He felt panicky, desperate. He could not force his new wife. It would hurt her, and she would never learn to trust him. Better to wait until another time, when she had gotten to know him better. What would it hurt to wait? Wearily, he pulled away.

Rhiannon tried to control her frantic breathing. She was glad he had stopped touching her, but her relief could not overcome her guilt and fear. Maelgwn sat on the edge of the bed, turned away from her. Obviously, he was disappointed, perhaps angry. She had failed him.

She had not meant to refuse him. The first part of his lovemaking had been pleasant, even enjoyable. His body felt warm and smooth; his mouth tasted good. But as his kisses became insistent, his hands probing and eager, the throbbing fear had overtaken her. She could not forget how big and powerful he was; despite his attempts at gentleness, he was bound to hurt her.

She glanced again at the motionless figure of her husband, the moonlight outlining the thick muscles of his back. She had caught only a glimpse of his naked body before he got into the bed, but she had marveled then at his broad shoulders, his lean torso and long legs, the fluid grace with which he moved. The raw power of her husband's form made her shiver. It was madness to resist the attentions of such a man. Somehow she must appease him.

Rhiannon fought to control her desperate thoughts. Esylt had once told her that a woman's power was even greater than a man's. A man could overpower a woman by force, but a woman could overpower a man by making use of his desire. Intrigued, Rhiannon had asked the methods of seduction, and Esylt had explained in detail the techniques a woman could use to enthrall a man's body.

A thrill of mingled hope and fear chased down Rhiannon's spine. Dare she try such a thing with Maelgwn? If she attempted to pleasure her husband, he might forgive her earlier rejection. Sitting up, she moved toward the still form on the edge of the bed.

The gloomy weight of despair pressed against Maelgwn's chest. He should never have married. He had feared taking another wife would be disastrous, and he had been right. Clearly, Rhiannon did not want him, and he had not the skill to win her compliance. He had failed, and failed in a way that a man, especially a king, should not fail.

Soft hands touched his naked back. Maelgwn started. Rhiannon was behind him, gently stroking him with her small fingers. He held his breath as her touch grew more intimate, probing deep into his tense muscles. What was she doing? Did she mean to entice him into loveplay once again?

Her hands moved to massage his neck. He sighed with contentment. He could feel her body close to his, the slight tickle of her hair brushing along his spine. Her hands moved lower, expertly kneading the sore muscles of his back, then reaching to his buttocks. He knew he should turn and begin to kiss her again, but he was afraid to try again, and this . . . ah . . . this felt so good, his worry and frustration almost forgotten.

She heard him sigh, and a half-smile formed on her lips. Her skillful fingers had not failed her. Although his body was not familiar to her, her hands knew exactly what to do. She could guess which muscles were most likely to be stiff and sore, and she concentrated her attentions there. The act of touching him gave her a strange sort of satisfaction. Maelgwn's skin was thicker and firmer than a woman's, but surprisingly soft. Heat rose from his body, carrying with it the warm, rich scent of maleness. She inhaled deeply, entranced.

Maelgwn groaned softly, and Rhiannon knew it was time to be more daring. She pressed her face against his back and moved her fingers forward to caress his chest, then lower. He inhaled sharply as she grasped his shaft in her fingers.

She touched him tentatively at first, then grew more confident as he swelled and stiffened with each caress. She stroked the length of his shaft, playing with the sensitive tip, twining her fingers around his flesh. Shimmers of delight ran along her fingertips. How marvelously a man was made, all velvet softness overlying rigid heat. Breathlessly, she reached her other hand to touch the silky pouches where he carried his seed. Closing her eyes, she leaned deeper into Maelgwn's strong back and concentrated on the rhythm her fingers had found.

He shifted his thighs apart, feeling her delicate fingers caressing, stroking, enflaming him. Dear God, it felt good! Where had she learned to do this? She knew exactly the right pressure, the exact rhythm to drive him wild. His mind was flooded with sudden, intense pleasure. He did not care where she had learned her skill, only that she continued to use it. Ahhhh . . . he would not last long!

His shaft was big, hard and throbbing in her hand. She tried not to think about him putting it inside her. If she could pleasure him well enough, he might not force her to couple with him this night.

Her arms grew tired. Rhiannon changed position, leaving the bed and moving around to face him. As she slipped to her knees, Maelgwn opened his eyes and stared at her, his pupils dark and dilated. Rhiannon fought back her fear. There was a technique, Esylt had promised, which unfailingly ensorceled a man's body and his will. Did she have the courage to try it, Rhiannon wondered? Was she brave enough?

Quickly, she pulled her eyes away from her husband's gaze and leaned over his thighs. With trembling fingers she lifted his shaft and took it in her mouth. He tasted salty and warm, his silken flesh stroking against the sensitive recesses of her mouth. She forced herself to relax, to ignore her fear of choking. Surely it was better to have his shaft between her lips, rather than inside her body, holding her down, thrusting into her.

Maelgwn's harsh, impassioned moans gave Rhiannon a thrill of accomplishment. She could hold this mighty warrior captive with her clever fingers, the subtle pressure of her mouth. It pleased her to please him, to feel him shudder and urge against her lips.

Maelgwn groaned deeply. Who would ever have thought that Ferdic's daughter would be like this? She was beautiful, so small and perfect, as lovely as a summer's day, as deliciously fair as a springtime flower. The sleek strands of her hair blanketed his thighs. His fingers sought her face as he pushed into her exquisitely sweet mouth. His thoughts spun dizzily. He wanted to last, to prolong the extraordinary pleasure. He could not wait . . . he could not wait . . . "Ahhhhhhhhh!!"

She held her breath as Maelgwn found his release. He paused a moment, breathing hard, then released her, his hands slipping away from her hair. His warm seed slid down her throat. She swallowed, choked, then looked up at him, blurry-eyed. In the moonlight she could make out the expression on Maelgwn's face. His stern features were suffused with tenderness, the hard planes softened with warmth.

A strange sense of triumph came over her. Esylt had not lied. There was magic in the things a woman could do to a man, the artful techniques she could use to secure his affections.

"Rhiannon." Maelgwn lifted her up and pulled her close. Leaning back, he rolled awkwardly into the bed, still clutching her to his chest. Rhiannon closed her eyes as she settled herself against her husband. His heart thudded against her ear, fast and strong.

Maelgwn sighed with contentment. How perfectly she fitted beneath his arm. How light and fragile and warm she felt. He reached for Rhiannon's face, stroking her slightly pointed chin and fingering her small lips. His wedding night had ended strangely, but it was not without its pleasures. There would be time to do his duty in the morning, to coax his lovely bride into more conventional forms of lovemaking. For now he was tired, utterly replete.

Rhiannon shifted slightly, so Maelgwn's body did not press against hers so heavily. From his long, deep breaths, she knew he slept. She herself was far from the oblivion of dreams. Her mind spun with the dizzying wonder of what she had done. Could it be true? Had Maelgwn really whispered words of love as he drifted to sleep? Nay, she would not believe a word of it. Narana insisted you could not trust what a man said in the aftermath of lovemaking. By tomorrow the spell would be broken. Maelgwn would remember the first part of their wedding night, that she had not been responsive, that she had refused to welcome him into her body. His anger would return, banishing the softness which made his face almost unbearably handsome.

Rhiannon moved again, trying to escape Maelgwn's fierce embrace so she could crawl beneath the blankets. Near dawn, she finally stopped listening to his deep breathing and fell asleep.

Chapter 6

Maelgwn woke slowly, aware of the soft warmth of a woman next to him. It reminded him of the old days, when he slept in his old tower room at Caer Eyri with Aurora. Opening his eyes, he saw dark red hair streaming over the bedcovers. A lock of it was entwined in his fingers. He disentangled his hand and raised himself so he could gaze at his new wife.

Rhiannon slept like a child, sprawled on her stomach with the blankets wrapped around her middle and clutched tightly to her chest. With her skin flushed with the warmth of sleep, she looked as pink and fragile as a summer rose. He recalled the memory of her small, wet mouth upon him, her long hair covering his thighs. His shaft swelled with desire even as he fought the urge to wake Rhiannon and attempt lovemaking again. She had not acquiesced to his attentions the night before. Rousing her out of a sound sleep did not seem like a good way to win her compliance.

He brushed a lock of hair from Rhiannon's face and admired her delicate beauty. It had felt good to touch her and hold her in his arms the night before. Despite her small size, her body fitted comfortably with his, like a well-balanced sword that felt sure and right in his hand.

And yet, for all the pleasure she had given him, his wife was unwilling or unable to allow him to come inside her body. She had lain stiff and frozen next to him. Her heartbeat had been as frantic and fast as a terrified hare's. Her behavior recalled a frightened virgin, but she was obviously experienced. He could hardly remember the last time a woman had satisfied him so expertly, and Ferdic had vouched for her lack of innocence.

He frowned. It did not make sense. Why did Rhiannon fear lovemaking when clearly she had experienced it before? Did her dread of his touching her stem from the same source as the fear he sensed when they met in the weaving room?

Maelgwn felt a vague irritation as the ache in his groin failed to go away. He was too old to deal with a woman's inexplicable and irrational moods. He had been patient so far, but he would not endure rejection forever. A flash of anger mingled with his burgeoning lust; he decided to wake her.

As he reached out to caress Rhiannon, she moved restlessly in her sleep. A frown crossed her brow, and a long sigh escaped her petal-like lips. She turned over to lie upon her back, and the poignant sweetness of her features struck him. It was startling how young she looked, how vulnerable. A protective urge rose up inside him. He did not want to force this shy, delicate creature to his will, to aggravate her obvious unease with him. He would wait until night to consummate the marriage.

Maelgwn took one last look at his new wife, then hastily dressed and left the room.

* * *

She was in the forest. The sun shone down on her through the trees. She felt safe and relaxed, and yet she was concentrating, trying to remember a spell Llewenon had taught her. Above her, birds twittered noisily, interrupting her thoughts. One bird was especially loud; its chirping drowned out all the others. She wanted to throw a branch and scare it away, but she could not move. The bird's cry grew louder and louder.

"Rhiannon."

She sat up suddenly. The memory of the dream left her. Lady Gwenaseth stood by the bed. "I'm sorry to startle you, Rhiannon, but it worried me when you didn't wake. You've slept nearly the whole morning away. You must have something to eat. I brought you some bread and cheese, and some apricots from the priory at Conwy. They have a fine orchard there."

Gwenaseth held out a basket of food. Rhiannon sat up and took it eagerly. She had been too nervous to eat well the last few days. Now her body cried out for nourishment.

"I'll leave you then," Gwenaseth said as Rhiannon bit into the bread. "Taffee will stay and help you dress." She gestured toward a plain, brown-haired slave woman waiting by the doorway. "When you are ready, meet me in the kitchen of the great hall. I'll show you around the fortress."

Rhiannon nodded, her mouth full. She looked uneasily at the slave. She had never had her own servant before and had no idea how to command one.

Without a word, the woman named Taffee began to tidy the room. She gathered the wine and cups from the table and picked up the wilted flowers scattered on the floor. Then she came to the bed and began to straighten the bedclothes. Rhiannon wrapped one of the blankets around her nakedness and went to sit in a chair by the table. Her worst hunger was satisfied. Now she savored the taste of the delicious golden fruit Gwenaseth had called an apricot. It was shaped like a small apple, only softer and sweeter.

Her thoughts drifted, slowly shifting from the dream to the reality of her luxurious surroundings. A vague anxiety nagged at her. Maelgwn had left without waking her, which meant their marriage was still unconsummated. Rhiannon's unease deepened. By Brigante law, the marriage bond remained invalid; the wedding agreement could be easily broken. Even now Maelgwn might be informing her father that he did not want her for his wife, that he had found her cold and unresponsive.

A wave of panic urged her to her feet, prepared to go to Ferdic and argue for another chance.

"My lady, are you well?" the slave asked, regarding her curiously.

Rhiannon nodded and sat down. Her thoughts were foolish. If Maelgwn had gone to Ferdic, she would have known immediately, for her father would waste no time in confronting her. It appeared Maelgwn did not intend to disavow the marriage—yet.

She was certain the sex magic she had practiced on him had helped sway his decision. He had liked how she touched him; he had liked it very much. A smile formed on Rhiannon's lips as she recalled the feel of his flesh beneath her fingers, the hot wonder of his maleness filling her hands and mouth. Esylt had not lied. Sex magic was amazing. The pleasure of it could almost banish the horror of that night in the forest with Llewenon.

"My lady?" The slave had finished the room and stood by Rhiannon, waiting expectantly. "Would you like me to do your hair or help you dress?"

"My hair," Rhiannon murmured, still caught up in her own thoughts. "It would be helpful if you could comb it out and braid it. It's too hot to wear down."

"But Maelgwn likes his women to wear their hair free and loose."

"How do *you* know?" Rhiannon asked, thoroughly surprised that a slave would make such a suggestion.

"Because his first wife always wore hers down," Taffee answered smugly, beginning to comb the tangles from Rhiannon's tresses. "She had long, thick hair, like yours, only wavy. She flaunted it, often leaving it unbraided. The other women resented her sometimes, but Maelgwn reveled in his wife's beauty."

Rhiannon was too startled to interrupt. Taffee continued, "You could hardly blame Maelgwn for enjoying his wife's appearance. She was tall and slim with full breasts and a body that made every man want to bed her. She had Roman blood, though, and looked it. Perhaps that explained her charm for Maelgwn. It seems he favors foreign-looking women," she added pointedly.

The servant's words dismayed Rhiannon. She did not need a reminder of her small breasts and childish features, the foreignness of her red hair and freckles. She wondered if the slave woman was deliberately being malicious. Taffee stood behind her, attending her hair, and Rhiannon could not see her face to guess her intentions.

Rhiannon decided she wanted to hear more. "Did you serve Maelgwn's first wife too?" she asked.

Taffee laughed. "I was but a child then, a serving girl in the kitchen. Besides, Lady Aurora was too fine and proud to allow someone like me to wait upon her. Lady Gwenaseth herself served Maelgwn's first wife. Now, she says I will serve you. It's true that I can mend a tear or make a braid quicker than anyone."

The slave woman's boasting rankled Rhiannon, but she had to acknowledge Taffee's efficiency. She had speedily combed and braided Rhiannon's hair, as well as tidied the room. At any rate, Rhiannon was not inclined to refuse Taffee's services. She had spent too much of her life answering to Narana's beck and call not to appreciate the luxury of having her own body servant. Besides, Taffee's inclination to chatter about Lady Aurora intrigued Rhiannon. She wondered how much more the woman would tell her.

"Maelgwn's first wife, Aurora. He loved her very much, didn't he?"

A sharp assessing look lit Taffee's gray eyes as Rhiannon turned to look at her. For a moment Rhiannon worried that she had revealed her doubts too openly. To her relief, Taffee's answer was not mocking, but grave and sure.

"Aye, he loved her. Too much I would say. A king can hardly afford to marry for love."

The shrewd, matter-of-fact words soothed Rhiannon as she walked to the great hall to meet Gwenaseth. Maelgwn might not desire her body or want her as his wife, but he needed her. The army of Brigante warriors she brought him more than justified their marriage.

"I'm glad you're here," Gwenaseth said as soon as Rhiannon met her in the kitchen. "I have much to show you."

Rhiannon's tour of the fortress began in the kitchen of the great hall and progressed to the bakehouse, the granary, storerooms and cellars, the brewery, the buttery, the newly built kiln and finally, the garden. Struggling to keep up with Gwenaseth's rapid pace, Rhiannon tried not to gawk at the many buildings and the constant bustle of servants and workers along the pathways of the fortress. She was reminded that this was no petty chieftain's ragged hill-fort, but the stronghold of a powerful overking. Her father told her that Maelgwn the Great received tribute from a vast network of fishing villages, farmers and herdsmen. After he conquered the rest of Gwynedd, his wealth would be even more astounding.

"I don't know how you keep track of everything," she told Gwenaseth in an awed tone when they finally took a break from the tour to enjoy an afternoon repast of barley bread and honey in the feasting hall. "There are so many things to think of, so many people doing the work."

Gwenaseth shrugged. "I helped run my father's household when I was a girl of only eight winters. Degannwy is much bigger, but the work is the same. You will learn, I'm sure. In no time at all, the slaves and servants will answer to you as mistress as well as queen."

Rhiannon paused between bites. "Me? I could not begin to manage so many people."

"Of course you can. As Maelgwn's wife you must look after things while he is away on campaign."

"Maelgwn expects me to take charge of his fortress?"

"I assumed you would want to."

Rhiannon put her bread down, her appetite utterly gone. Not only was she to lose her freedom; she was also expected to take on a heavy load of responsibilities as Maelgwn's queen—responsibilities she had no training for.

Gwenaseth frowned. "Perhaps I assume too much. Maelgwn has never discussed your role in his household." Her face grew thoughtful. "I will speak to him about it later. For now, we must attend to other matters." She rose and gestured for Rhiannon to follow.

"I'm surprised your mother didn't train you to supervise slaves and servants," Gwenaseth said as they walked toward a cluster of workshops. "Most Cymry girls learn such skills early on."

"My mother is dead. And my stepmother—she was too busy with my brothers to take an interest in me."

"I'm sorry. My own mother died when I was a babe, and I always felt her absence. Your mother," Gwenaseth asked gently, "was she a Brigante woman?"

Rhiannon shook her head. "Nay, a foreign princess. I know very little about her. My father seems uncomfortable with the subject."

"Perhaps she died when you were born. That always makes it hard for a man." Gwenaseth smiled. "I'm glad Maelgwn has married you. He grieved far too long for his first wife. He will be happier now, and he does need an heir."

Rhiannon looked away. So far, she had done poorly at conceiving a son for her husband.

"Here we are," Gwenaseth said cheerfully as they reached the weaving room. "Maelgwn told me to have some new gowns made for you. Let's see what sort of fabric we can find."

Rhiannon followed Gwenaseth into the busy workroom. A half dozen women smiled and nodded at her as they entered. By daylight, the room did not appear threatening at all, and Rhiannon looked with interest at the variety of materials and equipment used for the making of cloth. Gwenaseth went rapidly to a large chest in the corner and began to pull out pieces of dyed fabric. She put aside some pieces immediately. Others she held up to Rhiannon, squinting to imagine the effect.

"I like this deep green, and the blue and gold weave perhaps . . . Your hair is too vivid for the saffron and certainly the red . . . you look best in the soft colors of forest and sea."

She dug further down in the chest and pulled out a shimmering piece of cloth in a shade the color of violets. "This piece is very small; it must have been left over from something else. You are so tiny, though, there might be enough. Maelgwn wanted you to have at least one truly exceptional gown. No other woman of Degannwy is likely to have a gown made of real silk."

Rhiannon stared in awe at the exquisite cloth, overwhelmed to think Maelgwn wished her to have something so fine.

Gwenaseth put aside the fabric and turned to Rhiannon. "Now we must measure you. You'll have to take off your gown."

Rhiannon glanced at the open door uncertainly. Gwenaseth shook her head. "No one will bother us. The men are all off planning the summer campaign."

Rhiannon stripped to her shift and stood as still as she could while Gwenaseth measured off strips of leather to mark her size.

"How small your waist is!" Gwenaseth said in admiration. "I can scarce believe I was once almost as tiny as you." She smiled ruefully. "Bearing children has filled me out."

"I wish I were larger," Rhiannon said wistfully. "Especially my breasts. Men seem to prefer full-figured women. Maelgwn's first wife—was she much larger than me?"

"You must not worry about that," Gwenaseth chided. "Maelgwn is not one to turn away from a beautiful woman, no matter what her size or shape."

"I am not beautiful!"

"Of course you are, Rhiannon. I find no flaw in your features or your form, and any woman would envy your extraordinary hair. In some light it looks as bright as a flame; other times it appears dark and rich, like wine."

"Red hair is common among my people. I would rather have dark hair like the Cymry, or golden hair, as I've heard the Saxons have."

"You must not wish to be something other than what you are," Gwenaseth said gently. "Your beauty merely needs a little enhancement, some new gowns and jewels to set it off." She slapped her forehead suddenly. "The jewels! I near forgot them!"

Gwenaseth led Rhiannon to her own chamber, and while Rhiannon admired her collection of seashells and baskets, searched through another chest. She finally pulled out an intricately carved box, fashioned from some dark gleaming wood and fastened with strips of enameled bronze. Opening the box, Gwenaseth held it out.

Rhiannon gasped. Never before had she seen such dazzling jewelry. Bracelets, neck pieces, earrings and rings crammed the box to the top. Most pieces were not of bronze or silver, but of gold, and set with a rainbow of brilliant stones that sparkled in the light.

"What treasure you have!" Rhiannon exclaimed.

"No, what treasure *you* have," Gwenaseth answered. Rhiannon looked up, perplexed.

"These jewels have been in Maelgwn's family for years. Some of them belonged to Cunedag, his great-great-grand-sire," Gwenaseth said. "Maelgwn is the last of his line, and you are his queen. It's only appropriate that you use them to adorn yourself."

"I could not," Rhiannon breathed. "They are much too beautiful."

Gwenaseth nodded. "I admit many of the pieces are rather gaudy, but some would suit. We might ask Maelgwn if the smith could use the metal and stones to make something special for you."

Rhiannon reached to touch a necklace set with glittering green stones. "These remind me of cats' eyes."

"Those are emeralds," Gwenaseth supplied. "They come from very far away—beyond Rome, in a land of great heat and strange and miraculous beasts. The color flatters your pale skin and bright hair. And this . . ." Gwenaseth held out a necklace of large amber beads. "This blends well with your coloring and is simple enough to wear every day. There are earrings to match."

Rhiannon hesitated, reluctant to accept the finely made necklace. She had never worn anything more ornate than a few bronze and enamel wristbands and the simple gold torque Esylt had given her when her bleeding times began. The idea of wearing these fantastically beautiful jewels made her uncomfortable.

Gwenaseth saw her unease and spoke pointedly. "Maelgwn expects you to display his wealth. What will the other Cymry princes think if they see their overking's wife in plain gowns with her neck and wrists unadorned? They will think Maelgwn has squandered the fortune he inherited from Cadwallon. You would not want that, would you?"

Rhiannon shook her head, feeling more disconcerted than ever. The role of Maelgwn's queen appeared more and more confining. She was expected to run his household, to deck herself in uncomfortable and ostentatious finery. Her life was no longer her own.

Reluctantly, she allowed Gwenaseth to fasten the amber necklace around her neck. In an effort to change the subject before Gwenaseth insisted she wear the heavy earrings as well, Rhiannon fingered one of the more garish pieces and said, "I had no idea Maelgwn was so wealthy. Where did all these things come from?"

"Cunedag was something of a pirate, raiding the coast of Britain for years before he settled in Gwynedd and married a Cymry princess."

"I've heard of Cunedag," Rhiannon responded. "My people also claim him as an ancestor."

"I had forgotten Maelgwn's grandsire and Ferdic's great-grandsire were brothers. In a way, you and Maelgwn are related; distant cousins perhaps. That makes it even more fitting you should wear these jewels."

"It's odd to imagine Maelgwn and me as kin. We are very little alike."

"The blood tie is not strong. Maelgwn's line has bred dark, like the Cymry, while the Brigantes have kept the fiery coloring of the Irish line. But both peoples are big. Maelgwn's family were all tall, except for his mother. She was tiny, like you. Oddly enough, she was also named Rhiannon."

"But she was dark-haired, like Maelgwn," Rhiannon pointed out.

"Dark-haired?" Gwenaseth stared in surprise. "How do you know?"

"Esylt told me."

As soon as she spoke, Rhiannon realized her mistake.

Ferdic had taken her aside before they left Manau Gotodin and warned her not to mention Esylt to Maelgwn. There had been some falling out between the two of them years, ago, Ferdic said. Esylt had gotten over it, but Maelgwn had not. He still harbored some bitter grudge toward his sister.

Gwenaseth's eyes rounded. "Esylt? Surely you don't mean Maelgwn's sister? You couldn't have known her!"

Rhiannon hesitated. Her instincts rebelled at the thought of lying about her relationship to Esylt. She had given up a great deal to please her father and marry Maelgwn; she would not deny the woman who had offered her the only love and tenderness she had ever known.

"Aye. It is Maelgwn's sister I speak of. She told me about her family. She often talked about Maelgwn," Rhiannon continued. "How handsome he was, how courageous and gifted in battle."

Gwenaseth's soft hazel eyes grew cold and hostile. "It's odd she should speak of Maelgwn so fondly when she very nearly destroyed him!"

Rhiannon looked down and clasped her trembling hands together, determined to defend Esylt. "I know that there was trouble between Maelgwn and his sister long ago, but I . . ."

"Trouble? Is that what Esylt called it?" Gwenaseth jerked away, clearly beside herself with anger. "Obviously, Esylt failed to tell you how she plotted to have Maelgwn killed and his kingdom destroyed!"

"Nay!" Rhiannon's voice came out in an anguished whisper. "Esylt would never have done such a thing. She *loved* her brother!"

"Loved him!" Gwenaseth sneered. "She had a strange notion of love. To plot his death, to betray him to his enemies . . ."

"That was Aurora! His wicked wife betrayed him!" Rhiannon put a hand to her lips, appalled by the words that had slipped out. She should not have dared to attack

Aurora, the wife that Maelgwn loved, that everyone seemed to admire.

"Did Esylt say that? That bitch!"

Rhiannon began to shake, torn between her loyalty to Esylt and her dread of alienating Gwenaseth. "You must understand," she implored. "Esylt was kind to me. She cared for me as no other did."

The anger and outrage in Gwenaseth's face eased. "Esylt was kind to you?"

Rhiannon nodded, relieved to have a chance to share what Esylt had meant to her. "She . . . she did not live at my father's camp, but she often came to visit in the summer. She used to comb my hair and tell me stories . . ." Rhiannon's voice choked. How bitter and lonely her upbringing had been. Ferdic considered her a possession, a trinket he could barter away to the highest bidder as he had with Maelgwn. Her stepmother, Narana, treated her as a nuisance, another mouth to feed, another body to clothe, another annoying distraction to keep Narana from making sure her own hair was beautifully braided, her skin smooth and soft so Ferdic would not stray from her bed. Only to Esylt had Rhiannon mattered. Only Esylt had bothered to love her.

"I'm sorry." Gwenaseth spoke stiffly, her expression brittle and controlled. "If you were fond of Esylt, I should not speak ill of her. But I warn you, Rhiannon, Maelgwn must not hear of your affection for his sister. He hates her. It would be unwise to let him find out you even *met* Esylt."

"But I . . ."

"No." Gwenaseth shook her head firmly. "You must promise you will not speak of Esylt to Maelgwn. If he guessed you were close to his sister, he would never trust you again. Except as a political alliance, your marriage would be finished."

Rhiannon felt crushed, powerless. To please her husband, she must forever deny the one person who had loved her. It was almost too much to be borne.

"Promise me," Gwenaseth insisted.

Rhiannon clenched her teeth and slowly nodded. "Aye, I promise."

Chapter 7

Gwenaseth trembled as she left the weaving room. God above, would the past never cease to haunt them! She had been so happy to see Maelgwn married to that sweet-faced young woman. The darkness was over at last, she thought, and now there would be happiness and sunshine . . . and darling, red-haired royal babies. Who could have dreamed that Maelgwn's new wife was probably the only person in all of Britain who cared for Esylt?

Turning the corner sharply, she nearly ran into a slave carrying a large cauldron of water. Gwenaseth shook her head in disbelief as she sidestepped the man at the last minute. Rhiannon and Esylt—what an absurd association. The one so shy and guileless, the other the most manipulative, evil bitch in creation. What could Esylt have possibly seen in Rhiannon?

The question gave Gwenaseth pause. Had Esylt guessed Rhiannon would be married to Maelgwn? Was it possible she had plotted with Ferdic to form this alliance, hoping that someday, through Rhiannon, she might regain control over her brother? It was too far-fetched. How could Esylt have been certain the marriage between Rhiannon and Maelgwn would actually take place? Besides, if Esylt had intended to manipulate Rhiannon, she would not have used kindness and fond words, but threats and intimidation.

Gwenaseth rubbed her face wearily, puzzling over the connection between Rhiannon and Esylt. According to Ferdic, Rhiannon's mother was a foreign princess, and Rhiannon bore the same name as Esylt's mother. Was it possible . . .? Gwenaseth stopped walking and froze in dread at her own thoughts. What if Rhiannon were really Esylt's daughter, begotten by Ferdic?

It could not be true. There were no rumors Esylt had ever borne a child, and Rhiannon looked nothing like Esylt. It was ridiculous to think Esylt could have concealed such a thing all these years.

Gwenaseth pushed the thought firmly from her mind, and went to see to the preparations for the evening meal.

Maelgwn's eyes took in the neat rows of soldiers moving in formation before him. It held a thrill, even in practice, to see the flash of swords and armor in the sun and feel the power waiting there, the muscles of a hundred men at his command. With these troops, he would conquer his disloyal allies and unite Gwynedd again.

"They look sharp," Gareth said in satisfaction. "The Brigante troops are in superb condition. Even after drilling all spring, our own men scarcely measure up."

"The Brigantes have fought nearly every season, and after the long march here, they're primed for campaign. How long before we set out?"

Gareth shrugged. "As soon as we organize the command and get our supplies together . . . a few days, a week at most."

A week. Maelgwn felt a vague stirring of regret. He had

been married only a day. He scarcely knew his wife—indeed, he had not properly bedded her yet. Now he must leave her for several weeks, perhaps months. Still, he had worked toward this goal for almost two years.

Gareth appeared to guess his thoughts, for he smiled and spoke sympathetically. "Barely wedded and you must bid your wife good-bye for the fighting season. It's harsh, my lord. But then, such is the lot of queens."

"Aurora never liked the constant traveling I had to do; I hope Rhiannon better understands what it means to be married to a king."

"She seems like a gentle sort," Gareth offered. "Quite a beauty too, in a different sort of way. I've never had a redhead myself."

Maelgwn smiled uneasily, remembering Rhiannon's thick, vivid hair filling his hands as she pleasured him. In truth, he had not "had" Rhiannon yet either. It embarrassed him to think how easily his new wife had put him off. He should have finished things this morning. Since he had not, he must take her to bed as soon as the evening meal was over. This time her reticence would not deter him; gently, firmly, he would make Rhiannon his wife in all ways.

He did not see Rhiannon until she joined him in the great hall for the evening meal. She appeared as strained and distant as ever. He attempted to bridge the tension between them by teasing her.

"Gwenaseth said you lay abed half the day, Rhiannon. Do you enjoy the luxury of being my queen?"

Rhiannon gave him a startled look, then turned away. "I will try to get up earlier tomorrow, my lord."

Maelgwn felt a stab of irritation that she would take his light words to heart. He reached out and patted her shoulder with a tender gesture. "It's no matter to me; you may sleep as late as you wish." He leaned close to add provocatively in her ear, "I suspect after tonight you may well need your rest."

Rhiannon gave him such a wary, frightened glance, Maelgwn tensed with aggravation. He had only meant to flirt a little, to entice her with the thought of a night of pleasurable loving. She acted as if he had threatened her!

Maelgwn rubbed Rhiannon's shoulder gently, trying to soothe her. Her body felt stiff, and he sensed the fear hovering over her like a dark cloud. As he glanced from his wife's strained face to the crowd surrounding them, he realized that anyone watching would think he had chastised his wife most severely.

Maelgwn pulled his hand away. Curse it! No matter what he said to Rhiannon, it seemed to be the wrong thing. How was he to deal with this baffling, frustrating woman?

The rest of the evening, Maelgwn concentrated on his duties as host and ignored his wife. Almost everyone else had left the hall before he finally admitted that he could delay no longer in confronting Rhiannon.

Glancing her way, he saw how tired she looked, her lovely eyes smudged in shadows. A sinking feeling enveloped him, but he struggled against it. He no longer expected Rhiannon to be enthusiastic about their lovemaking. It would be sufficient if she responded enough to allow him to enter her without causing pain.

He took her hand and led her to their bedchamber, pausing in the anteroom outside the wooden door. Carefully, he tipped up her delicate face and kissed her. Rhiannon did not respond. He drew back and searched her face. For a moment, thick auburn eyelashes veiled her eyes, then her gaze met his. The apprehension he saw distressed him. His fingers probed her body, searching for the soft breasts hidden beneath the heavy wool. Her eyes widened; her lips parted, but not with desire.

Her mute, silent fear undid him. What did it matter if

she did not scream? Her dread showed clearly on her features. He jerked his hand away, breathing hard. Her eyes watched his. Stricken. Imploring.

Dear God, what did she want? What was he to do? Abruptly, Maelgwn turned and left, striding off into the night.

Rhiannon stared after him, the cold despair encircling her. Her husband surely hated her now. She could not pretend she desired him. Her husband's attentions aroused the most terrifying sensations. When Maelgwn put his arms around her, she felt trapped, helpless. When he kissed her, she could not breathe. His caresses evoked the memory of Llewenon's clawlike fingers.

It was madness. Maelgwn was nothing like Llewenon. He was boldly handsome, enticingly fair to look upon. She knew his touch could be exquisitely pleasing. Still, she could not banish her fear.

Shaking, Rhiannon went into the elegant bedchamber and began to undress. Clad in her shift, she climbed into the big bed and pulled the blankets up. She took several deep breaths and tried to make herself relax. Maelgwn might return at any time, and she dared not refuse him again. Perhaps if she kept her eyes open as he touched her, she could endure it. She would let her eyes linger over her husband's proud features and admire his gleaming dark hair. She would reach out and caress him, reminding herself of the smoothness of his skin, the solidity of his thick muscles. Somehow she must make herself accept the idea of his massive shaft invading her, his huge body pressing so close to hers.

She would do it. She would will herself to allow Maelgwn to kiss her and touch her the way he had before. She would try to please him.

Rhiannon lay back and stared into the darkness, waiting for her husband to return.

* * *

Balyn crossed the courtyard shortly after dawn. The sight of Maelgwn leaving the council room startled him. The king was usually an early riser, but with Maelgwn so newly wed, Balyn had expected him to lie abed later than this. A glance at the still-darkened building aroused his curiosity even more. "Why are you up so early?" he called across the misty courtyard. "Are you anxious to set out on the war trail?"

Maelgwn approached Balyn and spoke in a weary voice, "Nay, it's not the coming campaign which keeps me awake, but worry about my wife."

"Rhiannon? What's wrong?"

Maelgwn gave a deep sigh. "I don't know how to explain it. My wife . . . Rhiannon is afraid of me."

"Afraid?"

"Aye. It has been like this since the night she arrived. I have only to touch her, and she all but recoils in terror."

"Jesu, the bedding must have been difficult!"

"Difficult? Nay, impossible. For all I know it must be done, I have not the courage to force her."

"You mean . . . you have not yet . . ." Balyn's voice was shocked.

"I know I can't delay any longer. I'm going to her now." Through the dim light, Maelgwn's blue eyes met Balyn's brown ones beseechingly. "Say nothing of this, Balyn. I would not speak of it again."

"Of course, Maelgwn. But I can't understand . . . Did she refuse you? Was she unwilling to honor her vows?"

"She did not refuse me. Indeed, the first night, she pleasured me well in other ways."

"She pleasured you, and yet she would not allow the marriage to be consummated?"

Maelgwn nodded. "Rhiannon fears penetration. She found no fault with touching me."

Balyn's broad brow furrowed with a frown. "Are you certain her actions are motivated by fear?"

"Of course. Her dread is palpable. I have only to touch her, and she tenses as if I mean to strike a blow."

"Unless it is an act," Balyn said thoughtfully.

"An act?"

"Don't you think it odd, my lord, that a woman would pleasure her new husband, yet refuse to lie with him? I can't help doubting Rhiannon's fear. I suspect she plays some sort of game with you. Why would a woman avoid only the act of consummation? Unless she intends for the marriage to remain invalid."

"Balyn, you imply . . ."

"What if Ferdic instructed Rhiannon to delay consummation of the marriage? You have said you do not trust Ferdic—what if he planned some crude scheme to embarrass you? Or, what if Rhiannon hopes to thwart her father's wishes? Perhaps she has in mind another suitor. If you went to Ferdic and rejected her for her unwillingness in bed, he might agree to void the marriage contract. He would no doubt beat her for the embarrassment she has caused him, but in the end, Rhiannon would be given to the man she truly desires."

"But Rhiannon's fear appears so real, so convincing."

"She's a woman, Maelgwn. Who of us men can truly guess what transpires in a woman's heart?"

Maelgwn stared at his friend and officer, feeling his blood run cold. He felt sorry for Rhiannon, pitied her for her fear and shyness. What if Balyn were right, and her reticence only an act? It did not seem possible. But then, Ferdic's boyishness had fooled him years ago. His daughter's innocent face might mask even greater deceit.

Anger replaced Maelgwn's sympathy for his new wife. If Balyn were right, Rhiannon had manipulated him with a cold-hearted finesse that would have done even a bitch like Esylt proud.

Balyn watched suspicion darken the king's face and abruptly regretted his warning words. The Princess Rhiannon truly seemed shy and gentle. What if he was wrong? "Of course, I might be mistaken," he added hastily. "We don't really know that Rhiannon has deceived you."

"Nay, but something is clearly awry. I hadn't thought of it before, but now I see that mere maidenly shyness could not account for Rhiannon's behavior. Ferdic informed me the night they arrived that she was not a virgin."

"Not a virgin? But who . . .?"

"Ferdic did not say, and I did not ask. Rhiannon has lain with a man, so it's unlikely she fears lovemaking as much as she pretends."

"Perhaps you should confront her, ask her outright why she fears you."

"I asked her the first night she arrived, and she was unwilling or unable to tell me the truth." Maelgwn unclenched his fists and met Balyn's eyes. "I have given Rhiannon more than enough chances to explain. It is time I took what Ferdic has so insistently thrust upon me."

Maelgwn turned to go. Balyn reached out a restraining hand, suddenly finding himself in the role of Rhiannon's defender. "A word of advice, Maelgwn. Go slowly. If you treat Rhiannon too harshly, she could panic. If you rape her, you risk souring things for good."

"Have more faith in me than that," Maelgwn answered coldly. "I know a thing or two about women. For all that Rhiannon has baffled me these last few nights, I intend to make her see things my way from now on."

Maelgwn started across the courtyard, determined to go to Rhiannon immediately. Gareth, who was also an early riser, intercepted him before he reached his bedchamber. His master horseman had a dozen questions about transportation for the combined army, and Maelgwn was busy until well after sunrise. By the time he reached his bedchamber, Rhiannon had gone.

Realizing he had no idea where his wife might be, Maelgwn went looking for Gwenaseth. He finally found her coming out of the bakehouse carrying a basket full of fresh loaves.

"Where's Rhiannon?"

"She's probably in the weaving room."

Maelgwn frowned. "I don't want my wife burdened with menial tasks. We have seamstresses aplenty."

Gwenaseth gave him an exasperated look. "Rhiannon takes great pride in her needlework. She *offered* to help sew her new clothes."

"You're certain she enjoys it?"

"Sewing seems to be one of the few things that interests her—that and pottery. She asked to visit the kiln again this morning. I must say, Rhiannon is not what I expected in a Brigante princess. She is so quiet, so unassuming." Gwenaseth sighed and her eyes met Maelgwn's, misty with memories. "Remember how Aurora fought with you over managing the household at Caer Eyri? It was one of the main sources of conflict between her and Esylt. But Rhiannon has no interest in being mistress of Degannwy. The very thought of it seems to distress her."

"My wife is free to do whatever she wishes," Maelgwn said sharply. He turned away from Gwenaseth, seeking to hide his own inner turmoil. The mention of Aurora aroused the familiar ache of grief. Aurora had despised sewing and done as little as possible. She had also been ardently responsive in bed.

Maelgwn forced himself to walk toward the weaving room, reminding himself that he could not afford to dwell on the past. He had a new wife now, and somehow he must deal with her. Rhiannon's strange behavior nagged at him. Her fear had been so convincing. Could anyone feign that kind of desperation?

There were several women in the weaving room, and they stared at Maelgwn uneasily as he entered. Rhiannon was the last to be aware of his presence. When she finally looked up and saw him, she gave a little gasp of surprise.

Sewan, Balyn's wife, gathered up her things. "It's time to feed the children," she said meaningfully. The other women quickly followed Sewan's lead. In a few moments, the small room was deserted, save for Maelgwn and Rhiannon.

Maelgwn went to stand beside his wife. She kept her eyes on her lap, idly fussing with her needlework. Her hands trembled, and Maelgwn noticed a mistake in her embroidery. For a moment, sympathy almost won out over his anger. Nay, he told himself sternly, he would not be put off this time.

"Rhiannon."

She looked up at him. Her dark liquid eyes reminded him of flowers glowing in the dim purple of twilight. For a moment, they stared at each other. Then Maelgwn reached down and grasped Rhiannon's shoulders, pulling her up so he could kiss her. Her body went limp and yielding in his arms. Maelgwn felt a wave of relief. Perhaps Balyn was right, and she would give in easily once she knew his determination.

He explored her small, luscious mouth languidly, tenderly, and was rewarded by her fragile body melding to his. Instinctively, his tongue probed deeper. Rhiannon shuddered against him, making him intensely aware of the way her breasts crushed against his chest and her slim hips met his thighs. His thoughts focused on the delicious heat burning in his loins. Without releasing her, he reached down and rested his hand on the small of her back, subtly urging her against his erection.

She could feel how big and hard he was! His kisses were not tender now, but rough and insistent. He held her so tightly, she could barely breathe. She must try to relax; she must remember that he was her husband and let him do what he wished. No one had ever died from lovemaking, and since she was no longer a virgin, it would not hurt so much. Desperately, Rhiannon clutched his neck, trying to will the fear away. If she could concentrate on breathing slowly and rhythmically . . .

Maelgwn found himself overcome by his urgent desire. He had been without a woman too long, and Rhiannon was so heartbreakingly lovely, so sweet. He released her and glanced around the room. A strange setting for their first time, but it would do. There was even a large pile of unspun wool in the corner that could serve as a bed. Maelgwn went to the door and shut it tightly. Sewan and the other women would warn others away; it was unlikely they would be interrupted.

He returned to Rhiannon and led her over to the pile of wool, but did not lie down with her. Instead, he held her tightly against him and reached down with both hands to pull up her gown. Impatiently, he buried his fingers in the lush warmth of her buttocks. She was so soft . . .

Rhiannon smothered a cry against Maelgwn's chest. Cerrunos save her! She could not go through with it! His hands touched her bare flesh. Soon he would be pressing her down beneath him. Fear clawed at her throat. She could not stand it, she could not! He was going to hurt her!

Rhiannon's body went rigid. Maelgwn released her slightly and moved his fingers to stroke the silken skin of her back as he tried to soothe her. The familiar frustration ate at his patience. Rhiannon did not want him. She endured his touch now, nothing more. So be it, he thought angrily. There had to be a first time, and it seemed likely Rhiannon would find it distressing, no matter what he did. He moved his hand lower, seeking the warm, secret place between her thighs.

A flurry of energy fanned out from Rhiannon's small form. Her small fists beat desperately against his chest, and her mouth beneath his was frantic. Finally jerking away, she cried out.

Maelgwn watched, stunned, as Rhiannon backed away from him, her eyes wild, her chest heaving. He followed her, determined to finish. Pushing her down on the pile of wool, he pulled up her gown with one hand and forced her legs apart with the other.

He was fumbling with his trousers when she whimpered. It was an inhuman sound, low and wordless. It jarred him back to his senses. He saw the frightened creature who cowered beneath him. Rhiannon's eyes were stark with terror, her small features a mask of agony.

The anger left him, replaced by shame. He had never raped before, not even in the passion of battle. Men who relished hurting women were cowards. A real man aroused the woman and made her desire lovemaking. But this woman?—Maelgwn felt the aching weight of failure. Would this woman ever want him?

With shaking fingers he helped Rhiannon up. He could not stand to look at her. He helped her brush the lint off her dress, staring fixedly at the vague pattern of the brownish red wool. Then he turned and left the room.

Rhiannon trembled so badly she could hardly walk. She groped her way to a stool and sank down. Her mouth was dry. Her body ached with fatigue. She felt as if she had been fighting for her life. She shook her head. It was over; she was safe. Except, it would never be over.

Rhiannon stared at the door, her breathing harsh and ragged. Once again she had failed her husband. How much more would he endure before he complained to Ferdic, and her shame was known to everyone—Brigante and Cymry alike? She closed her eyes. If only she could talk to Maelgwn, explain what Llewenon had done, explain her terrible fear.

She could not do it. She had buried the memory of the rape deep in the darkest part of her mind. To speak of it with a man, especially an angry, frightening man like Maelgwn, was unthinkable. There had to be some other way out of this wretched tangle. If only Esylt were here— Esylt would know what to do, how to deal with her brother.

Rhiannon stood, fighting a wave of homesickness and grief . She needed to escape this fortress, this prison. She needed to walk among the trees and smell the wild, restless air.

The thought of the woods lured her to the door of the weaving room. Rhiannon pushed it open and stepped out into the muddy courtyard. She walked warily past the great hall. A few servants saw her, and either nodded or ignored her. She passed several buildings before the fortress gate came in sight. Two rosy-cheeked, dark-haired boys chased a brindle-marked hunting dog in circles near the open gate. Above them, a lone sentry stood in the watchtower.

Swiftly, Rhiannon approached the gate. She slowed as she walked through it, trying to keep her pace unhurried and nonchalant. Thinking of her bright, uncovered hair, she winced. If anyone saw her, it would be remarked upon.

She shook her head stubbornly, and her heavy braids swayed against her body. On the morrow, Maelgwn might lock her away, or her father beat her for displeasing her new husband. But for this moment, she was free, and she meant to make the most of it.

The track sloped down to the coast road. Rhiannon veered in the other direction, heading for the river and the verdant green of the forest beyond.

Chapter 8

Gwenaseth was in the root cellar looking over supplies when Maelgwn found her. When he called her name, she jumped up and gasped in surprise. "My word, Maelgwn. What do you mean by sneaking up on me like that?"

"Elwyn said I might find you here. I thought I made plenty of noise."

"What do you want?"

Maelgwn hesitated. As much as he disliked confiding in a woman, especially one as sharp-tongued and opinionated as Gwenaseth, he had no choice. For two days he had avoided Rhiannon, seeing her only at the evening meal, where he had been scrupulously polite and formal. After that, he said good-night to her at the bedchamber door, then went off to his council room to spend the night tossing and turning on his bedroll.

The strain was making him moody and irritable, although it was doubtful anyone except Balyn guessed the true cause of his bleary eyes and short temper. Ferdic had departed yesterday, apparently convinced that Maelgwn was delighted with his bride. His men continued to make lewd jests regarding his status as a newly married man, adding to his misery.

"I need your advice about Rhiannon."

Gwenaseth sighed. "She is a puzzle—so shy and wary. I've found it difficult to befriend her."

"I have no one else to turn to, Gwen. No man can advise me in this." He gave Gwenaseth a pleading look. "It's been days since the wedding, and I still haven't been able to bed my wife."

Gwenaseth's mouth dropped open. "God above, why not?"

Maelgwn turned away, fists clenched. "She fears me, nay, she is terrified of me. Other than forcing her, I can't think how to manage it."

"Why didn't you say something before this?"

"Obviously, I'm embarrassed by my situation."

Gwenaseth took a deep breath. "Of course, I'll help you. But I can't understand . . . why did you let things go on so long?"

"I'm at loss; I've never had a woman act this way before."

"What happened?" Gwenaseth asked. "What went on the first night?"

Maelgwn began to pace as he described the events of his wedding night. He saw Gwenaseth's eyes widen as he explained what Rhiannon had done to him. "That's what makes the rest of Rhiannon's behavior even more baffling," he continued. "For a time, I even considered she wanted the marriage to remain unconsummated to thwart her father's plans. I no longer believe that. I think Rhiannon truly wants things to be right between us, but her fear will not allow it."

Gwenaseth's eyes remained questioning, and Maelgwn went on to describe what happened in the weaving room. "That time was even odder," he finished wearily. "One minute she was willing and responsive, the next, wild with panic. In all my days, I've never heard of a woman acting so.''

"Perhaps she didn't care to be tumbled on the floor of the weaving room like a serving slut," Gwenaseth said acidly. "Perhaps she has more decency than that."

"Haven't you been listening, Gwenaseth? She wasn't outraged, she was out of her mind with fear!" Maelgwn jerked around as if to leave.

"Wait," Gwenaseth called. "I'm sorry. I should not have said that. You're right; Rhiannon's behavior is peculiar." Gwenaseth sighed again, her forehead etched with furrows of worry. "I've known only one other woman to act as Rhiannon has. Years ago, I knew a coastal woman who was brutally raped in an Irish raid. Afterwards she would scarce allow her husband to touch her, although their relationship had been passionate before. The memory would not leave her, and the mere sight of a naked man aroused her dread."

"Surely you don't think . . . who would dare rape Ferdic's daughter?"

"I can't imagine. Still, it seems a likely explanation."

Maelgwn pressed his lips into a grim line. The thought of Rhiannon being violated infuriated him. How could Ferdic have let it happen?

"If Rhiannon has been raped, I'm not certain I can help you," Gwenaseth went on. "The woman I knew never got over her fear. She finally allowed her husband his rights, but she never found pleasure in the act."

"I won't accept that. I refuse to endure a wife who looks at me with dread. Rhiannon *must* to learn to trust me."

"Then you must win her trust. Have you taken the time to talk to her, to woo her with gentle words and little gifts?"

Maelgwn shook his head. "I had not thought it necessary. After all, this marriage was not one of choice, but political expediency."

Gwenaseth rolled her eyes. "Any woman, even a princess, wants to think her husband values her for more than her dowry."

"Your point is well taken," Maelgwn said thoughtfully. "I've sought to know Rhiannon's body, but not her heart and mind. I think it's time for a change in tactics."

Maelgwn left the cellar, feeling relieved to at last have a plan. He had never wooed a woman; they had always sought him out instead. But he had won over a considerable number of chieftains with persuasion and subtlety. With Rhiannon, it was more a matter of winning the trust of a wild animal. She was so skittish, so wary. Still, some part of her had responded to him that first night. Her touch had not been merely skilled, but filled with yearning. Beyond his obligation to consummate the marriage, it might be worth a great deal to win Rhiannon's gentle trust.

"Rhiannon."

She woke with a start. Maelgwn bent over her, calling her name. "I'm sorry if I frightened you, Rhiannon. I want you to come with me. I wish to show you something."

Rhiannon sat up slowly. It was very dark and quiet, surely it was still night.

"Get dressed," Maelgwn whispered. "I'll wait for you outside."

Rhiannon fumbled breathlessly for her clothes. She pulled on her gown, found her sandals, then touched her hair distractedly. It was hopeless; she could not fix it in the dark.

She crept outside, into a world of mist and shadows. The fortress was amazingly quiet. The bark of a hound broke the eerie silence, sending a tremor of fear down Rhiannon's spine.

"Rhiannon."

She turned with relief at the sound of Maelgwn's voice. His tall form materialized only inches away in the mist.

"Cold?"

She nodded. She had not thought to bring her cloak, and the damp air chilled her skin. Without a word, Maelgwn took off his cloak and draped it around her. It came almost to the ground, but it was warm and smelled comfortingly of Maelgwn.

Maelgwn took her hand and led her to the fortress gate, then called up softly to the guard. The man came down, and the two men pushed hard on the massive gate until it opened with a creaking sound.

Thick, almost palapable darkness closed around them. Rhiannon clutched Maelgwn's hand more tightly.

"Where are we going?" she whispered.

"The cliffs above the sea."

"How will we find our way?"

Maelgwn's warm chuckle startled her. "We'll follow the sound of the ocean," he said. "Listen."

The unmistakable crash of the surf sounded in the distance, a vague, roaring rhythm. Rhiannon still felt anxious. She did not like walking blind in the dark. Why was Maelgwn taking her to this place in the middle of the night? What did he want with her?

She strained her eyes, trying to see the man who held her hand and trod silently next to her. She could scarcely make out his form, and his face was completely hidden. It might not even be Maelgwn; it might be a spirit or a demon. Nay, his hand felt too real, too hard upon her own.

Rhiannon's fear intensified. She had wronged Maelgwn by denying him his marital rights. He had every right to possess her body, and she had refused him. Perhaps he meant to make her pay. If he took her away from the fortress, he could satisfy himself where no one would hear her screams. Once they were alone by the sea, no one would ever know or care what he did to her.

"Rhiannon, what's wrong?"

She had stopped walking, her body frozen in dread at her thoughts.

Maelgwn sighed. "You think I mean to hurt you, don't you? Listen to me." He turned her so his face was very close to hers. She still could not see him, but his breath felt warm against her face.

"I promise I won't hurt you. It's not meant to hurt, Rhiannon, but to feel wonderful."

His hand came up to touch her face, and Rhiannon relaxed slightly. She recalled how he had cupped her chin in his fingers after she had pleasured him on their wedding night. She sensed kindness in this man, despite his powerful body and fierce manner. Mayhap over time she could even learn to trust him.

They began to walk again. Maelgwn paced his long strides so she could keep up with him. The dazed feeling from waking up suddenly vanished, and Rhiannon was keenly aware of the feel of the damp air against her face, the rumbling of the sea, the shape and scent of the man who walked next to her.

The crashing of the surf grew louder as they neared the cliffs, and the mist thinned slightly as dawn crept upon them. Rhiannon experienced a vague disappointment. She had found safety in the darkness, a kind of peace in this silent, mysterious journey. Maelgwn did not seem as threatening when she could not see him. She enjoyed his invisible presence next to her, his musky male scent warm in the cool air, the hardness of his strong fingers gripping hers.

Now, she would have to see his face and try not to flinch from his hard, proud features, those probing, passionate eyes. As the sky lightened with morning, her fear lingered, ready to swoop down upon her.

They reached the cliffs above the beach. Maelgwn stopped and pulled her close, nestling her against his chest. Rhiannon tried not to look at him. She closed her eyes, expecting the pressure of his kiss. Instead, Maelgwn grasped her chin with his fingers and turned her toward the east. "Watch," he said.

The sky had begun to glow with the milky pink of dawn, and a luminescent mist floated on the horizon. As they watched, the haze thinned, revealing the peaks of the mountains dark in the distance. The colors of the sky deepened and then grew brighter, glowing with shades of orange, rose, violet and gold. Slowly the sun rose, stealing color from the sky and burning away the mist as the far-off highlands blurred to blue-gray again.

"How beautiful," Rhiannon whispered. "It's as if the world were beginning again."

"It's not a sight you can see from anywhere in Britain but Gwynedd," Maelgwn answered. "The sea, the mountains, the misty air—that is the magic of this land. It speaks of ancient mysteries, forgotten gods, barely remembered dreams." He sighed softly. "When I was young, I loved the highlands best. I once thought never to leave them. Now, I find the sea calls me, too."

He turned to look at the ocean. "I love to watch the waves, breaking and breaking, forever and ever. It reminds me how very short and insignificant life is, that a man should never measure himself against the eternity of the sea."

Maelgwn stroked Rhiannon's hair gently, and she felt a strange contentment. She had not seen this side of her husband before. There was a contemplativeness about him she had not known in her father or other men. Maelgwn was not merely a warrior, obsessed with fighting and victory, nor was he like Llewenon, who was obsessed with power of another sort. He seemed set apart . . . solitary . . . searching. She could feel his deep connection to the land and the sea, the bond he experienced with the place he had grown up in and now ruled.

Rhiannon looked up at her husband, watching him stare out at the sea. The morning light made his hair seem lighter and softened the fine lines in his face. Even his mouth did not appear so stern. All at once, she was able to stop thinking of him as a king and see him as man. She recognized his haunted look, the wistful sadness in his eyes. Like her, he sought something far beyond this place, perhaps even this time. Llewenon had often bragged that he could visit the spirit world, although she no longer believed it was true. But this man—perhaps Maelgwn the Great was really strong enough and brave enough to go to the other side.

Maelgwn glanced at her and smiled. "Come, let us walk some more. We have the whole beach to explore."

Chapter 9

Maelgwn led Rhiannon to the path that ran down the cliffs to the beach. He held her hand tightly as they climbed down the narrow, rocky defile. In one place a large rock blocked their way, and Maelgwn picked her up and lifted her over it. He paused before releasing her and kissed her. Even through the cloak, she felt the heat of his body, the strength of his muscles as he held her. She realized she was no longer afraid, but enthralled by his maleness. She clung to him as he kissed her, then he released her and they continued down the path.

They reached the beach and walked out onto the damp sand. The scent of dying sea creatures, stranded by the retreating tide, mingled with the clean ocean air. Maelgwn led her out further, until they were a few paces from the waves.

"It's breathtaking," she said, staring at the endless gray waves stretching out to the distant horizon.

"Have you ever seen the ocean before?"

She shook her head.

"Would you like to go in?"

Her face lit with eagerness. "Could I?"

"Of course. I'll hold the cloak. Take off your sandals and wade in."

Rhiannon bent down and removed her shoes. She held her gown up to her knees and walked gingerly into the water. She gave a shriek of surprise. Maelgwn laughed. "The Irish Sea is cold even in summer. Don't fall in or you will freeze before I can get you home."

Rhiannon waded farther out, scarcely hearing his words. Despite the icy chill, the waves felt good upon her legs. The ocean was like a mouth, sucking you in. She tensed her body against the next wave, feeling the power of it, then closed her eyes. How easy it would be to let the ocean carry her away to the faint green glow at the bottom where the spirits lived.

Maelgwn watched Rhiannon jump and dance among the waves. Her childlike delight in the ocean surprised and tantalized him. The carefree water sprite cavorting wildly in the rainbow mist of the seaspray bore no resemblance to the wary, silent woman he had wed. This was another Rhiannon, an even more lovely and enchanting one.

Hope filled him. He had not yet found the words to ask Rhiannon about her life, her feelings, but perhaps there was another way. Already he felt closer to her, as if he had gained some small part of her trust. If only he could overcome her terror of physical joining.

Rhiannon continued to play in the water, holding her skirts high, almost to her thighs. Maelgwn stared at the paleness of her legs flashing above the seafoam, surprised at how much he desired her. Rhiannon's delicate, fragile-looking beauty aroused him more than the earthy, voluptuous women he usually took to bed. Was it her dazzling coloring—the cool white skin, fiery hair, her eyes like blue cornflowers? Or was it the mystery of her? When he looked into Rhiannon's eyes, it seemed he saw far-away, forgotten things, as if he were slipping into a beautiful dream. Something about Rhiannon made him want to possess her with a longing greater than he had thought to feel for a woman again.

He turned to look at the lonely expanse of beach, pleased he had given into the impulse to rouse his wife from her bed to see the sunrise. Again spending the night in an agony of wakefulness, he had given up his quest for sleep long before dawn and gone out to walk in the night air. It was one of those nights that seems like a dream, when the spirits walk in the silver mist and the voices of the dead beckon on the wind. He felt close to something, some profound message waiting in the darkness. As his feet found their way to his bedchamber, he remembered the woman sleeping there and realized he had need of her, a need for companionship and human warmth on a night of spirits.

Maelgwn looked back at the waves. Rhiannon had waded out quite far. Feeling a strange fear, he called out to her, shouting her name. Rhiannon came to him slowly, reluctantly, like a child summoned from play. But she did not look unhappy. She was smiling, a radiant smile. He noticed how white and even her small teeth were. She looked altogether different when she smiled, more womanly. He had not noticed before. Or could it be that he had never seen her smile?

The waves had soaked her dress almost to the waist, and the shape of her slim legs and hips was clearly visible through the damp fabric. Maelgwn felt the tightening tingle in his loins.

"May I have your cloak?" she asked through chattering teeth. "I'm so cold."

"You shouldn't have gone in so far," he chided as he wrapped her tightly in the cloak and held her close. Her damp hair smelled of sea spray, the fresh, tangy scent of the ocean. The pressure of her body against his aroused him further. He turned her face up with his fingers and began to kiss her. She settled willingly into his arms. Maelgwn gasped at the fire that burned through him. He nibbled her lips, sucking the wetness from Rhiannon's mouth with his own, then forced his tongue between her lips, searching, searching . . .

Abruptly, he released her. His body ached with need, but his mind remembered her fear. His desire was too urgent, and he sensed that she feared his raw passion more than anything. Even he was appalled by the untamed fever which was urging him to rut with her on the beach like a stallion gone wild with the irresistible scent of a female in heat.

But as a man, he had the means to control his lust, to slow down and take time to pleasure his wife, to make her ready for his loving. It had been a long time since he had sought control. His couplings in recent years had been quick and violent, satisfying his body before his emotions could be touched. Mingling with his passion was a dread that echoed Rhiannon's. A part of him feared making love instead of merely coupling. What if this woman came to mean more to him than he intended?

He turned to stare at Rhiannon. Her cheeks were flushed, her eyes dazed but not yet fearful. It was only a flicker, but he could sense longing in her face, almost imagine she desired him. He felt very close to her, as if their spirits had touched briefly. It came from the mood conjured up by the sunrise, the mountains, the sea. Like him, she responded to the land and heeded its call. Now something else primal called him. He wanted to lay her down upon the soft sand and love her like the waves washing over her. He would be the sun and pierce her body with his light . . .

"Maelgwn?"

He shivered at the touch of her hand against his chest. He could feel the fire of her caress burning down his body. He looked into her eyes and saw tenderness. She knew his need and sought to gratify it. Her delicate fingers moved lower, finding the tie to his trousers. She did not fumble. Her touch was easy and sure. She freed his shaft from his clothes and began to stroke him. The flame shot down his body . . .

"No," he moaned. She released him and backed away. "Not like that, Rhiannon. Any woman can satisfy me that way; I can even do it myself. What I want is *you*."

Her eyes burned with agony. She wanted to please him, but her fear held her hostage. Frustration boiled up inside him. Should he let her pleasure him? It would take the edge from his lust but brought them no nearer to joining their bodies.

"Take off your clothes, Rhiannon."

Her eyes went wide. He softened his voice. "At least let me satisfy myself that way."

She took a quick breath and looked around the open beach. "Here?"

She was right. He might be king and call the beach his own, but some things demanded privacy. Without a word, he picked her up and began to walk toward the cliffs. Beneath the ancient rocks, several large boulders formed a slight shelter. He stopped and put her down.

"I . . ." he paused, trying to find words for what he had to say. "I know you fear me. I will try not to push you."

The look of mute gratitude in Rhiannon's eyes sent a chill down his spine. Her fear of him was deep and terrible. He reminded himself it was also unfounded. For her sake as well as his own, he must break through the barrier between them. If he did not possess her, they would both go mad.

"I'm not going to hurt you, Rhiannon. I want to teach you the magic of your body. There is pleasure to be had between a man and a woman, wondrous pleasure. If you will let me, I will show you. But first, you must take off your clothes." Seeing her fear deepen, he added, "I won't do anything you don't want me to." He pulled Rhiannon to him, trying to soothe her. "I promise," he whispered into her hair. "For now, I only want to look at you. You are so lovely. I want to enjoy the sight of you. Please . . ."

He released her, and she began to undress slowly. First the cloak, then the wet gown. She paused at her shift, but only a moment, then she pulled it over her head and stood naked before him.

Maelgwn sucked in his breath. She was even more beautiful than he had imagined. His eyes moved down her body slowly, lingeringly: pale skin warmed with only a scattering of freckles, delicately rounded breasts, the nipples rosy pink, upturned and inviting, her waist no wider than a handspan, then the triangle of deep red curls, like a bronze shield, guarding the mysterious passageway he could not stop thinking about. His eyes swept over her again, taking in the grace and perfection of her form. Everything about her was small but exquisite. He wanted to devour her.

"Turn around," his voice was harsh, faltering with desire.

After a second's hesitation she obeyed him. This view was beautiful too. The veil of hair swinging over the narrow back, the faint outline of her ribs barely visible through the translucent skin, the tiny waist, the achingly plush, rounded bottom. Maelgwn held his hands at his sides, scarcely trusting himself not to touch her.

"Rhiannon," he whispered. She turned around, her cheeks flushed with embarrassment. He almost laughed. "Do not look so miserable. I like what I see. Indeed, I can scarce remember ever seeing any woman so beautiful, so irresistible . . ."

Rhiannon stared at her husband; the huskiness in his voice made her throat go dry. She could feel his need, guess his hunger. His eyes were dark, the pupils nearly swallowing the blue of the irises. Her heart pounded, and it took all her determination to keep from bolting across the beach.

"Lie down." Maelgwn spread his cloak upon the sand and gestured toward the makeshift bed. Trembling, Rhiannon moved to obey him. Her pulse thudded in her ears; her legs felt so weak it was a relief to sink down upon the cloak. Maelgwn joined her, settling himself beside her. His eyes moved over her like a caress, burning a pathway across her exposed skin. She could feel the heat of his body next to hers.

"Does this . . . are you frightened of me now?"

She shook her head, wishing she did not have to lie.

"You are my wife, Rhiannon. It is only natural that I take pleasure in the sight of your body."

"But I am too thin, too little for you." Her words of protest seemed to startle Maelgwn. He reached out, as if to touch her, his large, tanned hand moved to within inches of her breasts. She sucked her breath, and he pulled his hand away. She saw the clench of his jaw, a flash of frustration in his eyes. He appeared to struggle with himself, then he spoke:

"You are beautiful, Rhiannon. All of you. I like the way you are, so small and perfect." His face flushed with passion, and his voice fell lower. "I would like to see more. I would have you spread your legs for me."

Horrified, Rhiannon shook her head. Maelgwn's eyes met hers, hot and pleading. "If I cannot touch you, at least allow me to know you that way. Please."

She shivered, then slid her legs apart. She closed her eyes, feeling a wave of shame rush over her. No man had known her body except Llewenon, and he had used it, sating his lust with ruthless cruelty. The horror of the memory made her open her eyes.

Maelgwn watched her. His dramatic blue eyes fixed upon her face. A slight smile curled his mouth. "You are beautiful there too, Rhiannon. Like a flower, a sweet flower."

She stared at him. A strange ache was building inside her. This man had not mauled her nor used her as if she had no feelings. He watched her with tenderness and something akin to worship. It thrilled her to know that he wanted her. It was as if he shared part of his power with her.

Maelgwn abruptly turned away and leaned against a nearby rock. She sensed the tension in his body. He trembled, and his hands clenched in frustration. Her heart went out to him. It was unfair to deny him. If he would not let her relieve him as she had before, she must find some other way to satisfy him.

"Maelgwn." Her voice came out frail and shaking. "If you want to touch me . . . it is all right. Only tell me . . . tell me you will not hurt me."

His eyes were so grateful, so warm. She moved toward him and allowed him to pull her to sit between his legs. Her back rested against his chest, and he held her tightly, crushing her breasts with his arms. "Ah, Rhiannon," he sighed, his mouth nuzzling against her hair. "Do you know what I see when I look at you?"

She shook her head as he continued in his soothing musical voice. "I see skin as cool as the sea, as fair as moonlight. But I also see hair as bright as the sun, as brilliant as a flame. I have known your coolness, Rhiannon. Now I wish to know the fire of you." He stroked her hair softly. "It is a wonder it does not burn my fingers, your hair is so vivid and rich. And here . . ." His hand slid down her body, pausing at the juncture of her thighs. She held herself very still as he caressed the coarse curls.

"Here it is even redder, even hotter. Do you know what

I think, Rhiannon? I think there is heat and fire there, there in the darkness between your legs. Let me touch you there . . . let me feel the flame.''

His voice was a raspy whisper, shivering across her skin. It seemed to ignite something within her, a kind of heat, a hungering ache. She slid her legs apart, fearing and welcoming him.

His fingers were gentle, almost reverent. She could feel him coaxing her to relax, to trust him. The heat grew; the rest of her body felt fevered and tingling.

"I can make you wet with desire for me. I will be patient. I will take my time. I will take as long as I need to make you want me.''

It was like drowning, or what she imagined drowning to be like. Her breath would not come fast enough. She was dizzy and weak, but it felt pleasurable. Her will dissolved, her body felt boneless and weightless, melting into the strength and warmth of Maelgwn's chest and shoulders, vibrating to the warm, coaxing, seductive sound of his voice.

"You are beautiful, Rhiannon. A lovely pink flower sweet with nectar.'' His stroking ceased its teasing rhythm and grew more intense. Maelgwn eased her thighs further apart and slowly urged a finger into her aching center. Rhiannon shivered convulsively.

"Feel how good it feels," he murmured. "It will feel even better when I am inside you.''

The pressure of his finger increased, making her tense, but still she did not want him to stop. A strange weakness filled her. She needed him, needed him to keep touching her.

"You are wet," he whispered. "I have made the flower spill its sweet nectar. I cannot pleasure you more . . . except by coming inside you. Will you let me, Rhiannon?''

She did not answer. She was too enthralled by the sound of his voice and the throbbing energy building within her.

She felt sad and frustrated when he slid away from her and stood to undress. Without his touch to entice and distract her, the fear returned. She closed her eyes, afraid to watch him, afraid to think about what he would do next.

He returned to kneel beside her, so close she could almost taste the salty, earthy scent of him. His hands moved over her body. His fingers explored her breasts, then glided over her hips, reaching around to caress her buttocks. The feverish heat returned as his hands stroked and squeezed, shaping her flesh into patterns of pleasure. Rhiannon's hips arched upward, her thighs opened slightly. Still, she stiffened as Maelgwn covered her. She could feel his shaft hard against her thigh, like a weapon. Then it moved away, and she felt the soft tickle of his hair upon her belly. Startled, she opened her eyes. Maelgwn was leaning over her breasts. She watched as he took one of her nipples in his mouth and suckled.

A strange energy flowed through her, half pleasure, half subtle, exquisite pain. The pain faded as she grew used to his rough, hungry mouth. She gasped in wonder and closed her eyes. Her hips pressed against his body. The fever inside her burned deep, shooting along her legs. She could not help moving, her body urgent against Maelgwn's. He held her down gently, his mouth working upon her breast as if he suckled sublime delight from her body. He switched to the other side, and Rhiannon moaned, thinking she would burst apart from the bliss of it.

Then Maelgwn's mouth left her, and she opened her eyes to look at him. His lips were soft and wet. The fierce blue of his eyes seemed to have melted. He looked tender and very beautiful. She reached up to stroke his wind-burned skin, enjoying the pleasing harshness of it. His wild, wavy hair framed his face with darkness. She pulled him down to her, realizing she desired more of this wonder he had taught her. He kissed her, enveloping her mouth with wet, throbbing pressure. As his tongue penetrated her lips, she felt a moan vibrating in his chest. His body trembled and heaved, like a great river washing over her. His tongue entwined with hers. She clung to him, fearful and excited.

He broke away, and his eyes fixed upon her, glassy with passion. "Please, Rhiannon. Let me." His hand slid down her belly, easing closer and closer to the juncture of her thighs. "Relax," he whispered. "Think of the flame within you. I'm going to touch the flame and make it glow even brighter, even hotter. I'm going to make magic inside you."

She moved her legs apart, and his hand found the warm wetness between them, caressing her with light, rapid strokes. She closed her eyes and gave in to the feverish longing his touch evoked. The rhythm built and then ebbed, throbbing and tantalizing, bringing her to the brink of completion but never fully satisfying her need. She moaned and twisted her hips in search of the magic he had promised.

"Now," he murmured. "Now, I will touch you with something even better."

He covered her, easing his body lower, and she felt his hand guide his shaft against her flesh. She felt a shivering light ecstasy, then the comforting pressure she had longed for. The pressure increased, deepening, filling her. She tensed, but there was no way to get away. Maelgwn's body held her down.

Panic surged through her. He was too big, too overwhelming. She shifted her hips; the movement made Maelgwn groan. She went utterly still. He brought his mouth next to her ear, whispering her name and kissing her neck. She forgot her fear as she listened to his voice, as low and vibrant as the wind through the reeds. Then Maelgwn pressed himself deeper within her, and the terror returned. Would he consume her, steal away her very soul with his body?

"It's all right," he whispered. "See, it does not really hurt. Relax and feel how good it is to have me close to you. I want you, Rhiannon. I want you so badly!"

She felt his control snap. He cried out her name again, then his hands moved beneath her hips, holding her tightly as he began to move inside her. He was huge and powerful, and he rocked and urged within her until her body seemed on the verge of shattering. She reached for his strong shoulders and clutched them, bracing herself against the tumultuous rhythm that rampaged where their bodies were joined. He was part of her now, his body so close it became one with hers. The energy that was each of them swirled and mingled in a dark, hot void. She surrendered to the magic and held on.

Fierce, pounding rhythms, older than anything except the sea and the rocks around them. Life itself crushed into a moment. Dazzling, aching flesh and the sensation of falling . . . falling. She heard Maelgwn's cry of ecstasy and shared it briefly. Then it was over, and the world swam around them in light and sound as they became separate creatures again. Her cheeks were wet with tears, but she was happy. She lingered her fingers over her lover's damp, burning skin.

He raised himself from her, still panting for breath. His eyes were a distant misty blue. A passionate ache filled Rhiannon, more poignant than anything she had ever known. It choked her throat and filled her eyes with tears. It was incomparable what she had shared with this man, what he had given her. All Llewenon's talk of magic had not prepared her for this. The magic was beyond pleasure or pain; it was a gift from the gods, a glimpse of the light of the other side.

She knew Maelgwn felt it too, for he turned to watch

her with dazed, wondering eyes, and when at last he spoke, his voice was stunned and tender.

"Ah, Rhiannon. Now that I have had you, I will only want more."

Chapter 10

"Have you told Rhiannon we leave tomorrow?" Balyn asked as he walked from the practice field beside Maelgwn.

"No, but she must expect it. The purpose of our marriage was to join Brigante forces with Cymry so I could win back Gwynedd."

"Even if she expects it, she may not be pleased to watch her new husband go to war, especially now he's begun to spend so much time in her bed."

Maelgwn gave Balyn a quick glance. "Is it so obvious?"

"I should think so. A few days ago you were glowering and snarling around the fortress like a wet wildcat; now you appear as mellow and contented as one of Gwenaseth's pet kittens. It's not hard to guess you've overcome your problems with Rhiannon."

Maelgwn shrugged. "There's much less tension between us these days."

"Lludd's balls! Don't be coy, Maelgwn," Balyn chortled. "There's no shame in admitting you enjoy your wife. She's a lovely young woman, and it's been a long time since you've had anything so fine to warm your bed. I would think you were in your dotage if you didn't lose a little sleep making the most of these few nights you have before we leave.''

Maelgwn opened his mouth to protest, then closed it. His passion for Rhiannon surprised him, but there was nothing shameful in it. He had once felt this way about Aurora. *But he had loved Aurora,* he reminded himself. He could hardly say he loved Rhiannon. He did not even know her.

He allowed himself a small smile. ''Now that Rhiannon has overcome her fear, we get along exceptionally well.''

''Did you find out the reason for her odd behavior?''

Maelgwn's face darkened with a frown. ''Gwenaseth had some thoughts on the matter, but I'm not certain I agree with her. Perhaps it was no more than simple shyness. Rhiannon's still as skittish as a wild creature if you catch her unawares.''

A wild creature, Maelgwn mused as he took leave of Balyn and walked across the courtyard. The image would not leave his thoughts. For all that she had finally let him explore her body—every delicious inch of it—Rhiannon's mind remained as much a mystery to him as a hind's.

He headed briskly for the weaving room, knowing he would be likely to find his wife there. She looked up when he entered; her face colored prettily, and a slight smile turned up the corners of her mouth. Like him, it seemed she had only to see him to be reminded of the pleasure their bodies shared. She put down her sewing and came to greet him. Maelgwn ignored the other women in the room and pulled her into an embrace.

''Do I embarrass you?'' Maelgwn asked as they left the weaving room. ''Would you rather I didn't kiss you in front of others?''

''Oh, no, my lord. I mean . . . you may do whatever you wish.''

"That is not what I asked, Rhiannon. I inquired as to your feelings."

Rhiannon took a deep breath. What could she tell Maelgwn? It still astounded her to see a warrior, a *king*, showing warmth and affection to a woman before others. "Your kindness pleases me, although I suspect that some of the women look askance at your familiarity."

"There will always be those who are jealous of you, Rhiannon. You must not let them cause you distress." Maelgwn pulled her close, snuggling her against his chest. "If you like me to touch you, I will continue doing so. We have little time left. I leave tomorrow for war."

Rhiannon tensed. Despite its inevitability, she still dreaded Maelgwn's leaving. They barely knew each other, had only begun to build a sense of trust between them. Now he was leaving.

"Don't look so sad." Maelgwn smiled teasingly. "Although I admit it warms my heart to know my wife regrets my departure, I don't want you to worry. With any luck, I will return long before the leaves fall."

"You'll be gone the summer then?"

"A couple of months at most. I know the Brigantes will be anxious to return north. And I . . ." He leaned over to whisper in her ear. "I will be anxious to return to my wife."

A hot thrill filled her at the sound of Maelgwn's seductive, compelling voice. She could scarce believe this passion that moved between them, this impatient, dizzying hunger that forced them to seek out the bedchamber in broad daylight and kept them sleepless long into the night. Maelgwn had taught her so much in a few short days. She had gone from fearing his touch to reveling in it.

"Let us say good-bye now, Rhiannon. I will sleep alone tonight. I must rise early, and I don't want to wake you."

Rhiannon looked toward the sprawling wooden building that housed their bedchamber. Maelgwn nodded. "I fancy seeing you naked by daylight one more time ere I go."

They walked together without speaking. Rhiannon felt her breath quicken with every step, and the ache inside her deepen. She remembered the incredible things Maelgwn had already done to her. The feel of his mouth nuzzling her most sensitive, intimate parts. The shock and wonder of his shaft entering her. The satisfying but almost painful sensation that filled her as he teased her nipples with his fingers and suckled her greedily.

They had barely entered the bedchamber and closed the door when Maelgwn drew her to him so hard the air left her chest. He grasped her hips with his hands and lifted her so her pelvis pressed against the hardness of his erection. "How would you like it today, Rhiannon? There must be some position we have not tried yet. Aye, I am sure there is."

Rhiannon nodded, too breathless to speak. It was all new to her, so overwhelmingly intense. At times she wondered if Maelgwn truly had stolen her soul. When he touched her body, she seemed to become a different person—a bold, sensuous woman, eager for every delight he could teach her.

He hiked up her gown so she was naked against him, then slid his fingers deep in the cleft between her legs. "Mmmmm," he moaned. "You spoil me. I no longer have to spend time arousing you. You are so eager and willing, if you are not careful I will grow lazy in my lovemaking. Aye, I do feel lazy," he added. "Perhaps today, I will let you do the work. I will let you pleasure me."

He released her gently, and she slid down his body, her legs so weak and trembly she could scarce stand. "The bed . . ." she gasped.

"Aye, we would be more comfortable in a bed, wouldn't we?"

He picked her up and carried her to the bed, then released her so she could sit down. She undressed hurriedly, her fingers shaking and clumsy. It took Maelgwn longer, as he had boots and trousers to unfasten, but at last he stood beautifully, gloriously naked. Rhiannon leaned toward him and traced the sleek lines of his muscles with her fingers, glorying in the hard, substantial planes of his body. She trailed her fingers down the broad expanse of his chest. The faint pattern of dark hair dwindled to a narrow line, then widened as she reached his groin. She glanced at Maelgwn's face, and saw his nostrils flare and his eyes narrow as she grasped his shaft in her fingers. She stroked him, applying all her skill to the warm, silky shape that filled her hand. Maelgwn closed his eyes and, half-smiling, moaned.

She found a rhythm and followed it. Maelgwn's face flushed and his mouth curved in dreamy pleasure. She watched with satisfaction as his breathing quickened and his body tensed in anticipation. Abruptly he reached out a hand to grasp hers. "I want to be inside you," he growled, his eyes like glimmering blue flames.

She nodded and moved onto the bed. He lay down beside her, then motioned her to climb astride him. "You ride this time, Rhiannon."

He was so big; she doubted for a moment whether he would fit. She positioned her body over his, then cried out as he thrust upwards, impaling her body with his. She paused, motionless, panting, overwhelmed by the explosion of feeling that throbbed through her. Maelgwn reached up to fondle her breasts, still smiling, but slit-eyed with passion.

"The view is beautiful. It amazes me that I did not think to try it before." He squeezed her nipples until her hips moved of their own accord, a slow, pulsing rhythm that stole her breath again, and made Maelgwn clutch her buttocks.

"Aye, *cariad,*" he moaned, reaching up to sprawl his fingers in her hair. "Make the fire burn even hotter. You scald me now. Make me seethe with madness."

She used all her strength to rock to and fro, rubbing herself against him until sweat glowed upon her skin and her muscles trembled with the effort. Her head fell back, her long hair swept over his thighs. Maelgwn's hips met hers, pushing upwards, penetrating her even deeper. She shivered with the ecstasy of it. He grabbed her tightly and bucked against her, bouncing her furiously. Exhausted, Rhiannon sank down upon his sweaty chest, her whole body a rippling mass of rapture. Maelgwn still thrust inside her, touching her womb, her soul. Consciousness seeped from her, and she was lost, lost in a heaving world of darkness and light.

"Sweet Heaven!" Maelgwn's harsh cry roused her, and she pressed herself more tightly against his pounding heart. She soothed him, stroking his fevered brow, smoothing his thick, damp hair. This time it was she who cradled him, clutching him to her as she would an overwrought child.

At last his breathing slowed. He groaned once, then his eyes opened as he slipped out of her. "Perhaps it is true what they say about the dangers of taking a younger woman to wife. A few more times like that will slay me."

"You talk nonsense," she chided. "You are alive and strong even now. You are the one who seeks the heights of pleasure. I am content with only a little of your loving."

"You are a rare woman then," Maelgwn said with a faint smile. "Most women can easily outlast a man. It must be your red hair, *cariad*. For all your cool demeanor, you are a fiery lover. What an enchantress." His smile deepened. "You've certainly given me reason to finish my battles quickly. I will come home to you as soon as possible. I'm sure you can teach me a thousand pleasant ways to die in your arms."

Rhiannon buried her face against his chest, uncomfortable with his jest. While not a youth, Maelgwn appeared as strong and formidable as any man. She could not endure the thought of his dying. Now that Esylt was dead, Maelgwn was the only one who cared for her.

"Tell me of your battle plans." She smoothed her fingers over the sparse hair that darkened his skin. "Are you certain you are ready?"

Maelgwn laughed. "I've had two years to think strategy. I assure you, we are ready. We'll march along the coast and do battle with the coastal chieftains as we come to them. First, we will take on Rhodderi—he's been a thorn in my side for years. If he gives in without too much of a struggle, we'll move south to meet Maelgrith, Arwistyl and Cynan. By then, we will know if the mountain men support us or if we must subdue them as well."

"It sounds like many battles and much danger."

"Not really. I don't expect to meet each region's army in pitched battle. If one chieftain capitulates, the rest will follow. You know enough of war, Rhiannon, to understand that if a few strong chieftains decide to support me, my task will be easy. The first battles will count heavily, but with the Brigantes behind me, I don't see how we can lose."

Rhiannon watched him skeptically. Aye, she knew enough of war to know that a battle commander must appear confident no matter what the odds. She could not tell if Maelgwn truly thought this campaign would be easy, or if he only hoped it would be so.

"You plan to unite all of Gwynedd?"

"It is not so large a kingdom, only a small corner of Britain. My father did it, and my great-great-grandsire, Cunedag, controlled even more territory. At one time he ruled settlements from Catraith in the north to the black mountains in the south."

"I have heard of Cunedag. Gwenaseth said you and I were distantly related through him."

"If I counted all of Cunedag's spawn as kin, I could call most of the British princes 'cousin.' Cunedag was a very busy man, especially with the women. I imagine I have kin in Ireland and Brittany as well as the north."

"And you, my lord, have you sons scattered throughout your kingdom?"

Maelgwn looked surprised for a moment, then a look of sadness crossed his face.

"Nay, I have no offspring that I know of. There was the babe with Aurora that was born dead and another born to a servant girl that did not live much longer." He sighed regretfully. "It has bothered me sometimes. My father had five healthy sons by my mother and numerous bastards, but my seed does not seem to take so easily. I must be with a woman often to get her with child."

Rhiannon rubbed her palm across her husband's rough cheek, relieved by his words. If Maelgwn believed he must lie with her regularly for her to conceive, he would be less likely to stray from her bed. It was welcome news. Having learned to enjoy Maelgwn's attentions, she had no desire to share them with other women.

"And your father's other offspring—they are all dead?" she asked, still stroking his face.

"As far as I know. No one has come forward to make a claim since I became king. The last of my kin died a year ago."

Rhiannon's fingers stilled as she realized Maelgwn spoke of Esylt. She glanced down at his face, searching for a hint of his mood. The pensive look in his eyes heartened her. Perhaps Gwenaseth had overstated Maelgwn's harsh feelings toward his sister.

"Did you have any sisters?" she coaxed, beginning to smooth Maelgwn's thick, wavy hair.

"One. She died last winter. We were not close."

She watched his face intently. Did she dare to ask him about Esylt? For all his animosity toward his sister, surely he could not hate her as much now that she was dead.

"It's strange what one remembers about the dead, isn't

it?'' she began softly, still twining her fingers in his hair.
"I'm sure you can recall happy times with your sister,
perhaps childhood memories . . ."

Rhiannon's voice trailed off as Maelgwn jerked upwards.
His face flushed. "Esylt be damned! I'm glad she is gone.
I hope she is in hell now, paying for what she did to me.
My sister betrayed me, she sought to destroy everything I
loved!"

Rhiannon leaned away from Maelgwn, startled by his
vehement response. She had never seen him so angry, and
it frightened her. Even so, she felt the need to soothe him,
to let him know that Esylt eventually regretted what she
had done to him. "Perhaps you misunderstood your sister's
intentions," she whispered. "Perhaps she did not really
mean you ill."

Maelgwn's eyes narrowed. "You do not know the story,
do you? Of course not. Ferdic would not think to tell you
how he and my treacherous sister plotted to wrest away
my kingdom."

Rhiannon flinched. She should not have pursued the
subject. Gwenaseth was right. Maelgwn's hatred for his
sister was all-consuming. He would never listen to anything
said to defend her.

"I will tell you the story." Maelgwn sat up against the
back of the bed. His expression was harsh and controlled.
Only the movement of his fingers twisting a piece of the
blanket into shreds revealed his banked-down fury.

"In the fall of the year I married Aurora, Ferdic's father,
Cunedda, your grandfather, asked me to come to his aid
against the Picts. Cunedda and I were allies, so I went to
Manau Gotodin and helped him chase after an elusive
enemy who refused to meet us in battle." Maelgwn looked
up, his eyes glinting with bitterness. "Meanwhile, Gywrtheyrn, a chieftain to the east, gathered a huge army and
prepared to invade Gwynedd. If Aurora had not warned
me, I would have returned to find my people conquered

and my kingdom destroyed. But Aurora sent me a message warning that there were rumors I was soon to be brought down by treachery. When I returned, I found the source of the rumors—my sister's lover. Esylt had bragged to him of her plot to see me ruined. She planned it all with Gwyrtheyrn and Ferdic.''

Rhiannon held her breath. The look on Maelgwn's face was one of helpless pain. Esylt's betrayal had angered him and hurt him deeply.

Maelgwn turned away suddenly, as if guessing she read his expression too clearly. He retrieved his tunic from the floor, then shrugged it on over his shoulders. ''It was a very complicated plot,'' he continued. ''The raids in Manau Gotodin were not really carried out by the Picts, but by Ferdic and his men. Ferdic used it as an excuse to take part of Cunedda's army north, allegedly to fight the Picts. His real scheme was to gain control of his father's lands and set himself up as king of the Brigantes. My involvement was meant to distract Cunedda from what was happening until it was too late. With me and much of my army in the north, Gwyrtheyrn thought to easily take over *my* lands. Ferdic, Gwyrtheyrn, my sister—they planned this together. They meant to divide Gwynedd between them.

''But they failed,'' Maelgwn continued coldly. ''After receiving Aurora's message, I returned to Gwynedd and gathered my army. We marched east and met Gwyrtheyrn in battle in the lowlands. It was a bloodbath. I lost many men—warriors I've never replaced. Gwyrtheyrn was killed and the plot thwarted. Cunedda, too, took warning from Aurora's message. He went north to confront his son, and Ferdic and the rest of the usurpers fled into the wild forest.''

Maelgwn leaned back against the bed again and sighed heavily. ''In the end, Cunedda was unwilling to punish his son. He took Ferdic back among his warriors, and when Cunedda died of a fever two years later, Ferdic became king. I suspect that you, living with Ferdic's mother, never heard what your father had tried to do."

Maelgwn was silent, lost in thought. Rhiannon leaned toward him. This tale of Ferdic's treachery did not surprise her, and Gwenaseth had warned her about Esylt's betrayal. Still, she had many questions. "You're sure of Esylt's part in the plot?" she asked. "It seems Gwyrtheyrn and my father were the true villains."

Maelgwn's eyes flicked to hers. "I am sure. They could not have planned this without Esylt's help, and she bragged of my impending defeat to her lover."

"The man could have lied."

Maelgwn shook his head. "He knew I intended to kill him. He would have gained nothing by lying. Besides, Esylt acted guilty enough. Even as I marched toward the battle with Gwyrtheyrn, she fled north and joined up with Ferdic."

"But why did she do it?" Rhiannon pressed. "Her betrayal makes little sense. Ferdic and Gwyrtheyrn would never have given Esylt—a woman—any real power."

"She did it because she hated Aurora!" Maelgwn's voice shook. "Once Esylt knew I meant to honor a foreign woman as my wife, she made up her mind to destroy me."

Rhiannon considered Maelgwn's agonized explanation for his sister's actions. It was true Esylt despised Aurora, but she would not have used that as a reason to ruin her beloved brother. There had to be some other motivation for Esylt's traitorous actions. What it was, Rhiannon could not guess.

Maelgwn gave her a probing look. "You're naturally kind-hearted, Rhiannon, and I suspect it is your nature to make excuses for the failings of others. But you can make no excuse for Esylt. She was evil, pure and simple."

Rhiannon opened her mouth to protest. Maelgwn raised his hand to her lips and silenced her. "Esylt was exactly like my mother. Neither one of them could ever think of anything or anyone but themselves. Their hunger for power was a poison that ate away their souls. I thought at one time I was like them, that I was cursed as they were. I feared the evil would eat me up as it did them.''

Rhiannon reached for his fingers and kissed them. ''Do not say such things, my husband. You are a good man, a good king. You are not cursed.''

Maelgwn gave her a haunted look. ''Sometimes I wonder if the reason I have not sired any living children is because my seed is meant to die out, and the evil perish with it.''

Rhiannon tried to suppress the shiver Maelgwn's words sent through her. What darkness her husband carried in his heart. There was a kind of madness in the way he hated Esylt. Gwenaseth was right. If he ever found out what Esylt had meant to her, Maelgwn would hate her as well.

Maelgwn reacted quickly to her shudder. ''Ah, Rhiannon, I didn't mean to frighten you. If you bear my children, I'm sure they will not be cursed.'' He reached out and touched her cheek fondly. ''You are so pure and innocent. Perhaps your sweetness will purge the sin of my family. I see nothing in you of Ferdic . . . no greed or maliciousness. Whoever your mother was, she must have been a kind, gentle woman.''

Rhiannon pulled away from his caressing fingers. ''I am not pure,'' she said stiffly.

''What?'' Maelgwn stared at her, then his eyes slowly registered understanding. ''Oh, that. I care not about the innocence of your body, Rhiannon. It is the purity of your spirit I admire. I can look into your eyes and know you have no malice in you.'' He pulled her down to lay against his chest.

Rhiannon allowed him to hold her close, but her heart still raced. The secret of her relationship to Esylt weighed heavily on her mind. Could she keep it from him? If she did, what sort of trust could there ever be between them?

Maelgwn sensed her lingering unhappiness. ''What's

wrong, Rhiannon?'' he asked. ''Did I frighten you with my talk of a curse?''

''Your anger frightens me,'' she whispered against his chest. ''Your unwillingness to forget the past, to forgive.''

Maelgwn lifted her up so he could gaze into her face. His eyes were gentle, reassuring. ''Lovely Rhian, I'm sure you will never do anything I cannot forgive. There will be times when we argue, but all husbands and wives do that. My temper is fierce, I know, but usually I get over my moods quickly.''

''But what of . . .?'' Rhiannon hesitated, unable to say Esylt's name. Maelgwn's tender mood vanished, as if the mere thought of his sister afflicted him with rage. He shook his head grimly, his jaw clenched in bitterness. ''The Christian priests say it is blessed to forgive, but I cannot. I have no doubt I will go to my grave cursing Esylt.''

He glanced at Rhiannon, visibly making an effort to shake off his vindictive mood. His heartbreakingly blue and compelling eyes met hers, and he reached to touch her hair. ''Speak of it no more. I don't want the demons of my past to ruin my chance for a new beginning with you.''

His hand moved down her back, slowly, thoughtfully. Rhiannon laid her head on his chest, struggling to relax, but unable to repress one final tremble of foreboding. Maelgwn felt it and moved his hand lower along her spine. As he stroked the curve of her buttocks, he urged his hips upwards so his swollen shaft once more pressed against her.

''Make me forget, Rhiannon, one more time. Make me forget the past, and I will do the same for you.''

Chapter 11

Rhiannon examined the dark blue tunic spread across her lap, gazing in satisfaction at the embroidery encircling the neck. No one could deny she was skilled at needlework. Even her inattentive father had recognized her abilities. She had seen only thirteen winters when Ferdic made her responsible for sewing his ceremonial clothes.

Her fingers stroked the complex twining pattern of leaves and serpents she had fashioned to decorate the luxurious garment. The design was slightly different from anything she had ever done before. She hoped Maelgwn would be pleased with it. At any rate, with winter arriving shortly, he could use another heavy tunic.

Rhiannon heard Gwenaseth's voice outside the weaving room and stood. A sigh of consternation escaped her lips, and she hurriedly put aside the tunic and replaced the precious iron needle in a leather case inside her basket of sewing supplies. Lady Gwenaseth always seemed displeased to find her in the weaving room. What did Gwenaseth expect? Did she really want Rhiannon to attempt to run

Maelgwn's fortress—even though she had no training in such things and no skill in ordering people around?

When Gwenaseth failed to enter the room, Rhiannon walked restlessly to one of the looms and perused the plaid cloak she was weaving for her husband. She smiled with pleasure at the rich pattern of crimson and indigo, thinking how kingly Maelgwn would look with the thick mantle draped over his shoulders. Deep shades suited him, much as vivid ones befitted her father. The subtle, jewel-like tones would make Maelgwn's dark hair gleam even blacker, his brilliant eyes appear even more striking.

Rhiannon's smile faded. She had begun the cloak soon after Maelgwn had left with his army, never expecting to finish it before he returned. Now it was almost complete, and there was still no sign of her husband and his men. A twinge of worry creased her brow. Two moon cycles had passed, and little word had reached them on how the army was faring. Had Maelgwn's hope the campaign could be finished quickly been overly optimistic?

"Rhiannon!"

She turned to see Gwenaseth hurrying into the room. Her fair skin was flushed with color, and she panted for breath. "The army's on their way home," she announced. "The messenger said they'd been victorious, so I assume that means the other chieftains have agreed to Maelgwn's terms. The sentry sighted the troops, so they'll be here soon."

Gwenaseth paused, catching her wind, then gestured to Rhiannon's clothes. "I've sent Taffee to find your new lavender gown. It would hardly do for you to welcome home your husband in *that.*"

Rhiannon felt a flash of irritation at Gwenaseth's tart words. The loose, plain gown she wore was comfortable and was perfectly suited for the life she led. If she wore her good clothes, they would only get stained with dye in the weaving room or smeared with clay as she made her pots. And she could not imagine traipsing through the woods in bright silk and embroidered lamb's wool. Of course, now that her husband was home, she would have to resume her efforts to appear as the kind of queen Maelgwn wanted. The thought of it somehow dampened her pleasure in her husband's return.

Gwenaseth rushed off. Rhiannon followed her from the weaving room. She crossed the busy courtyard full of excited woman and children and busy servants. Inside the king's bedchamber, she stripped to her shift and put on the lavender silk gown. The fabric felt delightful against her skin, but she could not get used to the way the garment clung to her body. Gwenaseth insisted it should fit snugly around her tiny waist and slim torso, but Rhiannon doubted whether it flattered her. She had no generous curves to stretch the fabric enticingly, and she feared that the clinging shape only emphasized her slightness.

Rhiannon found the matching amethyst jewelry in the box of treasures at the bottom of the chest and adorned her neck and wrists with the gleaming stones. As she replaced the box, her hands touched a smooth, heavy object. She slowly lifted the polished bronze mirror, fingering the ornately designed handle. The mirror had belonged to Maelgwn's first wife, and Gwenaseth insisted Rhiannon should have it. Rhiannon raised the mirror to gaze into it, then hastily put it back into the chest of clothes. There was no point looking at her reflection. Except for the jewelry and the clothes, she looked exactly the same as always. She could not hope to compare with the beautiful creature Taffee had described when she told Rhiannon about Maelgwn's first wife.

And yet—Rhiannon almost reached for the mirror again. Before he left, Maelgwn had appeared to find her appearance pleasing. He mentioned the bright color of her hair several times, and his passion for her slender body had been astounding. Could it be he thought her comely?

Esylt had often complimented Rhiannon on her appearance. Perhaps her brother also saw something in Rhiannon that others did not.

Her thoughts were interrupted by shouts from the courtyard, and she realized that Maelgwn and his army must have arrived. She hastily shut the chest and pushed it back into the corner, then hurried from the bedchamber and ran across the courtyard to join the rest of the crowd thronging the gates.

Another shout went up, and Rhiannon stretched on tiptoe, struggling to see over the excited mob. The army advancing up the trackway to the fortress was an impressive sight. Brilliant banners streamed wildly above the gaily attired troops, crimson and green for the Brigantes and deep scarlet and gold for the Cymry. The whole assemblage sparkled as the sun glinted on the fishscale-like mail shirts and gleaming bronze helmets, and gilded the gold and jewels of daggers and swords. The dazzling colors of the warriors' plaid war cloaks swirled and seethed in the light like the waves of a many-hued sea.

Rhiannon held her breath as the army approached. The convoy was led by a handful of mounted warriors. A knot formed in her stomach as she spotted Maelgwn in the lead. On his proud gray stallion, he looked so beautiful, so magnificent. It amazed her to think she was wedded to such a splendid warrior. How strange to think of herself as a wife welcoming her husband back from war. She had often watched Narana greeting Ferdic as he rode into their encampment. Ferdic usually gave Rhiannon's stepmother an absentminded kiss, then went off to recount his exploits around the feasting fire.

Remembering Ferdic's attitude, Rhiannon felt a flutter of nerves, and she edged away from the press of eager wives and children. Maelgwn had been very attentive to her before he left, but that was probably because her body was new to him. It was common for a warrior to give himself over to the comforts of a woman before he left to face the hazards of war. Now that the danger was over, Maelgwn would no doubt spend his first few hours home around the fire with his men, bragging of their victories.

The army entered the gates with a clatter of hooves and jubilant cries. The crowd moved aside. The confusion and noise intensified. The men leading the army dismounted, and servants and slaves came to take their horses. The crowd swelled forward again. Rhiannon watched as Gwenaseth, Sewan and the other women all but threw themselves into their husbands' arms. The tension inside her deepened, and she was on the verge of fleeing the noisy courtyard when she heard someone call her name.

She glanced around and saw Maelgwn coming toward her, a captivating smile on his face. She moved shyly to meet him, surprised and pleased as people stepped aside for her. She was even more surprised when Maelgwn pulled her into his arms for an ardent kiss. "Rhiannon, my love." His gruff whisper sent chills down her body, and her lips seemed to burn where his had pressed.

Maelgwn's eyes met hers, an extraordinary, glowing blue. "I have my kingdom back, as I promised you. But that is not the only reason I am so happy. Rhiannon, I want you to be the first to meet . . . my son."

Releasing her, Maelgwn gestured to a young boy waiting behind him. Rhiannon blinked, gazing in amazement at the child, who stood only a few inches shorter than she. From his soft cheeks and slender limbs, she guessed him to be about seven winters. There could be no doubt as to the child's sire. He had the same intense blue eyes as Maelgwn, the same lean, graceful build. But his coloring surely came from his mother. His soft brown hair was streaked with lighter strands, and his skin had a golden sheen. With his deep-lashed eyes and fine features, he was as lovely as a girl.

"Rhun, this is your stepmother, Queen Rhiannon."

The boy bowed slightly, then thrust a bunch of wilted wildflowers toward her. "My lady."

Rhiannon took the offered bouquet and tried to smile. She was shocked, but knew she must appear pleased for Maelgwn's sake. Besides, she felt sorry for the boy. It had been overwhelming for her to meet Maelgwn's people. How much harder would it be for a child?

Maelgwn took her hand and pulled her close as they were carried along with the crowd into the fortress. "I'll explain when we are alone," he murmured in her ear. "For now I'd best go wash. I'll meet you in the hall."

As she headed toward the feasting hall, Rhiannon tried to gain control over the tumult of emotions assaulting her. It had all happened so fast. First, Maelgwn's eager greeting, then his startling introduction of his half-grown heir. What did it mean for her? Would Maelgwn be less eager to seek her bed now that his need for a son was not so pressing? Would he do as she'd feared and take a mistress? Rhiannon felt tension steal through her as she took a seat in the half-filled hall.

A few moments later, Maelgwn sat down beside her and immediately began conversing animatedly with the soldiers around them. Rhiannon took a deep swallow of the rich wine—imported from Gaul and a rare treat even for coastal dwellers.

"Would you have some roast lamb?" Maelgwn asked her, with his eating knife poised over her trencher. Rhiannon shook her head, too nervous to think of food. She felt Maelgwn's eyes on her face, then his hand warm and reassuring on her arm. "Don't look so sad, *cariad,*" he whispered. "After the feasting, I will give you my full attention, I promise you."

Rhiannon tried to smile back. She could not let Maelgwn see her anxiety over Rhun. She would concentrate on celebrating his good fortune in winning back his lands, her pleasure in her husband's safe return.

Maelgwn was obviously overjoyed by the presence of his son. He smiled and laughed often. With the brooding intensity gone from his face, he looked even more like the boy who sat across from them, eating with relish. She must pretend she shared Maelgwn's happiness. She should also be thinking of ways to make Rhun comfortable in his new home. After all, she was his stepmother now.

She turned to congratulate her husband, to express her relief at his return, but Maelgwn had begun a battle tale. His voice was low and serious, and everyone seated around them had stopped eating to listen.

"I remember trying to decide if I could take on all five of them, or if I should make a run for it." Maelgwn leaned back from his food and shook his head at the memory. "Christ's name, I thought my days were numbered when I saw Rhodderi and his four sons waiting for me in the clearing. They're all red-headed—except for Rhodderi, who is going silver fast, and they looked like a pack of copper-colored wolves planning their kill, their eyes shining and their faces hot for blood."

"Where were Balyn and Elwyn? Where were your other men?"

Gwenaseth's question sent a shiver down Rhiannon's spine, and Balyn's angry response made her feel ill.

"Well you might ask that. The fact is, Maelgwn was alone, unprotected and riding around in a God-forsaken bog." Balyn shot his king a look of disgust. "I hope you were scared, Maelgwn; I hope you were so scared your teeth rattled in your head. Perhaps now you'll think twice about chasing after your enemies by yourself."

"You went after them alone? All five of them?" Gwenaseth sounded shocked.

"Rhodderi and his sons would have gotten away if I hadn't pursued them immediately. If they had escaped and joined what was left of their men with Cynan's forces, their army would have outnumbered ours, and they certainly know the country better. The tide of the whole war was at stake. I didn't have time to worry about my own safety."

"If you had been captured or killed, the whole campaign would have been meaningless," Balyn grumbled. "You're not some young, wild-eyed warrior, Maelgwn. You know you must keep a guard around you at all times."

"Ah, but I knew you would come to rescue me," Maelgwn answered with a smile. "Just as you have for so many years."

"So tell us . . ." old Torawc interrupted impatiently. "After you captured Rhodderi, did he agree to surrender his lands, to cease his raiding?"

"Aye, he did. He saw the futility of resisting further. After he gave in, it was only a matter of time before the rest of the chieftains agreed to pay me homage. Men flock to follow a leader who wins, and I am winning once again."

Rhiannon barely heard Maelgwn's exultant words. She was still imagining him cornered by five fierce, bloodthirsty soldiers. The image made her shudder with fear. She laid a hand on his arm, reassuring herself that her husband was still whole and healthy. He glanced her way, and she was once more aware of the glow of happiness that radiated from him, making him even more handsome than usual.

Her eyes lingered on the sheen of his dark hair in the firelight, the way the skin around his eyes crinkled when he laughed. The open neck of his tunic drew her eye to his broad, muscular chest, and she remembered the bliss of nestling close to his warm strength. A rush of love filled her. She vowed she would do whatever she could to keep him content.

The conversation returned to warfare, and Rhiannon found her attention wandering. Across from her, Rhun squirmed on the bench he shared with Elwyn and Gwenaseth, jerking around every few minutes to glance behind him. Rhiannon looked and immediately saw what drew his eyes. Maelgwn's best hound, Belga, sprawled next to the fire, surrounded by a litter of wriggling pups. Rhiannon felt a surge of sympathy for Rhun. At his age, sitting still—for more than the few minutes it took to eat—was torture. She took pity on the boy and pulled on Maelgwn's tunic.

"My lord," she whispered when Maelgwn turned to her. "Perhaps Rhun would like to leave the table. I could show him Belga's pups."

Maelgwn's smile was so warm and glowing, it hurt Rhiannon's eyes to look at it. "What a wonderful idea, Rhiannon. Show him the puppies—and be sure that he picks the best of the litter for his own." Leaning over to kiss her, he added, "You are both so good for me. You will keep me young forever."

Rhiannon tapped Rhun on the shoulder and gestured wordlessly toward the dogs. The boy smiled with delight and raced to the hearth.

"Maelgwn says you may pick one to be your own dog," Rhiannon told him as Rhun fondled one of the plump, squirming creatures.

"In truth, I may have one?" Rhun looked up with wide-eyed wonder. "For my very own?"

"Of course. You will need a dog when you go hunting with your father."

"My father. That sounds so strange," the boy mused. "I'm glad I will have my own dog. I had one when we lived at Colwyn, but I had to leave it behind. My mother said it was not fair to bring it all this way."

A dozen questions sprang to Rhiannon's lips. The boy appeared unaccustomed to having Maelgwn in his life. Could it really be true that Maelgwn had not known about the boy until recently? And what of the boy's mother? Would Maelgwn bring her to Degannwy?

Rhiannon suppressed her questions, thinking it unfair to pry secrets from a child. She lingered beside Rhun for a moment and savored the tender scene of the soft, mewling puppies turning up their tight, milk-swollen bellies in ecstasy as Rhun petted them. Then she realized she had need of the privy and made her way across the crowded hall.

The free-flowing wine had made the privy a popular place tonight, despite the stink, and Rhiannon had to wait her turn. She moved around to the side and stood half-hidden in the darkness, barely listening to the group of women gossiping nearby. Only when she heard the name Rhun did she take note of their hushed voices.

"There is no doubt he is Maelgwn's son," Gwenaseth was saying. "Anyone can see by looking at him. But where did he come from? Why did Maelgwn keep him hidden all these years?"

"I think Maelgwn is as surprised as anyone else to find he has an heir," a plump older woman named Melagran suggested. "He must have learned about Rhun only recently, or he would have brought him to Degannwy sooner. The king is clearly thrilled to have a son. He near shines with happiness this night."

"But the boy? Who does he belong to?" a third woman broke in. "Why would his mother keep him secret until now?"

"Dewi told me that Maelgwn presented the boy to his men soon after Rhodderi surrendered at Colwyn. He said the prince's mother is some woman named Morganna that Maelgwn knew years ago."

"Morganna!"

Rhiannon near jumped at the shock in Gwenaseth's voice. She crept forward from the shadows and listened more intently.

"Aye, I'm sure Morganna was the name."

"Oh, I don't doubt you." Gwenaseth's voice sounded bitter. "Maelgwn often shared the bed of a woman named Morganna when he lived at Caer Eyri, even after he wed

Aurora. I never heard she was with child though. It seems strange no one knew, especially Maelgwn.''

"Well, he knows now, and he has apparently forgiven this woman for keeping his son a secret all these years. Dewi told me Maelgwn has brought this Morganna to live nearby. He had his men set up her household in a fishing village up the coast.''

"Oh, poor Rhiannon," Gwenaseth sighed.

"You think that this woman means something to Maelgwn.''

"Aye, I suspect so. She was a beauty in a coarse sort of way. You can see some of her in Rhun. But it was her body that bewitched Maelgwn. I'm not sure Rhiannon can compete with such a voluptuous woman.''

"Oh, aye," Melagran added with a note of disgust in her voice. "Men never seem to get over their fascination with big breasts. It is as if they were still little babes, greedy to suck at their mama's tits.''

The women drifted away, and Rhiannon could no longer hear their conversation clearly. She closed her eyes, feeling the waves of disappointment wash over her. She had been a fool to let herself care so much for Maelgwn. If she had once hoped to hold her husband's interest, now she knew there was little chance of it. There was no denying that men were enthralled with generously endowed women. She recalled peeping out from her blankets as a child, watching her stepmother proudly offer her big, round, white-skinned breasts to Ferdic as she sought to entice him into loveplay. For all Ferdic's casual regard for his wife, he had not often resisted when she tempted him thus.

Rhiannon wiped her sweaty face. If Morganna's body was not enough to lure Maelgwn, the fact that she had given him a son was sure to make him cherish her. Rhiannon wondered gloomily why Maelgwn had to discover he had a son *this* summer. She had so little claim upon her husband's heart. Now even that little bit was threatened.

Rhiannon used the privy, then walked listlessly to the king's chamber. She had expected too much. She had been so happy to have Maelgwn back, to feast her eyes on his glorious handsome face and to feel his warmth next to her. Even meeting Rhun had not ruined her pleasure. Despite what his existence might mean for her own sons, she liked the boy, and she could see he made Maelgwn happy. But Gwenaseth's pitying words tore all hope from her. It would be torture to watch her husband go to another woman. Even if Maelgwn came to her bed occasionally, she would always wonder if he would not rather be somewhere else.

Rhiannon let herself into the bedchamber with a deep sigh. It was agony to love. Why had Maelgwn done this to her? Why had he made her love him?

"Rhiannon?"

She feigned sleep as she heard Maelgwn's heavy step on the stone floor, tensing as the ropes supporting the mattress creaked with his weight as he sat down on the bed.

"Rhiannon, are you asleep?"

She heard him sigh softly, then stand up and begin to undress. She thought of his beautiful body—his strong, regal neck, the hard muscles in his arms and legs, his splendid shoulders. She wanted him, but she also wanted desperately *not* to want him.

The bed groaned again, and Rhiannon felt Maelgwn's body next to hers. She willed him to go to sleep.

A strong arm reached out and pulled her close. Maelgwn felt warm, almost hot. His fingers caressed her slowly, tugging lazily at the linen shift she wore.

"I'm home, Rhiannon. There is no reason for you to wear clothes to bed. I would have you naked."

She had no choice but to obey him. She squirmed away to pull the shift over her head, barely finishing undressing before he grasped her tightly and pulled her against his own hot nakedness.

"I know we should talk, but I have waited for this . . . for so long . . . so many weeks." His voice was muffled, husky, caressing her ears as his hands caressed her body. She could feel the fire burning, the fire Maelgwn awakened in her. She wanted to push him away, to cry out. It was not fair that he could do this to her, to make her want him so badly. She ached for it, for their joining. She felt his erection, hard and demanding against her belly, then his mouth, sweet and slow, devouring her. He kissed her face, her neck, her breasts, then suckled her so fiercely she cried out.

"That's right—moan for me," he whispered.

Maelgwn's fingers eased between her legs and gently probed. Rhiannon arched her back, melting into the delicious sensation. What did she care if Maelgwn loved her? As long as he touched her like this, she was content. She spread her legs and pulled Maelgwn to her. Savoring the maleness of him, she stroked his smooth chest and shoulders, then ran her hands down his back to his buttocks. She tightened her embrace until Maelgwn manuevered himself inside her. She moaned again. She had forgotten what it was like, such sharp, painful pleasure. She began to writhe, her fears forgotten as she heaved and shuddered in ecstasy.

"Rhiannon."

His voice was as soft and mellow as the night air drifting in through the window. Rhiannon closed her eyes more tightly and did not answer.

"Rhiannon?"

She heard him sigh, then murmur as if to himself: "We need to talk, *cariad*, we really do." Maelgwn rolled sideways from her, stretching out on his back.

Rhiannon stiffened. She did not want to hear Maelgwn's words of tenderness, of reassurance. She must learn to take what he gave and want no more, and his words stirred dreams within her that could never come to pass. Maelgwn shifted position on the bed, and Rhiannon waited anxiously until his breathing grew even and deep.

Somewhere outside, a bird sang a heartbreakingly lovely song. Rhiannon stared into the darkness, wide awake.

Chapter 12

"Maelgwn!"

He turned to see Gwenaseth running toward him with a determined look on her face.

"I must talk to you about Rhun," she said.

"What about him."

"Have you given any thought as to who will look after him?"

Maelgwn shrugged. "I expect he will sleep with the other unmarried soldiers in the barracks."

"Maelgwn, he's a *boy!* Those coarse, foul-mouthed men aren't proper companions for a child. Who's going to see that he takes a bath occasionally, that he combs his hair and wears a clean tunic?"

"I'll have Balyn or Gareth keep an eye on him."

"It's not the same. He's used to having his mother around. He's always had a woman care for him."

"Well, his mother isn't here, and he's too young for a wife, so what do you suggest?"

Gwenaseth's mouth twitched. "Don't be exasperating! Obviously, you should appoint someone to look after him—and I don't mean me. I have enough to worry about with my own children."

"I could ask Rhiannon."

"Of course you should. She's his stepmother now. Besides, she seems to have taken a liking to him. Although I doubt she has the authority to keep a strong-willed young boy in line."

"I'm sure she'll manage. Anyway, Rhun will be spending most of his time at his lessons with Father Leichan or training with me." Maelgwn turned to leave.

Gwenaseth stopped him with a hand on his arm. "There's another thing I wanted to mention."

"Of course there is," Maelgwn said resignedly.

"I feel I have to say something about Morganna."

"What about her?"

"I really don't think it's proper for you to have brought her to live so close to Degannwy."

Maelgwn tried to keep his voice calm and reasonable. "Look, Gwen, I know you never liked Morganna, but you must admit it would be cruel of me to take Rhun away from his mother completely. As you said, he's only a boy. It'll do him good to visit Morganna now and then."

"But think of Rhiannon, Maelgwn. She's barely been wedded to you one sun-season. Now she must accept your former mistress living a half-day's walk from Degannwy."

"There's no need for her to know."

"Don't be pigheaded, Maelgwn! Even if you don't tell her, Rhiannon will find out just the same. The gossip about Morganna is everywhere, running like wildfire through the fortress. Rhiannon's not deaf; she's certain to overhear something. When she does, she's bound to be angry. It might well sour the goodwill growing between her and Rhun."

Maelgwn weighed Gwenaseth's words carefully. Although he doubted Rhiannon would react with anger, he had not considered that she might resent Rhun. If

Rhiannon had a son, it would be tricky enough to keep the two boys from being rivals. He did not need to sow seeds of dissension so early on.

"You are right, as usual," he answered. "But tell me, Gwenaseth—what is your answer for me this time? I have promised Morganna and Rhun, and I can't go back on my word. I don't intend to seek Morganna's bed, if that's what you're worried about. But I can't send her away, either."

Gwenaseth's small jaw set stubbornly. "If you're determined to bring that whore here . . ."

"Morganna is not a whore!"

"Oh, no. Certainly not." Gwenaseth's voice was harsh with sarcasm. "You gave Morganna grain and wine and jewels now and then, but it was surely never payment for her favors."

"Damn you, Gwenaseth, you hate her because of Aurora."

"Aye, I do. It near broke Aurora's heart when she found out you were seeing another woman."

"That's a lie! I never bedded Morganna after I married Aurora."

"Aurora thought you did, and that's what matters."

Maelgwn clenched his fists in frustration. "Do you expect me to regret bedding Morganna? Because of one of those nights, I have Rhun. Sweet Aurora, bless her soul, did not live to give me a son, but Morganna has. I think I owe her something for that."

Gwenaseth's eyes narrowed. "Stubborn and so sure of yourself—the priory did not change you, Maelgwn, not one whit. You're obviously not going to listen to me, so I'll stop wasting my breath."

Gwenaseth turned and stormed off. Maelgwn, his own temper flaring, resisted the urge to call her back. She was right, but that did not make his dilemma any easier to resolve. Morganna had played on his guilt at taking her son away. Now he would pay for his weakness. He had

allowed his joy in finding Rhun to blind him to the consequences of the promises he made, but consequences there
would surely be.

Rhiannon, he thought with a sharp stab of guilt. He had
to explain.

"Taffee! Where's Rhiannon?"

"I wouldn't know, my lord. I haven't seen her since this
morning."

Maelgwn met the servant's insolent stare. "Help me,
Taffee. I've already looked in the weaving room, the
kitchen and the bakehouse. Where else might she be?"

"Mayhap she left the fortress. She does that, you know—
disappears for hours into the forest or down the coast."

"Alone?" Maelgwn asked in a shocked voice.

"Aye, alone. Who would go with her?"

Maelgwn gave Taffee an incredulous look and strode
off toward the gate. "Eleri!" he bellowed up at the guard.
"Get down here."

"Where's Rhiannon?" he demanded when the nervous
sentry reached him.

"She went for a walk. She promised not to go far, no
more than a short ways into the forest."

"A short ways! It takes little time for a woman to be hurt
or abducted. Rhiannon is my queen. She must always be
guarded. At the very least a boy should accompany her,
and if she goes very far, a footsoldier."

Eleri flushed. "Aye, my lord. I had not thought of her
being abducted. I see now that she needs better protection." He shrugged sheepishly. "I'm afraid it is hard to
remember Rhiannon *is* queen. She is so shy and quiet,
and she talks to everyone in the same soft voice and acts
as if she were no one special . . ." Eleri's voice trailed off
as he realized he was blundering further. The king was

already angry. It was probably unwise to suggest that his new wife behaved less than royally.

To Eleri's surprise, Maelgwn's anger seemed to ease. "You are right," he said thoughtfully. "It is easy to overlook Rhiannon. I do it myself sometimes."

"Ho, Maelgwn! Why are you chastising this young soldier? Your morning might be better spent thinking up ways to entertain your guests."

Maelgwn turned and smiled at the handsome, red-headed soldier who accosted him. Gavran was commander of the Brigante forces. He and Maelgwn had grown surprisingly friendly over the summer campaign. Gavran could be as jovial and mocking as Ferdic, but somehow his good humor was not nearly as aggravating. There did not seem to be any malice behind his teasing wit and ready grin.

"What? Have you already bedded all the wenches in the fortress and lost your booty gambling with my men? You northern savages are amazing. I had expected those pursuits to keep you busy for at least a fortnight."

"Oh, I've found a few women who please me, but I must let them get their rest or they'll never be able to handle me tonight. As for the gaming—it's only fair that I give your men a day of respite from my skill. I don't want to be blamed for breaking up marriages when the Cymry wives realize all their baubles and jewels have been lost to me."

Gavran gestured toward the fortress gate and continued, "I do have the urge to see more of the country here though. Perhaps do some scouting for a hunting trip before we return home. I don't suppose your game here compares to that of the northern forests, but it might make for decent sport."

"They say a twelve-point buck was spotted just a few days ago. Do you think that worthy enough quarry for a mighty hunter such as yourself?"

Gavran whistled. "Twelve points, eh? Aye, that might tempt me. When can we have a look?"

"I was thinking of going out to the forest this morning, although I had other prey in mind. It seems Rhiannon has gone off to the woods by herself." Maelgwn's face grew grim. "I'm not so secure in my kingship of Gwynedd that I mean to let my wife wander unescorted."

"Don't worry overmuch about Rhiannon," Gavran answered as the two men fell into step on the muddy pathway leading from Degannwy. "It's not likely that anyone could sneak up on her in the woods. She grew up in the forest, and she's spent as much time there as any hunter. She can creep among the trees and hide in the bushes like a wild thing. Ferdic used to tease her that she was a wood fairy instead of a girl. It made her flush very prettily when he called her that."

"Wood fairy! You might reassure me if I believed in magic and enchantments. However, I don't, and the idea of Rhiannon facing an enemy alone in the woods with no more than her wits and fleet little feet fills me with dread."

"Perhaps she could put a spell on them before she ran," Gavran answered lightly. "Rhiannon was very nearly apprenticed to our bard and magician. She spent hours with him, helping him gather plants and listening to his talk of spirits and spells. Surely he at least taught her how to turn men into toads. You might keep that in mind and do your best not to anger her, Maelgwn."

"Cease your jesting, Gavran. You don't really mean to tell me that Rhiannon trained to be a sorceress."

"May Lludd strike me down if I'm lying. Sorceress may not be the right word, but Rhiannon must have learned some craft in all her time with Llewenon. No doubt she would have learned more if Ferdic hadn't sent Llewenon away. Strange business that. No one ever knew what Llewenon did to offend the king. He simply disappeared one day, and Ferdic forbade anyone to speak of him. It was a loss for the tribe. Llewenon wasn't much of a healer, but he was a fine bard. He had a real silver tongue."

"Jupiter, I don't know my wife at all!" Maelgwn gave Gavran a startled look. "I never dreamed Rhiannon dabbled in the magic arts."

"The old ways are still strong in the north. Every tribe has a healer or two, someone who knows how to use plants and potions to aid in healing, to set bones and clean wounds. Very often those wise ones also claim to be able to predict the weather, to protect the tribe from evil influences or to cast spells that make men fall in love or behave heroically in battle. I wouldn't let Rhiannon's training bother you," Gavran continued with a brief shrug. "She's too kind a soul to use her knowledge for anything evil. She'd likely never use anything on you worse than a love potion."

"I'm not worried, only curious." Maelgwn frowned. "Most women have secrets, but Rhiannon is a virtual treasure trove of them."

Rhiannon shuffled her feet among the dry leaves, wondering why she could not find the peace and contentment the forest usually brought her. As much as she longed to forget Degannwy and Maelgwn and all her troubles, her worries pursued her even here. She could not escape the dull ache of jealousy that nagged at her like a sore tooth.

Stopping, she sighed. She had let down her guard and allowed herself to think she could mean something to Maelgwn. She had dared to believe in dreams, to indulge her naive fancies. Now she would pay for her foolishness.

A slight sound in the distance made Rhiannon tense. She should go back. She had promised the guard she would not go far, but she could not bear to return to the fortress yet, to endure the looks of pity in the other women's eyes, the whispering behind her back. No doubt they

all wondered what she would do about Rhun's mother,
and if there would be trouble between her and Maelgwn
over his mistress. Rhiannon took another step down the
path away from the fortress. She was not ready to return
to Degannwy. She might never be ready.

Wandering on, she listened to the birds, trying to pick
out familiar voices and give them names. She studied the
ground, watching the colorful leaves tremble in the
autumn breeze, noting the location of different herbs she
knew. She came upon a bush of blackthorn berries and
picked one and ate it, relishing the tartness. It was the
taste of fall—bittersweet and poignant.

Rhiannon walked until she reached a small clearing
where the sunlight shone in dancing patterns through the
thinning yellow poplar leaves. She sat down among the
leaves and gathered some in her skirt. Tossing bunches of
them up in the air, she watched them fall and whirl away
in the breeze. The idle act seemed to lighten her heart.
She had not played like this in months.

"Rhiannon!"

The call came faint and far away, but the voice was
unmistakable. Rhiannon stood up quickly.

"Maelgwn, I am here," she answered as loudly as she
could.

There was silence, then a vague rustling sound in the
distance. In a few moments, Maelgwn appeared next to
her. She jumped slightly in surprise.

"You see," Maelgwn said with a smug smile. "You are
not the only one who can move soundlessly in the forest."

"What's wrong? Why did you call for me?"

Maelgwn's smile disappeared. "You should not be walking in the forest alone. In the future, you may not leave
the fortress without an escort."

Rhiannon stared at her husband in dismay. How could
he do this to her? If she could not seek out the solace of
the woods, she would never be able to endure her life at

Degannwy. She opened her mouth to protest. Before she could speak, they both turned at the sound of someone else approaching.

"Maelgwn, I see you've found your wood fairy after all," Gavran announced jovially as he entered the clearing. "And she hasn't turned you into a toad yet."

"She hasn't had a chance," Maelgwn responded.

Rhiannon looked from one man to the other, baffled by their banter. She nodded to Gavran, then turned as if to leave. "I must be getting back. I . . ."

"What did I just say, Rhiannon?" Maelgwn barked, his face grim. "I told you that you must not go walking in the woods alone."

Rhiannon froze at his sharp words. She was unused to Maelgwn directing his anger at her, and it especially upset her that he displayed it in front of her countryman. She fought to make her voice meek, to stifle her resentment. "I'm sorry, my lord. I am accustomed to coming and going as I please. It is hard to remember I must be escorted. I will try to remember your wishes in the future."

She waited stiffly, expecting Maelgwn to take her arm and escort her back to Degannwy. Instead, he gestured to Gavran dismissively. "You're welcome to scout for the stag," he told the Brigante man. "I've found my quarry here." His eyes shifted over Rhiannon thoughtfully. "If I don't blunder about and scare her away for good, that is."

Gavran smiled broadly. "I'll leave you to your wood fairy then. Remember to watch out for spells and enchantments. I'd hate to go back and report that the Cymry king has been carried away to fairy land."

Gavran walked off noisily, likely scaring any game for miles, Rhiannon thought. Maelgwn moved toward her, his face intense. Rhiannon struggled not to flinch, to control her shallow breathing. For all his hot temper, Ferdic had never struck her. But her father's anger was mostly loud bluster, while Maelgwn's temper was rumored to be as quick and devastating as lightning. She watched her husband uneasily, trying to gauge if he meant to beat her. If he intended violence, she would not bear it meekly, but try to run before he could land a blow. She felt sure she could escape him in the woods.

Maelgwn lifted his hand, palm flat. Rhiannon hesitated, and it was too late as Maelgwn's flesh met hers. He grasped her chin in his fingers, lifting it so she faced him. Rhiannon sucked in her breath. She'd missed her chance to flee.

Maelgwn swore softly. "God help me, what a mess I've made of things. Again." Rhiannon watched him, wary and confused. Maelgwn's grip relaxed and his fingers moved to stroke her cheek. "You're as pale as a wraith, Rhiannon."

His touch was tender, caressing. Rhiannon felt her fear ease. Maelgwn apparently did not mean to hurt her.

Maelgwn drew her against him, still fondling her face. "I meant to reassure you, Rhiannon, not give you more cause for fear." His fingers lingered, soothing. "Did Ferdic beat you?" he asked.

Rhiannon shook her head. The pain inside her welled up, rendering her mute. What did it matter if Maelgwn struck her? That sort of suffering was easier to deal with than the heartache throbbing within her.

"Look at me," Maelgwn coaxed.

Rhiannon took a deep breath and obeyed him. His face looked sorrowful and somehow perplexed. She glanced away, but he grasped her chin again. "I don't want to see fear in your eyes, Rhiannon. I may lose my temper again. Indeed, I undoubtedly will. But I don't want you to think I will hurt you."

She nodded. The serious look in his eyes worried her. He had sought her out for some reason, and her instincts told her it concerned Rhun's mother. She had no desire to discuss the subject.

To distract him, she said, "We should go back."

"Why?"

"I . . . I must see to my sewing. If I spend all day away from the fortress, the women will think me lazy and too proud to work."

"The women be damned."

Rhiannon looked up, startled. Maelgwn's gaze was intent, unsettling. What did he want?

Rhiannon leaned forward and put her arms around Maelgwn's neck, expecting him to kiss her. When he did not respond, she slid her hands down his chest, trying to work her fingers between their bodies so she could touch his groin.

"Nay, Rhiannon." He grasped her hands in his own. "It would be better if I talked to you first."

She waited, filled with foreboding.

Maelgwn took a deep breath. Even now, as Rhiannon stood within his embrace, he felt her remoteness, her stifling unease. Like him, she sought to use the intimacy of their bodies as a substitute for sharing their thoughts. She did not want him to really know her, and he had been cowardly to go along with her reticence. It had been easy, as Eleri had said, to forget that Rhiannon was his queen, his wife.

He had thought of her often while he was on campaign —wondering how she was faring, imagining her fine-boned, delicate body beneath his. But he had been reluctant to examine his feelings for her, and even more reluctant to think about what she might want from him.

Now he had no choice but to settle things with her, to at least set out in words how he meant to deal with her. A twinge of guilt nagged him as he realized he was primarily speaking to Rhiannon to assure Rhun's future and that of his unborn sons. He ought to have more to give Rhiannon, more than kindness and consideration. But he did not, not yet.

"I must explain to you about Rhun," he began. "I didn't

mean to surprise you. I only discovered his existence a few weeks ago.''

He felt Rhiannon stir uneasily, and he tightened his grasp, determined she should listen. ''I remembered the woman, of course,'' he continued. ''But I never knew she was with child. I could blame her I suppose, but once she gave me her reasons, I could not fault her decision.''

He sighed heavily, trying to think of a way to broach the painful subject. ''She had the baby a few months before Aurora's time to deliver. Thinking that I had a legitimate heir on the way, she decided to keep Rhun secret. When Aurora died in childbirth, it might have seemed natural for her to tell me then that I had a son that lived, but she decided against it, believing that I was too distraught over Aurora's death to accept the child.'' Maelgwn grimaced. ''She was right. I was a monster after Aurora died. As filled with anger and hate as I was, I could not have loved Rhun.

''The fever struck soon after,'' Maelgwn continued. ''She wanted to protect Rhun, and she was not sure he would be safe even in my household. She took him to a small fishing village, not very fine, but prosperous, with a steady living to be made from the sea and the nearby fields. They did not have much, but Rhun grew up strong and healthy, untouched by the inevitable politics of a king's court. In a way, it may have been the best thing for him.''

Rhiannon had grown very still. Her breathing was so light and soft, he could scarcely detect it.

''I'm not sure why she finally decided to tell me about Rhun,'' he went on. ''Mayhap she heard my army was successful again, or decided it was unfair to deprive Rhun of his rightful inheritance. It could be it took that long for her to wear out her anger.'' He suppressed a smile, remembering Morganna's dark eyes narrowed in wariness, the bitterness in her voice as she explained eight years of silence. Morganna had always been easygoing and complacent. Motherhood had changed her. Now she was a she-cat, eager to defend her offspring with claws and sharp teeth.

"I could scarce believe it when she came to my camp," he recalled, so lost in the memory that, for a moment, he almost forgot the woman he held in his arms. "Morganna wouldn't let me see Rhun until morning. She said he needed his rest. What a torturous night of waiting! I was afraid to close my eyes, afraid that if I fell asleep, I would wake up and find it all a dream."

Rhiannon touched him softly, comfortingly. Maelgwn stared into the leaf-strewn clearing. "When I finally met him, it was so strange. It was like looking at myself twenty-odd years ago. It was very nearly the greatest day of my life."

He looked down and smiled sheepishly, wondering if Rhiannon thought him a fool. Her face was, as usual, grave and serious, and her violet-shaded eyes watched him intently. "Rhun was polite when we met, but he's only a boy. I think he was relieved when I dismissed him and he could be off playing again. You should have seen him dart out of Morganna's hut. Like a falcon he was, a glorious, little golden falcon." He paused, savoring the memory.

He bestirred himself to go on, to get to the heart of the matter. "Morganna knew I was going to take him with me. She cried and begged me not to take him away from her altogether." Maelgwn paused. The memory made him uneasy. It was not like him to be swayed from his better judgment by a woman's tears. But had it been her tears, or was it the long-ago memory of Morganna's bountiful body spread out to receive him—her generous breasts with their huge nipples like full-blown roses, the light brown hair between her legs glinting in the firelight?

He forced the memory away. He no longer desired Morganna. After Rhiannon, it was like comparing bland, unleavened bread to a piquant, perfect apple. One was filling, but easy to give up, the other, tantalizingly addictive.

But Morganna still aroused his guilt. He felt he owed her for those distant nights of pleasure and the son that was their fruit. Against his better judgment, he had settled his debt. Now, gauging from the feel of Rhiannon's stiff body in his arms, he would pay in another way.

"I have brought Rhun's mother to live at Penryn, a village east of here," he said abruptly. "I wanted you to hear this from me, instead of the wagging tongues around the fortress. I know that Morganna's presence nearby may be difficult for you to bear, but I have given her my promise. I can't send her away now."

He paused, trying to assess Rhiannon's mood. Jealousy was a dangerous thing. It sometimes festered beneath the surface, rotting a seemingly healthy relationship from within. But how was he to know what Rhiannon thought if she did not speak?

"You are my queen, Rhiannon. I will keep to your bed and hope to beget more heirs. I promise that any son you bear shall have an equal share in my kingdom with Rhun."

She said nothing, but still seemed worried and unhappy. Maelgwn tensed in frustration. How was he to reassure this woman? To let her know he cared for her feelings?

Sighing, he turned away. When he glanced back at Rhiannon she was watching him. Her beautiful eyes searched his with a kind of helpless hunger, compelling him nearer. His fingers reached out and touched her breast, surrounding the small, applelike shape and rubbing the sensitive peak against his thumb. Perhaps it was not right to do this, but he could not help himself. He knew no other way to reach his wary, silent wife.

Rhiannon felt her nipples tighten at her husband's caress. She felt torn, manipulated. Maelgwn had said he would not set her aside, that her children would be his heirs. Did he tell her this out of kindness? Duty? Or the selfish urge to placate her so she would not trouble him with her jealousy?

Maelgwn's lips sought her neck and moved lower, nuzzling the soft skin above Rhiannon's gown. He was coaxing her, seducing her. Her mind struggled to ignore the delicious, numbing contentment his touch evoked. Every time she lay with this man and gave in to his powerful magic, he stole another piece of her soul.

Maelgwn slid to his knees, then pulled her down and eased her beneath him. Rhiannon sighed and closed her eyes, unable to resist him any longer. He kissed her mouth with languid slowness. Her body went limp; she floated in a cloud of tingling pleasure. Maelgwn lifted himself away from her, and she heard the jangle of his sword belt as he loosened it, then tossed it to the ground.

She felt him lean over her again, his breath warm on her face. "I have told my secrets, Rhiannon," he said. "Now you must tell me yours. Is it true you are an enchantress?"

Her eyes sprang open. She saw Maelgwn above her, his blue eyes misty with passion. He smiled lazily. "Gavran said you trained with a magician in Manau Gotodin. He warned that you would bewitch me. Verily, I think you have, for I can think of nothing except your beautiful body."

The spell shattered. Rhiannon wriggled away from Maelgwn and sat up. Her body went tight with fear. Gavran had told Maelgwn about Llewenon. Soon her husband would ask questions about her apprenticeship with Llewenon. Questions she could not bear to answer.

"I was only jesting," Maelgwn soothed. "I don't believe in magic spells anyway. But it would be nice to have a healer at Degannwy. Bleddryn is a decent army surgeon, but he doesn't know much about fevers or birthing babies. You have a gentle way about you. I'm sure you would make a wonderful healer."

Rhiannon shook her head. "I know very little, next to nothing. My training is incomplete."

"I will not force you, of course," Maelgwn said. "I only thought it was a way you could help out."

Awful images rushed into her mind. Collecting herbs in the forest with Llewenon, his gray eyes watching her. The healer's hand resting on hers as he showed her how to prepare a poultice. His smooth, seductive voice in her ear, explaining the proper method to decoct a sleeping potion.

Rhiannon sprang to her feet. She gave Maelgwn one last desperate look, then dashed off into the woods.

Chapter 13

Maelgwn stared in astonishment at the silent, empty glade. One moment Rhiannon lay pliantly beneath him. The next she had vanished as swiftly and silently as the wood fairy Gavran said she resembled. The memory of the look of desperation on his wife's face left him stunned. What was wrong? What had he said to throw her into a panic?

He shook his head in bafflement and set out after her. In her turmoil, she had left something of a trail behind, and he was able to track her passage through the dry leaves and underbrush.

He found her among a thicket of birch saplings, squeezed in tightly, her arms wrapped around her knees, her face pressed into her lap. He made his way into the thicket and reached for her shoulders, trying to drag her out of the tangle of branches.

"Nay, stop! Stop!" she cried out hoarsely. Her fingers grasped desperately at the underbrush.

"Rhiannon, it's me, Maelgwn."

She gave no sign that she had heard him. She remained crouched down, her face turned away.

Maelgwn swore in exasperation, then used his much greater strength to gradually loosen her grip so he could pull her free of the thicket and into his arms. Even then she fought him, her delicate, fine-boned body thrashing violently.

Maelgwn's heart pounded as he grappled with his frantic wife. He felt as if he had caught a wounded bird in a trap, and he was half-terrified the creature in his grasp might destroy itself in its desperation to escape. Still, he held on, gripping Rhiannon's fragile wrists tenderly in his hands and cradling her close. "Relax, Rhiannon, relax. It's Maelgwn."

She stilled slightly, and he pulled her body tight against his and lifted her head so he could gaze into her eyes. They were filled with wild anguish, like swirling pools of fear.

Maelgwn took a deep breath. He released Rhiannon's wrists and embraced her, pressing her pale, lovely face into his chest. "It's all right, Rhiannon," he whispered. "You are safe. I'll let nothing harm you, I promise."

She rested against him, still and silent. He felt the rapid thudding of her heart and waited for the fear to leave her. The minutes passed, and she sighed softly at last, as if exhaling the tension from her body.

"Rhiannon, please, tell me what's wrong. Tell me what distresses you."

She shook her head, her disheveled hair rubbing against his chest.

"If you will not talk to me, you must share your unhappiness with *someone*. Gwenaseth, perhaps?"

Again, she shook her head. Maelgwn felt a surge of helplessness. If Rhiannon refused to reveal the source of her suffering, how would he ever know how to help her?

"Why not? Don't you like Gwenaseth?"

Rhiannon lifted her gaze to his and gave him a startled

look. "Of course," she answered. "She has been very kind to me. I truly admire her."

"I don't mean that, Rhiannon. I mean ... don't you consider her a friend?"

Rhiannon's eyes grew wary. "I feel she disapproves of me somehow, that I disappoint her."

Maelgwn's sense of protectiveness toward his wife deepened. He had not realized how alone Rhiannon was, how vulnerable. He knew his people treated her with respect and deference, but had no one at Degannwy thought to offer her friendship?

"What of your home in Manau Gotodin? Was there anyone there you were close to?"

Rhiannon considered for a moment, then answered. "Aye, I did have a good friend once, but she is dead."

"I'm sorry." Maelgwn was almost afraid to press Rhiannon further. Softly, he asked, "How did she die?"

"It was a fever that took her—last winter."

He nodded, wondering how to proceed. Although her friend's death obviously grieved Rhiannon, it did not seem related to her earlier panic. Talk of healing had aroused her sudden flight. Healing, how curious. Gavran had implied that Rhiannon was quite skilled, that she had spent a great deal of time training with a magician and herbalist named Llewenon. Yet she vehemently denied having any useful knowledge. What was it about healing that disturbed her?

He watched Rhiannon intently. Her beautiful eyes remained distant, as if she looked into the past and dreaded what she saw there. Anger twisted inside him. Someone or something had damaged his young wife, crippling her vulnerable spirit in a way he was powerless to mend. Had she been abused? Raped as Gwenaseth suggested? But who would dare rape a chieftain's daughter? Only a man who was very powerful, very sure he could survive Ferdic's wrath.

Only another chieftain, or—Maelgwn's breath caught—a magician.

Shards of facts shifted in his mind, then abruptly fell into place, forming a horrifying picture of betrayal and cruelty. What if this healer, Llewenon, had taken Rhiannon against her will? That would explain her abhorrence of the healing skills he had taught her, as well as her earlier fear of sexual penetration. It would also explain why Ferdic had banished a respected bard and healer.

Maelgwn's jaw clenched. He darted a swift look at Rhiannon, then glanced away. He wanted to confront her, to find out if his guess was true. But he could not. The wound to Rhiannon's spirit was too deep, too grievous to risk disturbing. He would not have her flee from him in terror again. He must ascertain the secrets of his wife's past by other means.

He tightened his arms around Rhiannon, keeping her face pressed against his chest so she could not see his expression. He wanted to kill the man who had hurt this fragile, lovely woman, and Ferdic too, for failing to protect her. But for now, he had no chance to seek his revenge. He could only hold Rhiannon and comfort her, and swear to protect her as best he could.

He stroked her luxuriant hair. "Ah, *cariad*, it is all right, my darling, my love. I will not let anything hurt you now."

"There he is," Gavran whispered.

Maelgwn squinted in the direction the Brigante man pointed toward, peering into the mist-shrouded forest. Gradually his eyes made out the shape of a huge stag, not thirty paces ahead. The deep red of its body stood out like blood against the dull brown of the late autumn foliage.

"My God, look how big he is!"

"I've seen bigger in the north," Gavran boasted. "Still, there are few as splendid as this."

The two men stared in awe at the prey they had tracked for hours. Every inch of the stag displayed grace and power—the magnificent rack of antlers, the sleek, intelligent face, the mighty shoulders and flanks. In the forest, this beautiful creature ruled supreme. Here he was king, and the two men acknowledged his royalty with a soundless salute.

The stag turned his head, uneasy. His dark eyes watched for movement. His nostrils sniffed the air for danger.

"We'll both have to shoot," Maelgwn whispered. "With two lucky shots, we might bring him down. Otherwise, we'll have to track him through the forest. I don't relish that."

Garvan nodded. They had gone out alone, with no dogs, horses or other men. It had seemed like a grand, heroic thing to do this morning, two men, stalking their prey with only their wits, muscles and bows. Now they recognized their foolishness. If their arrows did not swiftly cause a mortal wound, they might end up following the animal for hours in the dense woods. Once they brought him down, they still had the problem of transporting the carcass back to Degannwy.

The two men gave each other a wary look, then nocked their arrows. Despite the cool autumn air, sweat dripped down their faces. The stag lifted his head again, sniffing the air.

"On your signal," Maelgwn whispered.

Gavran nodded. "Now."

The arrows flew with a shriek, and the stag leaped into the air. They barely saw the blur of his body as he sailed a few dozen paces and then crashed to the ground with a thundering sound that echoed through the forest. The two men let out whoops of delight.

"We did it!"

"Aye, two perfect shots."

They stared at each other for a second, their faces

flushed with excitement; then they embraced exuberantly, pounding each other brutally on the back.

Their celebration finished, they hurried toward the fallen animal. The stag sprawled awkwardly on the ground, his legs askew beneath him. His majestic head leaned to one side, the neck broken by the force of the arrow driving through it. The other arrow was lodged deep in his chest, impaling his heart. His glassy eyes were empty of life, but his flanks still heaved slightly and his legs twitched spasmodically.

"A king," Maelgwn whispered.

"Aye," Gavran agreed.

It seemed natural to lower their voices; they could almost sense the great stag's spirit hovering nearby, floating on the dim, moist air.

With a fierce heave, the two men rolled the stag on its side, and Maelgwn deftly slit the belly. After pulling out the intestines, still steaming with life, he reached deep into the warm mass and found the stag's heart. He paused from his butchering and began to dig a hole in the damp, cold ground with his huge hunting knife.

"What are you doing?" Gavran looked up from his struggle to retrieve his arrow from the stag's neck.

Maelgwn glanced at him almost sheepishly. "I'm making a sacrifice. In honor of this great king."

"I thought you were a Christian."

"In part," Maelgwn answered. "I am other things as well."

Gavran smiled, showing the big, white teeth the Brigante were famous for. "Say a prayer to the horned god, Cerunnos, for me as well. Ask him to see me safely home."

Maelgwn nodded solemnly, then went about his task of burying the heart. When he was done, he bowed his head and whispered his words of thanks. He could not explain why he did it, and no doubt the monks of Llandudno would have called him a blasphemer, but in the darkness of the woods, it seemed right that one king should show honor to another.

They finished butchering the deer, covering much of the carcass with dirt and leaves, then each slinging a hindquarter over their shoulders.

"We should have brought horses," Gavran said with a groan beneath his burden.

"Aye, but then we would have had to bring the hounds and the other men. It wouldn't have been the same."

"No, it wouldn't have been the same," Gavran agreed. "It was a superb hunt, and one I will boast about for years."

"No doubt you are eager to be home to begin your boasting," Maelgwn said.

"Aye. I am eager to be home, but it is not to sit around the fire and talk of hunting. It is my wife I miss . . . and my three small sons."

"Haven't you found any women here to your liking?"

"You know I have sampled nearly every wench in the fortress," Gavran answered with a smile. "Still, it is not the same. There is nothing like a Brigante woman. Tangwyl has the thickest, softest red-gold hair and the loveliest white breasts . . ."

"Stop!" Maelgwn complained. "If you keep this up, I will want to go home to her myself."

"Ah, but you have a Brigante woman of your own now, Maelgwn, the fair Rhiannon."

"Rhiannon hardly seems like a Brigante woman, so delicate and small she is. Tell me, Gavran, do you know anything of her mother or her mother's people?"

Gavran shook his head. "Only the stories the women tell. That Ferdic, when he was just newly a man, came home from campaign with a tiny, red-haired babe, claiming that she was his own off a foreign princess. Rhiannon was raised first by Ferdic's mother and then his wife."

"A strange tale."

"Aye, especially for a man like Ferdic. He's shown little

interest in Rhiannon, at least until she became a woman and he realized he might make a good match with her.''

"So, you don't think Ferdic holds his daughter dear,'' Maelgwn said contemptuously. "I thought as much. The girl has been neglected and perhaps more.'' He turned to Gavran abruptly. "I recall you mentioning a man named Llewenon, the bard and healer Rhiannon trained with. What more can you tell me about him?''

Gavran frowned in concentration. "He was an odd one, kept to himself mostly, but then, most of the Learned Ones are like that. After he disappeared, he wasn't really missed, except for his tales around the fire. The man could weave a fine story.''

"What of women? Did Llewenon seek any of the Brigante women to warm his bed?''

"Not that I know of, although he could have met them in secret. Why do you ask?''

"It is only a thought . . .'' Maelgwn's voice trailed off. He did not know how to broach the subject of Rhiannon's possible rape. It was an awkward topic to bring up with one of his wife's countrymen, but it seemed the only way to discover the truth.

"Does it still trouble you that Rhiannon took training from such a man?'' Gavran asked.

"Not exactly.'' Maelgwn met Gavran's gaze. "Do you . . . is it possible that this man, Llewenon, took Rhiannon off alone and raped her?''

Gavran looked startled. "Did Rhiannon tell you this?''

"She has not told me anything at all. It's only a feeling I have.''

"I suppose it's possible. She was in his company a great deal . . . alone in the forest. And such a thing would explain how Llewenon fell out of favor with Ferdic. If he learned his daughter was violated, Ferdic would have been furious. Not because of Rhiannon, but for the offense against his authority." Gavran glanced at Maelgwn. "Why does it matter? Are you dissatisfied with your agreement with Ferdic?"

"Of course not," Maelgwn answered, then paused. He did not want to discuss Rhiannon's odd behavior, nor could he tactfully vent his fury at Ferdic with one of the Brigante king's own men. He shot Gavran a rueful smile. "I only seek to understand my wife a little better. Who among us would not like to glean better knowledge of their mates?"

Gavran laughed. "Don't waste your time, Maelgwn. There's no understanding women. I've been married for well-nigh seven years, and my wife is yet a mystery. I've come to believe it's better this way. I fear if I knew the truth of her thoughts, I would not like it!"

Maelgwn chuckled agreeably, then fell silent. Since the incident in the forest two days ago, Rhiannon had seemed much more relaxed. She smiled frequently, and he had even seen her laugh openly when she and Rhun played with the puppies. It was obvious she was trying to put the past behind her. For her sake, he must do the same.

But someday—Maelgwn's jaw clenched—someday he would speak to Ferdic about Rhiannon. He would discover the whereabouts of this monster, Llewenon. He would track him down and see him punished for what he had done.

"What troubles you, my lord?"

"What? What do you mean?"

"You looked so angry just now."

They were in the bedchamber; Maelgwn lay on his back while Rhiannon gently massaged the front of his thighs. He was bone weary. His muscles still screamed from the torture of carrying the stag's carcass so far. Still, real relaxation eluded him; he kept thinking about his conversation with Gavran, about this man Llewenon and the gruesome way he deserved to die.

"It was nothing. Merely a grimace of pain." He turned over so Rhiannon could ease his aching shoulders, and no longer see his face. She moved over him. Her small, delicate fingers probed deep into his tight muscles, making him groan.

"It must have been a grand animal," Rhiannon said.

"Aye, he was magnificent, a twelve-point rack."

"Think how many years it took for him to grow so big."

Rhiannon's voice sounded wistful. Maelgwn felt a twinge of irritation. He suspected Rhiannon had more sympathy for the stag than for him.

"Think how many years it took for me to grow fool enough to attempt this madness of hunting without horses. Lludd's balls! I am too old for such pain!"

"You're not old," Rhiannon soothed. "Why, there are hardly any gray hairs on your head yet, and your stomach is hard and lean."

"It's not my stomach that hurts tonight, but my back and legs. Ahhhhgghhh!"

"From the way you grunt and groan, I'm not sure this is doing any good."

"Aye, it is . . . right there . . . ahhhh!"

Rhiannon continued to stroke him, trying to soothe her own worries as she eased Maelgwn's sore muscles. Her husband had such a strange expression on his face tonight. It was a look of brooding hatred. She wondered who it was directed toward—but in her heart she knew. Esylt. His sister might be dead, but Maelgwn had not eased in his desire for revenge against her. It burned inside him, a white-hot, unappeased loathing.

She closed her eyes as she stroked the thick muscles of her husband's back and shoulders. If only she could make the pain in his heart go away as easily as she assuaged his sore body.

Chapter 14

"You wish me to go riding with you? Right now?" Rhiannon's fingers stilled on the clay pot she was shaping in the workroom near the kiln.

Maelgwn gave her a reassuring smile. "I promised I would take you to the woods sometime, and we're not likely to have another day so fine as this one." Sensing her hesitation, he added, "The clay will be here when you return, as will your sewing."

Rhiannon nodded slowly. Maelgwn turned and started toward the door. "I'll meet you at the stables."

Maelgwn walked toward the corner of the fortress where the horses were kept. He knew Rhiannon loved to walk outside the fort. Still, she appeared reluctant to go with him. Would he never win his wife's trust? Would she always be wary?

He met Rufus at the entrance of the stables. "Is Cynraith saddled yet?" Maelgwn asked.

"Aye, my lord. And the little pony too, although I hardly think the puny beast a fittin' mount for a queen. Are you sure Lady Rhiannon wouldn't rather take Sawyl?"

"Docile Iau reminds her of her homeland. Given the short distance we are traveling, the pony will suit."

Rufus led Cynraith and Iau out. Maelgwn reached to stroke the stallion's glossy neck as he waited for Rhiannon. Iau nickered softly, as if jealous. Grinning, Maelgwn turned to give the shaggy little pony a measure of his attention. He did not expect Rhiannon to be long. She would have to wash the clay from her hands and change to a looser gown for riding, but unlike most women, she would not take time to fuss with her hair before meeting him. Her lack of vanity did not detract from her natural beauty, but only emphasized it.

At last she came, walking toward him with the light, rapid steps that made her able to move so silently in the woods. She smiled at him shyly. Her cheeks flushed a lovely rose hue. He suspected she was pleased he had asked her to go riding with him, despite her earlier hesitation.

Maelgwn lifted Rhiannon up on Iau, then mounted himself. They rode through the gate and down the hillside trackway. A soft wind blew in Maelgwn's face, and he breathed deeply of the air, scented with sea and sunshine. The breeze bore a hint of winter but was not yet cold. It was one of the mildest autumns he could recall.

Rhiannon rode silently beside him, and Maelgwn felt no urge to converse with her. He was content to enjoy the presence of his wife, to appreciate her pleasure in the moment. As soon as they left the fort, he sensed a quickening of Rhiannon's senses. Like an animal, she responded to the wild elements around her. Her body relaxed, her breathing deepened. Even her face looked different. There was an alertness in her expression, a glow in her eyes.

They reached the forest. Maelgwn dismounted and helped Rhiannon off her mount, then tethered their horses to a pine tree. He took her arm and led her among the stands of alder, beech and oak. Beneath their feet, the fallen leaves rustled, making a soft, soothing music.

Yellow agrimony and purple loosestrife still bloomed in clearings, and majestic purple and white spikes of foxglove poked above the dingy gray-brown carpet of fallen leaves. Maelgwn recalled that foxglove was poisonous, yet prized by healers to treat ailments of the heart. He wondered if Rhiannon knew the uses for the other plants they saw. He suspected she did, for as they walked, she examined the underbrush with a critical eye.

Silently, Maelgwn cursed Llewenon. His abuse of Rhiannon had not only damaged a sweet and innocent woman, it had robbed the Cymry of a skilled healer. Maelgwn would never be able to ask Rhiannon to use her knowledge of plants and healing to aid his people. To do so would risk damaging the fragile trust he hoped to build with his wife.

Maelgwn sighed. He could not indulge his anger toward Llewenon now. He had brought Rhiannon to the forest to ease her anxieties, not arouse them.

They progressed deeper into the woods. Away from the sunlight, the air was cool and moist, and scented with the dark, pungent odor of decay. Dry and dying bracken and horsetail ferns covered the ground, and dark red bryony berries glowed like drops of blood on the vinelike plants curling around the low branches of trees.

The path narrowed, so only one of them could pass at a time. Maelgwn gestured for Rhiannon to go ahead of him. Following, he admired the grace of his wife's movements, the rich color of her braids as they swung against her slender body. A lazy, tranquil mood crept over Maelgwn. There was a sense of timelessness here. These woods had existed for centuries before his great, great grandfather Cunedag settled in Gwynedd. They would be here for centuries after Maelgwn.

He halted as Rhiannon paused beneath a huge, old oak and looked up at the tree's nearly bare branches. Her lips moved slightly, and Maelgwn guessed she whispered a prayer to Nemetoma, the ancient personification of the trees. The skin prickled slightly on the back of Maelgwn's neck as he stared at his wife.

As a boy, he had sometimes felt the eyes of the Old Ones upon him when he walked in the forest, but never had his awareness of them been so strong.

Rhiannon turned to face him and raised her eyes to his. Maelgwn felt her spirit reach out for him—as if she touched him, despite the handful of yards that stood between them.

He walked toward her, drawn by her mystical gaze. "When I am with you, I sense . . . I feel as if I have been here before . . . in another time, another lifetime."

Rhiannon nodded. "The forest is crowded with spirits. Perhaps they remind you of your other lives."

Her words made a shiver run down Maelgwn's spine. He watched his wife intently, somehow half-expecting her to vanish before his eyes. She was so elusive, mysterious and yet, irresistible. He pulled her close, seeking the reassurance of her warm, lithe body in his arms.

She reached up to touch his face and sighed. "Autumn is my favorite time of year. Such a magical time, the world poised between regret and hope. Plants are dying, the birds have begun to leave, animals prepare for the hardship of winter. But there is a sense of completion in the air. The dying plants are heavy with seed; the animals mate. Even in the end of things, there is a beginning."

As her soft, light voice caressed his ears, Maelgwn felt heat fill his loins. Although he had not consciously brought Rhiannon to the woods to make love to her, it seemed right. When she lifted her face to look at him, Maelgwn leaned down to meld his lips to hers, slowly and thoughtfully.

Rhiannon kissed him back breathlessly, savoring the warm, firm pressure of his lips, the sensual pleasure of their tongues touching. It startled her how easily Maelgwn had fallen under her spell. She wanted him—so badly her body ached. But she could not have asked him to love her, here among the dying splendor of the fall forest. Yet, he had known; his body answered the hunger of hers.

She felt his hands slide beneath her braids and stroke her nape with a luxurious, gentle rhythm. Rhiannon sighed and leaned into him. The feel of his swelling arousal against her belly made spirals of longing unfurl along her body. She slowly slid her hands along his chest and stroked the hard muscles beneath his tunic. Her fingers inched down to the tie of his trousers.

Maelgwn released her and allowed her to unfasten his clothes. She took his silky, hot shaft in both hands, enjoying the power of him, the raw strength and irresistible need that quivered within her grasp. The sense of control she felt at this moment intoxicated her. She could make him moan with delight or increase his desire to unbearable intensity with the magic of her fingers.

Slow and easy—she wove patterns in his flesh until his whole body seemed to vibrate. Then she slipped to her knees and took him in her mouth, savoring the salty, sweet taste of him, the warm pressure of him against her lips and throat.

"I cannot last . . . that way." He gasped and lifted her face.

She watched him spread his cloak on the ground, making a cushion beneath it with the dry leaves. Rhiannon stripped off her own garments and stretched out naked on the cloak. She looked up at Maelgwn, glancing shyly at his proud, purplish erection. The thought of him inside her made more warm wetness seep between her legs.

Maelgwn knelt over her. He reached out and ran his fingers through her hair, fanning it out around her face. "My autumn woman," he whispered. "She is the color of berries and bright leaves and frost upon the ground. She will keep me warm all winter."

He leaned down and kissed her. He body shuddered.

His mouth moved lower, nuzzling her neck and shoulders. As he reached her breasts, his lips grew greedier, rougher. His teeth grazed her nipples; he sucked them until they were taut and aching. His mouth grazed her belly and still lower. She closed her eyes as the rough skin around his mouth scraped over her flesh, teasing her deliciously.

Then his hot, demanding mouth sucked raggedly on the inside of her thighs. She cried out. His lips moved closer and closer to the melting, aching center of her. She flinched as he stuck his tongue deep inside her, but he held her tight, his strong hands kneading her buttocks.

Her mind was flooded over and over with waves of rapture. She knew nothing except his firm hands stroking her, the tantalizing pressure of his mouth, the soft tickle of his long hair against her thighs. Her hips twisted and writhed, and she could feel the flame burning inside her, catching and swirling like a fire in the wind.

Her legs were weak and trembling when he pulled his mouth away and turned her over. She rested on her hands and knees as he entered her from behind, burying his whole shaft within her with one glorious thrust that instantly took her to the heights of passion yet again.

He moved inside her, a deep rhythm, like the rolling waves of the sea. Ripples of pleasure rocked through both of them. He rubbed his lips in her hair and stroked her breasts, her belly and the softness below, twining his fingers in the hair there. Rhiannon moaned and grasped his forearms, digging her fingernails into his skin. Her body struggled to adjust to the pressure of his shaft entering her from behind, to accept the aching massiveness of him. She lingered between indescribable pleasure and almost-pain. Then came oblivion as Maelgwn pushed her to the ground, pumping into her as if he would beat them both into the earth, into the darkness before life began.

Rhiannon heard her own cry of release—like the scream of a vixen, wild and haunting, ringing through the forest.

Then came Maelgwn's triumphant moan as the fire of their love coursed through him like lightning.

Slowly, their spirits returned to the peaceful glen where their bodies lay strewn in a sweaty tangle of limbs. Rhiannon eased herself from beneath Maelgwn. She looked up at the canopy of branches above them and watched the sunlight trickle down in little spangles of light, mellow with the sleepy, ancient gold of fall. If only it could always be like this, their spirits touching, their bodies entwined.

Maelgwn reached out and caressed her face. "Rhiannon, did I hurt you?"

She shook her head.

"It is a kind of lovemaking that a man likes once in a while," he added apologetically. "I usually try to be more gentle."

Rhiannon gazed at him. A nearly unbearable love filled her. How could Maelgwn hurt her when his fierce passion fed her very soul? She could never deny the pure animal urges of his beautiful body. It was the essence of him, the male splendor of him that completed her femaleness and made her whole. Together they made magic, as ancient and timeless as the rocks and the wind.

"If I died now, I would be content," she told him solemnly.

Maelgwn laughed. "You don't wish for much, do you Rhiannon? Why, with any luck, I've planted a babe within you." He patted her flat stomach. "You must carry it and mother it. You have your whole life as a woman ahead of you."

Rhiannon felt a twinge of unease at Maelgwn's practical words. For a time she had forgotten the future . . . and the past. When their bodies were joined, it did not seem as if there was anything in the world that could come between them. Maelgwn's words brought her sharply back to the present.

"Does it matter so much if I have a baby, now that you have Rhun?" she asked.

"Well, another son would be nice . . . or a daughter. I would enjoy a little red-haired lass I could spoil and tease." Maelgwn reached out to twist a strand of her hair in his fingers, and his voice grew more serious. "Still, I lost one wife to childbed, and I don't have my heart set on risking you so soon. You are very young, Rhiannon; if you do not conceive right away, it is no matter."

Rhiannon sighed and laid her head upon Maelgwn's chest. He was so good to her. She loved him so much.

Chapter 15

"Maelgwn!" The urgent voice pierced his dreams. "There's a messenger at the gate."

Maelgwn sat up, groaning. Though three days had passed, he was still sore from the hunt. He tossed the blankets over Rhiannon, then eased himself out of bed and moved stiffly across the cold floor to unbolt the door.

"I'm sorry to wake you, my lord." The sentry gestured apologetically as his naked king confronted him. "There's a man at the gate who claims to be a messenger from King Ferdic. I'm reluctant to let him in at such a late hour, but he insists he must speak to you tonight."

"Find Gavran." Maelgwn ordered. "He can vouch for his countryman. If Gavran knows the messenger, bid him in."

The soldier hurried off. Maelgwn found his clothes on the floor and began to dress.

Rhiannon bestirred herself from the warm covers. "What is it?"

"A messenger from Ferdic."

"What can it be?"

Maelgwn shrugged sleepily, then pulled on his boots and left the room.

Rhiannon moved to the edge of the bed and shivered as the warm blankets fell away. She was wide awake now, and she could not shake the feeling that something was wrong. A chill wind blew through one of the windows, making the unfastened window covering flap ominously against the wall. Rhiannon jumped from the bed and hurried to the wall where her gown was hung.

She dressed and went out. In the dark courtyard, she paused and gazed up at the sky. There was a tang of moisture in the air, and her instincts told her a storm was on the way. Her sense of unease intensified. Ferdic would not have sent a messenger unless the matter was grave. The fact that the messenger asked to see Maelgwn and not Gavran implied the business was between the two kings.

Rhiannon's hand shook as she opened the door to the feasting hall. Across the long room, Maelgwn and his men gathered around the fire. Balyn and Elwyn turned at her approach, and Rhiannon was apalled by the pitying look she saw in their eyes.

Maelgwn broke away from the group and advanced toward her. He took her hand and spoke in a gentle voice. "Rhiannon, it's your father. He sent word he is dying."

Rhiannon stared at her husband. She shook her head, as if shaking off an unpleasant dream. "My father has never been sick. He can't be dying."

For a moment, no one spoke, then the weary, begrimed messenger stood and addressed her: "I'm sorry, Princess Rhiannon. There is no doubt; the healers say he will not last past the first hard frost. He took a leg wound this summer, and the blade must have been tainted. Soon after the battle, he began to ail, and now the poison has spread up his thigh."

Rhiannon swayed on her feet. Maelgwn reached out to

steady her. She jerked away and gave him a stricken look, then bolted from the hall.

Rhiannon raced back across the courtyard to the bedchamber. Once inside, she fumbled with the heavy door, barring it behind her, then went to the bed and sank down on the mussed covers. She closed her eyes as she heard the sound of heavy footsteps and the rattling of the door.

"Rhiannon? Rhiannon, open the door."

She put her hands to her ears, trying to block out the sound.

"Rhiannon, please! I swear, I will break it down!"

Maelgwn's deep voice was impossible to ignore. At first it was coaxing, then it became more insistent and demanding. The anger she heard finally frightened Rhiannon into obeying him.

She hurried across the room, unbarred the door, then raced back to the bed.

She turned away as Maelgwn approached her. His voice was impatient, frustrated.

"The gods above, Rhiannon, I know it's a shock, but there's no reason for you to act like this. Ferdic never gave a thought for your happiness. He gave you to me as if you were some trinket he'd tired of. I won't have you grieving as if the world has ended because your wretched sire is dying."

Rhiannon tensed even more. She did not need to be reminded how little she meant to her father.

Maelgwn sighed and sat down on the bed. When he spoke, his voice was noticeably softer. "I'm sorry. My anger makes me unkind. Ferdic is your only kin, and it is natural you should care for him. But . . . don't ever bar the door against me again, Rhiannon. It makes me . . . beside myself."

She felt him reach out and touch her hair, stroking it. She lifted her head, pulling it away from his caressing

fingers. "Please don't touch me. It makes it so much worse
. . . knowing that I must give you up."

Maelgwn's fingers went still. "What are you talking
about?"

"The alliance . . . if Ferdic dies, the alliance will be finished, and you will . . . you will send me back to Manau
Gotodin." Rhiannon took a sharp breath and turned her
face away.

Maelgwn made a sound of consternation, and she felt
his strong hands upon her. She tried to resist him, but he
pulled her onto his lap, cradling her in his arms. "Nah,
nah, Rhiannon," he whispered close to her ear. "I would
not . . . could not send you back . . . even if Ferdic's successor should make war upon me. You are mine now, and I
will not give you up . . . ever."

She refused to believe the tenderness in Maelgwn's voice.
She tried to push him away. "But it is ruined now. The
Brigantes will no longer fight for you, and our marriage
will be meaningless."

Maelgwn held her tight as he spoke in a low, solemn
voice. "As a blood tie between our peoples, aye, perhaps
in that way our marriage will be meaningless, but as a bond
between a man and a woman, it has not lost its meaning
for *me*. I tell you again, Rhiannon, you are mine, for better
or worse. I will not forsake you because your father has
the poor timing to die at the height of his power."

Rhiannon turned to look at her husband. "Why do you
hate Ferdic so much?"

"Well . . ." Maelgwn paused, as if choosing his words
carefully. "He has not done right by you, Rhiannon, and
that is hard for me to forgive."

"You hate him because of me?" she asked incredulously.

"Obviously, his plotting years ago does not help, but I
can overlook that. His treatment of you goes beyond what
I can endure. He had a responsibility to protect you, to
seek revenge against anyone who hurt you . . ."

A harsh, angry look crossed his face. For a moment, Rhiannon watched him in puzzlement, then she relaxed into his embrace. She could scarcely believe her good fortune. Despite everything, Maelgwn meant to keep her as his wife. Even more amazing, he hated Ferdic because of her. She rested her head against her husband's broad chest in astonished relief. This was not the moment of reckoning she had feared. Her husband truly cared for her, more than she imagined.

Her contented reverie was broken as Maelgwn shifted her off his lap. "If you are to go to him, I must be making arrangements."

"Go to him?"

"You didn't stay to hear the rest of the message. Ferdic wishes to see you before he dies."

"Me?"

Maelgwn nodded. "Mind . . . if you do not want to go, it will not matter to me."

Rhiannon took a deep breath to steady her nerves. "He is dying. I can't refuse him. Anyway, I don't hate him as you do. My father . . . he did the best he could for me. It's only that Ferdic thinks all women are unimportant."

"Perhaps." Maelgwn released her and stood up. "If you do not hold his treatment of you against him, I will try not to either." He moved toward the doorway. "I will be back soon; it should not take long to make arrangements for your journey. You must sleep. I'm sure Balyn will want to leave very early."

"You . . . you're not coming with us?"

Maelgwn shook his head. "I can't afford to leave my lands unprotected when they're so newly won. You will ride back with Gavran and his men. Balyn and Elwyn will go along to escort you home. You'll be safe with them."

Maelgwn left, and Rhiannon undressed again and crawled under the furs and blankets in the cold bed. She stared up at the ceiling. Maelgwn did not mean to set her aside, despite having the perfect reason to do so. It was hard to believe he was really that pleased to have her as his wife, but it must be true.

Rhiannon chewed her lips thoughtfully. It was dangerous to hope for the future, but she could not seem to help herself.

Despite the late hour, most of Maelgwn's officers were still gathered around the fire talking when he entered the great hall.

"Well," Balyn said, looking up quickly, "Is she going?"

Maelgwn made a pained face. "Aye. As hard as it is for me to understand, Rhiannon seems to care for Ferdic."

"He *is* her father," Gareth pointed out.

"Aye, and she has apparently not yet realized her misfortune. At any rate, it gives us an opportunity to find out about Ferdic's successor. I saw Gavran here earlier. Did he suggest who it might be?"

Balyn shook his head slowly. "He said Ferdic's sons are too young to even consider, and his brothers . . . well, there are several and none of them live at Ferdic's camp. Gavran couldn't even begin to guess the most likely contenders."

"Damn!" Maelgwn turned and began to pace. "Of all the ways I thought Ferdic might let me down, this is the most unexpected!"

Balyn cleared his throat. "You think the alliance is finished?"

"I don't know. It depends on who comes to power."

"What about Rhiannon?" Rhys's voice was low and cautious.

Maelgwn turned to him coldly. "If you think I mean to repudiate my marriage because Rhiannon is no longer an asset to me, you are wrong. Ferdic's death changes nothing. I may have married Rhiannon because she brought me a dowry of Brigante warriors, but now that she is mine, I

intend to keep her. There is a limit to how much I will let
political goals determine who sleeps in my bed."

"Blessed Jesu!" Balyn exclaimed heartily. "That is good
news. After Aurora's death, I feared you would never care
for a woman again."

Maelgwn's voice grew even frostier. "Balyn, if you are
to set off at first light tomorrow, you'd best seek your bed."

"Do you think we will arrive in time?" Elwyn asked as
the men filed out of the hall.

"You mean before Ferdic dies?" Maelgwn shook his
head. "I don't know. Ferdic is tough and young—if he
truly wishes to see his daughter before he goes to the spirit
world, he'll have to hang on to life for another week or
two."

The ride to Manau Gotodin was cold, wet and miserable.
Even Rhiannon, who had grown up in the north, was dismayed by the brutality of the wind in the hills and the icy
cold mists rising from the bogs and lowlands. Their pace
was further slowed by the Brigante footsoldiers who accompanied them. Finally, anxious lest Ferdic die before they
reached Catriath, Rhiannon and her mounted escort went
on ahead.

The first few nights, Rhiannon had slept in a tent with
Enid, the Irish bodyservant who accompanied her because
Taffee could not ride. The two women woke up so cold
and exhausted each morning that Elwyn and Balyn finally
put aside their embarrassment at lying so close to their
king's wife and agreed to share their tent with Rhiannon
and the slave woman. Bundled between the two men, they
were finally able to get a good night's rest.

As the journey progressed, Rhiannon was grateful for
the men's company as well as their warmth. The more she
thought on it, the more anxious she became at facing her
father on his deathbed. It seemed very odd that he should

ask to see her now, after ignoring her all her life. She
guessed that Ferdic must have something important to tell
her and could not help fearing what it might be. Only her
sense of responsibility to her dying sire kept her from
calling a halt and asking the men to turn back.

At last, they reached the dense forests of Manau Gotodin.
Even half-frozen and coated in silvery frost, certain clearings and streams brought back memories for Rhiannon.
Here there would be an abundance of berries in the fall—
she had picked some once with Bouda. And over that hill
was the sacred grove where Llewenon had taken her that
awful night. She shivered a little at the memory, but to
her surprise, the anguish was not as intense as she remembered. Somehow time and Maelgwn's tenderness had
healed her pain a little.

It was late when they arrived in the valley where Ferdic
made his winter camp. In the gray, dreary light, no one
spotted them until they were almost to the low wall that
surrounded the lodges. Several warriors came out to welcome them and lead them into the encampment. The
Brigante men nodded to Rhiannon and exchanged polite,
formal greetings with Balyn and Elwyn, but no more was
said.

If the subdued manner of the men had not warned her
how grave things were for Ferdic, one glance at Narana's
face convinced Rhiannon that Ferdic was indeed dying.
Her stepmother's eyes were red from weeping and her
strong jaw tense with pain. Narana did not speak to Rhiannon but took her arm firmly and led her to Ferdic's lodge.

After the freezing cold, the inside of the lodge was stifling; it reeked of the humid, putrid scent of the sickbed.
Ferdic lay on a pallet of sheepskins by the fire, and as
Rhiannon neared, she saw his face clearly in the glow of the
flames. Despite being prepared for the worst, she gasped
involuntarily. Could this wasted creature really be the man
she had once held in awe? It was hardly a man at all, but

rather, a yellowish, grayish shadow that breathed with a harsh, rasping sound.

"Father?"

Ferdic turned to look at her, and Rhiannon felt tears of pity flooding her cheeks. Ferdic had always been lean, but now the bones of his face pushed painfully against his skin. His brilliant, turquoise eyes glowed with feverish agony. With his feral mask and blazing eyes, he reminded Rhiannon of a wildcat—cornered but still fighting furiously— facing down his adversary with the last vestige of his strength. His valiant struggle hardly mattered, Rhiannon thought with sinking heart. The enemy that baited him and circled the reeking bed was Death, and sometime within the next few hours or days, Death would surely win.

"Rhiannon." The voice was faint and weak. "I am glad you have come."

"Father . . . I . . . let me look at your wound . . . let me send for someone."

"Nah, nah," Ferdic answered wistfully. "It is too late for that. When the healer finally came from the north, he told me I was dying. Even you should know enough of healing to see I am beyond help."

"I wish . . ." Rhiannon stopped. What did she wish for, she wondered? She was ashamed to realize that her thoughts were for herself. She wished with all her heart that Ferdic had asked to see her long ago, when she could have offered him love instead of pity.

"The messenger you sent . . . he said you wanted to speak with me?"

Ferdic glanced at other people in the lodge—Narana, a man dressed in the plain robe of a Learned One, the healer no doubt, and an old woman. "Leave us," he told them abruptly. When they hesitated, his eyes glittered with some of the old fire, and he raised his arm in an impatient gesture.

Narana and the two caretakers filed out. Rhiannon

watched them go, as frightened as ever to be alone with her father. What would he say to her? What did he want after all these years?

"Sit." Ferdic gestured to some skins near the bed-place, and Rhiannon hurried to obey him.

For a very long while, Ferdic was silent. Finally he sighed softly. "Once I promised never to tell you these things . . . but now, the person I promised is dead . . . and you, you are still alive. You have the right to know the truth."

"What truth is that?"

"Have you never wondered, Rhiannon, who your mother was?"

"I thought I knew, a foreign princess, you always said."

"Aye, a foreign princess she was. A princess of the Cymry."

"The Cymry? But that is Maelgwn's tribe." Rhiannon felt a tingle of foreboding along her spine.

Ferdic's mouth quirked, as if in amusement. "Who was the only woman who cared for you, who saw that you had decent clothes and jewels and were educated as a princess, who near murdered me herself when she found out my bard had violated you? It was Esylt, of course. she was your mother."

Longing overwhelmed Rhiannon . . . then despair. If she could have chosen anyone in the world to be her mother, it would have been Esylt, the handsome, dark-haired woman who had cherished and loved her. But Esylt was dead, and it was too late for anything except regrets. Except . . . except . . . An awful thought gnawed at the edge of her consciousness. *Maelgwn!*

Rhiannon's veins seemed to run with icewater even as the smoky, humid air of the tent became unbreathable. She turned horrified eyes to Ferdic. There was a thoughtful look on his fevered countenance as he answered her unspoken question.

"Why did I allow you to marry Maelgwn, the man who

is your uncle by blood? It was part of the plan, of course—
Esylt's plan.''

Rhiannon's eyes widened even further. "Esylt's plan?"

Ferdic lifted a wasted hand, then dropped it limply.
"Don't look so dismayed, Rhiannon. It's not so close a tie
as to be forbidden. I know the Christians might frown upon
the practice, but among the Celtic tribes it is customary to
mingle royal blood with royal blood. Your kinship is only
a little closer than that between cousins, and such marriages are common enough.''

"But Esylt and Maelgwn—he hates her!''

"So he does.'' Ferdic's eyes glittered again, and his
cracked lips formed a grotesque smile. "I enjoyed that
aspect of the marriage—knowing how Maelgwn would feel
if he ever knew the truth.'' The mockery of a grin faded
quickly. "But there were other more obvious advantages
as well. While I have no fondness for Maelgwn as a man,
he is a strong leader and promises to be a power in Britain
for years to come. I liked the thought of having control
over a southern king.''

Rhiannon was too overcome to speak. Ferdic filled in
the silence with his weak, raspy voice. "In the end, it was
Esylt's choice. I suppose you were her peace offering to
her brother. She wanted you to love him, to make him
happy.''

Rhiannon swayed on the cushion of skins. Ferdic shifted
his own frail body, as if trying to make himself comfortable,
and began to tell the story.

"On one of her visits to Catraith, Esylt got herself with
child. For some reason, she did not kill it as she was wont
to do. She went north and had the babe in secret. Then
she sent for me.'' He smiled the death's mask grin again.
"I was very young, and she was quite skilled in bed. It did
not take much to convince me to claim the babe. Besides,
there was to be a great reward in it.''

Rhiannon took a deep breath. She wanted to run from

the tent and never hear another word. But she could not. Even if it killed her, she had to know.

Ferdic fixed his heated eyes on hers. "The price of my compliance was Esylt's betrayal of Maelgwn. I was not willing to wait for Cunedda to die so I could be king. I wanted my father out of the way, and my only chance was to have Esylt cause trouble for Maelgwn so he could not come to Cunedda's aid. Esylt did her part most admirably. She conspired with Gwyrtheyrn to overthrow Maelgwn."

Ferdic's eyes narrowed thoughtfully. "Our plan almost succeeded. If that bitch, Aurora, had not sent Maelgwn a message warning him, he would never have been able to muster his army to defend his kingdom in time. Once Gwynedd fell, it would have been easy for me to defeat my father and take the kingship of Manau Gotodin for myself."

Rhiannon shook her head in agony. "How could she do it? How could Esylt betray her brother? I thought she *loved* him?"

Ferdic lifted his wasted shoulders awkwardly. "Love, hate—for Esylt, they were always intertwined. She was jealous of her brother; she hated him for being a man. He wielded the power that she, as a woman, would never have. It was only later that she came to regret her betrayal, to realize what she had lost." Ferdic's voice faded; Rhiannon felt a renewal of her panic. A dozen questions whirled in her mind, tormenting her.

"Father . . . please . . ." She breathed the words to the sallow, corpselike man beside her.

Ferdic's eyes flickered open. "Father?" He shook his head. "I am not your father. Though, for a time, I thought I might have sired you—certainly I bedded Esylt enough that it was possible. But one time when we were arguing, Esylt told me about the night you were conceived. She took two lovers to bed that night—I wasn't one of them."

Ferdic sighed wearily and continued. "No one ever

guessed. You had that red hair, and it was enough. If you had been a boy, I don't think I would have agreed to continue the deception. But a daughter . . ." He made a careless gesture with his wasted hand. "A daughter hardly matters—as long as she is pretty and obedient, one is as good as another."

"And my real father—did Esylt say who he was?"

"One of the men who bedded Esylt that night was a lusty warrior, big and dark-haired. The other was a young Irish slave. She took him to bed while the soldier watched. It was the boy's first taste of a woman, and Esylt recalled that they laughed at him, at his awkward fumblings."

"Stop," Rhiannon whispered. "I don't want to know anymore." Her stomach threatened to heave itself up.

Ferdic nodded. "I cannot blame you for not wanting to know, but it's easy to guess the rest. Although the Irish slave did not live to be a man, it's clear he would not have been much of one. He's to blame for your small stature."

For a long while, Rhiannon stared into the fire. She thought that Ferdic surely slept, but when she glanced at him, she saw his eyes were half-open, watching her.

"No wonder you never cared for me," she said bitterly. "I was not yours, and I was a bastard . . . begotten by a slave."

"Ah, Rhiannon, do not fret yourself over who your father was. You must have got some good of him, for you are fair of face and sweet of temper, as a woman should be. As for my loving you . . . it wouldn't have mattered if you had been my own. Like all men, I wanted sons."

He extended a clawlike hand, as if to touch Rhiannon's trembling form. "If it matters so much, know that Esylt cared for you, likely more than she ever cared for anyone. It ate at her, that she could never claim you as her daughter. When she knew she was ill unto to death, she sent me a message begging me to honor her wishes, to see you married to Maelgwn. She knew he would look after you."

Ferdic's face twisted, as if the pain of his ruined flesh had deepened. "I have honored her wishes, but I would not go to my death with this dread secret upon my conscience." His eyes widened slightly, their jewel-like vividness fading. "I have told you all. Now sit with me as a daughter should."

Stunned beyond thought, Rhiannon reacted instinctively to the plea in Ferdic's voice. She reached out and took the dying man's bony, feverish fingers in her own.

Chapter 16

"Christ save us! What could have happened to her?"

Balyn's toe scuffed restlessly at the new-fallen snow outside the tent where Rhiannon slept. His eyes met Elwyn's. It was getting dark, but the gray twilight filtering through the trees was enough to illuminate the worry on both their faces.

"The gods only know," Elwyn replied. "But it must have been something terrible. What ails Rhiannon goes beyond mere grief over her father's passing. I'll never forget the look on her face when she came out of Ferdic's lodge . . ." He shuddered.

Balyn's hand came up to scratch at the stubbly beard he was growing for the winter. "They say that sometimes when a dying man's soul passes out of his body, it rushes around the room like a great wind. That would scare me too—if I were to see it."

Elwyn nodded. "And Ferdic died even as Rhiannon sat with him, holding his hand."

Balyn again scraped at the pattern he had made in the snow. "But what will Maelgwn make of Rhiannon's distress?

He told us to keep her safe . . . how can we bring her back like this? Pale as a wraith, whispering to herself, her eyes distant and wild . . . I could make no sense of anything she said, except when she begged us to take her away from Catraith. That's another tangle. Maelgwn told us to find out the most likely contenders for Ferdic's kingship, and we've had no time to do that. Still . . .'' Balyn sighed and his eyes met Elwyn's. ''If Maelgwn were here and had seen Rhiannon's face, he would do the same as us. We can always return later to find out the news.''

''Another winter trip—Gwenaseth will be beside herself,'' Elwyn said glumly. ''These winter journeys distress her even more than my going on campaign—she says she cannot rest easy with me so far away and the weather so uncertain.''

Balyn looked up at the cloudy, sullen sky. ''This winter promises to be a fierce one, and I would prefer to wait it out at Degannwy.'' He flexed his shoulders. ''I swear, every inch of my body hurts from sleeping so many nights on the cold ground.''

''Let's go to bed then,'' Elwyn urged wearily. ''We have a long way to go tomorrow.''

The two men went into the tent and took their places on either side of Rhiannon and the slave woman. Several times in the night, the queen woke them as she moaned and thrashed in the grip of a nightmare. Once she called out the name Esylt, and the two men lifted their heads to stare at each other in the darkness of the tent. They said nothing about it, not then, nor in the morning either.

''You're back? Already?'' Maelgwn looked up in surprise as Balyn and Elwyn entered the council room. He was looking over winter supply tallies and had not heard the sentry's call to open the gate.

"Aye, my lord." Elwyn wearily took a seat across from Maelgwn. "Ferdic died the day we arrived, and we did not stay longer than to rest our horses and resupply."

"The decision came that quickly? Who's the new king?"

Balyn shook his head. "It's not decided yet, nor even much discussed. We didn't hurry back because we had news."

"Why then?" Maelgwn asked sharply.

Balyn hesitated, then took the bench next to Elwyn's. "Rhiannon insisted we return."

"Rhiannon insisted?" Maelgwn shoved aside the tally sheets; his blue eyes narrowed. "My wife is not usually one to insist on anything."

"Rhiannon was, is, very distraught. She begged us to take her away from Catraith."

Maelgwn stood. "Rhiannon and her father were hardly close. I don't see how she could be so overwrought with grief that you couldn't stay a few days longer."

"I'm not sure if grief has disordered Rhiannon's mind, but something has," Balyn said. "She does not speak, and her eyes scarcely rest upon anyone with recognition. She was alone with Ferdic when he died. I'm afraid . . ."

"She is ill?" Maelgwn interrupted with a frown. "I knew it was unwise to send such a delicate woman on a long winter journey."

"I would not say she was ill, at least not in her body. But her mind . . ."

Maelgwn glared at the two men. "What is it? What are you trying to say?"

Balyn and Elwyn exchanged looks, then Elwyn broke the strained silence. "We think Rhiannon saw Ferdic's spirit leave his body, and the experience has disordered her wits."

"His spirit? You mean his 'fetch'?" Maelgwn grimaced in disapproval. "I don't believe it. I have seen dozens die, and not once have I observed a man's spirit leave his body, at least not the way the bards speak of it."

"I didn't believe it either, at first," Balyn began. "But Elwyn pointed out that Rhiannon has had some training in the magic arts, and perhaps . . ."

Maelgwn gave Elwyn a cold look. "Where did you hear this?"

"Gwenaseth told me Rhiannon had spent time with a magician and healer who served her people."

"Forget it. Rhiannon is uncomfortable with that part of her life; I don't wish it discussed."

Elwyn gave Maelgwn a puzzled look. "Of course, my lord. I only mention it because I thought it might explain why she was able to see things which ordinary people do not."

Maelgwn struck his fist on the oak table. "This talk of spirits and fetches is worse than slaves' gossip. Give me the facts. What's wrong with Rhiannon?"

Balyn took a deep breath before answering. "When she was led out of Ferdic's lodge, she appeared stunned, unaware of anything around her. The woman put her to bed, and we went to the meeting lodge to see if we could learn anything of Ferdic's successor. A short time later, Rhiannon burst into the lodge, utterly frantic. She begged us to leave for Degannwy immediately. We had a terrible time convincing her to wait until the next day when our horses were rested." Balyn shrugged uncomfortably. "After that, she did not speak at all, except to cry out and rave in her sleep on the journey home. I tell you, Maelgwn, your wife is not herself."

Maelgwn regarded the two men for a moment, then walked toward the door. "I will go to her," he said. "Perhaps Rhiannon can give me an explanation that makes more sense than yours."

* * *

Maelgwn walked rapidly across the muddy courtyard; on the way, he met Gwenaseth. "Rhiannon is sleeping," she said, her eyes flashing a warning.

Maelgwn nodded curtly and continued on. In a few strides he reached his chamber and knocked sharply. Hearing no answer, he pushed the door open and entered. The lamp was unlit, and with the hides over the windows to keep out the cold, the room was illuminated by only the faint glow of the hearth. He went quickly to the bed, where he could see Rhiannon's small shape wrapped tightly in the blankets and furs.

She murmured in her sleep as he sat down. He reached out and touched her cheek. It felt cool and soft, exactly as he had remembered. She mumbled something unintelligible as he pulled the blankets back. He ran his hand over her body, feeling the warmth of her beneath her shift. Immediately aroused, he shed his trousers and climbed into bed.

She stirred as he kissed her neck. She smelled of the forest—the clean, sharp scent of pine trees, wind and smoke. His kisses grew more passionate. He felt her awaken, and her body stiffened beside his.

"Rhiannon, my love," he soothed. "It's Maelgwn."

She jerked away and her elbow caught him hard under the ribs. He reached for her again, grappling with her, pulling her down to the bed. His grip tightened as she fought him. "Rhiannon!" he cried. "What is it?"

She struggled frantically against him, but his weight held her pinned to the bed. "Rhiannon, it is all right."

"No!"

Maelgwn eased his hold on Rhiannon, trying to think. Balyn and Elwyn had said something was wrong with his wife, and he had not believed them. But the truth was this—Rhiannon's frail body strained against his; her breathing was so harsh and rapid it made his own breath catch in his throat. He was reminded of the first time he tried to bed his wife, only now her struggle against him was even more desperate, untempered by any sort of reason.

"Rhiannon," he said gently. "Tell me what's happened. Why do you fear me?"

She did not answer, but shook her head violently. Her long hair whipped around, entangling them both. With one hand, Maelgwn pulled it back and gazed into her face. Even by the dim firelight, he could read the anguish on her countenance. She was panting and her body trembled. It seemed as if—but perhaps he imagined it—it seemed she bared her teeth at him.

Abruptly, he released her. His own hands shook. He recognized the look of awful desperation in her eyes. As a boy, he had once come upon a fox trapped in a snare. In its frenzied struggle to escape, the creature tried to gnaw off its own foot. The stark look of terror glimpsed in its eyes had remained with him since.

He got up and backed slowly from the bed. "All right, Rhiannon. I will go away. But you must talk to someone, you must tell someone what has befallen you."

The expression on Rhiannon's face did not change, and even after he had dressed and left the room, Maelgwn could still see it clearly in his mind. Rhiannon looked— he tried to force the thought away but could not—his wife looked as if she had gone mad.

Gwenaseth approached the king's bedchamber briskly. Maelgwn's mind was obviously addled. The queen had seemed rather odd and despondent since returning from the north, but that was normal for a young woman who had journeyed a long distance to watch her only kin pass away. As for Rhiannon turning Maelgwn from her bed—

even a wife should be allowed to decline when she felt
melancholy and fatigued. Maelgwn had obviously over-
reacted when he said Rhiannon recoiled from him in
dread.

Gwenaseth entered the anteroom outside the king's
chamber and prepared to knock. The door was ajar, and
she could hear Rhiannon's voice. Gwenaseth pushed the
door aside, expecting to find Taffee or one of the servants.
Rhiannon was alone. She sat by the fire, dressed only in a
shift, staring into the glowing embers that scarcely lit the
room. Her arms were wrapped around her body, and she
rocked back and forth with an eerie rhythm.

Gwenaseth approached quietly, afraid to startle the
young woman. When she was a few paces away, Rhiannon
spoke, her voice a low, broken murmur.

"Esylt . . . oh, my mother! How could you? What shall
I do? What shall I do? Oh, Esylt, answer me—tell me what
it is I should do!"

"Esylt" and "mother"—the two words collided in Gwenaseth's mind. She sucked in her breath. It made sense,
terrible sense. Esylt, who had never been kind or tender-
hearted to a soul, had made Rhiannon feel loved. Of
course. She was Rhiannon's mother!

"Why did you have me, Mother? Why? Why did you not
kill me when I was still inside of you? Oh, save me from
this misery; make me die!"

Walk away! Pretend you haven't heard! The thoughts
formed in Gwenaseth's mind, but she could not act upon
them. The agony in Rhiannon's voice was too heartrending
to hear. Someone had to comfort this young woman, to
help her with this.

Slowly, deliberately, Gwenaseth went to Rhiannon and
put her arms around her. For a moment the smaller woman
relaxed against her, then Rhiannon stiffened and raised
her face to stare at Gwenaseth with huge, devastated eyes.

"You heard me. You know."

Gwenaseth nodded. "Did Ferdic tell you?"

Rhiannon made a vague gesture of assent.

Gwenaseth took a deep breath. "I'm sorry, Rhiannon, truly I am. I didn't mean to listen, but perhaps it's for the best. You need not bear this thing alone."

Rhiannon bowed her head. "I cannot make myself tell Maelgwn. You must do it for me."

"Tell Maelgwn!" Gwenaseth gasped in horror. "You must not! He must never know!"

Rhiannon shook her head, her eyes closed. "I will not live this lie. I will not have him hold me and speak words of love . . . all the while knowing . . ." she broke off, her voice a smothered gasp.

Gwenaseth tightened her grasp upon Rhiannon's shoulders. "Listen to me, Rhiannon. You cannot tell him. Ever. You will go on as if everything was as before. You must!"

Rhiannon's eyes opened, wide with shock. "How can you say such a thing? Knowing what I am to Maelgwn, knowing how he would hate me if he knew who my mother was?"

"That is exactly why you must do as I tell you!" Even to her own ears, Gwenaseth's voice sounded strained. Somehow she must convince Rhiannon to disregard the horrible secret she learned at her father's deathbed. "It would destroy Maelgwn; surely you don't want that, Rhiannon."

She saw the younger woman hesitate. There was a flash of hope in her eyes; then it was extinguished, smothered by the despair and grief that lay there. "But if there should be a child . . ." Rhiannon shook her head, her face a mask of agony. "I would not curse a child to that, to be unloved, unwanted . . ." Her voice trailed off, a mere whisper, etched with the longings of a lifetime.

Gwenaseth gave her a little shake. "It would not be so. You would love your child, and so would Maelgwn. He need never know the rest."

Rhiannon shook her head. "But the truth of my parentage—secrets always come out in the end."

"Nay, they do not. No one knows, save you and I. Therefore, it is up to us. If we are determined, we can take *this* secret to our graves."

Rhiannon looked doubtful. Gwenaseth licked her dry lips. "Think of it, Rhiannon. If you had not gone to Manau Gotodin, if Ferdic had died but a day or two sooner, you would never have known the truth. All you have to do is pretend your father's deathbed confession never occurred."

"Aye, there is that too," Rhiannon said sorrowfully. "Ferdic is not my father."

"What?"

"He told me my father was an Irish slave, a young boy Esylt took to bed for fun." Another grimace of pain crossed Rhiannon's features.

Gwenaseth silently cursed the dead Brigante king. What had the man been thinking of? Had he intended to ruin Rhiannon completely? If so, he had well-nigh succeeded. Rhiannon's face looked haunted, utterly devastated. Still, she was strong; beneath all that delicate beauty was a core of sterner stuff. There had to be. After all, she was Esylt's daughter.

"I know you've had a shock, Rhiannon, but you must think seriously about this. If you care for Maelgwn, consider how the truth will hurt him. Could you bear to see him suffer so? Would it not be better to keep your secret and save him the pain you have just endured?

Rhiannon's anguished face was suddenly imbued with tenderness. "I love him so; I would not see him hurt for anything!"

Gwenaseth's heart leapt with relief. This, then, was the means to ensure Rhiannon's silence. "Think of it," she coaxed. "Maelgwn has already lost one wife and grieved for her overlong. If he should lose you—by any means—

I fear for his mind. It is not merely idle talk to say you could destroy him. If you love Maelgwn, you must put Ferdic's words from your thoughts and continue on with your life as if your journey to Manau Gotodin never took place."

Rhiannon sat in silence for some time. Gwenaseth moved to leave. She was halfway to the door when Rhiannon called to her.

"Gwenaseth, tell me the truth; my husband is my uncle. Is it not unseemly for me to lie with him?"

Gwenaseth turned; exhaustion seemed to be seeping into her very bones. "Perhaps it is mad of me to think so, but I wonder if it is not the very nearness of your blood which makes you suit Maelgwn so well as a wife. You appear to bring the king peace and happiness. How can that be wrong?"

After Gwenaseth left, Rhiannon stared after her, wondering. Did she dare believe Gwenaseth's words? Could the love she felt for Maelgwn possibly be stronger than the curse of betrayal and hatred Esylt had entangled them in? She wanted to believe. It was the only alternative to despair. And yet . . . Another shudder racked her. If Maelgwn ever learned the truth, he would surely kill her. How was she to lie beneath him, accept his body, knowing he despised the very blood that flowed in her veins? And a child— Gwenaseth was wrong about that. She could never risk bearing a babe to Maelgwn; she would not risk dooming another living being to the pain and grief she had known.

Gwenaseth entered her house and sank down on the bed. She wondered suddenly if she had done the right thing. Her first instinct had been to protect Maelgwn. Gwynedd needed him to be sound of mind and at ease with his future, and all decisions must be directed toward that goal. Preserving his marriage was essential, and any deceit involved could be forgiven in light of the greater good.

But what about Rhiannon?—a voice whispered. *This is her life you are meddling with as well.* Gwenaseth sighed. She cared for Rhiannon, truly she did. Despite her doubts about the girl in the beginning, she had been won over by Rhiannon's sweet temperment, her kindness. As far as she could tell, there was no trace of Esylt's evil in her daughter. Rhiannon made a fine wife for Maelgwn, and in the long run, that was what mattered. Besides, what was best for Maelgwn was truly best for Rhiannon. If Maelgwn ever found out the truth, Gwenaseth did not doubt he might kill Rhiannon. Hiding the truth from Maelgwn was the best way to protect everyone involved.

But could Rhiannon do it?—Gwenaseth wondered with a shiver. Could anyone keep such a terrible secret? What if Rhiannon slipped up, perhaps talked in her sleep or mentioned Esylt's name without thinking? Nay, she would not think about that. As she told Rhiannon, they must put it out of their minds. They could tell no one, not even Elwyn. As much as Gwenaseth trusted her husband, he was too open and honest for her to dare burden him with something so dangerous as the truth of Rhiannon's parentage.

With a deep sigh, Gwenaseth lay down on the bed. She flexed her shoulders, feeling as if a great weight was bearing down upon her. Her mouth twisted into a grimace. How right her instincts had been. At last she knew the mystery of Rhiannon's haunted eyes, and it was as she had thought—she did not want to know at all.

Chapter 17

Rhiannon's hand jerked at the sound of Maelgwn's angry bellow in the courtyard. Ruby-colored drops oozed from where she had stabbed herself with her needle. She glanced quickly at the other women in the weaving room, sure they guessed she was cause for Maelgwn's foul mood. Neither Gwladus, working at the loom, nor Melangell and Sewan, busy carding raw wool in the corner, bothered to look up. It was obvious they did not blame her for the rift with her husband, but instead, took her side in a show of feminine sympathy.

Rhiannon went back to sewing and tried to block out the sounds from outside the room. Every crescendo of Maelgwn's deep voice made her shudder. She felt profoundly guilty for her role in his distress. A week had passed, and their relationship had deteriorated to one of strained avoidance. A dozen times she had made up her mind to go to Maelgwn and tell him the truth of her parentage. Another dozen times she decided to pretend nothing had happened and welcome him back to her bed. She was unable to act upon either decision. Instead, she did nothing. Each night, she slept, or tried to sleep, in Maelgwn's chamber, while he bedded down in his council room.

They were at a stalemate, and Rhiannon was unsure how it would ever end. Maelgwn would not come to her unless she asked, and she seemed incapable of committing herself to a relationship based on deception.

The voices in the courtyard rose again. Rhiannon tensed as she heard Rhun's young voice mingled with Maelgwn's much deeper one. This time Sewan looked toward the door, then glanced her way. Rhiannon felt her face flush. Sewan obviously expected Rhiannon to intervene between her husband and her stepson. Did she dare? Such a confrontation might force them to face the deeper chasm that loomed between them these days.

"Nay! I won't let you." Rhun's voice, distraught and tearful, pierced the silent weaving room. The sound pulled painfully at Rhiannon's heart. She put down her sewing and started toward the door, jumping back in surprise as Rhun came hurtling into the room. He threw himself at Rhiannon and grabbed her skirts.

"Don't let him!" he cried. "Don't let him cut it open."

Rhiannon looked up in dismay as Maelgwn entered the room. His face was flushed, his blue eyes angry. "He has a wound on his hand, Rhiannon. He let it go too long, and now it's festering. If it isn't opened and cleaned, his hand . . ." Maelgwn didn't finish; his voice shook. It was clear he was beside himself with worry.

Rhiannon looked from her husband to the trembling boy in her arms. "Rhun," she whispered, putting a hand on his shoulder. "Let me look at it. Please."

Rhun darted an anxious glance at his father, then held out his hand. Rhiannon took it carefully. One look and she knew Maelgwn was right. The cut had closed up, but the edges were red and raw, the area around the wound swollen. More ominous yet, a thin streak of red flared up the boy's arm.

Rhiannon kept her eyes trained on the wound and tried to keep the concern from her face. The poison in the wound had begun to spread; if it was not stopped, the boy could lose his arm, or even his life. Her thoughts moved rapidly as she tried to recall what herbs would best draw the poison out.

"Rhiannon, please, don't let them cut it open!" Rhun's pleading voice jerked her back to awareness.

"Tell him, Rhiannon," Maelgwn urged. "Tell him that he must let Bleddryn see to it."

Rhiannon glanced at the boy. "Rhun," she whispered. "Maelgwn is right; the wound must be tended to."

Rhun whimpered.

"Don't be a baby, Rhun. 'Tis nothing. You will never be a soldier if you don't learn to care for your hurts!"

Rhiannon shot her husband a reproving glance. "He's only a boy. Stop shouting at him."

Maelgwn opened his mouth, as if to protest, then closed it again.

"Rhun." Rhiannon made her voice as soothing as she could. "Would you let me tend it for you?"

Rhun watched her, wary. "Will you have to cut it open?"

"Aye," she replied gravely. "I will. 'Tis the only way."

Rhun stared at her, then nodded. "I will let you. I've seen you with Belga's puppies. You're gentle with them."

Rhiannon glanced at her husband. "This is no place for tending wounds. Why don't you take him to our bedchamber? I'll have Taffee bring some hot water and some clean linen rags." She frowned. "Do you think Bleddryn has any healing herbs?"

Maelgwn shook his head. "I don't know. Some, perhaps. What do you need?"

"Some cross-wort or wood sage, or perhaps some goldenrod. If Bleddryn has none, see if any of the women might.

It is not enough to clean the wound now; we must have something to draw the poison out." She turned back to Rhun. "Your father is going to take you to his bedchamber. I will meet you there. On the way, why don't you get one of Belga's puppies to hold. It will take your mind from what I am to do."

The boy nodded obediently and left the room. Maelgwn had not moved; he stood at the door, staring at her. Rhiannon gave him a defiant look. "Do not fear, my lord. Treating poisoned wounds is among the simplest of healing skills."

"I don't doubt you, Rhiannon. I . . . I am very grateful."

Rhiannon's eyes met his again, and this time she did not try to hide her anxiety. "Don't be grateful yet. For all its smallness, the look of the wound is bad. It is very like what killed my fath- . . . Ferdic."

It had gone as well as could be expected, Rhiannon thought as she gazed upon the sleeping boy. The puppy had served to distract Rhun from the pain. He had scarcely looked up as she cleaned the oozing wound. He could not know how serious it was. But Maelgwn did. She could feel his eyes boring into her as she worked on the boy. Her husband was sick with dread for his son, and well he should be. If the cleansing herbs did not halt the poison's spread . . .

Rhiannon turned the thought away impatiently. She would not think of that. She had done what she could, and the boy was healthy and hardy. The chances were he would recover completely.

She reached down and smoothed a lock of hair from Rhun's forehead. What a beautiful child he was, with his gleaming hair the color of autumn leaves, his plump pink mouth, his thick, dark eyelashes sweeping low over downy golden cheeks. A lump formed in her throat. He was so sweet and innocent; he trusted her so readily. How could she betray that trust? How could she reveal who she was to Rhun's father and throw all their lives into turmoil?

A shudder passed through her, and she shook her head. She could not do such a thing. Her secret had the power to rend apart not only her and Maelgwn's lives, but also Rhun's. Gwenaseth was right; for the sake of everyone, she must learn to live a lie; she must pretend that Ferdic had never told her who her mother was.

Going to the table, she began to put away the things she had used to prepare a potion to make Rhun sleep. Doubts still swept through her, undermining her plan. Her chief remaining worry was what would happen if she ever bore a child to Maelgwn. She could not risk the chance he might somehow find out the truth and reject the child. Somehow she must make sure she did not conceive. There were herbs she could take to prevent conception, but they might be hard to find this late in season.

Frustration made Rhiannon's temples pound. Every time she came to a decision, she found a reason to back out of it. Perhaps her indecisiveness stemmed from the finality of her choice. Once she made up her mind to keep the truth from Maelgwn, there could be no turning back. She would be stuck with the decision the rest of her life.

Rhiannon went to the bed and again stroked Rhun's brow, searching for a hint of fever. There was none. She let out the anxious breath she had been holding. Hearing footsteps behind her, she turned and saw Maelgwn approaching. He moved cautiously, as if he feared she would send him away.

"Rhiannon, I am grateful." Maelgwn nodded toward the sleeping boy. "You were wonderful with him. He trusts you."

"You said yourself that he was used to women, that he had not shed his ties to his mother."

"It is more than that." Maelgwn's eyes were vivid with

tenderness. "You do have the gift of healing, even if you deny it."

Rhiannon sighed. "I will deny it no longer. If I can, I'll use my skill to help your people."

"They are *your* people too, Rhiannon," Maelgwn said softly.

Rhiannon glanced uncomfortably at her husband, uneasy with the entreating look on his face. In his own way, he was asking her to be his wife again, to heal this rift between them.

"You look tired, Maelgwn. Perhaps you should go to bed yourself."

Maelgwn's glance flickered to the bed where the sleeping boy lay, then a look of pain crossed his face. "Of course, you will keep the boy beside you this night." Turning stiffly, he walked from the room.

Rhiannon watched him. A band of grief was constricting her chest. She could not stand to watch her husband suffer so. She would have to settle this thing once and for all. Tomorrow she would do it; tomorrow she would find the strength.

The next morning, Rhiannon dressed, tense and contemplative. She put on her fur-lined boots and her warmest cloak. After a quick glance at the sleeping boy and a word to Taffee, she closed the bedchamber door softly behind her and slipped out into the courtyard. It was still dark, but she could see a tinge of light in the east. A few sleepy servants were about, carrying water for washing and food for breakfast. She hurried to the stables and met the stablemaster in the doorway.

"Rufus. I need a horse—I wish to go riding."

The old Roman stared at her a moment, then nodded his head. "Aye, you may take Sawyl; she is gentle enough and needs the exercise."

Within a few minutes, Rufus had the mare saddled and ready. He helped her up, and Rhiannon directed the horse toward the gate.

The sentry's expression was similar to the stableman's when she told him her wishes. He looked at her in surprise, then climbed down.

"You should take a guard," he told her as he turned the pulley to open the heavy gate. "Maelgwn insists you should always be accompanied whenever you leave the fortress."

"I won't go far. If I wait for you to find a man to go with me, I'll miss the sunrise." Rhiannon's eyes were pleading.

The man sighed. "All right, but hurry back. There'll be hell to pay if the king learns I let you go alone."

She rode along the trackway by the river, smelling the salt marshes and watching the black-backed gulls and other water birds that stayed during the winter. Then she turned the horse sharply and headed toward the gray shadow of forest that spread over the hills further inland. Her riding had improved a great deal and taking the horse would be much faster than walking. She had little time before Maelgwn rose and noticed her absence.

The woods were mostly bare and drab, except for the dark pine trees. She left her horse tethered to an alder tree and entered the forest on foot. The sunrise was beginning to warm the dull morning sky, but she had to walk briskly to keep the chill off. She saw a bush of red bryony berries, now dried to the color of old blood, and recalled passing them with Maelgwn. The memory evoked was sharp and bittersweet. It had been fall then, the forest a blaze of color with the turning leaves and bronze glow of the sun. Now it was a silent pattern of shadows and leafless trees; underfoot, a carpet of mosses and dried grasses whispered as she passed by.

She walked slowly, feeling the gods of the woods all around her: Nemetoma, the goddess of the trees; Uiska, goddess of streams and springs; bold Cerrunos, the stag god. Rhiannon bowed her head and murmured a plea to all of them for protection.

She came to the great oak tree where she had lain with Maelgwn. The leaves that had made their bed were gone now, scattered by the wind, and the oak's boughs were almost completely bare. The pale morning light filtered down coldly through the empty branches. Tears came to Rhiannon's eyes, remembering. Their lovemaking that day had been magic of the rarest kind. For those moments, no one in the world had existed for her but Maelgwn, beautiful, passionate Maelgwn, with his burning eyes and warm mouth, his sleek muscles and broad chest. In his arms she had forgotten Llewenon and Morganna and Rhun, and everything else that troubled her.

Love for Maelgwn washed through her, as sharp as pain. For days she had denied the truth, that her decision was ultimately a selfish one. It had nothing to do with protecting Rhun or even Maelgwn. It was herself she meant to please. She loved Maelgwn. She could not bear to give him up, even if he hated everything she was. The love she felt for him was so strong, it made everything else unimportant. She felt bonded to Maelgwn; blood to blood, flesh to flesh, heart to heart.

And yet, she dared not bear Maelgwn's child. If she did, she might unleash the curse that haunted them both—her, the unloved, unwanted bastard, and Maelgwn, burdened by a legacy of betrayal and treachery that left him wounded beyond healing.

Rhiannon retraced her steps through the forest, her eyes searching the underbrush. Here and there, she paused and used her knife to dig among the dried leaves and plants that covered the forest floor. Despite the cool air, sweat trickled down her forehead as she searched.

Llewenon had once mentioned that the roots of the stinking gladwin could be used to prevent pregnancy. Rhiannon was much less familiar with the contraceptive properties of the plant than with those of rue and wild carrot seeds, but she could not be too choosy this late in the season. She would be lucky to find enough of any herb to last her through the winter.

Relief swept through her as she finally located some dried purplish stalks. Using her knife, she dug out several of the plant's reddish roots. She sniffed them and her nose wrinkled at the sharp, pungent smell. Aye, this was it—no wonder they called it stinking gladwin.

Llewenon said the roots must be boiled in wine and the resulting decoction drunk. Rhiannon presumed it must be taken daily, although she was not sure. A twinge of anxiety crossed her mind; it worried her to dose herself with an herb she had so little knowledge of. Still, she had no choice. Even if she risked her own health, it was better than getting with child.

Rhiannon gathered a large number of the roots, put them in the leather bag which she had brought, then secured the bag at her waist. Her task accomplished, she hurried back through the forest, anxious to return to Degannwy before Maelgwn noticed she was gone and questioned the sentry.

When she returned to where her horse waited, she tied the bag to the saddle, then mounted and set off for the fortress.

The mist that swam along the valley thickened, and Rhiannon felt the chill air begin to penetrate her cloak. The newly risen sun had crept behind a cloud; it would be another dreary, drizzly winter day.

Maelgwn stood in the watchtower, watching the horizon anxiously. He had risen early to check on Rhun. When he found Rhiannon missing from his bedchamber, he had not immediately been alarmed. Then he ran into Rufus in the courtyard and learned that Rhiannon was riding—alone. He had rushed to the gate, determined to thrash the guard on duty for disobeying orders. Only when Mabon explained how Rhiannon had begged to go alone did Maelgwn's ire cool slightly.

Things were strained enough with Rhiannon as it was. He did not need to distress her even more by punishing the guard for responding to her pleas. Maelgwn let Mabon off with a fierce warning that if he ever disobeyed orders again, he would flay the man himself.

Maelgwn looked toward the north, toward the coast, straining his eyes in the grayish light. His empty stomach twisted with fear. Anything could happen to Rhiannon. She might become disoriented and lose her way. The wolves that had moved down from the hills might attack her. And there was always the danger she would be kidnapped by one of his enemies. If she did not appear in a few moments, he would set out after her.

He glanced in the other direction, and his heart leaped in his chest as he saw a rider approaching the fortress. He tore down the ladder to the tower. In a flash, he was mounted and riding out the gate to meet his wife.

She slowed when she saw him.

"Rhiannon, where have you been?"

"Riding," she answered.

She looked so wistful and sad; he could not bear to be angry with her. "If you had but woken me, I would have gladly joined you."

Rhiannon gave him a small smile. "I will—next time."

Maelgwn almost held his breath at her words. It had been so long since she had given him any hint that she welcomed his company. To see her smile, however tentatively, to hear her words of encouragement—it gave him back some of the hope he had almost lost.

They rode into the gate together, and more than a few of the people who saw them grinned, seeing their king and queen out riding so early. At the stables, Maelgwn helped Rhiannon off the winded horse. When she did not immediately move away, he leaned down and kissed her. To his delight, her lips parted in welcome. His blood rushed through his veins, and he could not hold back, no matter how he tried. His mouth slanted hard over hers, drinking in the sweetness he had been so long denied. She tasted as he remembered, wild, intoxicating. Breathless, he finally paused. He would not push things; he would take this kiss as a beginning.

"Rhun is up and about," he said as he released her. "Taffee changed his bandage and announced that his hand looks almost as good as new. Do you want to see him, or join me for a morning meal in the hall?"

Rhiannon's soft lavender blue eyes regarded him in a manner that could only be called seductive. "I vow I am not a bit hungry. If Rhun is well, I see no reason not to return to bed."

Maelgwn's mouth gaped open. It was rare for Rhiannon to behave flirtatiously. It was especially startling now, when he feared he had lost her forever. For a moment, he was too stunned to respond. "Aye, I imagine we will not be missed," he said faintly.

He could hardly control his ardor as he walked Rhiannon to the bedchamber. He kept her hand firmly in his own. Once they reached the room, he was even more reluctant to let her go. She pulled away—and then began undressing.

Maelgwn watched her, his hands fumbling with his own clothes. It did not seem possible she meant to welcome him to her bed again, and without a word of explanation. Doubts crowded his mind, and he paused, half-dressed, to watch her uncertainly. It seemed he should question her, find out why she had shunned him and what had changed her mind.

She turned toward the bed, with her long, bright hair

swinging provocatively above her buttocks. He immediately abandoned his skepticism. What did he care what had swayed her decision? Some baffling woman's mood or a return of her old fear of lovemaking brought about by her visit to her homeland—it did not matter what had caused her to reject him. All that counted was that she wanted him once more.

He finished removing his clothes and crawled into the cold, rumpled bed. When he pulled her slender body against his, he found she was trembling, and for a moment, he was uneasy. Would there be wariness in her body when he entered her? Would she wait until then to pull away?

His thoughts seemed foolish as Rhiannon turned and pressed her breasts against his chest. He groaned as the warmth of her skin ignited his. Then he held her face with his hands and kissed her deeply. She smelled of the forest scent he loved so much. It clung to her hair, her small pink lips and cool white skin.

He ran his hand down her body, touching the curves he coveted most. Her nipples hardened at his caress, and his fingers found warm wetness when they fondled between her legs.

Panting, he pushed her thighs apart. It was madness, but he could not wait. He had to satisfy himself that she meant to accept him. He closed his eyes and pressed his shaft against her silky opening. When she did not tense or pull away, he pushed into her harder, deeper. Her body welcomed his, melting with the exquisite, boneless receptivity of a woman in need of a man. A thrilling tremor rippled down the entire length of his body, and he threw back his head and sighed deeply.

Ah, Rhiannon! She was his again.

Chapter 18

She was back in the dark, gloomy forest of Manau Gotodin, walking with Llewenon as he told her about different plants and roots. He led her farther and farther away from camp, until they reached a great grove of oaks where the huge trees had cut off the sunlight to form a clearing beneath their boughs. Llewenon took her to the center of the clearing and ordered her to remove her clothing.

She knew at once what was going to happen, but she could not make her legs work to run away. She was paralyzed, her body as stiff and unyielding as the oaks around them. As she watched in dread, Llewenon reached beneath his white robe and pulled out a small knife with a crescent-shaped blade. It glittered in the moonlight that filtered through the trees.

Llewenon held out the knife. "I'm going to purify you," he said. "It must be done—it is the only way the gods will accept you."

The knife pierced her gown. It felt cold against her skin. There was a sharp pain, and blood spurted from her body, splattering Llewenon's face and white robe. She tried to scream, but her voice was as useless as her legs. The knife cut into her again and again.

Rhiannon woke with a gasp. It felt as if the knife still

gouged her belly, twisting in her flesh. Her body was slick with sweat, the pain so intense, she felt sick. She tried to get out of bed, but the room spun around her. At last, she was able to lurch to her feet and stagger over to the chamber pot. She vomited, then lay down on the floor, too weak to move.

She closed her eyes, realizing all at once what was happening to her. This was the third day she had taken the decoction made from gladwin roots. As always, it tasted wretched, but this time it had also upset her stomach. She had lain down, hoping if she rested, the nausea would go away. Instead, she had fallen asleep and had that awful dream.

Rhiannon shivered with dread. The stuff was poisonous, either that, or she had taken too strong a dose. Surely now, after she vomited, she would begin to feel better.

The pains returned, sharp, knifelike. They gnawed at her belly, reaching deep, all the way to her spine. Rhiannon twisted, trying to escape the agony. Her legs trembled, her insides convulsed and shuddered. She could feel the perspiration trickling down her body, and there was more wetness between her legs. When she looked down, she saw the bottom half of her gown was stained black with blood.

Rhiannon suppressed a scream, then fainted as the pain intensified.

"How is she?" Maelgwn's voice was harsh; his blue eyes dark with worry.

"Well enough." Bleddryn patted him reassuringly on the arm. "She is young and strong, and losing a babe this early is not usually dangerous."

"But the blood . . ." Maelgwn shook his head, repressing the horrible memory.

"It's clear you've never seen a babe birthed; it was no more bloody than that."

"I never knew miscarrying caused such pain."

"She was scared, and no doubt distressed about losing the babe. Rhiannon is a nervous sort, a little high-strung perhaps. She will come around."

Maelgwn clutched sharply at Bleddryn's arm. "Are you sure?"

The plump physician shrugged. "The bleeding has stopped. When she heals, there is no reason to think she will not conceive again." He turned away. "Let her rest the night; she should be much better by morning."

As Bleddryn stepped out of the passageway between buildings, he was stopped again, this time by Lady Gwenaseth.

"How fares the queen?"

"As I told the king, she is as well as can be expected. She miscarried, but nothing is amiss."

"What made her lose the babe?"

Bleddryn yawned. "She is rather slight; perhaps her body is not yet ready for childbearing."

"Taffee said Rhiannon was sick."

"A touch of fever perhaps, or something she ate. It might have caused her to lose the babe, but I doubt it." He gave Gwenaseth an irritated look. "If you have no more questions, I'll be getting to bed."

Gwenaseth's forehead wrinkled in thought as she watched the physician cross the courtyard. She had not even known Rhiannon was carrying, and now the queen had lost the child. It seemed altogether too sudden.

The king's chamber was quiet as Gwenaseth entered on tiptoe. Rhiannon appeared to be sleeping soundly; she made no movement as Gwenaseth moved past the bed.

Seeing a cup on the table, Gwenaseth lifted it and sniffed the last few drops on the bottom. She grimaced at the awful smell, then glanced toward where Rhiannon lay.

Maelgwn entered the room, and Gwenaseth's face softened with sympathy. "I'm sorry, Maelgwn. I did not even know she was with child."

Maelgwn shook his head. "Nor did I."

The king sat down on a stool beside the bed. Gwenaseth went to smooth the covers over Rhiannon's sleeping form, then left.

Four babes of his seed, and only one had made it to the world of the living.

Maelgwn's hand trembled slightly as he reached out to stroke Rhiannon's disheveled hair. Dear God, how afraid he had been! When he had found Rhiannon and seen the blood all over the floor, he thought she was dying. For a moment, he had relived the despair of Aurora's death in childbirth. Then reason took over and he ran to find Bleddryn.

Rhiannon stirred at his caress. "Maelgwn," she whispered.

"Hush, Rhian, you must sleep."

Her face in the lamplight was forlorn and wretched-looking. Maelgwn yearned to tell her that he did not care about the babe, that all that mattered was that she was safe. But he worried that bringing up the subject would distress her, and she obviously needed to rest.

He touched her face, feeling the fragile bones beneath her smooth skin. "Sleep now. Bleddryn promised you would feel much better in the morning."

Obediently, she closed her eyes. Maelgwn watched her, repressing a shudder of deep relief. He would have to think of some way to spare Rhiannon this risk in the future. He could not endure standing helplessly by as another wife faced the dangers of childbearing. There were ways, surely, to prevent conception. He had heard of herbs that disrupted a woman's cycle or, if placed in the woman's body, poisoned a man's seed before it could reach her womb. And there was always withdrawal . . . or abstinence. He grimaced. For him, Rhiannon's body was like water to a thirsty man, bread to a starving one. He could not keep his hands off of her. And yet, they must be more careful in the future.

He glanced down again at his wife's sleeping form. He could no longer deny it. He loved Rhiannon. His fear for her went deeper than the haunting memories of losing Aurora. This scare had taught him how much he needed Rhiannon. She had healed his pain, made him whole. He could not think of life without her.

A half-sob rose in his throat. He had not wanted this; it was terrifying to love a woman so much. But there was nothing he could do now. Nothing but do his best to keep this small, fragile woman safe.

"It's mine, Dewi! Papa said I could have it!"

"Hush, boys! If you can't be quiet, you must go outside!"

Sewan's exasperated voice carried easily to where Rhiannon sat by a glowing brazier in the weaving room. She leaned further over her work, struggling to hide her distress. It took only the sound of a baby crying, or the sight of a mother comforting her little one, to remind Rhiannon of her terrible mistake.

What a fool she had been! The herb she took had not prevented conception, but ended a pregnancy already begun. Her bleeding times were often irregular, and she had never bothered to count backwards to the last one. If she had, she would have realized she had not bled since before she went to Manau Gotodin.

A sick sense of loss filled her. In her concern for avoiding conception, she had never considered that a baby might have already started inside her. Now it was too late. The babe was dead; she had killed it.

Sewan returned from shooing her children into the

courtyard and approached Rhiannon. "The embroidery on that tunic is exquisite. I wish I had your talent for needlework."

"I am making it for Rhun, to gift him with on Midwinter's Eve—or the Yule season as your people call it."

Sewan reached out to pat Rhiannon's shoulder. "I'm sure you will have your own son someday. You've been wed to Maelgwn only a half turn of the seasons. There is plenty of time for other babes."

Rhiannon nodded stiffly. The women of Degannwy were extraordinarily solicitous these days, and Maelgwn drove her half mad with his tender concern. He had not pressed her to share his bed, even after Bleddryn pronounced her healed, and she knew he would not. It would be up to her to take the fateful step, to welcome him into her body and risk him starting another babe.

Rhiannon repressed a shudder. "I'm not feeling well, Sewan." She stood slowly. "Perhaps I will go lie down."

"Have you been drinking your milk as Bleddryn suggested? Perhaps I should brew some snakeweed tonic for you. It's said to be good for ailments of the womb . . ."

Sewan prattled on, holding Rhiannon's arm as they walked toward the king's bedchamber. Rhiannon endured Lady Balyn's admonishments resignedly. It would not do to reject Sewan's gentle nagging. She should be grateful that Maelgwn's people cared so much for her welfare.

"Rhiannon?"

Gwenaseth peered in the doorway. "Sewan said you were ailing, that you had gone to lie down."

Rhiannon rose from her stool by the fire. "I'm better now. It was a passing thing; I still feel lightheaded sometimes."

Gwenaseth nodded knowingly as she entered the room. "It's the loss of blood. You must eat more meat at meals

. . . and take some tansy steeped in wine to keep up your strength . . ."

"Must the whole fortress play nursemaid to me?" Rhiannon said sharply. "I half expect Rhun to begin pushing food upon me and worrying whether I sleep well!"

"But you are still thin and pale," Gwenaseth countered. "We are only concerned for you."

For a moment, Gwenaseth thought she saw a flash of resentment in Rhiannon's eyes. Then it was gone; the queen took her seat and stared into the fire.

Now, Gwenaseth decided quickly. *Now was the time to ask Rhiannon about the miscarriage.* She might not have another chance when Rhiannon's guard was down.

She pulled up a stool next to Rhiannon's. "Your loss of the babe was very sudden—and rather violent too. Women do not usually bleed so heavily when they lose a babe early on."

Rhiannon did not look up, but Gwenaseth saw a slight tremor in her shoulders.

"You once told me, Rhiannon, that you would not bear Maelgwn's babe. I can't help wondering if you took something to make yourself lose it."

"That's absurd. You know everyone hopes that I give Maelgwn another heir." Rhiannon's voice was soft, almost inaudible. Her hands in her lap began to tremble.

"But you, Rhiannon, you don't really wish that, do you?"

The only sound in the room was the crackle of the fire. Gwenaseth held her breath, wondering if what she was doing was wise. Was it right to force this fragile woman to admit she had killed her own child? The queen had not regained her color since the miscarriage, and she appeared to have lost weight as well. Her pallor and slenderness had not damaged her beauty, but instead gave her features an unearthly, ethereal quality. There seemed no substance to Rhiannon; she was a shadow of a woman, reduced to a dazzling flame of bright hair and huge, haunted violet eyes.

"Rhiannon, please. You dare not try such a dangerous thing again. Next time you might take too much; next time you might die."

"Do you think I do not know that!" Rhiannon abruptly looked up, her eyes bright with anguish. "It was a mistake. I did not even know I was with child. I took the herb thinking it would keep me from conceiving. I'm such a halfwit that I did not consider I might have already conceived during the last moon cycle."

Gwenaseth took a deep breath. "You did not know you were pregnant? Truly?"

Rhiannon shook her head. Gwenaseth relaxed slightly. At least Rhiannon had not killed her babe deliberately. There was hope she might be able to convince the queen that bearing Maelgwn's child would not be so dreadful.

"Then you will not try it again?"

Rhiannon sighed. "I don't know. I don't know what to do. There are days I wonder if it would not been better if I had died along with the babe. Maelgwn might grieve for me, but in the end, he would heal, he could marry again and have a chance to found the dynasty he dreams of."

"Oh, Rhiannon, don't say such things!" Gwenaseth gathered the queen into her arms. "My poor child. I am so sorry. It is not fair that Esylt did this to you, that she should burden you with her terrible secret."

"Nay, Esylt is not to blame," Rhiannon answered in a muffled voice. "She did not mean to hurt me; she sought to protect me."

Gwenaseth shook her head. Poor Rhiannon. Even now, she would defend Esylt. She had not an inkling what kind of woman her mother had been. "Hush. *Hush.* You must forget this. You must forget that Esylt was your mother, and all else that Ferdic told you. Live for the present, Rhiannon. Maelgwn loves you, all he asks is that you be happy. He told me that he does not even care if you ever conceive again, if only you will smile and love him as you used to."

"How can I? Knowing that Esylt is my mother, knowing how he hates . . ." Rhiannon broke off with a horrified gasp. Her body went stiff in Gwenaseth's arms. Gwenaseth jerked her eyes toward the door. She sucked in her breath as harshly as Rhiannon had. Maelgwn stood in the doorway, as still as a statue.

Chapter 19

Gwenaseth tightened her grip on Rhiannon, fearing the queen would faint to the floor. "Maelgwn, how long . . ."

"Long enough." He spat out the words. His eyes locked with hers.

She tried to meet them fearlessly. "We were speaking of Rhiannon's miscarriage. I was telling her not to fret—that there would be other babes."

"Nay, you were not. You were speaking of . . ." Maelgwn's voice choked, and the color returned to his face. Gwenaseth could sense the rage building inside him.

She released the trembling queen and stood. "It's all in the past, Maelgwn. Rhiannon had nothing to do with this."

"She is Esylt's daughter!"

The hatred in Maelgwn's eyes made Gwenaseth flinch. The unthinkable had happened, and she did not know what to do. One thing was certain, she reasoned, as her mind was beginning to function again—she could not leave Rhiannon in the room with her half-crazed husband.

She groped for the queen's arm and kept her eyes focused on Maelgwn.

His eyes gazed off into the distance. His words were directed to a dead woman, a ghost from his tormented past: "Ah, Esylt—I thought that your poisonous hold over my life had ended. But I was wrong. Even from the grave you manage to spin your web of corruption and treachery."

Gwenaseth took a deep breath and gently pulled Rhiannon from her seat before the fire. Perhaps if they walked slowly and quietly past Maelgwn, he would let them leave.

They had almost reached the door when Rhiannon pulled away and turned to her husband. "Maelgwn, please, let me explain. Let me tell you why . . ."

Rhiannon's voice died, and Gwenaseth guessed the reason when she faced Maelgwn. No one could see the look on the king's face without knowing terror. His features wore an expression of barely controlled violence, of wrath so great it transformed his face into a mask of murder, a visage of death.

"You!" Maelgwn ground out in a tortured rasp. "You knew, and still you married me, you came to my bed, you made me love you . . ."

Rhiannon shook her head, reduced to muteness by the look on her husband's face. Gwenaseth stepped between the queen and Maelgwn.

"Nay, she did not know. She only found out the truth when Ferdic told her on his deathbed."

"That was weeks ago!" Maelgwn turned his fury-darkened eyes to Gwenaseth. "You've made a secret of Rhiannon's parentage all this time. You never meant to tell me, did you?"

"Some things are better left as secrets, and this was one. Blame me, not Rhiannon. I convinced her to conceal the truth."

"You meddling little witch!"

Gwenaseth took a step back in fear. "Maelgwn, I . . ."

"I want you out of this room. Out of my life! Be gone with you!"

Gwenaseth glanced uneasily at Rhiannon. The queen looked as if her wits had fled her. Gwenaseth took Rhiannon's arm again, trying to lead her to safety. Maelgwn stepped forward. He grasped Rhiannon's hair and jerked her head up so she faced him.

"My lovely wife . . . my niece . . . the daughter of my beloved sister."

With a swift jerk of her hair, Maelgwn flung Rhiannon to the floor with all his strength.

Gwenaseth screamed. "Dear God, Maelgwn, you'll kill her!" She hurried to help Rhiannon up, then confronted Maelgwn, her eyes blazing. "She's a sweet, innocent girl. She had no part in this."

Maelgwn moved threateningly toward Gwenaseth. His eyes flared like twin blue marshlights. Before he came close enough to grab her, Gwenaseth's nerves failed her. She released Rhiannon and fled the room.

Rhiannon gazed at Maelgwn, frozen like a hare before the hunter.

"Why?" Maelgwn whispered. "Oh, God, why?"

The despair in Maelgwn's voice made Rhiannon's heart twist in her chest. Her husband looked as if he were in terrible pain. His unseeing eyes stared straight ahead; his forehead was beaded with sweat. She understood exactly how he felt. She had endured such loss, such emptiness after Ferdic told her the truth. Now Maelgwn was experiencing a like anguish. She could not bear to see him suffer.

She touched his arm. "I know," she said softly. "It seems so cruel, so unfair. But I don't believe Esylt did this to us out of hatred. I think she hoped we would be happy, that we would come to love each other."

"Esylt!" he hissed. His tormented eyes met hers. "She planned this foul deception to destroy me!"

"Nay, she did not," Rhiannon shook her head. "She did not mean . . ."

She gasped in fear as Maelgwn seized her again. She felt his hands dig into her arms, as if he would crush her very bones. His eyes had gone black and senseless again. The rest of his features were distorted with anger.

"You are of her blood! You, too, are evil!"

"Nay!" She swayed and stepped back as he released her. The sound of Maelgwn drawing his knife echoed through the room.

"I should kill you. That would end the evil once and for all."

Wings of terror beat through Rhiannon, as though her heart might leap from her chest. The gods help her! She was afraid. She must escape; she did not want to die. Her will returned, as hot and raw as the blood surging through her veins. Her eyes measured the distance to the door, then veered back to Maelgwn.

Do not look before you move—a voice said. *He must not expect it.*

"Maelgwn, I . . ." What to say to distract him? She dared not mention Esylt; to do so might incite him further. "Gwenaseth," she whispered. "Do not blame her for this."

"Gwenaseth?" Maelgwn sounded startled, as if the name confused him.

"I didn't mean for her to know. She only found out by accident; she was trying to protect me."

The look of befuddlement on Maelgwn's face deepened. It was clear he had forgotten Gwenaseth, that she did not even exist in his tortured world. Rhiannon watched her husband warily. There seemed to be a slight relaxation in his stance. *Now*—the voice whispered. *Now!*

Rhiannon's muscles responded, sending her body into flight toward the door. Maelgwn lunged a second later. His hand flashed out. The knife caught Rhiannon's thigh.

A burning sensation, then a sudden loss of balance.

Halfway to the door, Rhiannon fell. A shower of stars followed her down. Her stunned state lasted a few moments, then she rolled over to see Maelgwn looming above her. His eyes were still frenzied, his breathing came in gasps.

"Go," he said. "Take your things and go. Otherwise, I will have to finish."

Rhiannon got to her feet. Pain throbbed along her thigh, and warm wetness trickled down her leg. A wave of uncontrollable trembling seized her, but she shook it off.

The room seemed gray and wavy, as if under water. She went to where her cloak was hung and her boots lay out to dry. Bending awkwardly, she put the boots on, then wrapped herself in the cloak. She walked unsteadily toward the door. She did not look back at Maelgwn.

The courtyard was nearly deserted. Rhiannon walked across it in a trance, her body stiff and slow. She reached the open gate and stepped outside the fortress. The cold sea breeze struck her face, sharpening her dimming consciousness.

She walked unsteadily down the track from the fortress. By now she limped badly, and there was a pulling and heaviness in her leg. The blood pooled in her boot and grew cold. When she glanced down, she saw that she was leaving a trail of blood behind her on the muddy ground.

The voice inside her told her to head toward the sea. The sound of the waves would soothe her and help her think, and she could wash there.

How tired she was. She walked across the sea grass which led out to the promontory above the ocean. The pain deepened and then ebbed, like the waves crashing below. The tangy sea scent filled her nose, and she listened vaguely to the mournful cry of the water birds. She seemed to be floating; the sounds of the sea came to her from far away. She fought the urge to stop and rest. She had to get to the water, to wash and stop the bleeding.

She stumbled on the pathway down the cliffs. When she

looked down to secure her footing, she saw the glitter of blood on the rocks. She must keep moving.

The soft sand of the beach was even more difficult to walk on than the rocky pathway. She stopped for a moment, breathing heavily. Everything seemed to be fading, as if a thin mist hung before her eyes. She heard a ringing in her ears, or was it the sound of the sea, crashing and thundering? She was almost there; the blue-gray waves danced in the misty light.

She sank down near the edge of the dark water. It was terribly cold, and her gown felt slimy and unpleasant against her skin. She removed her cloak, then stripped off the soiled garment. Shivering violently, she again wrapped herself in the cloak and walked to the water. She held the cloak out of the waves and washed off the streaks of dazzling red blood that ran down her leg. Wincing, she examined the wound on the side of her thigh; it still seeped blood. She covered it with a piece of seaweed, holding it tightly against the gash.

She tried to leave the water, but the soft sand sucked at her quivering legs. Her strength seemed to be trickling away with her blood, and it took all her resolve to pull herself from the lapping waves and stagger to the dry beach. Then she sat down and numbly wrapped the cloak around her. She was safe at last.

The blood pounded in his head. His body felt hollow, like a husk, a shell. Maelgwn still clutched the knife, holding it before himself for protection. He recalled Rhiannon trying to escape and remembered sending her away. Still, it seemed he was not alone in the room. The shadows crowded forward, moving toward him, blocking out the light. He whirled around. There was nothing there, but he could smell the sharp, unpleasant perfume Esylt always wore. Dread filled him.

He looked toward the corner where the fire smoldered. A haze of smoke drifted across the room toward him. He blinked and tried to see through the murky air. The hair on the back of his neck stood on end; his mouth opened in a silent scream. Esylt—she was there, standing quietly in the shadows. Her hair was as black as a raven's wing in sunlight, her skin as white as frost upon the moonlit hills. She moved closer, so close he could see a pale blue vein pulsing in her throat.

His eyes moved up to meet Esylt's. Her eyes gleamed with triumph and exultation, sparkling like hot blue stones. She threw back her head and laughed.

Maelgwn swayed, feeling the sweat soak his clothes. He reached out, intending to grasp his tormentor's thick flowing tresses. His fingers found dry, empty space, and fear curled more tightly around his heart. He reached out again, and his knife clattered to the floor. He could not breathe. A hand seemed to be squeezing his chest, pressing the air from his lungs. He swayed, then righted himself. He could feel the force like a vise around his heart. It was a living thing, a choking mist. He struggled against it, using all his will to stay on his feet and maintain a grasp on his fading consciousness. He was as sure of it as he had ever been of anything—if he swooned now, the ghosts would possess him; he would die.

Slowly, almost gently, the thing left him. His vision cleared. He was panting. His throat was raw, his body rank with sweat. Weakly, he groped his way to a stool by the fire and collapsed upon it. The fire still smoldered, filling the room with darkness. He closed his eyes against it. He felt defeated, despairing, helpless. Beyond the years, across the hills of Britain, defying even death, Esylt had worked her final wicked vengeance. She had come to remind him he could never be free of her cold, evil touch. It was as if she were a part of him; some foul putrefaction that could not be cut out without leaving a mortal wound. And now, through Rhiannon, Esylt had bound him to her even more dearly.

He stood with a gasp. The horror of his thoughts was draining his strength, his very life from him. But he would not give in; he would fight. He would find some weapon that would free him.

Maelgwn crossed to the corner of the room and opened the bronze-bound chest. He began to search through it. Beneath the piles of clothes and jewels, he found the cross he had worn in the priory. He lifted it up. The rubies set in the center caught the light from the fire and glinted like drops of blood. He clutched it to his breast and closed his eyes, waiting for the sense of peace, of forgiveness to come upon him. He felt nothing; the grinding dread in his chest did not ease.

Opening his eyes, he stared at the cross. The thing was cold, empty, without life. He dropped it with a sense of wretchedness. Even the true God, the *Christos,* had no power here. His struggle was with the ancient forces, with gods so old no man recalled their names.

He ran his hands across his sweat-soaked face and repressed the urge to weep like a child. What was to become of him?

"Maelgwn?"

Balyn stood in the open doorway, trouble written on his broad, open face. "Gwenaseth came to me with this story . . ." He paused, clearly uncomfortable with what he was about to say. "She said you and Rhiannon quarreled. She implied that you . . . you attacked Rhiannon."

Maelgwn met Balyn's gaze squarely. "It is true."

Balyn took another step into the room. "But why?"

Maelgwn hesitated. It seemed ill-fated to speak the words aloud. Still, Balyn must know sometime. Maelgwn's jaw clenched as he answered. "Rhiannon is Esylt's daughter."

"Her daughter!" Balyn gasped, then quickly crossed himself. "By the light! You believe this?"

"How can I deny what I heard from both Rhiannon and Gwenaseth's lips?"

Balyn's mouth worked. "I cannot imagine . . . Rhiannon . . . she seems so shy and gentle, without even the usual womanly guiles. Looking at her, you would not think it." His eyes jerked to Maelgwn's. "I can see no hint of Esylt in her. None."

"Rhiannon herself confirmed the truth. She even attempted to defend Esylt."

Balyn's eyes widened. "Nay, she did not! Blessed *Jesu* ! It's no surprise you struck her."

"I didn't strike her. I stabbed her with my knife." Maelgwn walked wearily toward where Balyn stood by the door. "There are bloodstains here which must surely be hers."

"Must be . . .?"

Maelgwn shook his head. "It comes to me from a distance. I recall that Rhiannon was injured, but I don't think severely. I urged her to flee. If she had stayed here, I could not have contained myself. I would have killed her." He turned, regarding the room warily. "Her presence reminded me too clearly of Esylt, and my sister has a very long reach as it is. Even now, I sense her with us, hovering in the shadows of the room, laughing at me."

Balyn crossed himself once more. His dark eyes bulged with dismay and fear. "You are saying that Esylt knew you were to wed her daughter? That she had a hand in this?"

Maelgwn closed his eyes again, wishing he could avoid the horror of the truth. "Aye, she knew. I guessed that she must, and Rhiannon confirmed it."

"But why?"

"A bitter jest, I presume." He opened his eyes. "My sister did not need much of a reason to be cruel."

"But Rhiannon—to do that to her own daughter. I didn't think even Esylt capable of such heartlessness."

Maelgwn exhaled softly. "I never truly understood my sister. I thought once that I did, but that was many years ago. Long before the sickness began to eat away her soul." He shook his head, trying to clear it. Memories pulled at his thoughts, tugging him into the past. He had once loved Esylt, admired her even, as a younger sibling looks up to an elder one. How odd to think it had all led to this. "It was the curse of my family," he whispered. "My mother and brothers suffered from it too. Their quest for power was all-consuming; it finally destroyed them."

The two men were silent. Maelgwn could hear Balyn's harsh, almost-labored breathing. "What will you do then?" Balyn asked after a few moments. "What will become of Rhiannon?"

Maelgwn shuddered. He was cold. The fire was dying; he should send for a servant to tend it. He moved restlessly to the hearth and began to poke at the glowing ashes. As the flames flared up, the memories came to him, unbidden, relentless. Rhiannon lying beneath him, in his bed, on the morning-lit beach, beneath the rustling autumn boughs. He had known such satisfaction in her body, such contentment. That was over now. Never again could he look at her without imagining her soft violet eyes turned to cold, gleaming blue, her vivid hair besmirched to raven blackness, her delicate body transformed into his sister's full-blown, wanton flesh. The thought of it made him shudder again.

"I care not what happens to Rhiannon," he told Balyn slowly. "So long as I never again behold her face in this lifetime."

Chapter 20

Maelgwn's fingers worried the rough edges of the amethysts set in the hilt of his knife. His body ached, and the cold made him shiver. The fire before him was almost completely extinguished, and there was no more wood to feed it. He had sent Balyn for a servant some time ago, but no one had appeared yet.

He glanced toward the door, where the bloodstains made dark spots upon the paving stones, then he quickly looked away. It seemed like a dream, and yet the mess on the floor proved it had happened. He had stabbed Rhiannon, threatened to murder her. A cold whisper of guilt brushed his thoughts. Even in his most vengeful musings, he could not believe Rhiannon had any part in the planning of their doomed marriage. She was a victim, just as he was. Esylt had used them both—her closest living kin—to weave some murky, twisted pattern of hatred and vengeance.

He stood slowly, struggling to unbend his stiff muscles. Where was Balyn? Why did he not return? Without the presence of another living being, the ghosts that crowded the bedchamber gained form and substance. Any moment he expected Esylt's wraith to appear again, materializing out of the faint twist of smoke over the hearth. His eyes roamed the comfortable, well-appointed room. There was nothing here to fear, nothing but beauty and luxury. Esylt's curse did not linger in the vivid wall hangings, their colors shifting and glowing by the flickering lamplight. Nor did it dwell in the room's many graceful objects—their shadows wavering eerily as he watched. The curse was inside him, waiting for something to ignite it, like dry tinder set aflame by an errant spark.

He turned toward the door. He could flee this place, seek out the solitude of the hills and the sea. But there was no escape from the thing that haunted him. Better to stay here, to do battle with the specters as they crept from the dark corners.

His fingers again sought the hilt of the knife, and he recalled his murderous rage toward Rhiannon. At the time he had felt a kind of certainty that she must die; that only her death could save him. Some dark part of him still believed the spilling of her blood would cleanse his own soul. After all, the ancients taught that blood, especially the blood of an innocent, was a very potent thing.

Maelgwn's glance jerked to the corner where the chest stood open, its contents scattered. The ornate cross still lay where he had dropped it. A Christian icon, celebrating another death, a death which was said to redeem the evil in the world. The symbol was there again. To defeat the darkness, men believed something of light and beauty must perish. Perhaps that was what had incited him to such violence against Rhiannon. If he had not let Rhiannon go, if he had held her body in his hands and felt the blood and life trickle from her young, soft form—would he not have been freed from the curse?

A tremor racked him. Nay, his own soul was not worth such a price. It was the darkness itself which suggested such a thing. Even before the spread of the Christian faith, men had rejected human sacrifice for the cruelty it was. Sacrifice arose out of fear, the ugliness inside men that made them slaughter their own kind to win the gods' favor. If he had killed Rhiannon, it would have only put a greater stain upon his spirit. It was well he had let her escape.

"Maelgwn."

He started, then turned toward the door. Gwenaseth stood in the gleaming lamplight, her small form as stubborn and tenacious as the marsh reeds that bent to the wind but never yielded. A sense of deep weariness beset him. Gwenaseth would urge him to keep Rhiannon as his wife. He could not do it, nor could he bear to share his reasons with Gwenaseth.

"What do you want?"

"I want you to listen. Nay, you will hear me out," she continued as he made a gesture of protest. "You frightened me away once, but you will not do so again. I will have my say about Rhiannon."

"Speak then, if you must," Maelgwn said coldly. "But I give you fair warning, you cannot change my mind."

Gwenaseth took a step toward him. "Rhiannon is innocent, Maelgwn; she did you no harm. She tried her best to spare you from the truth. She even risked her life to keep from bearing a child she feared you would hate. She took some herb meant to prevent pregnancy. Instead, it made her body expell the babe she had already conceived. You know as well as I how dangerous such potions are. Rhiannon might have died."

Maelgwn's sight dimmed, and he saw Rhiannon sprawled on the floor, the black-red blood staining the skirt of her shift. He had feared she was dead when he first saw her; now he knew how close she had actually come to ending her life.

"Rhiannon did that without thought for herself," Gwenaseth asserted. "It was you and the babe she tried to spare."

"What she did was right," Maelgwn answered softly. "A child of our shared blood would be doubly cursed."

"Cursed! Of all the self-pitying nonsense . . ." Gwenaseth paused, her breast heaving. "Always, Maelgwn, you have worn Esylt's betrayal as a badge of your great suffering. But most men and women know grief and disappointment in their lives, often at the hands of those they love. Still, they go on; they forgive and forget. They do not let their bitterness eat up the rest of their lives."

"I cannot forgive and forget." The words hissed past his clenched teeth, echoing the rage that afflicted him. "Esylt's wickedness lingers on even now. She planned this wretched marriage. She used me!"

"And have you not wondered why? Why Esylt did this thing? After pondering on it for weeks, I have begun to suspect the truth is not so terrible as you would believe. From what I can see, Esylt loved Rhiannon. I don't think she meant to cause her grief by wedding her to you. In fact, I begin to believe she intended for you and Rhiannon to love each other."

"Oh, aye," Maelgwn answered in disgust. "She intended we should love each other—so that on the day we found out the truth, our suffering would be so much more bitter."

"I don't believe Esylt would sacrifice her daughter, the only fruit of her womb, to such a brutal scheme."

"Believe it!" He could hardly control his anger. What did Gwenaseth know of it? How could she dare to defend his sister? "Esylt never cared for another living soul in her life. She was incapable of love!"

"Are you certain?" Gwenaseth challenged, moving closer. "Are you sure she did not once love you, so much that she could not bear to lose you to Aurora?"

Maelgwn shook his head. He could not answer. Gwenaseth's question probed too near his grief at discovering his sister's betrayal. The anger and pain were so much more unendurable where you once had loved.

"Think, Maelgwn. Do you not owe Rhiannon something? You used her dowry to secure your kingdom, sated yourself upon her body, accepted her tenderness and care for your son. Do you not owe her a debt for that, for the happiness she brought you? Don't you owe her a chance to be a wife to you?"

"No," he answered flatly. "The marriage was based on a lie, intended or not. Be it fair or unfair, I have nothing to offer Rhiannon."

Gwenaseth moved closer still. He could see that her eyes were red-rimmed from weeping; her small features distorted. "At least do not commit this ... this murder. You injured Rhiannon. She has left the fortress, bleeding and in shock. Please send someone after her to make sure she is safe."

"It was only a flesh wound," he argued. "Nothing so grievous as to be mortal."

"Night is coming. The wolves will move down the hills. I beg you, Maelgwn, at least see that Rhiannon is brought inside the fortress."

A chill swept down Maelgwn's spine. Could he bear the guilt if Rhiannon were found dead outside Degannwy's walls? If the blame for her death could be placed on his angry banishment?

"Go, then," he said. "Send some men after her to bring her back. But by all the gods and saints, I beg you, do not bring her within my sight."

Gwenaseth nodded rapidly, then hurried from the room.

Again Maelgwn went to stand before the dying fire. His anger was spent; all that remained was a sick, empty grief that weakened him until he could scarcely bear his tormented thoughts.

He crossed quickly to the table in the far shadows of the room. A bronze ewer stood upon the smooth-grained, ancient surface. It would be full, as always, with the weak, sour wine the Cymry imported from Brittany. He took a hammered bronze goblet, the cup of it chased with birds and beasts of gold and silver, and filled it to the brim. He took a deep swallow, then another. Closing his eyes, he willed the liquid to flow in his veins, to sap the sharpness of his pain.

The sound of thunder aroused him from his uneasy stupor. Thunder in the month of the winter moon? He had seen it before, the lightning striking vividly above the frosted hills. Still, it was rare, a thing men talked about as if it were an omen from the old thunder god, Taranis— and an unlucky one at that. Maelgwn struggled to his feet. He must see to preparing the fortress for a storm.

He left the bedchamber and went out into the cloud-darkened twilight. The sky was a strange, milky pink, the softness of it shattered occasionally by a jagged streak of silver lightning. The rain had yet to begin, but the court-yard was already in turmoil. Dogs, horses and men hurried to and fro, setting up a frantic racket. Maelgwn saw Gareth trying to subdue a rearing horse. Maelgwn hurried to his aid; as the horse was calmed and led toward the stables, Maelgwn's eyes met Gareth's harassed face across the mare's withers. "Were you out with the search party?" he shouted.

"The search party?"

"Aye, I sent Gwenaseth for some men to look for Rhiannon."

"The queen is outside the fortress?" Gareth looked alarmed.

"I believe so," Maelgwn answered. "She was seen leaving some time past."

"I know nothing of it," Gareth insisted. He guided the horse into the dim stable, then turned and faced Maelgwn anxiously. "Pray to God they have found her by now. This storm promises to be a bad one. The beasts sense it; we've had rough work to get the horses in."

Maelgwn nodded and left. A light rain began to fall as he hurried toward the gate. Two men were trying desperately to push it shut against the furious gusts. Maelgwn joined their struggle. When it was finally latched, he grabbed one of the men by the sleeve. "What of the queen—have they found her yet?"

The man, Eleri, gave Maelgwn a wild-eyed look. "It's really not my place to tell you, my lord."

"Tell me what?" Maelgwn's grip tightened on the man's arm. "Did you not find her? Is she dead?"

Eleri shook his head. "Nay, 'tis not so sure as that. We followed the trail of blood to the beach, but found nothing. It was as if she disappeared."

A grinding fear started in Maelgwn's belly. "You are sure she did not leave the coast road and head for the forest instead?"

Eleri again shook his head. "The bloodstains were clear and bright all the way to the sand. It is as if she vanished into the air itself."

"She could have washed the blood off in the sea, then set out again for the woods."

The young soldier suddenly averted his eyes from Maelgwn. His features stiffened into an expressionless mask. "I don't think she could have made it much farther. There was a lot of blood; over time such blood loss weakens a man, let alone a woman. If she did make it to the forest, the wolves . . ." Eleri did not finish, but a slight twitch in his jaw gave away his gruesome thoughts.

The sick feeling in Maelgwn's guts deepened. "You're telling me that my wi- . . . that Rhiannon is dead?"

"Nay, I would not tell you such a thing," Eleri asserted. "It is not my place. I only report that the search has been called off. The lightning spooked the horses, and it was growing too dark to see, even by torchlight."

It took Maelgwn a moment to remember to dismiss the man. He felt stunned. Though he had drawn his knife on Rhiannon and threatened her, he had not actually confronted the reality of her death. He did not feel the relief he might have expected.

He nodded curtly to Eleri, then went to climb the ladder to the watchtower. He trod out on the wooden platform. The wind buffeted him about until he braced himself against the heavy oak planks and leaned into one of the notches cut for bowmen to defend the fort from. The rain was falling heavier now, whirled into torrents by the wind. His face and hair were quickly soaked. It was getting hard to see. The pallor of the sky had darkened to a roiling gray, and the storm seemed to suck the remaining light from the landscape. His eyes searched for a glimpse of the coast road, but he could see nothing.

Crack! A bolt of jagged fire shot through the sky. Maelgwn flinched as the lightning cast the hills around Degannwy into bright relief. A rumble of thunder followed, and an odd, superstitious thought came to him. Did this violent storm signal the old gods' displeasure? Did bold Taranis seek vengeance for the hurt done against Rhiannon? She was very much a child of the woods, a half-wild, half-magic creature. Why should the ancient deities she worshiped not avenge her life with the violent forces they controlled?

"Blessed Jesu! What ails you, Maelgwn?"

Maelgwn turned to see Balyn at the top of the ladder, his face contorted from screaming into the wind.

"Have you heard?" Maelgwn brushed back the strands of soaking hair the wind blew in his face. "Eleri reports they had no luck finding Rhiannon. He thinks she is dead."

Another flash of lightning shot across the heavens, and Maelgwn caught a clear glimpse of Balyn. His face was pleading. "Even if she lives, she'll not come home in this. Come inside, Maelgwn. You can wait as well by the fire."

"You think she is dead, don't you?"

Balyn's voice was so hoarse, Maelgwn could barely hear it over the sound of the wind. "I don't know what to think. We need to rest, both of us. Let us leave this place before we are struck down by a lightning bolt or drowned in the deluge." Balyn advanced, catching his arm. "Please, my lord, come."

Maelgwn cast one last glance out at the nearly invisible hills, then let Balyn lead him down the ladder. "I am so cold," Maelgwn said, almost to himself. "I don't think I will ever be warm again."

The men in the search party swore as they guided their horses down the mud-slick track from Degannwy. Although the storm had passed, the rain continued to fall throughout the night and into the morning. If the drizzle had turned to snow, the way would have been frozen and less treacherous. As it was, an unseasonably mild wind blew up the coast, thawing the trackway to a morass of mud.

They followed the coast road to the cliffs and dismounted. The hounds they had brought gathered around, sniffing the wet ground mournfully. The men tethered the horses together, and Gareth remained to watch them as the rest of the men and the dogs half-slid, half-stumbled down the pathway to the beach. By the time they reached level ground, the rain had worsened. Balyn's voice was barely audible above the sound of the downpour and the raging roar of the surf as he shouted instructions to the men. "Spread out and cover the whole beach. Bring me anything you find."

Maelgwn flinched at Balyn's words. What could they hope to discover on this storm-ravaged beach besides Rhiannon's broken body? He tried to force it away, but his thoughts dwelled on the image of Rhiannon's corpse, battered on the rocks and half-eaten by sea creatures.

As the men fanned out, Maelgwn looked up at the cliffs, his eyes envisioning the dark, ghostly forest that covered the slopes of the other end of the valley. If only Rhiannon had fled there instead of the beach. He had some hope that she would be safe in the woods, at least for a day or two.

He tore his eyes away and wandered aimlessly over the sand, unable to make himself approach the crashing surf. His fear of what he might find was too great. He neared the dark boulders on the edge of the beach with almost as much reluctance. Here the memory of the first time he had loved Rhiannon came to him with painful clarity. She had been so lovely in the morning light, so dazzlingly fair and lithe, skipping over the waves like an enchanted fairy-creature, as careless and lovely as a rainbow glimmering in the sea spray. But he remembered her fear, too, the terrible wariness in her eyes. It had taken all his patience and tender coaxing to soothe her dread and win her trust.

Yesterday he had betrayed that trust, he thought grimly. He had hurt Rhiannon as he vowed he would not, banished her from his life, exactly as he promised never to do. Guilt twisted inside him. The rage was gone; he felt empty and tired.

He turned toward the sea, watching his men. A group of them had gathered near the water, and he could guess from the way the dogs circled and the men bent their heads toward the sand that they had found something. He looked away for a moment, willing their discovery to be nothing of consequence. If they found a scrap of her clothes, even her bloody, ruined gown, it would mean very little. Rhiannon might well have torn her garments into strips to make a bandage or even stripped off her soiled dress altogether. He would not believe her dead unless they found irrefutable proof she had not fled the beach and found shelter elsewhere.

He braced himself as Balyn left the group of men and

walked toward him. The big man's hair was as wet and matted as a dog's and droplets of rain ran off his nose in a steady, incessant stream. He did not appear to be carrying anything, but as he reached Maeglwn, he extended his hand and held out a sodden object. Maelgwn blinked away rain for a moment before taking the small hide boot. He remembered the day he had brought home the wildcat pelt that lined it. "Wildcats are so pretty," Rhiannon had murmured, stroking the soft, spotted fur regretfully. "I hate to think of you killing them." But despite her qualms over the animal's death, she had used the pelt to line her new winter boots.

Maelgwn's hand crushed the boot until water streamed from it. Such a little thing, so insignificant, and yet so fraught with portent. How, truly, could Rhiannon have left the beach without her boots? The way to the forest was rough going, especially with the icy pools and sucking mire the storm had left. It would be an impossible journey for a barefoot, wounded woman.

"I'm sorry, Maelgwn." Balyn's voice was husky with regret. "We'll keep looking if you wish it, but the men are soaked and miserable, and the dogs can't find a scent. I was hoping we could return to Degannwy until the weather clears."

Maelgwn nodded. Why should he make his men suffer for a cause so hopeless? There was no chance of finding Rhiannon alive now, and the search for her body could wait.

"Aye, send them home."

The men were eerily silent on the way back to Degannwy. The only sounds were the rain and the incessant rush of water, the jangle of harnesses and the soft splish-splash of hooves on the soaked ground. As soon as they reached the fortress, the horses were hurried to the stables to be dried off and fed, while the men shed their sopping garments and gathered with the hounds before a blazing fire in the feasting hall.

Maelgwn did not join them, but trudged slowly across the courtyard to the small chapel that stood not far from his own quarters. The door creaked as he opened it, and the scent of damp and mold that assailed his nostrils as he entered reminded him that he had promised the abbott at Llandudno he would eventually build a chapel of stone to replace this hastily built wooden one. Aye, he would do it—as soon as he could spare men to drag the rock down from the old quarry in the hills.

Despite the air of disuse and damp that clung to it, the chapel was not poorly kept. Rushlights gleamed along the walls, and the altar itself was lit with several precious beeswax candles. There was no sign of the priest, but that was not unusual. Father Leichan was more of a scholar and clerk than a holy man. Except for mass on Sundays and the rites for weddings, funerals and the like, the priest spent most of his time away from the chapel in the secular pursuits of copying books and, recently, tutoring Rhun and a few of the other likely boys.

Maelgwn walked hesitantly toward the massive stone altar; the fine piece of masonry had been rescued from some building at the old Roman fortress at Segontium. Perhaps it had been an altar there, too, but certainly not of the Christian god. Now it was covered with a crisp, white linen cloth whose edges fluttered slightly in the drafts swirling through the cracks between the timbers.

He did not kneel, but stood watching the shadows the shifting candlelight made on the whitewashed walls. Why had he come? God would not hear him now. His thoughts were too consumed with hate and bitterness. But at least it was quiet here, and there were no unpleasant memories to haunt him. The smell of candles reminded him of Llandudno and the countless hours spent praying in the priory chapel. He had found peace of a kind there; a numbing, blind sort of faith that purged the worst of the pain from his soul.

He turned as he heard a creaking sound behind him. The door to the chapel slammed shut, and Maelgwn tensed as he saw a movement in the shadows by the entrance. For a moment, he wondered if Esylt's spirit had followed him. Then he saw Gwenaseth's hair catch bronze in the rush-light. He exhaled deeply.

"You startled me."

"Is it me you fear, Maelgwn, or are your sins at last begin to haunt you?"

Maelgwn sighed. He might have known Gwenaseth was not finished with him.

"So, tell me . . ." Gwenaseth stepped forward. The light cast deep shadows on her face. For a moment, she looked to Maelgwn like a haggard, old woman; and yet, that could not be, for she was a few years younger than he. "Are you relieved that Rhiannon is dead? Drowned, they said, washed away in the raging storm." Gwenaseth took another step toward him. "Your problems are finished now, aren't they? Now that Rhiannon has so conveniently vanished."

He did not answer, and Gwenaseth moved closer. "Tell me, Maelgwn, will you give Rhiannon the final honors as your queen? Will you see that your people mourn her, that a mass is said for her soul?"

"Of course."

"Hypocrite. Rhiannon cared nothing for those things; she took her comfort from the forest and the hills. She nourished her spirit with the growing things, the scent of wind and rain. She was of the old gods, the old ways."

"Aye, you are right. But we have no pagan priests here. I can only have Taliesin compose a song honoring her, one that does justice to her gentle spirit and ancient faith."

"But you will invite no kinsmen from her own land?" Gwenaseth mocked. "Seek out no Brigante warriors to tear their hair and weep for her?"

"I cannot. You know I cannot."

"Why?" Gwenaseth stood next to him now. He could see her ravaged face, the lines of anguish etched over her tawny freckles. "Do you fear the alliance will not hold once her kinsmen learn Rhiannon is dead? What will happen when they discover she died by your hand? What blood price will they demand for the murder of their princess?"

"I will pay it," Maelgwn said wearily. "I will pay it even if it beggars me. But not until this fall. For the future of Gwynedd, we must have another summer of peace."

Gwenaseth stepped back; suddenly she looked defeated. "It doesn't matter. None of it will bring Rhiannon back. And if the truth be known, she was not a princess of the Brigante anyway." She glanced up, her green-gold eyes probing. "You didn't know that, did you? Ferdic was not Rhiannon's father."

"What are you saying?"

"There was more to the story Ferdic told Rhiannon on his deathbed than merely the truth of her mother. He also denied being her father. He said Rhiannon's sire was an Irish slave."

"A slave?"

Gwenaseth's eyes narrowed coldly. "You knew, of course, of your sister's wanton ways. No man was safe from her cruel predations. Ferdic said Rhiannon's father was only a boy. I think, of all things, Rhiannon's knowledge of their liaison came as close as anything to shaking her faith in her beloved Esylt's character."

Maelgwn stepped back. "I don't want to hear about Esylt's foul habits."

"Think how Rhiannon felt. In one brief conversation with a dying man, she learned that not only was she blood kin to a woman her husband hated, but also a slave's bastard." Gwenaseth's chin quivered, and she looked away. " 'Tis a wonder she did not go mad. But she was strong, delicate little Rhiannon was. She made herself go on. I think she was able to do that because she loved you . . . and believed you loved her."

"Our marriage was based on a lie," Maelgwn argued. "You cannot blame me for being revolted by who Rhiannon was. Being born of my sister's flesh, her blood was irrevocably tainted."

Gwenaseth was next to him again, her face contorted with grief. "How could you do it, Maelgwn? How could you send her away? Rhiannon had no one. She was utterly alone."

"It's true," he answered. "Rhiannon had no one, and I failed her. But her mother failed her long before that. It is Esylt who bears the burden for Rhiannon's death, not I."

"Fool!" Gwenaseth's eyes flashed, and she brought her hands up, as if she would scratch his face. "Rhiannon loved you, can you not see it? She could have made you happy; her love might even have healed you."

Her hands fell to her sides in a defeated gesture. "Of course you cannot see it. You are too blinded by your hatred. After all these years, all you think of is some vague, ancient curse that no one believes in except yourself."

"The curse is real," Maelgwn answered stubbornly. "There was never any hope for love between Esylt's daughter and me."

"A curse," Gwenaseth's sneering voice echoed clearly in the small chapel. The sound of it was so cold and sinister, Maelgwn felt a twinge of fear. "So be it then. I will give you a curse, Maelgwn. I curse you with loneliness and grief the rest of your days."

He watched as Gwenaseth turned away. She walked quickly to the door and opened it. As the damp wind whirled into the chapel and made the rushlights tremble, she called out over her shoulder. "By the by, I am leaving Degannwy. I don't know if you will release Elwyn from his service with you, but whether or not he comes, my allegiance to you is finished. On the morrow I take my children back to my father's old fortress at Llanfaglon.''

After Gwenaseth left, Maelgwn hurried to the chapel entrance and shut the door against the wind and rain. He leaned against it, breathing heavily. It was foolish; Gwenaseth had never shown any soothsaying power, any influence with the spirit world. Still, he could not stop trembling, shaking like a man with the ague.

Her angry words echoed in his head, and darkness settled hard upon his spirit. He walked stiffly back to the altar, knelt, and began to pray.

Chapter 21

The wolf loomed near. Rhiannon could see its huge, gleaming teeth and smell its acrid breath. She watched in horror as the animal's fangs sank deep into her flesh. She tried to pull away, but her leg would not move. The beast's teeth sank deeper, down to the very bone. She screamed.

"Hush. You're safe."

The voice was soft. The hands that stroked her face felt tender and soothing. They pushed away the image of the wolf. But the fear would not leave her. Her life was in danger; she must get away!

"Be still, little one. No one will harm you."

Someone held her and smoothed her hair. She could feel hands brushing away her tears, arms cradling her in warmth and softness. She gave in to the feeling of safety and began to relax. The soothing arms left her, then returned. A cup was pressed to her lips. She was thirsty, and she drank the warm liquid willingly. Then everything faded to darkness.

* * *

"Will she live?"

"Of course. She lost a great deal of blood, but the wound is not a mortal one."

The voices were strange, foreign. Lingering fear made Rhiannon hesitate, then curiosity overcame her anxiety. She opened her eyes and saw that she was in a small dwelling lit by a low fire. She could barely make out the forms of a man and woman sharing a bed-place a few paces away.

"How do you suppose she cut her leg? Perhaps on the rocks?"

"Nay, not even a very sharp rock would cut so cleanly. I'm sure the wound is from a knife."

"Someone hurt her deliberately?"

"It would seem so."

Rhiannon closed her eyes and saw Maelgwn looming over her, the knife glittering in his hand. He had looked nothing like the husband she loved. The man who attacked her was a stranger, a bloodthirsty, murderous stranger.

Rhiannon shook off the wretched thought and turned her head, straining to hear more of the couple's quiet conversation. The voices faded to murmurs and soft sounds. It took Rhiannon a moment to realize that the man and woman were no longer talking, but making love. She held her breath, listening. It was agonizing to remember, to recall what it felt like to lie in Maelgwn's arms, to have him love her. She must not think of it.

Shifting her leg, she concentrated on the sharp throb in her thigh. Physical pain was easy to endure; in fact, she welcomed it. It meant she lived, that she had not yet slipped over to the other side. She had been very close, though. She remembered moving toward a great ray of light and hearing people call out to her, the voices of the spirits of the dead. They seemed to be urging her toward the light. Then the light faded, and she was flung back into her cold, aching body. She had felt great pain, the harsh, racking pain of rebirth. Then even that faded, and she slid gratefully into the silent, gray twilight of oblivion.

But now she was safe, and awake. The voices faded away, and it seemed she could hear the sea crashing in the distance. Rhiannon lifted her head and tried to recall how she had come to this place. Her last memory was of lying on the beach; these people must have found her there and brought her to their home.

Her eyes searched the small, round, sparsely furnished dwelling. Two large rocks near the fire served as seating places, and the space between the foot of her bed-place and the other held only a few storage baskets. Rough-looking garments of leather and fur hung from the daub and wattle walls of the dwelling, and the hearth was a circle of stones. Smoke from the fire streamed up through a small smoke hole in the blackened ceiling. Even the bed she lay on was of meager stuff. The sheepskins were matted and old. Every time she moved, the coarse, rough blanket scratched her skin. These were poor people, and yet they had taken her in and cared for her. Somehow she must repay their generosity.

The thought made her weary, and she lay back, allowing the numbing fatigue to seep through her.

When Rhiannon woke again, a woman was leaning over her. She had dark, almost black eyes, and her skin was a weathered brown. From the warmth in her expression, Rhiannon knew at once that this woman was the one who had comforted her.

"So, my little mermaid, you are awake. We wondered for a time if you would ever rouse."

Rhiannon licked her dry lips and tried to find her voice. "Where am I?"

"A place called Penmaenmawr. It's along the coast near the king's stronghold."

The mention of the king made Rhiannon tense. The

woman leaned closer. "Does your wound pain you?" she asked.

Rhiannon nodded, eager to divert the conversation away from the king.

The woman pulled back the blankets and bent over Rhiannon's leg, examining it with gentle expertise. "It's healing well. The redness is fading, and your skin is cool. I think the pain you feel is from the flesh tightening around the stitches."

Rhiannon looked down and saw tiny, dark stitches closing up the wound. "You're a healer?" she asked the woman in surprise.

"Aye, soothing fevers and toothaches, tending wounds, birthing babes—I manage well enough."

"I am grateful," Rhiannon said softly. "I know enough of wounds to recognize your skill. Without stitches, it would have scarred."

" 'Twould be a shame to leave a scar. The Goddess would not like to see one as fair as you marred for life."

The woman's dark eyes twinkled with a kind of amusement, and Rhiannon watched her warily. "What's your name?" she asked.

"Arianhrodd." The woman's eyes did not waver from her face. "What's yours?"

Rhiannon hesitated. If she told the truth, would Arianhrodd guess who she was? It was no use. She was not clear-headed enough to think of a lie. "I am called Rhiannon."

The look of interest in the woman's eyes intensifed. "You bear one of the names of the Goddess. No wonder She saved you."

"Saved me?" Rhiannon asked skeptically.

"Aye. When Ceinwen found you on the beach, he was sure you were dead. Your limbs were stiff and cold, and you were deathly white from loss of blood. You couldn't have survived much longer without shelter." She paused meaningfully. "I can't help but think the Goddess led Ceinwen to you, that She wished to see you live."

A chill wind seemed to pierce the hut's rough walls and trace a shiver down Rhiannon's back. This was the third time the woman had mentioned the Goddess. Rhiannon considered asking her to explain, then decided against it. "Where was my cloak?" she asked instead. "Was I not wearing a fine woolen cloak when he found me?"

"Nay, you wore nothing. Ceinwen told me he thought at first you must be a mermaid, so fair you were in your nakedness. He feared to touch you for dread that you would enchant him." The woman smiled, deepening the pattern of fine wrinkles around her eyes. "Fishermen tell such stories. The Goddess must have helped him conquer his fear, for he wrapped you in some skins and carried you to his boat."

"And brought me here?"

Arianhrodd nodded.

"Is Ceinwen,"—Rhiannon stumbled slightly over the name—"is he your husband?"

The woman laughed. "We do not call it such among our people. I have not handfasted with him, if that is what you mean. But he stays with me, and we both strive to serve the Goddess in our own ways."

Rhiannon could ignore the subject no longer. "Who is the Goddess of whom you speak so reverently?"

The woman's dark eyes appeared to gleam brighter in the firelight. "The Goddess is the mother of us all. She rules the earth, and the sea. She is the giver of life itself."

Rhiannon nodded thoughtfully. The worship of the Great Mother was very old, older than that of the God of the Hunt, although he was sometimes said to be the Goddess's consort. It was an ancient faith, and a primitive one. Rhiannon recalled Llewenon's scorn for the simple folk who honored the moon as an aspect of the Goddess.

How, he asked, could a female, even a divine one, possibly be stronger and more important than a male god?

Rhiannon almost asked the question of Arianhrodd, then changed her mind. It was not polite to question another's religious beliefs, especially when one was a guest at their hearth. Besides, the idea of a powerful female deity intrigued her.

"When you are better, perhaps you can go with us to one of our ceremonies honoring the Goddess," said Arianhrodd. "Since She seems to have chosen you, it would be well if you learned more of Her. Anyway," she added before Rhiannon could respond. "That will be some time off. For now, you must rest. Take some more of this broth. You should eat and drink as much as possible to help your body replace the blood you lost."

Rhiannon nodded. She was very thirsty, and as weak as a newborn kitten. There would be time for questions later. For now, she must try to recover her strength.

A few days later, Rhiannon wrapped the rough blanket around herself and managed to walk unaided to take a seat on one of the flat stones before the fire. It was only a few paces from the bed-place, but still her legs quivered with the effort and sweat broke out on her forehead. The wound was healing swiftly, but it was more difficult to recover from the loss of blood. She slept much of the time, and even when she was awake, her mind seemed too muddled to focus on much of anything. There was a benefit to her fatigue though, she decided. Not having the strength to think about the future also kept her from having to think about the past.

Seeing that the fire was burning low, Rhiannon reached out and added more wood from the pile. Guilt nagged at her when she thought about how much Arianhrodd and Ceinwen had done for her. She dreaded being a burden to these kind people, and she was determined to somehow repay them for what they had done. To do that, she would have to be well and strong.

The bleak, mournful sound of the wind came from outside the hut, evoking a sense of sorrow Rhiannon could not quite shake off. From childhood on, she had grown expert at shutting away unpleasant memories, but this time she could not seem to banish the pain. There was a knot inside her. A tight heaviness gathered in her chest. All it needed was a slight reminder and the turmoil inside her threatened to explode.

At least the fight against it kept her alive and gave her the will to go on living. She knew now that she did not want to die. She was not ready; there was something else she must do, some purpose intended for her life. She must find what it was, why her spirit had been returned to the world of the living.

"Rhiannon, you are up." Arianhrodd's face split wide with a smile as she entered the hut. She carried a basket filled with cleaned fish. She took it over to the fire and set it down. "I'm pleased you feel strong enough to rise by yourself."

Rhiannon shook her head. "I'm still wretchedly weak; my legs are next to useless."

"This is a beginning though. In a few days you will be able to walk outside. Then we must find something to serve as clothes for you. It would be unseemly to have you walking on the beach wrapped in a blanket."

Rhiannon looked down at the coarse cloth. "If I had needle and thread, I could stitch it into a garment. It would give you one less blanket, but I would replace it as soon as I could." She sighed. "If only I had a loom and some wool, I would gladly weave and sew all the blankets and clothes you could ever wish for."

"You have those skills?" Arianhrodd asked as she bent

down and put the fish in a pot of water and set it on the fire.

"Aye. I am slow at spinning, but much better at weaving and sewing."

"Then I will see to it that you have what you need."

"That is very generous, but you must know I can't repay you. I have no coin, no jewels, no possessions at all."

Arianhrodd gave her a long, searching look, and for a moment Rhiannon worried that she meant to bring up the subject of Rhiannon's identity. Anyone could guess from her pale, unweathered skin and uncallused hands that Rhiannon was neither a slave nor peasant. Arianhrodd must surely wonder who she was and who had wounded her. Still, the fisherwoman had not asked any questions. She must be waiting for Rhiannon to heal before broaching the subject.

Arianhrodd gestured to her own shabby garment. "We have furs and skins in plenty, but cloth comes dear. Your sewing skills are very welcome."

Rhiannon nodded, feeling pleased. Here, at last, was a way she could repay her rescuers. But there was another worry. Weaving and sewing took time, and the longer she stayed with these people, the greater the chance that Maelgwn would find her. Once he did, what would he do? Did he still mean to kill her? Would he punish Arianhrodd and Ceinwen for taking her in?

Shivering, Rhiannon wondered if she were endangering the lives of her rescuers by failing to reveal who she was. Yet, if she told them the truth, they might well return her to Maelgwn. Rhiannon sighed. She did not want to bring trouble to those who had helped her, but neither could she risk revealing her identity. She must believe that Maelgwn would not find her here. Perhaps he would not even attempt a search; perhaps he would be satisfied that she was gone from his life.

She felt better for a moment, then she remembered

the look on Maelgwn's face when he sent her away. Her husband hated her. Even now he might intend to make certain she no longer inhabited the same world as he.

"You look pale, Rhiannon." Arianhrodd's soft voice roused Rhiannon from her frightening thoughts. "I think you should lie down again. Come, I'll help you."

Wearily, Rhiannon allowed Arianhrodd to support her arm and guide her to the bed-place. She sank back and closed her eyes. Her grief over her shattered life was great, but not so great that she wished to die. She would do what she must to survive, and the gods forgive her if she entangled these innocent fisherfolk in the web of misery and hatred that connected her and Maelgwn.

Rhiannon slept awhile. When she awoke, Arianhrodd was still there. Arianhrodd brought Rhiannon some broth and helped her sit up so she could drink it, then the fisherwoman left for a few minutes. When she returned, she carried two large pots of water slung on a stick over her shoulders. She put them to heat on the fire and came back to the bed-place.

"I think it is time we bathed you, little one." Leaning over the bed-place, she smoothed a tangled strand of hair away from Rhiannon's face. "We must also comb your hair. Such a fine color," she commented. "I suspect you must have a trace of Irish blood; they are known for their fiery tresses."

Rhiannon watched the fisherwoman as she returned to the fire and added herbs to the pots of water. The sweet scents of rosemary and lavender filled the hut, and Rhiannon smiled faintly. Arianhrodd was very skilled with herbs and simples. From what Rhiannon could see, the fisherwoman had a large store of dried plants and roots in the baskets in the corner, and she obviously knew how to use them. But her talent for healing extended beyond a knowledge of plants and their uses. Rhiannon was sure that Arianhrodd possessed some sort of magic. A sense of contentment and warmth radiated from the fisherwoman, and Rhiannon could feel it mending her spirit even as Arianhrodd's skilled ministrations healed her wounded leg.

Rhiannon's eyes followed Arianhrodd as she continued her tasks. Try as she might, she could not guess the fisherwoman's age. Despite the lines around her eyes and her weathered skin, Arianhrodd's hair was a dark rich brown, and her plump body and graceful movements displayed the strength and vitality of a young woman. Arianhrodd's face was pleasant, but without any pretense to beauty, and she had surprisingly good teeth. There was something ageless about her—as if she would never grow old.

Next to Arianhrodd, the man Ceinwen seemed like a quiet, little shadow. He was lean and very dark, with a narrow face and fine features. In an odd, animal-like way, he appeared almost handsome. Ceinwen still had not spoken to Rhiannon, but came and went with the cautious silence of a wild creature that creeps to a man's dwelling for food and warmth, then returns to the woods. He brought home fish every day, and nearly every night— Rhiannon knew, because she dreaded the memories it brought her—the dark, silent man made love to Arianhrodd.

When the water was ready, Arianhrodd carried one of the huge heavy pots over to the bed-place and pulled the covers aside. With gentle fingers, she bathed Rhiannon. When she was done, she gestured toward the fire. "You will have to dry in the air; I mean to wash the blanket, so you will be without a cover for a time."

Rhiannon looked uneasily toward the door, and Arianhrodd shook her head. "Ceinwen will not return yet. There is nothing to fear."

Rhiannon grimaced at her own foolishness. When Ceinwen found her, she had been utterly naked, and he had carried her to his boat that way. It was absurd to pretend modesty now. Still, she had always been like that, ever since Llewenon's attack. She was never easy with her own nakedness, especially when a man was near. Only with Maelgwn had she overcome her apprehension.

Maelgwn—the unwanted memory sent a shaft of pain through her, so sharp her body jerked. Arianhrodd noticed. Her eyes sought Rhiannon's, and for a moment Rhiannon felt the other woman could read her thoughts as clearly as if she spoke of them at length. Then the connection was gone. Arianhrodd came to her and helped her over to the seating place by the fire. Sitting crosslegged on the dirt floor behind Rhiannon, Arianhrodd began to smooth the tangles from her hair with an ancient bone comb.

Chapter 22

Maelgwn dreamt he was sitting on a riverbank. Blinking, he watched the water foam, spilling white over the rocks. His senses were filled with the scent of the mountains—pine, rain, wind.

A familiar voice called him, and he turned. A girl was coming down the pathway toward him. Her dark hair hung down in two braids, and her eyes shone like the bluest of mountain skies. She carried a bundle in her arms. It was long and awkwardly shaped, and he noticed how tenderly her tanned fingers clutched it. He looked back at her face; she was smiling.

"What is it, Esylt?"

"I have something for you. I promised you long ago that I would bring it."

Maelgwn felt his face form a scowl. The object in Esylt's arms resembled a sword. She had brought his father's sword to him after Cadwallon died. He could still remember it—or had it happened in another time, another life?

"Look, Maelgwn . . ." Esylt's voice was warm and coaxing. "Come look. It is not what you think at all."

He approached cautiously, unable to resist the seductive charm of his sister's voice. She had a low, throaty voice, very unlike a woman's.

She pushed the bundle toward him. He could see the brown shimmer of her skin very clearly. Her hands were small and unscarred. He recalled holding her hands once, and how her skin had felt cool and smooth against his own.

He glanced down at the thing she held, and his heart seemed to stop. It was a baby. He stared at it, at its bluish white skin and froth of red hair.

"She is for you," Esylt whispered. Maelgwn heard the love and tenderness in her voice.

"For me?" His voice was weak and high-pitched. A boy's voice.

"Keep her safe for me."

He nodded, overcome with longing and fear. He took the babe and pressed it to his chest. He looked again at Esylt. She was halfway up the path. She waved at him with a light, airy motion. His eyes locked a moment with hers, and then she was gone.

He glanced down at the babe. It closed its little eyes tight and began to cry, a wild shriek of pain. The fear inside him grew, filling him to bursting. He started up the path, seeking help. A root caught his foot, and he stumbled and slid into the cold, foaming river. He went under and the current tore the baby from his arms; he flailed in the rapids, trying to recover the child. His fingers found nothing but sharp rocks and numbing cold. Then he was falling, down, down into nothingness . . .

Maelgwn sat bolt upright on his bedroll. The muscles in his legs clenched in agony; his body swam with sweat. Staring into the darkness, he tried to focus his eyes. He slowly made out the shadowy form of the oak table he used for his council meetings. It was only a dream. He shivered convulsively, then threw off the fur throws that covered him and stood. The cool air chilled his bare skin. Taking deep breaths, he tried to calm himself.

A dream, only a dream. He had dreamed the dream before, but never had it ended so terribly. In past dreams, the thing Esylt handed him was his father's sword. As he took it, he knew his father was dead, that he would be king. This dream was a nightmare. He clenched his eyes shut, but the image refused to leave him. A tiny, innocent babe, and he had lost it, he had let it drown.

He stumbled to the table and leaned on it heavily, feeling sick. Esylt still tormented him. She had sent the dream to weaken him, to poison him with guilt. And it was working, oh, how it was working!

Maelgwn took a deep breath and groped blindly toward the door. He threw it open and inhaled the fresh air. It was raining, a blessed, cleansing rain. He stepped into the downpour, feeling the icy drops cool his fevered skin. Standing naked in the darkness, he let the rain soak his hair and every inch of his flesh. In the distance, the torch of the sentry on the watchtower glowed faintly. Maelgwn wondered for a moment what the man would think if he turned his gaze back to the fortress and saw his king standing unclothed and unmoving in the deluge.

Gradually, the shivering that racked his body came from the cold and not the dream, and he went back into the council room. He dried himself on the furs from his bed, then went to light the brazier. His teeth were rattling in his head with cold by the time he got the flame burning steadily. He retrieved his clothes and dressed by the flickering firelight. The discomfort of his body had eased his panic; he no longer felt half-mad with anxiety. But the sense of guilt lingered. It was like a foul taste in his mouth, a dull throb of pain that vibrated through him like a harper's fingers strumming a tuneless song. He did not know how to banish it, but somehow he must.

He pulled on his cloak and left the council room. Treading rapidly across the courtyard, he paused near his bed-chamber. The serpent again uncoiled in his guts. There, in that place, he had threatened Rhiannon and stabbed her. The floor was still stained with her blood; no matter how much the servants scrubbed, he could see the mark of it on the paving stones. He hurried on, heading toward the gate.

"Mabon, get down here."

"What is it, Maelgwn?"

"I'm going out. I need help with the gate."

The sentry scrambled down, and the two of them pushed the gate open. As Maelgwn started down the trackway, Mabon called after him, "My lord, if anyone asks where you've gone, what should I tell them?"

Maelgwn did not answer.

His feet took him toward the place where the forest spilled down to meet the valley. It was still night. The world was made up of shadows; distinct shapes formed only as he grew very close to them. He was not afraid of wild animals or any of the other dangers which could beset a lone man outside the safety of the fortress. There was nothing in the darkness which terrified him as much as his own thoughts.

He walked on blindly, trying to outpace the fear that followed him from Degannwy. The light of dawn edged the sky as he entered the forest. He could see the ghostly, silver branches of the birch and oak among the dark pines. The sight of the woods, even in their stark, barren winter state, eased his dread. Perhaps in this place he could leave the fearful nightmare behind.

The sound of water was everywhere, a light, gay, bubbling voice rising above the wind. The rest of the forest was silent. Most of the birds had not returned yet, and the animals were still quiet beneath the spell of winter. But there was a sense of expectancy in the air. Mingled with the smell of damp earth was another scent, a faint breath of growing things, of plants stirring beneath the ground. Soon green would creep along the forest floor, banishing the dull grays and browns of winter. The first flowers would peek out—wood anemones, their deceptively delicate white flowers defying even the fiercest spring storms—and violets, hiding their rich purple beauty in small sheltered spots among the trees.

A wave of longing swept through him. How he craved the arrival of spring, the freshness of the air, the stir of life, the first early blossoms. And Rhiannon—how like a woods flower she was, so shy and sweet.

He paused, startled. What was he thinking of? Rhiannon was the poisoned spawn of Esylt. To remember her was to seek out suffering and disaster. He dared not forget that.

Taking a deep breath, he forced himself to recall the scene with Rhiannon and Gwenaseth in his bedchamber. He waited expectantly for the revulsion and disgust to overwhelm him. To his surprise, the sense of abhorrence failed to come. He looked around, wondering. Out here in the clean, rain-washed air, among the gleaming, moisture-laden trees, Esylt's taunting image seemed far away and blurred. Was it possible her power did not extend this far? Esylt was a creature of smoky fires, wine-heavy dreams, stifling, perfume-filled laughter. Perhaps she and her curse had no place in the pristine, quiet forest. Perhaps here he was free.

He walked on, doubting his feelings. It did not seem possible that something that had agonized him not two days before could fail to move him now. Esylt and her curse had haunted him for so long, consuming his thoughts, sucking the very life from his body. Could she really mean to leave him alone?

It began to rain again, and he shivered convulsively at the cold. No wonder Esylt had retreated from her cruel game. He was near-dead with fatigue and grief—perhaps he made poor sport, even for a ghost. He laughed grimly, then fell silent. He had never felt so weary.

Deep within the forest, he stopped walking. Ahead of him stood the great oak. He stared at the huge tree, filled with foreboding. He had not meant to come here, but somehow his feet led him to this place. A part of his mind sensed what was to come. There was a reason he had been brought here—something else in this tangle between him and Esylt. Something he had denied and buried fast beneath the anger and the pain. Now he would know it. His despair would be complete.

He tensed as the image came to him. He saw Rhiannon beneath him, her pale and vivid beauty surrounded by golden oak leaves. He remembered their pleasure, the feeling of their flesh moving together.

"Nay. It's not possible," he said aloud. "I could not have forgotten that." The memories flooded him, so poignant and intense they made him want to weep. No woman had ever made him feel what Rhiannon had. With her, he had known what it was to walk with the gods themselves, as if he transcended his own flesh and melded his spirit with hers.

"Nay," he whispered. He clenched his eyes shut in agony, barely able to face his own thoughts. He still loved Rhiannon. Even the hate he felt for her mother could not destroy his feelings. Part of it was desire, the hunger of his body for her cool white skin and the small, perfect sweetness of her form. But he also felt another, deeper craving. Recalling the morning they watched the sunrise together, he knew he had never known such contentment with a woman, such peace.

He reached out his hands, desperately, imploringly. "Rhiannon . . . I have lost you . . ." His voice choked; the pain throbbed through him. He relived the dream—of holding the babe, precious and fragile in his arms, then the despair as he dropped the child and saw it tumble into the water. It was a true dream. He had possessed Rhiannon for one brief span of time, and then, by his own hate and anger, he had lost her forever.

The knot of pain inside him suddenly tore free, nearly suffocating him. He had been so blind. He had let his lust for vengeance, his terrible rage, destroy Rhiannon. He was alone now, alone as he had been after Aurora's death. Again he had failed to keep safe the woman he loved, and this time, his failure was even uglier. It had not been fate that stole his wife from him, but his own cruel temper. The despair of his thoughts struck him like a blow, and he sank to his knees before the great oak.

He did not know how long he knelt, weeping. When next he knew, there was a presence beside him. It made no sound, only stayed there, waiting. Maelgwn forced himself to clear his vision and turn toward it. The creature was small and oddly shaped, garbed in some sort of rough, brown stuff. Its blue eyes showed bewilderment.

"Rhun?"

The boy's worried look eased, and he spoke shyly from beneath the muffling layer of the heavy leather hood.

"Papa, are you all right?"

"What are you doing here?"

The boy looked away, then fixed his eyes on his father defiantly. "I heard Balyn talking. He said you were missing. I . . . I couldn't help it. I crept out of the fortress and went looking for you." The words died away, and the boy glanced uneasily around the forest, as if realizing the risk he had taken in coming into the woods alone.

Maelgwn's first response was anger. He opened his mouth to chastise his son, but no words came out as a second thought came fast on the heels of the first. He reached out and grabbed Rhun's wrist. "How did you find me? How did you know where I was?"

Rhun looked even more uncomfortable. "I thought you

had gone looking for Rhiannon. I knew she always came here."

Maelgwn caught his breath. His son felt it too; there was something of Rhiannon's spirit in this place.

Rhun sighed. "I miss her. Why did she have to leave?"

Maelgwn wanted to look away, to hide his shame. He felt sure the boy could see his guilt.

"Do you think she is dead, Papa?"

Maelgwn shook his head; he could not answer.

"Balyn thinks she is dead," Rhun asserted. "He says she drowned. If that's so, and she never gets a Christian burial, is it true she'll go to hell?"

Maelgwn forced himself to respond. "I think not. Rhiannon was not a Christian; she believed in ... other gods. They will care for her spirit."

The boy nodded again, obviously comforted. Maelgwn felt no such assurance. It seemed likely Rhiannon's spirit would be uneasy in death. If, as the common people believed, ghosts were the spirits of those who had died wrongly, Rhiannon might well come back to haunt him. The thought made Maelgwn glance around the oak grove. He realized with a start that he was still kneeling in a pile of drenched leaves. He tried to stand, but the stiff muscles and joints in his legs refused to obey him. He nearly fell face first on the ground before sinking back on his knees with a groan.

"Let me help you, Papa."

He used the boy's small hand to find his balance, then stiffly jerked himself to his feet. Pain spread down his legs, stabbing into the muscles like a hundred knives. He staggered, then braced himself on Rhun's small shoulder. The boy swayed beneath his weight, and Maelgwn stamped his feet, trying to regain feeling in them so they would hold him.

"Can you walk? What's wrong?"

"I'm stiff from the cold. My legs won't work as they should."

"Lean on me. I'll help you."

The pain in his legs faded to a dull throb, not half as harsh as the ache of sorrow in his chest. Feeling his son's hand on his arm reminded him of Rhiannon. They both appeared so small and fragile—his son and his wife. Another spasm of grief made his body stiffen.

"Are you crying, Papa?" Rhun's voice was shocked.

"Aye. There is no shame in grieving for those you love." No shame. Maelgwn shook his head. Rhiannon's blood stained his hands. He had no right to play the bereaved husband.

"Maybe she's not dead," Rhun said. "Maybe some Irish raiders came in a boat and stole her!"

Maelgwn sighed. The boy's fanciful explanations were nearly unbearable to hear. They must both face the truth, that Rhiannon was dead; that he had killed her.

"Rhiannon disappeared during daylight," he told Rhun gently. "If there had been raiders, someone would have seen them."

Rhun sighed heavily, and Maelgwn stopped walking and faced his son. "I must tell you . . . I am to blame for Rhiannon's death, Rhun. We had a . . . a disagreement, and I sent Rhiannon away."

The boy drew in his breath sharply. His eyes were wide. "But you didn't mean for her to die, did you?"

Maelgwn searched his heart. Despite his murderous thoughts, he did not think he could have actually killed Rhiannon.

"Nay, I did not mean for her to die."

Rhun's face brightened. "Then Rhiannon will understand." As Maelgwn stared at him with pained, disbelieving eyes, Rhun continued. "Rhiannon was like that; she understood me when I did things I was sorry for. She always made me feel better."

He wanted to cry out like a wounded animal. But he dared not. Rhun would never understand his suffering. He must shield the boy from the awfulness of what he had done. Maelgwn pulled on Rhun's arm and strode forward. "Come. It is still a long way to the fortress, and I am soaked to the skin."

At last they could see Degannwy through the haze of rain. Maelgwn heard Rhun's slight sigh and knew the boy was exhausted. They would both need some warm wine or mead. They stumbled through the gate like an awkward, four-legged beast.

Balyn came rushing toward them as soon as they entered the gate. Maelgwn fixed him with a cold glare. "How does it come to pass that my soldiers let a boy search me out while they relax by the fire?"

"A fool bastard like you isn't worth wasting good men on!" Balyn barked back. Then his face softened with relief. "Come into the hall, Maelgwn. There's a joint of roast venison waiting."

"I need a warm bed more than food. I'm chilled to the marrow."

Rhun pulled at Maelgwn's arm. "Let me help, Papa. I'll fetch the wine and make a fire."

The boy ran off in the direction of the king's quarters, and Maelgwn watched him go with a feeling of dismay. He had not slept in his bedchamber since the night he sent Rhiannon away. He knew Balyn had the same thought when he looked up and saw the big man watching him.

Balyn shrugged. "You have to face it sometime. It was your place before Rhiannon, Maelgwn, and someday you will likely share it with another woman."

"Nay!" Maelgwn's eyes snapped with anger. "I won't have you dismiss Rhiannon as if she were some casual bed partner. She was my wife!"

Balyn took a step backwards, clearly startled. "But I

thought that ..." He swallowed. "What's happened, Maelgwn? What's wrong?"

Maelgwn turned away. "I killed her. I'm as guilty as if I had finished Rhiannon off with my knife."

"You were distraught. Any man would be after learning ... what you learned. You didn't know Rhiannon would fall into the sea and drown."

"But I wanted her dead. My intent was to see harm come to her."

"But it's for the best!" Balyn insisted. "If she had lived, you would have had to set Rhiannon aside anyway. Certainly you could not go on with the marriage. She would always be a constant reminder of Esylt's treachery."

"What if I was wrong? What if Esylt did not conspire for me to marry Rhiannon because she wanted to hurt me? What if she knew what her daughter was like and meant for her to be a comfort to me?"

Balyn's dark eyes bulged, and his big shoulders gave a visible shudder. "You can't believe that. It defies everything we know about Esylt."

"But it does not defy what we know about Rhiannon. She never harmed me. She offered me comfort and tenderness and ..." Maelgwn whispered the word, ". . . love."

Balyn was silent. When he finally spoke, his voice was slow and weary. "You're exhausted. You don't know what you're saying. Get some rest, Maelgwn. Do not, in your fatigue, fall prey to Esylt's wicked, deceitful lies."

Maelgwn made it into the bedchamber and collapsed on the bed. He was so tired; surely he could sleep anywhere, even in this accursed place. He closed his eyes and tried not to think as Rhun and a slave made a fire. The pain clawed at him, pulling him down.

"I'll take your boots off, Papa."

He opened his eyes and nodded, then closed them again. He could hear the grunting struggle of the boy to pull off his heavy, water-swollen boots. It reminded him of the times Rhiannon had helped him undress when he was tired from hunting. After she undressed him, Rhiannon would rub his sore muscles. Her touch was expert and soothing, and so gentle.

The thought nearly choked him, and he opened his eyes to banish the unbearable image. Rhun stood watching him from the foot of the bed. He looked very sad and young. Maelgwn wanted to send him away, but knew he could not. The boy felt Rhiannon's loss as well. As much as Maelgwn longed for the oblivion of sleep, he could not send the boy away. He would not turn away another innocent.

"Help me get these clothes off," he told Rhun. Maelgwn undid the tie to his trousers, and the boy dragged them down. Then Rhun aided him in removing the two wet, heavy woolen tunics he wore. Maelgwn lay back, completely naked, but too tired to pull the bedclothes up. He glanced up to see Rhun staring at him.

"What is it?"

"I . . . I was looking at your scars."

Maelgwn tensed. He remembered Rhiannon fingering each one and asking its history. To her, his scars had been frightening, a reminder that he faced death every time he went into battle. Rhiannon hated war. He had never bothered to think why, but it was obvious she had feared for him.

He forced the thought away and fixed Rhun with a stern look. "There are men who take pride in their scars, Rhun, as if they were proof of bravery. But I see each one as a failure—a failure that might well have cost me my life if Lady Luck had not smiled upon me."

"You see this one here?" He gestured to a welt on his arm. "I turned my back to face another man and he came at me from behind. If my enemy's balance had been better, and he had hit me a full blow, I would not have a scar at all. He would have cut my arm clean off and I would be dead."

Rhun nodded solemnly, his mouth working slightly.

"And this one." Maelgwn touched a long jagged crease that ran across his ribs. "The bastard caught me below my breastpiece. He hit a lung, and I coughed up blood for weeks. Had his sword struck an inch higher, I would have died where I stood. No matter how much armor a man wears, Rhun, there is always a place that is unprotected, where an enemy's sword can find its mark and end your life. A soldier lives by his wits and instinct. Never forget how frail your body is, Rhun, how closely death hovers."

The boy had gone pale, and Maelgwn forgot his next words. He could see the fear in Rhun's smoky blue eyes, and he silently cursed himself for aggravating it. Rhun confronted his father's mortality in every gruesome word. After the loss of his stepmother, it was bound to make him feel alone and desolate.

Maelgwn turned to stare grimly at the richly adorned walls. He was a fool—always hurting those he loved. Why could he not think before he spoke?

He brought his gaze back to Rhun. The boy still watched him, forlorn and uncertain. Maelgwn gestured toward the hearth where the slave had left some heated wine. "Fill my cup, then come and get into bed with me."

"What?" The boy looked surprised.

"You can sleep here tonight."

A delighted smile crept over Rhun's face as he hurried to get the wine. He carried it carefully to Maelgwn, who had finally found the strength to pull up the blankets. Maelgwn drank the warm liquid, then moved aside to let the boy get in bed next to him. Rhun snuggled against him like a puppy. Maelgwn set the cup on the floor beside the bed and sighed. He wanted desperately to be alone, to face the terrible darkness that reached out for him. But he could not deny the boy. He would not fail him as he had Rhiannon. The thought made the pain return, harsh and aching, but dulled slightly by the wine and the feel of the warm, young body next to his.

Chapter 23

"You should rest, my dear. You'll tire your eyes working so long."

Rhiannon looked up from her weaving and shook her head. She would not quit, though her leg ached and her eyes burned from trying to see by the dim firelight. The piece of cloth she had finished was pitifully small. At this rate, it would take many weeks to complete a tunic for Ceinwen and a gown for Arianhrodd. Still, she was grateful for her task; it kept her mind from wandering to forbidden thoughts of her former life.

Arianhrodd moved beside her and examined the finished cloth. "It is very fine," she said. "You are exceptionally skilled." Her gaze turned to the gown Rhiannon had fashioned for herself from the rough blanket. "It's like magic, the things you can create with no more than your hands and a needle and thread."

"Not magic, but years of practice. I have been doing needlework since I was scarcely old enough to hold a spindle."

Rhiannon spoke without thinking, but as she felt Arianhrodd's eyes upon her, she realized how strange her words must seem to these simple fisherfolk. Her upbringing as a princess set her apart in a way that was bound to arouse questions.

Arianhrodd's thoughtful look lasted only a moment, then she turned back to the meal cakes she was preparing. Rhiannon breathed a sigh of relief, grateful for the older woman's patience. Rhiannon grew stronger day by day, but her hosts still apparently deemed her too fragile to be upset with questions.

Some time later, Rhiannon finally set down the spindle and rubbed her weary eyes. Arianhrodd came to her with one of the warm meal cakes. "Eat this, and then you must lie down. If you do not rest, you will not have enough strength to attend the ceremony tonight."

Rhiannon looked up in suprise. "The ceremony for the Goddess is tonight?"

"Aye, if you had been well enough to venture out after dark, you would know that the moon waxes full. The Goddess's power is at its peak, and we choose this time to call Her down to us. Do you still want to go? You haven't changed your mind, have you?"

Rhiannon shook her head. "Nay, I want to go. I am very curious about your Goddess." She gave Arianhrodd a sudden, warm smile. "You have been so kind to me. I think I must learn about the deity who inspires such generosity."

Arianhrodd's face grew grave. "The Goddess has put you under Her protection. We, as Her servants, have no choice but to care for Her chosen one."

Rhiannon felt a shiver travel down her spine. There was something unsettling about the way Arianhrodd spoke of the Goddess "choosing" her. Rhiannon did not want to be marked as special. So far in her life, she had found being different a difficult burden to bear.

Anxious thoughts continued to plague her after she lay

down, and only the exhaustion of her body finally allowed her to sleep. When she woke, she guessed it must be hours later. Ceinwen and Arianhrodd were sitting around the fire, talking quietly. They both turned when they heard her stirring.

"Are you rested, Rhiannon?" Arianhrodd asked. "Do you feel strong enough to make the journey into the woods?"

"Aye. I didn't delay you, did I?"

Arianhrodd's smile was cryptic. "Of course not. We would not think of going without you."

A little past twilight, they set out for the forest. The barely risen moon floated in and out among the clouds, casting a soft, vague light on the barren coast. Ceinwen and Arianhrodd walked a little ahead of Rhiannon, holding hands and talking in low, expectant voices. Their excited mood made Rhiannon uncomfortable, and as they approached the dark woodlands, a sense of foreboding crept over her. She could not help remembering the things Llewenon had told her about the ancient gods, about their terrible vengeful natures, their demand for blood. Suddenly, she was no longer certain she wanted to see the Ceremony of the Full Moon.

Rhiannon began to lag behind, and Arianhrodd paused and turned back to face her. "What is it? Does your leg trouble you?"

"Aye, a little," she answered. It only pulled slightly when she walked, but she considered that complaining of pain might serve as an excuse for her to return to the hut.

Arianhrodd slowed and put her arm around Rhiannon to help her along. Ceinwen joined her on the other side. Rhiannon felt trapped.

"You're trembling, child. Are you cold?"

Rhiannon shook her head and tried to control her terrifying thoughts. She was being foolish. These kindly people had saved her life and cared for her for weeks. They would not let harm come to her.

"It will seem warmer as we go deeper into the forest," Arianhrodd assured her.

The trees did help block the wind, but the greater shelter did little to quell Rhiannon's uneasiness. Patches of snow shone beneath the pine trees, and the soft sheen of ice coated the bare branches of the oak and alder. As the moonlight touched the icy surfaces and made them glitter among the shadows, Rhiannon's breathing quickened. It seemed she was back in the darkened grove with Llewenon, staring at the small curved knife gleaming in his hand.

"Rhiannon, what is it?" Arianhrodd and Ceinwen stopped and watched her with concern.

"I . . . I . . ." Rhiannon's throat felt dry, her limbs rigid. She tried to break the mood, to focus on Arianhrodd's warm, familiar presence.

"I have to ask you . . . does the Goddess . . . does She demand sacrifice?"

"Sacrifice?" Arianhrodd sounded doubtful. "We give the Goddess gifts of food and drink to show that we appreciate her bounty—is that what you mean?"

Rhiannon shook her head. "Blood sacrifice," she whispered.

"You think we shed blood during the ceremony? Of course not. All living things are the Goddess's children. She has no wish to see blood spilled for her sake."

A shaft of moonlight shone down through the trees, and Rhiannon could see Arianhrodd's face quite clearly. The expression on the older woman's face was one of puzzlement.

"I wasn't sure. I've heard stories . . ."

Arianhrodd put a reassuring hand on her arm. "There are people who practice such things, but they are not worshippers of the Goddess. It's true that one of Her faces is an old crone who brings death, but that is because death

is part of life. The trees, the grain, the deer in the forest,
the hawk in the air—they all must die. We must die, too,
but while we live, the Goddess offers us joy and contentment. She teaches us to celebrate life and find beauty in the
world around us." Arianhrodd reached out and hugged
Rhiannon tightly. "I promise you there will be nothing to
fear."

Rhiannon drew away, ashamed. "I should not have
thought such things of you."

Ceinwen spoke, his face grave and troubled. "It is wise
to be wary. You do not know us well, and who could blame
you for being afraid, especially when you have obviously
been ill-used ..." The man broke off at Arianhrodd's
disapproving look, and Rhiannon guessed that the two had
discussed confronting her past and decided against it. Her
regret increased. Arianhrodd and Ceinwen were the kind-
est of souls. What had made her so distrustful and suspicious? *Maelgwn*—a voice inside her answered.

Rhiannon stepped forward, as if she could leave the
tormenting thought behind. Arianhrodd and Ceinwen
were quickly beside her. Ceinwen touched her shoulder
as they walked. "In the beginning, I was afraid, too," he
said in a soft, confiding voice. "It is an awesome thing to
face the Goddess, to feel Her power."

"Tell me—what is it like?"

Through some trick of the shifting moonlight, Ceinwen's dark countenance seemed to brighten. "It is to be
calm and excited at the same time. To feel the energy flow
through your hair and toes and fingertips. To be a part
of everything else in the world and yet be more yourself
than you have ever known."

Rhiannon shivered again. She felt something touch her,
a soft, invisible hand soothing the stiff muscles of her neck
and spine. She walked more quickly. "Let us hurry. I didn't
mean to delay you."

They made their way deeper into the forest. The strange

feeling did not leave Rhiannon, and now she was grateful for Arianhrodd and Ceinwen beside her. The spirits walked this night, and she did not want to be alone. The sweaty, human smell of her companions reassured her.

At last, they reached a clearing. It was not what Rhiannon had expected, merely an open place in the trees, bathed in the silvery, beneficent glow of the moon. The spooky shadows were gone, and the place seemed familiar, welcoming.

A huge oak had once spread its branches far over the forest floor, but now all that remained of the great tree was a large stump in the center of the clearing. Arianhrodd took her bag of supplies to the stump and began to prepare it, in much the way Rhiannon had seen the priest prepare the altar in the chapel at Degannwy. She spread a cloth over the surface, then put down a dish of oat cakes and a skin of mead as offerings.

As Rhiannon watched Arianhrodd, she noticed movement in the shadows around them. Men and women were slowly moving into the clearing. They arrived almost soundlessly, with the quiet grace of people who spend much time in the woods. Rhiannon saw no one she knew, but she grew anxious. What if one of these people recognized her? What if one of them sent word to Maelgwn?

The people gathered and seemed to take little notice of Rhiannon. Gradually she relaxed. Two men stayed off to the side in the shadows, and Rhiannon soon heard the deep thump of a drum and the soft melody of a pipe from that direction. The rest of the people joined hands in a circle, and Ceinwen came to draw Rhiannon into the group. Arianhrodd remained in the center by the stump.

As the people moved around the clearing in a slow circle, Arianhrodd lifted up her arms and began to speak in a low, melodic voice:

"Into our circle, we welcome the Great Lady, the Creator and Protector of all life. The Giver of rain and wind and

sunshine. She who brings forth life from the bellies of
ewes and mares and does and women. She who makes the
flowers blossom and the grain grow ripe and golden. She
who fills our hearts with laughter and our eyes with tears
of sorrow. She who gives us life. Diana, Rhiannon, Cybele,
Isis—by all names we call you. Hear us and breathe your
warm breath upon us!''

Rhiannon heard the people around her whispering their
own invocations to the Goddess. The mingled sound of
their chanting voices filled the clearing with soft music.
The circle moved faster. Rhiannon felt herself being pulled
along, her feet barely touching the ground. The hair upon
the back of her neck stood on end. A warm wind blew
through the clearing, and Rhiannon yielded to it, floated
upon it.

She was in the water. Everything was white and blue and
silver streaked with the gold of the sun. She floated on the
waves, bobbing up and down in the massive arms of the
Mother Goddess—safe, protected. Her thoughts spun out
finer and finer, into gossamer threads dancing over the
waves. Then the waves pulled her under, and everything
was dark and frightening. Down, down, down, into the
darkness she fell, until only the fine fragile threads of her
thoughts seemed to be holding her back from the bottom
of the sea.

Part of her longed for the bottom, where Esylt waited.
She saw Esylt's black hair curling around her face like thick
vines, her white skin blurred and almost blue beneath the
water. Rhiannon swam to reach her, her chest aching for
breath, her arms weak and frail with fatigue. It was so hard,
it hurt so much.

She was almost there. She reached out to touch Esylt's
face. It was not her mother's face which her fingers grasped
but the cold, still flesh of an infant floating in the murky
water. She sucked in her breath with a gasp of horror and
jerked her hand away. The babe floated, lifeless, pale and

eerily beautiful in the blue water. Another scream convulsed in Rhiannon's throat, and this time she could not hold it back. She breathed the cold sea-water; her lungs filled. She struggled against it, against death.

When she came to herself she was lying on the cold ground. Arianhrodd was very near, although her voice seemed to come from far away.

"Rhiannon? Are you all right?"

Rhiannon nodded numbly. The terrible fear was leaving her, but she still felt light-headed and breathless. "I . . . I was afraid," she whispered.

"Of what, Rhiannon? What did you see?"

Rhiannon shook her head slowly. "I'm not sure. I was in the water. I saw my mother. And then . . ." She could not go on; she could not tell them about the babe.

"What did your mother say? Did she speak to you?"

"I don't know. I couldn't reach her."

"It's just as well," Arianhrodd said with a slight sigh. "I don't think you are strong enough yet to visit the spirit world."

"The spirit world?"

"Aye. Where did you think you had gone?"

Rhiannon said nothing. Much of her life she had longed to cross over to the other side, to see what it was like. In the past few weeks she had done it twice, and found nothing but death and cold fear.

Arianhrodd helped Rhiannon to stand, and the people gathered around her began to move away. Rhiannon could not stop shivering. Ceinwen took off his ratty old wolfskin and draped it around her. Even then, it took a long time for her to get warm.

The rest of the night was uneventful. The people built a fire and cooked some savory stew which they shared as they talked. To Rhiannon's surprise, the strangers around her seemed genuinely concerned for her—although no one asked prying questions or brought up her strange experience during the ceremony. She could not help contrasting Goddess worship with the religious ceremonies of the Brigantes. At the festivals in Manau Gotodin, there had always been an element of danger in the air—a mingling of suppressed violence and sexual tension. Perhaps it was because there, cruel Llewenon led the ceremonies, and here, Arianhrodd was the leader. Her spirit of warmth and benevolence pervaded everything.

When the moon was high and the air black with the chill of midnight, people began to leave, disappearing into the forest as quietly as they had come.

"Come, Rhiannon, it's too cold to stay here all night." Ceinwen helped Rhiannon up from her spot near the fire.

"Where is Arianhrodd?" Rhiannon asked, glancing around the deserted grove. She realized she had not seen the priestess for some time.

"She usually goes off by herself after the ceremony," Ceinwen answered. "Drawing down the power of the Goddess takes a great deal of energy and leaves her very tired."

"She will be all right?"

"Arianhrodd is a very powerful priestess. I would not worry about her. The Goddess protects Her own."

Rhiannon was not entirely convinced, nor did she really want to be alone with Ceinwen. For all his kindness, he was a man, and she could not forget the last time she had been alone in the forest at night with a man she trusted. She shifted awkwardly against the pressure of his arm beneath her ribs, and Ceinwen released her.

"What's wrong, Rhiannon?"

"I'm afraid."

"Of me?" Ceinwen gazed at her with wide eyes. "It was a man who cut your leg, wasn't it? You still fear him."

Rhiannon shook her head.

"Tell me who he is, and your hurt shall be avenged."

Rhiannon stared at Ceinwen's dark, angry face. She was

touched by his concern, but she dreaded the thought of him confronting Maelgwn.

"I cannot tell you. Anyway, I don't want to be avenged. I have no desire to see anyone else suffer."

Ceinwen gazed at her a moment longer, as if trying to read her thoughts. Then he took her arm again and they began to walk.

"I would never hurt a woman," said Ceinwen softly. "I'm sworn to serve the Goddess . . . and all women."

Rhiannon wondered again about this strange religion Ceinwen and Arianhrodd believed in. It was odd to think that women should be honored, treated as more exalted than men. The Brigantes were a warrior race, and prized males above females in all things. The Cymry were a bit better in their treatment of women, but it was clear they still considered them inferior. She had been given to Maelgwn like a mare left to run with the stallion, and he had taken her body as no more than his due.

A feeling of anger crept over Rhiannon. If she was sure Ceinwen would not be hurt, would she not perhaps wish to see Maelgwn suffer a little?

The thought of his name evoked a sharp pang in her belly, a reminder of her loss. She quickly pushed the memories away. She was not ready to face what Maelgwn had meant to her.

"It's cold," she murmured to Ceinwen. "Let us hurry."

Rhiannon soon grew too numb and tired to think. She leaned heavily on Ceinwen, willing herself to take the next step, and the next. She scarcely remembered reaching the hut or climbing into her bed-place.

It was near morn when she woke. The fire was kindled but Ceinwen was gone. That did not surprise Rhiannon, for she knew the fisherman always left for his boat before dawn. But Arianhrodd was not back yet either, which concerned her.

Rhiannon rose quickly and went to the fire. She sat down

at the hearth and warmed her fingers over the flames. A dull heaviness filled her this morn. She could not shake the memory of her vision during the ceremony. It kept returning to her, the beauty of the glittering waves, the cold darkness of the sea below, the sight of Esylt floating with the seaweed.

Rhiannon closed her eyes tightly, as if she could block out the memory. It was her child that waited in the cold depths, the babe she lost. It had been a girl, she had seen that. A daughter with a face like Maelgwn's.

A deep, keening wail came from Rhiannon's throat. She could suppress the grief no longer. She had lost everything—her future, Maelgwn's love, their child. The pain crashed over her, and she rocked blindly, trying to hold her body together, to keep the agony from tearing her asunder.

Her child! A daughter, a sweet daughter. If she had not killed it, the babe would be with her still, growing under her heart. Soon it would be born, and she could hold it in her arms. It would be hers, and she would love it. She would not be so alone, so terribly alone!

When Arianhrodd came into the hut a few hours later, Rhiannon's grief was spent. She had returned to her weaving, and was considering the next part of the pattern for Ceinwen's blue and red tunic. She was dry-eyed but shaky. She nodded to Arianhrodd as she entered and called good morning, but did not trust herself to speak.

Arianhrodd approached her silently. She smelled of pine and sunshine as she took Rhiannon in her arms and embraced her.

Chapter 24

"Maelgwn!"

Maelgwn swayed slightly. Had he dozed, even dreamed? In the dim atmosphere of the chapel, he could not guess the time. Had he been kneeling for minutes? Hours? Days?

"Maelgwn!"

The call came again, more urgent this time. He stumbled to his feet. Searing pain shot down his calves. Damn the Christians for choosing this miserably uncomfortable position for praying. For a soldier, whose legs were invariably scarred with old wounds and the joints stiff from years of riding, kneeling was pure torture.

"Sweet Jesu, Maelgwn, I've been looking everywhere for you!" Balyn was beside him, shaking him. "It's the Irish. They've landed at a fishing village below Llandudno. It's a raid, Maelgwn."

A raid—how long had it been since he heard the word spoken in fear and dread? Two years or more. But the word had not lost its power to quicken his heartbeat. "Have you sounded the alert?"

"Aye."

"And our horses—we are ready to ride?"

"The men wait only for you."

In what seemed like seconds, he was armed and ready. He mounted Cynraith and joined his men at the gate. As they cantered down the coast road, Maelgwn felt the battle fever rush through him. How wonderful it was to be riding to face a real enemy, to know the wind in his face, to see the glint of polished armor and weapons all around him. Too long, he had been weighed down with sorrow and worry; it was time he took up his sword and acted like a warrior again.

The little fishing village was not far, but they rode like madmen to reach it, afraid they would be too late. A pall of smoke from the burning huts marked the place, but all seemed deserted. The village had been no more than a gathering of rude dwellings, poorly defended and simply poor. There was no wealth or supplies to steal here, few women or children to carry off as slaves. These raiders came for wanton destruction, nothing more.

Anger made Maelgwn spur his horse faster, and the others quickened their pace to match. As they drew abreast of the smoking village, they saw the raiders making for their little leather boats, called coracles. The Irish were burdened with what little booty they had claimed, but their number gave Maelgwn pause. His force was relatively small, and although their weapons and armor were superior, the Cymry would clearly be outnumbered. He calculated quickly, decided they had sufficient men to attack, then led the charge.

They hit the shoreline at a dead run, using the speed of their horses to cut down as many of the enemy as they could in one swift assault. But after the first shouts of fear and surprise, the Irish began to rally. The rocky, uneven beach made a poor battleground for mounted men, and the Cymry horsemen were quickly surrounded—three Irishmen to one defender on average. Maelgwn felt a twinge of unease. His men held their own, but only barely. If they couldn't scare the Irish off quickly, they might be forced to retreat.

The battlefield was grimly quiet, and sweat dripped down Maelgwn's face despite the cool breeze. His arm ached from lashing out with his sword. The attacking Irishmen seemed endless, their faces melding into a blur. The enemy's plan appeared to be to disable the horses so the Cymry would have to fight on foot. Four men rushed him at once. Maelgwn swerved, trying to guide his horse from their deadly swords. Cynraith was not so cautious. The stallion's eyes went wild, and he lashed out at the Irishmen with his huge hooves. Two of them ran, but the others pressed on, wielding their weapons dangerously close to the stallion's underbelly. Cynraith manuevered smoothly, gracefully, playing the deadly game with relish. Maelgwn held his breath. If only he could get close enough to use his sword.

One man miscalculated—a second slow, and his body was shattered by a powerful hoof. But the death blow cost Maelgwn as well. The impact made Cynraith stumble, and his rider, leaning to the side and pulled off-balance by the weight of his sword, found himself thrown from the saddle. Maelgwn landed awkwardly, one leg twisted beneath him. A scorching pain burned through his ankle. He ignored it and lurched to his feet in time to face his first challenger. The man was grinning, and he shouted some sneering curse in Gaelic.

The enemy's moment of gloating cost him dearly. Maelgwn had time to draw back his immense sword and swing it across the man's chest. The force of it knocked the Irishman off balance, and as he struggled to right himself, Maelgwn was upon him. He crumpled the Irishman to the ground with another blow to his legs, then loomed over him, his sword pointed at the man's unprotected throat.

Then a strange thing happened. As the warrior lifted his head to defend himself, his leather helmet tumbled off, revealing long, vivid red hair. A mist seemed to pass before Maelgwn's eyes. When he could see again, it was Rhiannon's face that looked up from beneath his sword. He froze, unable to take his eyes from the sight of his dead wife, staring at him with a look of utter dread. His grip loosened upon his sword. His knees buckled beneath him. A trickle of blood had begun at his victim's neck, where the sword had pricked it. Maelgwn gaped at the crimson stream blurring into the long red hair.

Abruptly, the face changed back to that of a young Irish warrior. The man's blue eyes bulged and then turned glassy.

"Maelgwn! For God's sake!"

He turned to see Balyn. The big man had a cut on his forehead, and the blood dribbled down his temple, mingling with the dirt and sweat. He looked angry.

"Maelgwn, what's wrong with you? You very nearly got yourself killed!"

Maelgwn stood up, struggling to keep his legs steady. He looked down at his opponent. The man was dead. Blood trickled from his slack mouth, and his body trembled with a ghastly quiver as life left it. Balyn's sword jutted out of the man's side at an evil angle.

"He had a knife," Balyn said in a strained, gasping voice. "If I had not come along when I did, he would have stabbed you for certes!"

Maelgwn nodded dumbly. The dead man's fingers still twitched near the fallen dagger. Thinking of what would have happened if Balyn had not come to his aid, Maelgwn shuddered. For a moment, he had been absolutely helpless.

"Blessed *Christos*, you gave me a scare!" Balyn's voice cracked. "What's wrong? Are you hurt?"

"Cynraith threw me, and my ankle turned. But it was more than that . . . for a moment . . . I couldn't see clearly."

"Let's get you out of here." Balyn grasped Maelgwn's shoulder and led him away from the battlefield.

The fighting was nearly over, and Maelgwn watched the last skirmishes from a grassy knoll. The Irish finally made for their boats. Only a few unfortunate men remained, surrounded by the angry Cymry. In moments the stragglers gave up and allowed themselves to be captured. They would be taken back to the fortress and made to serve as slaves. In a few years, if they lived, they might yet buy their freedom and return to their native land.

Maelgwn felt dizzy and weak, and the image of Rhiannon's terrified face flickered in his mind. It had been so real. His hands still shook at the thought of his sword slicing through the smooth white skin of her neck. And yet, it had not been Rhiannon at all—merely a wild-eyed Irishman whose tresses were a similar shade.

Maelgwn tested his ankle, trying to see how badly it was injured. Despite some swelling, he could walk. He began to search for Cynraith. The stallion had left the battlefield soon after losing his rider. Maelgwn found him grazing contentedly on the dried brown reeds and grasses along the shoreline.

"I'm glad they didn't hurt you," he whispered as he stroked the stallion's velvety nose. Cynraith tossed his head and stared back at Maelgwn with his dark, rust-colored eyes.

Maelgwn mounted, wincing with pain as he threw his injured leg over the horse's back, then rode back to the beach. It had not been a particularly bloody engagement, but the stench of death seemed to be everywhere, turning his stomach. He ignored the queasiness and forced himself to shout orders at his men. He knew they would do what was necessary without being told, but acting the role of commander helped him maintain control over his precarious emotions.

The Cymry returned the fallen Irishmen to the sea and gathered up the wounded. A few men remained behind to guard the captives. Maelgwn and the main part of the force rode home through the bone-numbing chill of winter twilight.

When they reached Degannwy, Maelgwn mumbled a few words to his officers and slipped away. He washed, stopped in the kitchen for a few bites of mutton stew, then sought the solace of his council room. He had barely lit the brazier and pulled up a stool when he heard the door open. He stiffened and put down the skin of mead. He dreaded company; even Rhun would be unwelcome tonight.

The shadow on the wall loomed gigantic, and Maelgwn guessed his visitor was Balyn. He took a swallow of mead, then another, before he turned to greet his friend.

"Balyn, come join me." His voice was forced. He could not pretend to welcome this intrusion, but neither could he send Balyn away. The man had saved his life. Again.

Balyn did not speak but dragged another stool over to the brazier and sat down with a huge sigh. A quick glance roused Maelgwn's guilt. Balyn looked awful. The wound on his temple was livid against his ashen skin, and his eyes were bloodshot from the cold.

"What a day!" Balyn sighed again.

"Aye," Maelgwn answered grimly. "What a day indeed."

"What happened, Maelgwn? Why did you let that damned Irishman nearly send you back to your maker?"

Maelgwn flinched. "Something made Cynraith stumble and throw me."

"I don't mean that, Maelgwn, and you well know it! I mean afterwards, when you stood there stunned—like a callow boy freezing up in his first battle. It was as if you were afraid to kill the murderous heathen!"

Balyn's insulting remark penetrated Maelgwn's dazed

state. He got to his feet, nearly upsetting the stool. "It was not the Irishman that frightened me, but what I saw in his face."

"What did you see?"

Maelgwn gripped the skin of mead more tightly. "I saw Rhiannon."

"What?"

"As I was about to cut the Irishman's throat . . . he . . . somehow he changed. I saw Rhiannon looking up at me, her eyes full of dread."

Balyn sucked in his breath and crossed himself. "Jesu, help you. You've seen a wraith, a demon!"

Maelgwn shook his head. "It was not a malevolent spirit. If anything, it appeared frightened of me."

Balyn clutched at Maelgwn's sleeve. "The spirit, this thing, it very nearly caused your death. You must go to the priest and ask for a prayer of protection, some charm to use against it."

"You forget yourself, Balyn. Christians don't believe in charms or spells."

"Mayhaps some holy water then, or a relic. There must be something that will ward off this demon!"

Maelgwn gave Balyn a hard look, then paced to the other side of the council room. He came back to face his friend. "I don't expect you to understand. I can't get the thought of Rhiannon out of my mind. It's as if she were trying to speak to me, to tell me something."

Balyn's mouth dropped open. "You're hoping it comes again, aren't you?"

Maelgwn froze. "You think it's possible—that I could seek her out?"

Balyn muttered a smothered curse, then grabbed Maelgwn by the arm. "Nay! It's mad! Sinful! To seek speech with the dead—it's, it's . . . you would be risking your soul!"

"My soul!" Maelgwn's face twisted bitterly. "I tell you,

Balyn, if I thought it would bring me peace, I would willingly seek out the archdemon himself. It would be worth any price to banish this terrible guilt, this gnawing sense of loss!''

Balyn released Maelgwn's arm and took a step back, his eyes wide and fearful. ''I must get Father Leichan. He'll know what to say. He'll know how to dissuade you from this blasphemy.''

Maelgwn sat down wearily after Balyn left. His friend's wild words gave him an idea. Perhaps he could seek out Rhiannon's spirit. He would go back to the oak tree, where his sense of her was strongest. If he sought the vision hard enough, surely it would come again.

Maelgwn went back to his mead and mused over the plan, and Balyn soon reappeared with the young cleric. The priest's plain brown cowl was pulled up around his face, and his round black eyes met Maelgwn's uncertainly. Maelgwn felt a stir of pity for the priest. Father Leichan was pious and sincere, and intelligent enough to understand most subtleties of faith. But Maelgwn did not expect him to be comfortable with what they were about to discuss.

''My lord, Balyn says you have need of religious counsel.''

Maelgwn smiled faintly at Balyn's quaint choice of words. He cast a glance in the stout man's direction, and Balyn gave him a look of near-dread. How typical Balyn was of a good soldier, Maelgwn thought. Loyal, disciplined and utterly fearless on the battlefield, but with a superstitious fear of the unknown which made him cling as staunchly to the new faith as he had once clung to the ways of the old gods. Balyn seemed unable to consider that there might be things that Christianity failed to explain.

''Tell me, Father, do you believe in ghosts?''

The priest looked startled. ''Of course not. The Scriptures teach that when men's souls depart their bodies, they either ascend to heaven to be with our Lord or are taken below to suffer eternal damnation.''

"There is no way, then, for a person's soul to linger in the earthly realm after death?"

Father Leichan shook his head resolutely. "Certainly not. That is an ignorant belief of the common people. Surely a well-educated Christian such as yourself should not be troubled by such superstitious fancies."

Maelgwn frowned at the young priest's rather credulous compliment. "Nevertheless, Father, I believe I have seen such a thing. A spirit—the spirit of my dead wife."

Father Leichan's brow furrowed. "Perhaps you were dreaming, my lord."

"Nay. I was wide awake. It was in the middle of a battle. I saw Rhiannon, Father, I saw her quite clearly."

The priest was silent. Maelgwn wondered what Father Leichan would say. He could not mimic Balyn and counsel the dangers of associating with spirits. He had just said they did not exist.

"Do you blame yourself for your wife's death?"

The priest's question surprised him. Maelgwn felt the guilt tightening like a noose around his neck. He answered in a low, shaky voice. "Whom else can I blame? I wounded her in my rage, then sent her away. It is my fault she was washed to sea."

Father Leichan nodded. "Your guilt still haunts you. You must ask God to forgive you and deliver you from these troubling visions." His soft voice grew softer, and he laid a consoling hand on Maelgwn's arm. "The Christ can forgive even murder if you are sincere, and you obviously did not intend for your wife to die."

"You don't believe me." Maelgwn's voice was cold. "You think I am half-mad with grief."

The priest did not answer; he moved his hand away.

"I saw her, Father. I can't help but think she seeks to communicate with me."

Father Lleichan licked his lips. "Such a thing—it would be a miracle. There are those who claim to see angels or even our Christ's mother, Mary. But for someone such as Rhiannon to appear among the living . . . it seems unlikely. She was not even a Christian."

"Aye, I had forgotten," Maelgwn said bitterly. "Rhiannon was not a Christian, therefore, she is doomed to burn in the fires of hell. I don't believe it. Rhiannon was kind and good—no just god would curse her so cruelly!"

He glared at the priest a moment, then waved him away. "Go. Leave me be."

The priest left quickly. Maelgwn gave Balyn a threatening look. He, too, quit the room.

Maelgwn took his place by the fire again. The warmth eased his aching leg; the mead numbed his emotions. But his mind still spun. He recreated the vision of Rhiannon, savoring it. If she had come to him once, why not again? Tomorrow he would go out and search for her. Perhaps on the beach or in the forest by the oak tree, she would show herself. It would be only her spirit, but it was better than nothing. If he thought hard enough, believed strongly enough, surely he could will some part of Rhiannon into existence again.

He closed his eyes, resting them from the flickering firelight. A strange peace enveloped him. Rhiannon and he, they had both believed in the other side, the realm of the spirits. If he was willing to journey there, he would find her. Perhaps, somehow, he could even bring her back.

The two women bent over the pile of dried herbs, comparing their lore. "You know a great deal," Rhiannon said. "More even than Llewenon. Of course . . ." She frowned slightly at the memory. "When he was my teacher, I was too obsessed with learning magic to devote my energies to the healing arts."

She looked up. Arianhrodd met her eyes warmly, and Rhiannon felt no uneasiness. She had finally confessed a little of her past—that she had trained with a healer in the North. She said nothing about Llewenon's attack nor how she had come to Gwynedd, and Arianhrodd had not pressed her for more information. The risk had been worth it, Rhiannon decided, for now Arianhrodd was eager to teach her about the medicinal plants that filled her baskets. They had spent quite a bit of time comparing information about preparation and storage as well as uses.

It was exciting to learn from someone like Arianhrodd; unlike Llewenon, she took a sincere interest in using her skill to help others and had greatly increased her knowledge through practical experience. Now that Rhiannon's leg had healed and she could walk easily, she accompanied Arianhrodd when she visited the nearby villagers and offered them her healing skills. So far, they had attended a woman giving birth, set a boy's broken arm and opened a putrefied wound on a fisherman's foot. To Rhiannon's surprise, the local people accepted her presence easily. If they found anything odd about her unusual coloring and smooth, unblemished hands, they kept it to themselves.

"This is plantain—excellent for healing burns," Arianhrodd was saying. "I mean to put in a good store of it. The news is that the Irish are raiding again. Ceinwen told me that a village down the coast from here was attacked and burned yesterday. Most of the people escaped to the woods, although they lost their homes and nearly all of their possessions."

Rhiannon's eyes widened. In the North, raids by the Picts were a constant danger. She had not realized that the Cymry faced a similar threat from their neighbors across the sea.

Arianhrodd nodded knowingly. "The Irish have harassed the coasts of Gwynedd for time out of mind. It is only the strength and fierceness of our warriors which keeps them from establishing permanent settlements. Ceinwen told me the king himself led the attack against the raiders yesterday.''

Rhiannon went still as a tumult of emotions fought inside her. The mention of Maelgwn aroused fear, curiosity and a deep, unwelcome longing. "Did the defenders prevail?" she asked woodenly.

"Aye. They killed ten Irish, captured several others and forced the rest to flee."

Rhiannon let out her pent-up breath. She was not sure which frightened her more—the thought that Maelgwn had been in a battle or the realization that he had been so close to her refuge with Arianhrodd and Ceinwen. She had been wrong to think she could stay with them beyond the time it took for her to heal and repay them with new clothes. Ceinwen's and Arianhrodd's hut was only a short distance from Degannwy, and the king's attention had already been drawn this way by the raid. It was only a matter of time before he heard of a small, red-haired woman newly come to the area.

Arianhrodd's dark eyes watched her, intent but not threatening. She leaned over to replace the plantain in a leather pouch, then returned it to the storage basket. "Enough of this," Arianhrodd said briskly. "Why don't we take a walk in the woods and see if the coltsfoot has come up yet? It also makes a fine salve for easing burns, and my supply from last year is sadly depleted."

They replaced the rest of the herbs in the storage baskets, then went out. It was a mild day, overcast, with a slight mist in the air and a gentle wind. Rhiannon was silent as they walked toward the woods. Her thoughts and feelings were wrenched in so many competing directions she felt unsettled and confused. The woods called to her, reminding her of the wild forests of Manau Gotodin and her plan to return there as soon as her leg healed and the weather grew warm enough for traveling. But Arianhrodd's comforting presence beside her made Rhiannon realize how safe and protected she had come to feel in the little hut on the coast. The plump, dark woman was like the mother she had never had. For all that Esylt had loved her and cared for her, there had been no true bond of understanding between them. With Arianhrodd, Rhiannon felt a connectedness and sense of peace she had never known with anyone else.

And then there was Maelgwn. She had tried to forget him, to remove the memory of him from her thoughts, or bury it beneath her fear and anger over what he had done to her. But she had been even less successful in forgetting him than she had once been in escaping thoughts of Llewenon. Perhaps it was because Maelgwn was king, and his name was on the lips of even the simple folk. Maelgwn was Gwynedd, and Gwynedd was he. As long as she lived in this place, she would be haunted by her husband's shadow over her life. He would never leave her in peace.

Rhiannon wrapped her arms around herself, as if cold. Arianhrodd saw and quietly offered Rhiannon the fur wrap she was wearing. Rhiannon shook her head; there was no garment that could ease the chill she felt. It came from inside her, from her heart.

Chapter 25

Maelgwn shifted impatiently as he waited for the next petitioner. Tonight was Candlemas, or Imbolc, as the herdsmen referred to it. Tradition required the local ruler to grant favors and hear disputes before the festival. Although it was an ancient and reasonable custom, this particular day, Maelgwn begrudged his part. Every minute spent in the smoky hall delayed his plan to seek out Rhiannon's spirit.

He pressed his hands to his temples, trying to soothe away the tension. It was nearly impossible to recall the numbing mass of traditions governing Cymry society. Without his bards, Taliesin and Aneurin, beside him, he would have been lost. There was a law for everything—even the payment that must be made for the killing of a man's barn cat.

Maelgwn's ill-temper eased slightly at the memory of the incident. Early in the day, an indignant farmer had come before him, demanding compensation for the loss of his best mouser. Taliesin had listened gravely and pronounced the verdict: the dead cat was to be picked up by the tip of its tail so that its nose touched the ground and grain poured over it until the cat's whole body was covered. That amount must be paid to the farmer by the man who had killed the cat.

Maelgwn's smile faded, chased away by fatigue and boredom. He glanced at Aneurin and Taliesin—they looked as restless as he. "Go," he said. "I'm sure I can deal with anything left."

They nodded gratefully and lost no time in quitting the hall. For a few minutes Maelgwn was alone; only the sound of the crackling fire broke the silence. He stood and stretched, relieved to think the stream of petitioners had come to an end. A lone man entered the wide doorway and walked toward him. Maelgwn's irritation returned. What did this one want of him?

The man was small and dark and dressed in poorly tanned leathers and a ratty wolfskin. A bow protruded over his shoulder, suggesting he was one of the rugged men who eked out a sparse living hunting and trapping in the woods. Maelgwn watched him with vague interest. The native huntsmen were superb archers. He often thought that if he could recruit them to his army, his need for warriors would be greatly reduced.

The man knelt before him. Maelgwn gestured curtly for him to rise. "Speak. What matter do you bring before me?"

The man licked his lips, and Maelgwn caught a glimpse of brown, broken teeth. "I come to you with news of your wife."

Maelgwn jerked back in astonishment. "My wife?"

The man nodded. "I know that the queen is said to be dead—drowned many weeks ago—but I have seen her alive."

Maelgwn gaped at the man, then cleared his throat, trying to keep his voice calm. "What do you mean?"

"I saw your wife in the forest, at a ceremony honoring

the Goddess, the Great Mother. She was one of the worshippers. She had long red hair, unbound, and she was very beautiful. I have seen her before, once when you were with her in the woods."

The memory of making love to Rhiannon beneath the great oak tree rose unbidden to Maelgwn's mind, filling him with longing—and then anger.

"You spied on us?"

"I didn't mean to bother you, my lord," the man said hastily. "I left as soon as I saw who it was. But I had a good glimpse of the woman. She was lying next to you, her head resting on your chest. It was the same woman I saw at the ceremony." His gaze met Maelgwn's, imploring, fearful. "I swear, my lord, I swear upon the lives of my wife and child. It had to be your queen. There is no other woman like that among the Cymry."

Maelgwn's mind raced. Rhiannon could not be alive; there had to be some other explanation. Perhaps there was a village girl who resembled her. Or maybe the man had simply made up the story and come seeking a reward.

Maelgwn fixed his eyes coldly on the huntsman. "What did you expect to gain with this story?"

"I . . . I'd heard you were grieved over your wife's death," the man quavered. "I thought news that she is alive would gladden your heart."

"Aye, and perhaps feed your family this spring as well." Maelgwn's eyes narrowed. "I'm not a lovesick fool, despite what some might think. It would bring me great joy to find my wife alive and unhurt, but if you are lying to me . . ."

The man gave a gasp of fear. "I swear, my lord. The woman was your queen. During the ceremony, the woman fainted, and we all gathered round to see if she was well. I saw her clearly. Her hair was as red as blood, her skin pale as the flowers of a wood anemone."

Despite his attempt at self-control, Maelgwn's hands began to tremble. The vision the man described was much like what he had experienced during the battle with the Irish. Could this be another sign that Rhiannon's spirit lingered in the world of the living?

"This woman . . . did she speak?"

"Only a little. After she fainted, the priestess asked her what she had seen, and the woman . . . the queen . . . she said something about her mother, that she had seen her mother."

Maelgwn clutched the thick oak table in front of him. "Her mother," he whispered faintly.

"Perhaps she said more later," the man added anxiously. "But that is all I recall."

In the quiet room, Maelgwn could hear the crackle of the fire, the soft sound of voices outside in the courtyard. He felt as if he were in a dream, a trance. Shaking off the mood, he forced himself to speak. "Was it a spirit, do you think? A wraith?"

The huntsman's eyes widened, and he made the ancient sign against evil. "Nay, 'twas not a spirit! I not only saw the woman, I held her hand. During the ceremony, we all joined hands and danced in a circle. I remember clearly how small her fingers were, how smooth and uncallused. Afterwards, she sat and ate with us. I've never heard of a spirit eating, my lord, nor fainting either!"

"Who else saw her? Who else could confirm what you've told me?"

The huntsman shifted on his short legs and fidgeted. "There were others there . . . I dare not say. The priestess, Arianhrodd, perhaps she would be willing to speak to you."

Maelgwn felt his composure returning, along with his suspicions. "Tell me about your priestess."

"She leads our ceremonies. She uses her powers to help us. She is a healer."

An obscure sect of Goddess-worshippers led by a priestess with magical powers—what could be a more likely setting for the reappearance of a dead queen? Maelgwn thought cynically.

"What powers does your priestess claim?"

The man shrugged. "She is skilled with herbs and potions and has the old knowledge of the stars and the way they move in the sky. She can go into a trance and visit the spirit world. Sometimes she speaks to the spirits on our behalf. Arianhrodd is not a witch," the man added, noting the cold look on Maelgwn's face. "She uses her knowledge only for good, and she is willing to share what she knows with anyone who wishes to learn. She teaches us that our own powers are as great as hers—if we are willing to learn to use them."

Maelgwn frowned. He had expected more extravagant claims for this so-called priestess, that she could curse a man to death, or bring the dead back to life. The woman the huntsman described sounded very ordinary, a surprisingly modest individual to act as a representative of the Great Mother Goddess.

"Where can I find this Arianhrodd?"

"She lives west of here, along the coast. The man who shares her hut, Ceinwen, is a fisherman."

"Can you take me there?"

The huntsman shifted uncomfortably. "I could tell you how to find her."

Maelgwn nodded. It was to be expected that the man would be afraid of the priestess. No matter how benignly the man portrayed her, she obviously had some hold over the minds of the forest folk. But did she have any real power? Was it possible she could help him communicate with Rhiannon's spirit? The idea excited Maelgwn, but frightened him as well. If he spoke to Rhiannon's spirit, what would he say? How could he atone for the terrible thing he had done?

A small noise made Maelgwn look up. He had completely forgotten the waiting huntsman. He gestured abruptly.

"Go to the kitchen and tell the Irish cook, Bridget, to give you a loaf and a jar of oil. Until I know more, that is all the reward I offer you."

The man's face split with a ruined grin. Maelgwn felt a vague stir of pity to think that such a pittance should please him.

After the man left, Maelgwn continued to sit in the empty hall. He knew he should get up, but still he sat, his body growing stiff and tired. He was afraid, afraid to find out the truth—whatever it was.

Arianhrodd knew she was about to meet the king of Gwynedd as soon as she saw the man on horseback. He rode a formidable-looking stallion, and his deep red and blue cloak and long dark hair flew behind him as he galloped down the coast. Arianhrodd glanced at the nearby hut. There was no time to warn Rhiannon. She could only hope the young woman would hear the approach of a rider and know enough to stay hidden.

The man drew his horse to a halt and asked her name. When she answered him, he dismounted gracefully and stood staring down at her. He seemed impossibly tall; Arianhrodd had never seen a man built in such spectacular fashion. Strength and danger emanated from his long, powerful limbs and immense shoulders. His face was handsome and arrogant, his beautiful blue eyes at once brooding and threatening. Arianhrodd stiffened and met his gaze resolutely. She would not be cowed by a mere man; she knew the power of the Great Goddess who ruled all men, even kings.

"I am Maelgwn, Prince of Gwynedd. My wife, Rhiannon, disappeared some weeks ago, presumably drowned. I have since heard a story that she was seen in the forest. It is said you were present the night she appeared."

He was direct, she would give him that. Someone must

have seen Rhiannon at the ceremony and gone to the king. Arianhrodd had not thought any of the forest folk would be so brave as to approach the king, but if there were a reward offered, some might take the risk.

"Well, what say you?" Maelgwn asked impatiently.

Arianhrodd cleared her throat and met his eyes challengingly. "It is said your wife drowned after you wounded her and turned her out of your fortress."

The king's blue eyes filled with rage. "How dare you?" he muttered. He took a step toward her.

Arianhrodd stood her ground. As dangerous as it might be to anger this man, her goading words had their purpose. She wanted to know if he had as little control over his temper as it appeared. If so, she would not consider having Rhiannon return to him.

She met his fierce gaze levelly. "Isn't it true you stabbed your wife, then ordered her away?"

Maelgwn's expression wavered. The anger vanished, to be replaced by a look of pain. "Aye, it is true. But it was not my intention that Rhiannon should die."

The anguish in his face surprised Arianhrodd. Perhaps the king genuinely grieved the loss of his wife. Still, she could not think of trusting him yet. Maelgwn's pain might be feigned. Indeed, he recovered quickly. The kingly mask slipped back into place, and when next he spoke, his voice was commanding.

"You have not answered my question. Was there a woman attending the ceremony who might be mistaken for my wife—a small, fine-featured woman with long red hair?"

Arianhrodd pretended to consider the king's question. "Do you believe your wife is alive?" she asked.

Maelgwn shook his head grimly. "In truth, I can't see how she could have survived."

"Then why come to me? The man was obviously mistaken."

"I don't think it was a living woman the man saw, but a spirit."

"Your dead wife's spirit?"

Maelgwn nodded. His gaze was unflinching. Arianhrodd regarded him with bemusement. She had not taken this proud, powerful king for a man who believed in spirits. Did he really imagine his dead wife's wraith walked the earth?

"Sometimes the Goddess takes the form of a beautiful young woman. If the man you spoke to was familiar with your queen, perhaps the Goddess appeared to him in the guise of your wife. I have heard she was a beautiful woman—lovely enough to be mistaken for a goddess."

Maelgwn looked away and sighed, a long aching sigh. "Aye, my Rhiannon was very fair." His gaze returned to Arianhrodd, and she saw his features tense with grief. "I come to you not because I think Rhiannon lives, but because it is known that troubled souls often linger among the living, seeking to set aright the things unfinished at their death. As foolish as it seems, I seek to communicate with Rhiannon, to settle things with her so she can be at peace." A faint, grim smile touched his lips. "There are those who say that Rhiannon's death has driven me to madness. Now you know of what they speak."

Arianhrodd could only stare at Maelgwn. While she had suspected Rhiannon's husband would eventually come in search of her, she had not anticipated this. The king was a worldly man, a warrior, a wielder of death and the essence of masculine power. He was also said to be a pious Christian. For him to express the wish to communicate with his dead wife's spirit was astonishing. Arianhrodd abruptly revised her opinion of the man who stood before her. Perhaps it was not a question of protecting Rhiannon from her husband, but finding a way to reconcile them.

Abruptly, Arianhrodd turned and began to walk down the beach. She gestured for Maelgwn to follow her, and he hesitated only a moment, then came after her, his long stride easily matching two of her steps.

"It is not easy to have speech with spirits," she said as he drew beside her. "To seek them out is to risk your hold on your own realm, the existence known as life. It is a dangerous thing for one unskilled. Of those who journey to the other side, many do not return."

She cocked her head sideways, awaiting Maelgwn's response. Something flared behind his eyes, some lingering resentment, perhaps that he must ask a mere woman for help. Then it was gone, and his expression grew thoughtful. "You say it is difficult, even dangerous. But is it possible? Can someone like me, untrained, unskilled as you call it—can I hope to succeed in my quest?"

"Of course it is possible. But you must vow to submit your will utterly to the Goddess." Arianhrodd paused, and her eyes searched Maelgwn's ruthlessly. "Her power is great, but She does not always show you what you wish. When Rhiannon speaks to you, you may not like what She says."

"So be it," Maelgwn answered stiffly.

Arianhrodd nodded. So be it, indeed. Soon they would know what lengths this man would go to in his effort to see Rhiannon.

"I will help you, if you agree to do exactly as I tell you. Tonight, I will send you a message explaining where and when the meeting will take place. You must follow my instructions without hesitation."

Maelgwn's face looked as solemn as a stone statue's. Arianhrodd added, "I must warn you. If you wish to converse with your wife's spirit, you must put your trust in the Goddess. Your life will be in Her hands."

Again, there was hesitation, the hint of resentment in Maelgwn's eyes. Arianhrodd waited, holding his gaze firmly with her own. Gradually the look of doubt faded and he nodded.

Arianhrodd turned away and continued to walk down
the beach alone. Her steps were slow and measured even
though her heart raced with excitement. Dealing with
Maelgwn had been remarkably easy; now there was only
Rhiannon to convince. Which would win out?—Arianhrodd wondered. Rhiannon's love for her husband or her
fear of him?

When Arianhrodd returned to the hut, she thought at
first that Rhiannon had heard her husband's voice and
fled. Then there was a small, scuffling sound in the corner
by the baskets, and Rhiannon stood up from her hiding
place among the herbs and medicines. Her freckles showed
dark in her ashen skin, and her eyes were wide with alarm.

"You know who I am," she whispered.

"What did you think, child? Your looks are uncommon,
and Ceinwen goes out every day and talks to the other
fishermen. As soon as he came back with the story of
Maelgwn's queen fleeing his fortress and being drowned,
we knew who you were." Arianhrodd went to the fire,
thinking to alleviate Rhiannon's distress by preparing her
a soothing draught.

"Why didn't you say anything?"

"We had no desire to upset you by reminding you of
events you wished to forget. I assumed, in time, the king
would come looking for you, and we would deal with it
then. That day is here."

"He's come to ask for me back! To have me put to
death!"

Arianhrodd looked up from the water she was heating.
"That would be very odd, considering he already believes
you dead."

Rhiannon sucked in her breath. "He truly believes
that?"

"So he said."

"But if Maelgwn thinks I'm dead, why has he come?"

"He came here to ask me to help him communicate with your spirit."

Rhiannon looked aghast. She stumbled over to the fire and sat down, her breathing quick and shallow. "What does he want with my spirit? Hasn't he cursed me heartily enough in this world? Is there no end of his hatred for me?"

Arianhrodd reached out and patted Rhiannon's shoulder. "He does not hate you, child. He regrets what he did to you; he seeks your spirit in order to make amends."

Rhiannon flinched. "Who is to say when the madness will come upon him again? It takes only the mention of Esylt to kindle his hatred into a blazing rage!"

"I have agreed to help him."

Rhiannon turned to Arianhrodd, panic-stricken. "You mean to send me back to him! To my death!"

"Nay, nay." Arianhrodd grasped Rhiannon's hand gently. "I will take every precaution to see that you are safe. Besides, it is not *you* I mean to send him, but your spirit."

Rhiannon gazed at her in puzzlement. Arianhrodd squeezed her hand and went on. "I mean to give the king a drug that causes visions. It will confuse him, blur his senses so he is not sure what he sees. Then, and only then, will I send you to him."

"But what if the drug also stirs his hatred? Even if he thinks I'm a spirit, he might still wish to destroy me."

Arianhrodd shook her head. "The substance arouses visions, but it also calms the spirit and soothes the mind. He will do you no violence under its spell."

Rhiannon considered this information with a wary expression. "I have heard of such potions. Still, I'm afraid."

"I wouldn't risk this if I thought Maelgwn meant you harm. I believe he regrets losing you; I think his love for you is very great, greater even than his anger."

"You cannot know," Rhiannon said mournfully. "You cannot guess why he despises me." Arianhrodd waited expectantly as Rhiannon spoke in a soft, halting voice. "Not only am I Maelgwn's wife, I'm also his niece. Esylt, the sister he hates, whom he blames for every misfortune of his life, was my mother."

"And for this he stabbed you and drove you out to the pitiless sea?"

Rhiannon nodded.

Arianhrodd was silent for a time. Rhiannon's relationship to her husband was convoluted, but that most likely only made the bond between them stronger. If Maelgwn transferred to Rhiannon the sins of her mother, perhaps he also transferred the love which begat his hatred.

She met Rhiannon's eyes reassuringly. "The man I spoke with on the beach was a tortured soul, one near sick with grief. I believes he loves you. That he sincerely wants you back."

Rhiannon shook her head. Arianhrodd continued, "I warn you, Rhiannon, before you decide whether you will take part in my plan, you must consider very carefully the power you hold over your husband. You have the means to heal him or toss him back into the pit of black despair. Which do you wish? Mercy for Maelgwn, or destruction?"

Rhiannon went utterly still, and her lovely eyes looked as agonized as Maelgwn's had. Arianhrodd could see that her will was torn, half-rent apart by the decision forced upon her.

Arianhrodd resisted the urge to reach out in pity. Instead, she made her voice stern. "Look beyond your fear and anger, Rhiannon. If you are truly a healer, you have a duty to aid Maelgwn, even if it imperils your own life. If you would help a wounded bird that lay helpless upon the sea rocks, how much more should you help a man, especially a man who carries the future of Gwynedd on his broad shoulders?"

Rhiannon shook her head. "Don't ask this of me. I can't do it. I fear him too much."

"It's not I who asks it, Rhiannon. It is the Goddess."

"You know this? She has spoken to you?"

Arianhrodd nodded, suddenly certain it was true. "I have seen enough of the future to know that Maelgwn the Great must live and prosper, or many will suffer. There is good in this man you have wed, and also a deep bond with the land, the Goddess's timeless flesh. She has chosen him, and it is up to all of us to protect the vessel of Her will."

Rhiannon licked her lips uneasily. "I cannot deny the Goddess, nor do I wish Maelgwn ill. But tell me truly, is there no other way?"

"Having seen the determined look in your husband's eyes, I know he will not be satisfied with anything less than confronting your spirit. And since I am not able to conjure the ghostly vision he desires, I must do the next best thing. I will send him a living, breathing woman, but one he believes to be dead." A faint smile formed on her lips. "With the aid of the drug, and your promise to speak no word to Maelgwn when you see him, I think my plan will serve."

Chapter 26

Rhiannon gazed out at the sea, watching the slow lap of frothy waves across the beach. The rhythm of the surf pounded in her ears, like the timeless heartbeat of the Mother herself. She had come to this place every day since her leg was well enough to allow her to walk there. Never before had the sea failed to soothe her, but today she was so oppressed by her thoughts that even the glimmering waves could not wash away her dread.

In a few hours, she would see Maelgwn again. The Goddess had willed it, and she would obey. Still, her heart twisted in her chest at the thought. Her terror did not arise from fear of death, nor dread of the physical pain she might endure if he defied the drug and attacked her. She feared seeing the hatred in his eyes again—knowing that her husband loathed who and what she was with all his soul.

Rhiannon got up from the rock she sat on, her thoughts so disturbing she could no longer remain still. She sighed heavily. There was nowhere she could go, no sanctuary to which she could flee. Even the forest was haunted. The woods no longer echoed with mystery and enchantment. Now they were full of memories, achingly lovely memories that tore her insides and rendered her helpless and empty. Llewenon's attack had not destroyed her refuge, but Maelgwn's love had. He had made her into a woman, a woman full of passion and grown-up dreams. She could never go back. She had lost the simple magic of the wild forest forever.

Anger rose in her, hot and choking. She had only wanted to be herself, to be free. But Maelgwn would not allow it, no man would. Men wanted your soul, to make your spirit so bound up with theirs you could never escape. It was not fair. She had not asked to be wedded to any man. She had passed from Ferdic to Maelgwn like a possession, mute and obedient. Even then, she had some hope she might keep her soul . . . until Maelgwn stole it with his beautiful body and harsh male hunger.

Rhiannon gritted her teeth as the longing swept through her. Would she ever be free of the insatiable craving to have Maelgwn hold her in his arms? He had plucked the strings of her heart to make sublime, enchanting music. The tune lingered, ceaseless, relentless, vibrating through every fiber of her being with a dull aching roar.

Listlessly, she walked back to the hut. A few days ago, she had dreamed of beginning again, inspired by Arianhrodd's example. Like the priestess, she wanted to live her life free of the constraints of men. Someday she might even be a priestess and serve the Lady as Arianhrodd did. She longed to feel the power of the Goddess singing through her, filling her body with invincible strength. She wanted to walk fearlessly to the other side and bask in the golden light of eternity. Now, her dream would never be. She belonged to Maelgwn, and again he claimed her.

Rhiannon entered the small dwelling and took a seat by the fire. Arianhrodd met her eyes and nodded slowly. Gesturing to the liquid she was preparing in a small bowl, she said, "The drug is almost ready. You should sleep, little one. Maelgwn will come for you at dawn."

By the time Maelgwn returned to the fortress, the feast of Candlemas had already begun. There were more than a few puzzled looks from those already gathered in the great hall. Father Leichan especially looked reproachful. Maelgwn considered how much more unhappy the priest would be if he knew where his king had been.

The feast dragged on interminably. In his inner turmoil, Maelgwn could scarcely keep his mind on his responsibilities. He forced himself to listen to his chieftains complain about the Irish raiders and their grievances toward one another. The herdsmen grumbled about their losses of cattle and sheep over the winter. He was polite to the young women—daughters of freemen and chieftains—who were pushed his way so he might consider them as wives or bed partners. By saying little and nodding often, somehow he got through it.

At last, everyone began to drift drunkenly toward their beds. The chieftains and their men went off to sleep in the barracks, or bedded down in the fire-warmed hall. The poorer farmers and servants sought the stables and other outbuildings. Finally alone, Maelgwn circled the inner courtyard, then climbed the gate tower to look out over the barren hills, faintly illuminated by the still-full moon that peeped out from behind the shifting clouds.

His eyes searched the coast road for the priestess's messenger. A deep, aching grief filled him. If Arianhrodd failed him, he did not know what he would do. His plan to visit the woods in search of Rhiannon's spirit seemed futile. He was very near to losing hope he would ever see Rhiannon, or her spirit, again.

Toward midnight, he gave up and climbed down. He headed back toward his council room, the one place in the fortress that was not filled with sleeping bodies. As he reached the door, a small man stepped out of the shadows and spoke his name. Maelgwn jumped like a startled buck. "In the name of Llud! How did you get in here?"

The man moved into the torchlight surrounding the doorway, and Maelgwn could see the amused expression on his dark, feral face. The visitor wore a rough, weathered leather tunic, and deep lines grooved the skin around his eyes. Maelgwn wondered if he was the fisherman Arianhrodd was said to dwell with.

"Do you have something for me?" Maelgwn asked. "Something from Arianhrodd?"

The man held out a packet of leather. Maelgwn took it and opened it. Inside was a little bottle made of reddish-brown clay and marked with strange designs.

"By the first light of morning, you must drink it all," the man instructed. "Then go down to the beach, to some place that was special to you and Rhiannon. There you will find your wife."

The man disappeared into the shadows.

"Wait," Maelgwn called after him. "What is this? What will it do to me?"

There was no answer from the darkness. Maelgwn looked down at the bottle he held in his trembling hands. He could have dreamed the man, but not the bottle. Stepping closer to the torchlight, he attempted to read the inscription. It was obviously not Latin. It seemed very old, very old indeed.

What was it? Poison? A shiver of foreboding ran through him. The priestess insisted he must trust her, and this was the test of her demand. If he did not drink the stuff inside the bottle, she must think to know somehow, and fail to send him Rhiannon. But if he drank it and it was poison . . .

Impatiently, Maelgwn shook off the thought. He sensed no evil in Arianhrodd. She seemed kindhearted and friendly, a simple peasant woman, albeit a remarkably fearless one. Her faith in the Goddess must give her the courage to treat him so peremptorily. He smiled slightly, remembering Arianhrodd's challenging expression. She expected him to do her will, and the message she sent was just as implacable.

"Maelgwn—you're still up?"

Balyn's hearty voice startled him out of his reverie. "Aye, and you?"

"Been to bed, but couldn't sleep. I kept thinking something was wrong. Is there?"

Maelgwn turned over the small bottle in his hand. "I might as well tell you. Someone should know if I don't come back. This bottle contains a drug given to me by a healer named Arianhrodd. She has promised to help me converse with Rhiannon's spirit." He paused and met Balyn's appalled look. "I mean to drink the stuff. It represents the only chance I have of seeing Rhiannon again."

"But it could be poison. What do you know about this healer? Why should you trust her?"

"She's a priestess of the Great Mother Goddess, an ancient sect dedicated to helping and healing. I don't believe she would harm me."

"But you can't be sure! You take a terrible risk."

Maelgwn shrugged.

Balyn's voice grew more frantic. "This is your *life* we're speaking of! Or, if you care so little for your life, what of your immortal soul? To willingly consort with spirits . . . with demons . . ."

"I don't fear for my soul," Maelgwn said coldly. "If you do, then pray for me."

"I will," Balyn whispered in anguish.

Maelgwn turned away, but not before Balyn stopped him with a trembling hand on his arm. "At least tell me where you're going."

"The beach . . . at dawn. If I'm not back by twilight, you may want to come looking for me."

As Maelgwn left the fortress, morning was merely a promise in the eastern sky, where the clouds broke open in a faint thinning of the night. A bone-chilling mist curled around the fortress walls and slunk across the barren hills. The mist followed Maelgwn as he walked. He felt its damp caress insinuating itself into the neck of his cloak and along the bare skin of his face. He shivered in the icy night air.

He walked briskly down the coast road. Impatience was spurring his steps. So far he felt no effects from the drug. It had tasted foul and slimy, reminding him of dead and rotting things. What was in it? Bat ear and eye of newt? He grunted in disgust. The priestess had likely given him some repulsive but worthless concoction meant to deceive him into expecting magic.

Magic! How foolish he was. Did he really think he could find Rhiannon's spirit and speak with it? What a waste of time! Rhiannon was dead. If anything remained of her, it would be a battered corpse. His lovely wife was gone, her beauty wasted on the indifferent worms that ate her flesh.

His brutal reasoning failed to quench the vague, yearning hope inside him. The huntsman insisted he had seen Rhiannon and held her warm, smooth fingers. Had it been a vision the man experienced, deep in an ecstatic trance? Or was it the woman herself, somehow saved from death and hiding in the woods like a wild thing? He had to find the truth. As long as there was even a slight possibility he could see Rhiannon again—hold her close to his heart—he must pursue it. He would not sleep soundly until he had exhausted every hope.

He reached the cliffs above the surf and paused to look down at the desolate beach, still swathed in impenetrable darkness. An uneasy sensation crept over him. His stomach churned, and a huge fist seemed to grab at his insides, twisting his stomach until it writhed in pain. Fighting the urge to vomit, he began walking again. The agony in his stomach increased, and he wondered again if the drug were poison. Had he been fooled by Arianhrodd's aura of warmth and benevolence? What if she was really a sorceress, who used magic to transform her hideous witch's visage into the open, hearty features of a Cymry peasant?

Maelgwn's stomach convulsed violently, and he bent over and tried to relieve the agonizing pain by vomiting. Nothing came up but a trickle of bitter liquid. It was too late; the drug already coursed through his veins, filling him with sickly faintness. When he tried to rise, he could barely straighten up. A strange weakness overtook him, paralyzing his limbs. He slumped to the frozen grass, wretched and gasping. His legs seized up to his belly.

Oh, the pain, the dizziness! He was helpless, too feeble to move or even cry out. Panic flowed through him. Was this how he would die? Would they find him here, frozen stiff, doubled up in agony like a sickened dog?

The thought made cold sweat seep from his skin. He had always counted himself brave, afraid of nothing, not even the damnation of the Christian god. The darkness that swarmed around terrified him. He did not want to die. He had too much left to live for . . . there was his son . . . his kingdom . . .

The weakness slowly passed. Gradually, his senses recovered, and he could feel the cool breeze blowing on his face, soothing the sudden fever that racked his body. His cramped gut loosened, and his eyes focused again. His body grew stronger and free of pain.

He got to his feet. It was odd, a moment ago he feared he was dying; now he was well. Indeed, he felt almost refreshed. The youth and vigor had returned to his body, and he was ready to beat any opponent. But he was not going into battle, he reminded himself—he was looking for Rhiannon. The messenger had told him to go to the beach at dawn, and he had lain senseless as the streaks of morning light crept deeper into the darkness. A new anxiety gripped him. Was he too late? Had his chance to meet Rhiannon's spirit already passed?

Maelgwn hurried down the cliffs as fast as the treacherous pathway would allow, stumbling on a few loose rocks. When he reached the beach, he realized with surprise that it was barely getting light. He had thought himself delayed for hours, but he must have lain stricken on the cliffs for only a short while.

He looked around, trying to decide where to begin his search. The messenger told him to go to a place special to Rhiannon and him. Ahead was the spill of boulders where he had first loved his shy, fearful wife. Maelgwn squinted at the rocks. One of them looked like a woman in long dark cloak. He moved closer, and the image disappeared. He paused, tense with frustration. Had the mist thickened? The edges of objects appeared blurred. He kept looking out of the corner of his eyes, searching for shapes that disappeared as soon as he turned his head.

He strained his eyes in the half-light and tried to decide. Was it here or further back they had lain? He could not remember. A gust of harsh wind blew past him, clearing his head. He blinked. For a moment he saw a glint of red among the rocks—the color seemed strangely out of place on the drab winter shoreline. He walked toward the place with cautious, unsteady steps. Aye, he had seen it. Dawn rapidly approached, brightening the frozen beach with misty light, and there was indeed a flicker of color among the gray rocks. He walked faster and reached the place, breathless and panting.

Damn! There was nothing there. His mind was playing tricks on him. He looked down longingly at the damp sand, willing Rhiannon to be lying there as she once had, a blaze of vivid hair and dazzling white skin. For a moment she was, but Maelgwn knew the image could not be real. It wavered and then faded, until he could see the pattern of the sand glowing through the transparent figure of his wife.

He turned away, and a surge of suffocating anger assailed him. Was this all that fraud of a priestess offered? Did she really think he would be satisfied with these vague apparitions, conjured up by his disordered mind? If he were wise, he would go back to the fortress, sleep off the drug and forget this foolishness.

Reluctantly, he started back. As he looked toward the east, his gaze was caught by the blazing colors of the sunrise. Delicate pink, glowing orange, a hint of sapphire—he could feel the colors, almost taste them. He paused and stared; the sky seemed to move, to swirl in vast waves of light. The sun turned into a churning spiral of flame. The air around him caught fire, and as he shifted his gaze toward the coast, the ocean itself seemed to be burning. The glow of the morning sun was reflecting on the waves in ripples of gold. Half-blinded, Maelgwn closed his eyes.

When he opened them, the world was normal again, a pretty winter's morn, but no more fantastic visions. Maelgwn glanced around uneasily. The drug had distorted his perceptions. Things were not what they seemed. Again, he saw the glint of red between the rocks, and yet, he knew nothing was there. It must be a reflection from the fading dawn sky. The flicker of red grew brighter. Perhaps it was . . . after all . . . Maelgwn ran to the place with his heart pounding.

Rhiannon stood in the shelter of the rocks, her eyes wide and fearful, her hair whipping around in the wind. For a moment, Maelgwn feared to move, even to breathe. Rhiannon stood mere inches away from him. He could scarcely believe it.

She did not look like a spirit. She was dressed strangely, in some sort of rough woolen tunic that barely reached to her knees. Her lips were almost blue with cold and she shivered violently. Even in his confused state, he knew the freezing wind should have little effect on a ghost. He reached for her, stretching out his trembling fingers, unsure what they would touch.

His hand grazed solid flesh, and he jerked it back in surprise. This was not a phantom, the misty apparition he had anticipated. The thing felt like a living woman.

Maelgwn closed his eyes, then opened them again. He knew his wits were addled from the drug, but surely they could not deceive him so completely. He reached out again. The woman felt real, and very cold. Instinctively, he pulled off his cloak and wrapped it around her. When she did not vanish, he dared to draw her against his chest. She warmed at his touch, and Maelgwn moaned. If this was truly Rhiannon, he knew there were things he should say, but his mind would not function. The relief he felt at holding her in his arms was too great to disrupt with the complexity of words.

Trembling, uncertain, he leaned over and kissed the delicate lips that beckoned him. It was Rhiannon; it had to be. No other creature evoked these feelings in him. The sweetness of her, the clean cool smell of her skin and hair—passion streamed through him, raw and desperate. He kissed her harder, deeper, reveling in the awesome splendor of her small mouth, the faint rhythm of her breathing. He was frantic with desire, utterly immersed in the wonder of her nearness. Tears streamed down his face, and his whole body shook. Only the need to breathe finally forced him to break off the kiss.

He stared down at Rhiannon's face, flushed pink from his kisses. She appeared as amazed as he felt. Her eyes were dazed, shocked. He opened his mouth to reassure her. He could not think what to say. His muddled thoughts flitted away as soon as he formed them. Then he knew. He would not tell her what he felt, he would show her.

He would explain with his fingers, his mouth, his body hard within hers. He crushed Rhiannon against his chest, trying to reason out his plan. It had been summer when he last loved Rhiannon on the beach; now it was much too cold, even with his cloak for a blanket.

The cave! The thought startled him, coming as it did, so suddenly, as if a part of him remained alert and wide awake, prompting from far away. The cave in the cliff wall would be the perfect shelter. Rhun and the other boys had gone there often before the weather turned so cold. They would have left supplies behind, mayhap even things to make a fire.

Maelgwn picked Rhiannon up and half walked, half stumbled to the cliffs. He searched steadily, instinctively, until he found the small opening in the cliff wall. He crawled in, cushioning Rhiannon against his chest as he pulled her along with him. The cave was dark and cold, and Maelgwn swore as he scraped his head on the low ceiling. He released Rhiannon and explored the cave floor with his fingers. His excitement built as his hands encountered first rags and rough blankets, then the hard, solid shapes of a flintstone and a lamp, still half filled with oil. With trembling fingers he struck the flint, once, twice. The cave flared into light, and Maelgwn used the first of it to drink in the sight of Rhiannon's face so close to his own.

Her eyes watched him, wary, solemn. He could scarcely contain himself long enough to light the lamp and push the rags into a pile. He gently removed his cloak from around Rhiannon and laid it down to form a makeshift bed. Then he reached for her.

He felt her shiver as he pulled her into his arms. She feared him; even now she thought he would hurt her. Anguish choked his throat. He had to show her how much he loved her, needed her.

He kissed her tenderly at first, beginning with her forehead, her blue-veined eyelids, her delicate cheeks. His mouth grew hungrier as it descended to her neck. He tore her gown slightly as he nuzzled her neck, and she pushed him away. With swift, graceful movements she removed the garment. She wore nothing underneath, and he could not stop staring at her, at the beautiful body he had never thought to see again.

He gasped and reached for her. She came passively, willingly into his arms. Suddenly, he began to weep, overcome with the pure joy of holding her. He wanted to look at her, to kiss every lovely glowing inch of her, but she would not let him. She pressed her mouth to his and arched her naked body against his bare flesh. His body responded with a stabbing jolt of answering desire. He could not wait; he must be joined with her now!

He was fumbling with his clothes when he heard a whispering voice, low, vibrant and unearthly. Along with it came a cool breeze, gently ruffling the hair along his neck. Maelgwn looked up, sensing another presence in the cave. The lamplight cast strange shadows over the uneven rock walls, and the flames flickered wildly in the slight draft from the cave entrance, but there was nothing there.

He looked down at Rhiannon again. Her face had changed. Her eyes were half-closed and far away. He had a panicky thought that she was leaving him, and he leaned down to kiss her, hard. Her lips burned him. Something burned him below, too—an incessant need that blotted out all his other thoughts. He lowered his mouth to suckle Rhiannon's breasts. They were fuller than he remembered, and as he sucked the velvety nipples, they seemed to swell, filling his mouth with the sweetness of milk.

The Goddess, Maelgwn thought with hazy surprise. She who feeds and nourishes all life. He drank the milk eagerly, feeling it fill his belly and seep into his veins, making him warm and strong.

His hand moved down to Rhiannon's smooth stomach, and it also seemed to swell. It grew firm and rounded, and he caressed it in awe, feeling the young life growing beneath the taut skin. The Goddess—he thought again—She who gives birth to all things.

He jerked back, struggling to see by the flickering lamp-light. It was only Rhiannon he held, her delicate body stretched out beneath him. She sighed slightly at his touch, and Maelgwn wondered if she felt the strange things he did.

Her eyelids fluttered and she reached for him, her fingers closing around his erection. Maelgwn gasped. The sensation was almost painful. He had never felt so aroused; he was near to bursting. He spread Rhiannon's legs and pushed his fingers inside her. Warm liquid soaked his fingers. He opened his eyes and stared at the glittering fluid. What was it—moonlight, sea water, some magic nectar? He bent to place his mouth on the moist, rosy opening between Rhiannon's legs for a taste. The stuff was sweet and filling, but like nothing he had ever experienced. The Goddess, his mind prompted him. She feeds all creatures with Her bounty.

He had no time to dwell on the wonder of it. Rhiannon touched him again, and he seemed to grow enormous in her delicate fingers. Maelgwn groaned with excitement. Never had he felt so virile and potent. His testicles were aching and swollen, bursting with his seed. He could wait no longer. With one swift movement, he entered Rhiannon, his body exploding with sensation as he sheathed himself inside her. He felt himself changing, his form altering, distorted by the ecstasy, the magic of their coupling. He was a stallion, thundering with his mare, her flanks heaving beneath him. Then a fox, his cock sharp and pointed, his teeth ripping into a vixen as she screamed her pleasure. Then a wildcat, all claws and liquid muscles, locked in passion with a lovely she-cat. Or a stag, his massive head held proudly as he mounted a trembling doe.

His body changed and swelled. He was every male,

flushed with the savage heat of procreation, the terrible aching drive to beget life. And Rhiannon was every female thing, soft and wet and welcoming.

Only gradually did he become a man again. His explosive lust slipped away. He felt chilled and empty—and afraid. He saw himself from a distance, his naked body sheltered by the solidity of the cave. His flesh was nothing compared to the ancient walls of rock, enduring silently for a hundred generations, or the sea, pounding against the cliffs, eating them away grain by grain. He was frail, insignificant. Someday he would die, his body rot to slime, then dusty bones. Nothing would be left of him.

Fear choked his throat, and he pressed against Rhiannon desperately, seeking her warmth to chase away his cold, empty visions. She moaned beneath him, and his fiery passion returned. He turned her over and entered her from behind, cupping her swollen woman's flesh as he drove into her, rubbing his face in her long hair. He was joined with her, her body becoming one with his. He wanted to love her forever, to merge her soul with his own. He would bury himself in her dreams, as he buried his body within hers now.

He neared climax, and the cave walls began to twist and turn all around him. The rock floor trembled beneath them. There was a shower of stars illuminating the cave, far, far into the darkness. Then there was a bright light, so intense he squeezed his eyes shut in agony.

And then there was nothing.

Chapter 27

Rhiannon shuddered as she turned away from Maelgwn's unconscious form. He looked so pale and vulnerable lying there. She had bunched up his clothes to make a pillow for his head, and she had covered him with his cloak, but she still worried that he would wake up wretchedly cold and stiff.

With swift, silent movements, she quenched the sputtering lamp, then crept from the cave. Outside it was daylight, and she hastened down the beach, glancing behind occasionally to make sure no one saw her. At the far end of the beach, Ceinwen waited for her beside his boat. She rushed toward him, nearly falling into his arms in relief.

"Rhiannon, are you well?" Ceinwen asked harshly. "Did the king hurt you? It looks as if you are limping."

Rhiannon shook her head. She was sore and exhausted, but she would not tell Ceinwen that. He might mistake Maelgwn's strenuous lovemaking for abuse.

The fisherman helped her into the boat. When he had cast off and they were at sea, away from open beach, she spoke in a hesitant voice. "Maelgwn's still asleep in the cave. I left some of his clothes outside the cave, as a marker of sorts. Will they find him, do you think?''

Ceinwen gave her a startled look, then lowered his eyes. ''You still worry about him, rather than yourself. Perhaps it is as Arianhrodd says, you are meant to return to the king, that the Goddess wills it.''

Rhiannon shook her head. ''Nay. I have obeyed the Goddess this time, but She cannot ask more of me.''

Ceinwen watched her curiously. She pretended not to see his puzzled look. She could not explain her decision. Her whole being was still on fire with the magic of Maelgwn's lovemaking. Despite her fatigue and the tremors of cold and weakness that racked her body, she felt light, buoyant, whole. Lying with Maelgwn had been everything she remembered and more.

Perhaps that was what frightened her. It was too good, too wonderful. She had known that kind of happiness before, and it had not lasted. It was impossible to forget how swiftly Maelgwn's love turned to hate, how abruptly and cruelly her hopes had died. She would not make that mistake again; she would not return to Maelgwn as his wife. Even the Goddess could not demand that of her.

Maelgwn shifted in the bed, trying to relieve the cramping in his legs.

''He stirs! He's waking!'' The familiar voice was resonant with joy. Maelgwn opened his eyes, curious to see what could make Balyn so delighted. He found himself in his bedchamber. Balyn stood beside the bed, watching him intently. The look of total exhaustion on his friend's face drew a startled gasp from Maelgwn's lips. ''By the gods, what happened to you?''

''Me?'' Balyn asked incredulously. ''I find you naked and half-dead in a cave and you ask what happened to *me?*''

The pieces shifted and sought each other in Maelgwn's mind. He remembered taking the drug and going to the beach. After that came wild, startling images. His forced his attention back to Balyn. "You look exhausted. How long since you found me?"

"The day before yesterday."

Maelgwn grimaced. The drug was powerful. Had he really slept two full days?

"Well?" Balyn's voice was hesitant, tinged with dread. "Did you see her? Did you meet with Rhiannon's spirit?"

The memories came to Maelgwn from a long distance, a different time and place, almost a different world. It was like being a child and learning to speak again. The things he had experienced were so primitive and elemental they could scarcely be described.

As he shaped the images into coherent memories, violent emotions washed over him. He felt the wonder, the nearly unbearable awe of seeing Rhiannon again and holding her in his arms. Then came his strange, mindless passion, the blinding urge to mate with her, to fill her womb. He recalled taking her to the cave, lighting the lamp, kissing and caressing her. Such strange loving it was. Not merely her body and his joining, but some confusion of senses that made him think they were a pair of rutting animals.

The remembered images jarred him, and he struggled to reduce them to something he could understand. He recalled Rhiannon beneath him, urging him on. She had reached for him, stroked his shaft, arched her body to receive him. But, nay! Was not it the Goddess Herself who cried and moaned Her divine pleasure and made the solid rock walls quiver and shimmer with motion and light?

He stiffened, shocked by the memory. Balyn met his eyes, clearly disturbed.

"Maelgwn, what is it?"

"I . . . I dreamed I mated with the Goddess Herself."

Balyn went dead white. He brought his hand up in an ancient sign of protection, completely forgetting in his dread that he was a Christian. "I warned you," he whispered. "I warned you what would come of this."

Maelgwn slowly shook his head. "Nay, it was not something to be feared. Nothing like that. Merely strange . . . and confusing."

"She's bewitched you," Balyn moaned. He ran his thick fingers over his sweaty face. "That woman, the priestess, she drugged you . . . stole your soul."

Maelgwn laughed abruptly. "I'd forgotten how much this sort of thing terrifies you. It was not awful, Balyn. Really. I would not like it to be like that every time, but, mind you, it was not awful. It was . . ." A caressing breeze seemed to lightly touch his neck. "For a time I felt a part of everything—the earth, the ocean, the sky. I suppose you could compare the Goddess's power to a flame or a great wave rushing through you. Afterwards, I felt empty, lifeless. But Rhiannon was there for me, so soft and sweet . . ." Maelgwn's body warmed at the memory, and he was suddenly astounded by the realization that Rhiannon was alive.

"It's true," he whispered. "I didn't dream that part." He met Balyn's alarmed gaze. "Rhiannon lives. I held her in my arms. I *loved* her."

"It was only a dream. You said so yourself."

"The Goddess—she was something in a dream, or a trance . . . But Rhiannon, nay, I did not dream her."

"Of course you did. Every man has wakened at one time or another to find his blankets damp with spew, his arms clutching the bedclothes like a lover. It was no more than that."

Maelgwn considered silently. The drug was powerful enough to make him sleep for days. Had it also given him visions of what he most wished for? He dismissed the thought. Even if his mind had been disordered, his body

could not lie. Two days had passed, and still it hummed
with the unmistakable warmth of pleasure deeply satisfied.
No wet dream could make a man feel as he did now. The
memory of Rhiannon's body was still on his fingertips. Her
moans still echoed in his ears. Against all reason, he knew
his wife was alive.

It was a mild day. The air seemed quiet and humid
with a lethargy that was almost summerlike. By the time
Maelgwn had ridden half the distance to Arianhrodd's hut,
his face was damp with sweat and the heavy wool of his
winter tunic stuck uncomfortably to his back and chest.
He fought to ignore the fatigue that radiated through his
limbs. The drug and the long hours in the cold cave had
weakened him more than he wanted to admit. But he
could not afford to rest; he had delayed too long already.
Two days had passed since he had met Rhiannon on the
beach. By now she might have disappeared again.

He urged Cynraith faster, goaded by a sense of panic.
The serene feeling he experienced on first wakening was
long gone. Even as he enjoyed the memory of holding
Rhiannon in his arms and loving her, he confronted the
fact that she had vanished again, leaving him with nothing,
no proof that their coupling had been anything more than
a vivid dream. The languorous satisfaction in his loins
faded, leaving him empty and yearning, doubting his memories. There was only one person besides Rhiannon who
could prove his memories were true. He intended to find
her and speak with her, before she vanished as well.

Arianhrodd was drying fish in the sun when he rode up.
She stood up as she saw him, her face expressionless. He
dismounted and looked down on her. "So, Maelgwn the
Great," she said, "did the Goddess send you your lady-
love?"

Her voice was smooth and faintly mocking. Maelgwn felt

his anger rising. How lightly this woman spoke of things which meant so much to him!

"Aye, Rhiannon came to me. Not her spirit, but the woman herself."

"You believe she is alive?"

Maelgwn's anger overflowed, and he approached Arianhrodd threateningly. "You lied. Rhiannon is not dead." He jerked his head toward the small hut not far from where they stood. "I have half a mind to tear this place apart piece by piece until I find her."

"You speak as if Rhiannon were a possession of yours that you have come to claim." Arianhrodd's voice was soft, but cool and warning. "In the eyes of the Goddess, Rhiannon is not your servant or slave, but a free woman who chooses her own destiny. She comes and goes as she pleases—and it seems she is not ready to return to you."

Maelgwn stepped back, abashed. Arianhrodd was right. He did often consider Rhiannon a possession. A beloved possession, but nevertheless, something he owned or had a claim upon.

"You've spoken to her?" he asked in a more reasonable tone. "She's told you she doesn't wish to return to Degannwy?"

Arianhrodd gave a slight shrug and gestured to the open beach. "Rhiannon is not being held against her will. If she wished to see you or return to Degannwy, she could do so at any time."

The harsh truth of Arianhrodd's words struck Maelgwn like a blow, igniting a terrible dread inside him. What if Rhiannon was alive, but he had lost her anyway? The thought so horrifed him, he reacted with fierce, defensive anger. He took another menacing step toward Arianhrodd. "You tricked me, manipulated me!"

Arianhrodd stood her ground, gazing up at him with calm, intent eyes. "A trick, Maelgwn? Can you deny you felt the Goddess's power? Can you deny you experienced something extraordinary?"

"I have no desire to know the Goddess's mysteries. I only want Rhiannon back."

"Can you not guess the two things might be connected?"

A tremor of anxiety moved down Maelgwn's spine as he stared at the small, dark-featured woman before him. A part of him feared Arianhrodd and the power she represented. As he met her implacable gaze, he reminded himself that she was merely a woman, and a poor, insignificant one at that. Her jet-dark eyes bored into his, reaching inside him. For a moment he felt her power, a warm, peaceful energy that made his flesh tingle.

He forced the warmth away. Pushing past Arianhrodd, he headed directly for the small hut behind her. He crouched down to enter the low doorway. Inside, he blinked, struggling to see. Across the smoldering fire and clutter of the small dwelling, he saw Rhiannon. She stood at a loom, as if she had been weaving. Her wide, startled eyes met his. Maelgwn held his breath, afraid she would vanish if he tried to touch her.

She wore the short, coarsely woven gown he vaguely remembered her removing in the cave. Her hair was plaited into two long braids that fell across her shoulders. Otherwise, she looked the same—delicate, fragile, impossibly lovely.

He wanted to go to her, to pull her into his arms, to feel the substance of her body, the heat of her flesh. Something held him back. Her eyes were cautious, wary. There was something different in her expression, a determination he had never seen before.

"Rhiannon . . . I . . ." He meant to say that he had come for her. The words died on his lips. "You're alive," he finally said. "I didn't dream it."

Rhiannon nodded almost imperceptibly. He had the sense she had prepared for this moment.

He swallowed, utterly at loss for words. "I . . . we . . . I thought you were dead. Drowned. What happened? Where did you go?"

"Ceinwen—a fisherman—found me on the beach and brought me here."

He nodded. Such a simple explanation, but still, somehow miraculous.

"The Goddess led Ceinwen to me, or I surely would have perished." Rhiannon's eyes seemed lit by a strange fire. "Perhaps now you will understand how much I owe Her."

Maelgwn shifted uncomfortably. The Goddess stood between him and Rhiannon. He resented Her interference; he wanted things to be as they had been before this strange deity had involved Herself in their lives. "What does the Goddess . . .?" Maelgwn gestured awkwardly. "What does She have to do with me? With us?"

Rhiannon turned away; Maelgwn could feel her spirit leaving him. He tried to maneuver around the fire to reach her and he hit his head on a basket hanging from the ceiling. Feeling big and clumsy, he got down on his knees and half crawled the last few steps to Rhiannon's side. She would not look at him.

"Please, Rhiannon, tell me, what does the Goddess have to do with us?" He wanted to touch her, but some instinct held him back. If he reached for her, he was afraid she would flinch. He could not bear that.

At last, she looked at him. He felt himself captured in her mystical gaze like a fish in a net. "My place is here, Maelgwn. I can't return to Degannwy."

"Why not?"

"I don't belong there."

"Of course you do!" His heart began to pound. Was Arianhrodd right? Would Rhiannon really refuse to return to him?

Rhiannon shook her head. "If I went back, I would be

called a witch, an enchantress. Your people believe I am dead. If I returned now, they would regard me with awe and dread.''

Maelgwn exploded. "How can you imagine I care what they think of you? I would *make* them accept you!''

"You cannot bend men's hearts to your will, Maelgwn. You can make them follow you to their death in battle, but you cannot banish their fear of the other side.'' She shook her head again. "It would not work. Their fear of me might taint their faith in you. I would not have you lose the kingdom you have fought so hard for—because of me.''

"My God, Rhiannon, don't you know that means nothing to me? If I can't have you, ruling Gwynedd is meaningless.'' A deep despair filled him. He meant his words. Even his dream of uniting the Cymry could not compare to the sense of completion and peace he had known with Rhiannon. He must make her understand. He grabbed Rhiannon's hips and jerked her to him. Before she could protest, he lifted the hem of her gown and placed his fingers on the angry red scar on her thigh.

"Is it because of this? Can you not forgive me for drawing my knife against you?''

Rhiannon's eyes met his, full of resignation. "You were distraught, confused. You did not mean to hurt me.''

"What then?'' Maelgwn gasped, clutching her tightly. "Why won't you return to me? Why won't you be my wife?''

Rhiannon swallowed, then her delicate lips moved, speaking so softly he could barely hear her. "I'm sorry, Maelgwn. I can't go back. I can't be your wife. I belong to the Goddess now.''

"The Goddess! How can She claim you? She might possess your soul, but I have possessed your body, your fleshly form. How can you deny that, Rhiannon? How can you?''

Rhiannon reached to touch his face. Her small fingers

glided over his skin. "I did not say I would not lie with you, Maelgwn. I did not say I would forsake your loving."

Maelgwn loosened his violent grip and took a deep breath. "What do you mean? You will not return to Degannwy—but if I came to you, you would couple with me?"

"I could not deny you that."

Maelgwn released her altogether, breathing heavily. Her words confused him. He had not considered this possibility. He had hoped she would agree to return to Degannwy and all would be well. He had also dreaded she would reject him and tell him she never wanted to see him again. But this, this in-between, unsettling state of possessing her body, but not her heart and soul. Could he endure it?

"What if there were a child, Rhiannon? To what world would he belong? Yours or mine?"

"There won't be a child."

"What? Would you kill it as you did the other one?"

Rhiannon gasped and took a step back. Maelgwn quickly realized his mistake. He reached for her, sorrowful and beseeching. "I'm sorry. I didn't mean that. Gwenaseth told me it was a mistake. But please, next time, trust me."

"Trust you!" Rhiannon exclaimed. "I find I am married to a man full of anger and hate, and I am supposed to trust him? The Goddess help me! You nearly went mad with rage when you found out who my mother was. Who is to say that if the babe had been born and sleeping in the room that day, you would not have dashed out its brains in your fury? And yet you . . . you taunt me for failing to protect it!"

"Dear Rhiannon, do you truly think that of me—that I would kill my own child?"

"I don't know," she answered tautly. "When it comes to the matter of Esylt, I'm not sure what cruelties you are capable of. Even now, you cannot find it in your heart to forgive your sister, can you?"

"Esylt has nothing to do with us."

"Esylt has everything to do with us! She was my mother. Her blood flows in my veins." Rhiannon held her wrist up to his face, forcing him to watch the blue pulse that throbbed there. "Even now, it makes you shudder to think of it. You are a fool, Maelgwn, if you think you can continue to hate Esylt and yet love her daughter."

Maelgwn closed his eyes and struggled for strength. A few weeks ago, he would not have been able to think of forgiving Esylt, of letting go of his hatred. But the loss of Rhiannon had taught him that there were worse things than forsaking the bitterness he had nursed for years. He took Rhiannon's wrist and brought it to his lips. "I cannot promise," he said softly. "But I will try to forgive Esylt. After all, she gave me you. Such a great gift must surely cancel out her other sins." Pulling Rhiannon close, he stood and cradled her against him, stroking her hair. "Please, Rhiannon, come back to me."

Rhiannon shook her head. "I can be your wife no longer. Ceinwen has said he will build me my own hut, so we will have a place to meet."

Maelgwn's blue eyes met hers, bright as flames; he leaned over and began to cover her face with kisses. His mouth moved lower, nuzzling the sensitive skin of her neck. Rhiannon sagged against him, wondering if she could deny this man anything.

Slowly, wordlessly, she summoned the strength of the Goddess. It came to her, a rush of energy that made her tremble from head to toe. She lifted Maelgwn's face with gentle but firm fingers, pulling his scorching lips away from her skin.

"Nay, you will not convince me. Nothing you can say or do will change what I have become."

Maelgwn gazed at her with mute, stricken eyes. Rhiannon closed her heart to him, to the aching pity that assaulted her every sense. He was a man, a king. It was unthinkable that he could really want her so much. In time, he would forget her. He would go on with his life.

"In a few days, when the moon is again full, come to me, and I will lie with you. We will make sex magic together."

Maelgwn shook his head. His eyes were full of bitterness, despair, but he said nothing. He stumbled slowly to the small doorway. Ducking down, he went out.

Chapter 28

Arianhrodd was waiting for him when Maelgwn left the hut. He expected her to be gloating, smug. Instead, the look she gave him was one of regret.

"What a tangle," she murmured as he swept past her.

He paused, confused by her sympathy. "I should think you would be pleased to learn that Rhiannon has chosen the Goddess over me."

Arianhrodd put a small brown hand on his arm. "Come. Walk with me in the forest. I think better when there are growing things around me."

Maelgwn hesitated a moment, then followed Arianhrodd over the rocky beach. Rhiannon had refused him. The return journey to Degannwy would be filled with failure and despair. Delaying would cost him nothing.

A short distance from the ragged shoreline, they entered the forest. The young birch and alder had begun budding, and the ground beneath their feet was spongy with moisture. Everywhere there was the sound of running water and the rich scent of wet earth. Maelgwn inhaled deeply, soothing himself with the sweet, indefinable fragrance of spring.

When they were far into the woods, Arianhrodd turned to him. "Do you mean to abide by Rhiannon's decision?"

"Do I have a choice?"

Arianhrodd's face lit with amusement. "You could take Rhiannon back to your fortress by force."

Maelgwn shook his head. "I want more than to possess her body. It's her heart and soul I crave."

"At least you know the difference now. When you came here, it appeared you would claim her by any means you could."

"I was wrong. I was wrong about many things."

He felt Arianhrodd's dark eyes probing him. He paused on the pathway and confronted her. "Why have you brought me here? What do you want of me?"

Arianhrodd spoke slowly. "It's a pity Rhiannon no longer wishes to be your queen. Things I have seen in the scrying bowl once made me believe she was meant to be your consort."

Maelgwn cocked his head skeptically. "Visions?"

"I don't pretend to see the future, but sometimes a certain pathway is revealed. Of course, Rhiannon is free to choose the course of her life."

Maelgwn sought the priestess's hypnotic gaze. This time he did not struggle against her power, but searched it for the answers he needed. "Think you there is a way I might win Rhiannon back?"

"There is always a way."

Maelgwn jerked away in disgust. Arianhrodd was exactly like the Christian holy men. She spoke in riddles, used vague, exalted words. And told him nothing.

"I'm going back." He turned and began to walk down the pathway.

"Are you giving up?"

Maelgwn whirled around. His fists clenched. His body

was ablaze with anger. "Why do you taunt me? What game are you playing with my life? With Rhiannon's?"

Arianhrodd met his fury with a look of bemusement. "It's no game. A test perhaps, but not a game."

Maelgwn took a deep breath and unclenched his fists. "Am I to presume I have failed the test?"

Arianhrodd did not answer. She turned and began to walk again. Maelgwn followed her warily, reluctantly.

Further along the pathway, Arianhrodd spoke. "It's odd. I have heard you are a just king and a wise one, but you are ever a fool when it comes to women. Several times now, you have sought to intimidate me with your size and strength. Did you never think to reason with me, to talk with me as you might with a man?"

Maelgwn forced himself to listen. He did not like what she was saying, but there might be a grain of truth in her words.

"With women you are ever on the defensive," Arianhrodd continued. "A little boy who must shout and raise his fists to be heard. But women are exactly like men, Maelgwn, except for the shape of our bodies. We have minds and feelings as you do. We appreciate being asked to do things instead of being ordered around. We appreciate being reasoned with instead of intimidated. You wouldn't try to win over an ally strictly by force. You would use persuasion as well."

"It's different between men and women."

Arianhrodd shrugged. "If winning back Rhiannon is important, I would think you would use any means available."

"You're suggesting I bargain with her? Treat her like a reluctant ally?"

"Perhaps if you discovered the real reason she refuses to return to Degannwy, you would have a better chance of changing her mind."

"The real reason? But she told me . . ."

"Told you what?"

Maelgwn shook his head, reliving the pain of Rhiannon's rejection. "She spoke first of my people not accepting her. And then we argued about children, and, of course, my sister. I would concede all those points, do whatever I could to work them out. But, still, I don't think she'll change her mind. It's the Goddess who stands between her and me." Maelgwn raised his face to Arianhrodd, grimacing. "The damned Goddess has stolen my wife."

He expected the priestess to flinch at his blasphemy. Instead, she smiled. "You have felt the Goddess's power and yet are unafraid to curse Her. If Her hold over you is so weak, how can She hold Rhiannon in thrall?"

"Rhiannon believes she owes the Goddess her life."

"Do you believe it?"

Maelgwn shrugged uncomfortably. "She was very fortunate to be rescued when she was. It could be interpreted as the will of a god, or goddess, or simply good luck. At any rate, I can't see that the Goddess needs Rhiannon so badly."

Arianhrodd's eyes crinkled with mirth. "And besides, you have a prior claim."

"Something like that."

"Then you must convince Rhiannon that the Goddess has released her from her debt. If Rhiannon believed it was the Goddess's will that she return to your bed and hearth, how could she refuse?"

Maelgwn gave Arianhrodd a wary look. "You're the one skillful in manipulating the will of men and gods. How do I convince my wife to return to my side?"

"There will be a price."

"There always is," Maelgwn noted ruefully.

Arianhrodd took his arm and drew nearer. Maelgwn felt the heat of her fingers even through his heavy tunic. Smelling the musky, warm scent of her, he was reminded that she was a woman as well as a priestess. She caught the quickening of his senses, and her face lit with laughter.

"What a fine consort you shall make for the Goddess. I'm sure she will be delighted to release Rhiannon from her pledge . . . and accept yours instead."

Stacks of wood and brush for the bonfires. Eight casks of Brittany wine. Two oxen slaughtered for the feast. Musicians, including a drummer and pipe player borrowed from Cynglass's court. A tale honoring the Great Mother Goddess, commissioned of Taliesin . . .

Maelgwn's eyes traveled down the scribbled list, then wearily, he pushed it away.

The idea for the ceremony had struck him as promising when Arianhrodd first proposed it. He had thought to easily gain acceptance among his people for a ceremony celebrating the coming of spring and the renewal of the Earth Goddess's power. He had not guessed how many Cymry had converted to the Christian faith, nor how stubbornly they would adhere to the proscriptions against worshiping other deities. A good share of the inhabitants of Degannwy wanted no part of any ceremony honoring one of the old gods. They would not defy him, but their faces showed the anxiety and resentment his plan aroused.

Maelgwn stood abruptly and began to pace across the council room. In four days the seed moon would rise high and bright. He had planned that his people would gather on cliffs above the sea, and Arianhrodd would call down the Goddess, invoking Her spirit to enter Rhiannon's body. He would wear the mask of the Stag God, the Goddess's traditional consort. There in the wild light of the moon and leaping fires, he and Rhiannon would be joined. Rhiannon would realize the Goddess meant for her to be with him. No longer would she resist his plea to return to Degannwy and take her place next him.

Maelgwn sank back into his seat again, uneasy. Was it fair to ask his people to violate their consciences for his sake? Was it prudent to involve the Goddess's power—a power he accepted as very real—in a matter that primarily involved the happiness of one man? Most of all, would their plan work? Would Rhiannon agree to her part in the ceremony, and would the experience alter her refusal to return as his wife?

Uncertainty gnawed at him. One could not participate in a ceremony half-convinced. When it came to the magic of the Old Ones, belief was everything. He must put his doubts aside somehow. He must believe the Goddess would not fail him.

Balyn approached the hearth in the great hall quietly, trying not to startle the slight, swarthy man who squatted before it. "Rhys," he whispered urgently.

The man turned and grunted.

Balyn jerked his head toward the doorway. "I need to speak with you."

Rhys rose and followed him out into the misty gray twilight. They walked silently to the fortress gate. Once outside, they braced themselves against the sea wind, tucking their hands into their tunics. The wind was chilly, and both men felt the loss of the fire's warmth acutely.

"Is this matter so secret we must freeze to death discussing it?" Rhys groused.

"Aye, it is."

Rhys's shrewd eyes searched Balyn's face. "Out with it, then. I don't mean to stand here long."

"What do you think of this Goddess ceremony Maelgwn has planned?"

"He's completely lost his wits."

Balyn's head bobbed in agreement. "It's a vile, loathesome plan. No good can come of it, only censure from the Church and ridicule from his enemies. Why, I wouldn't be surprised if Bishop Gildas denounced him publicly!"

"Maelgwn's never played the fool like this before. What's come over him?"

Balyn lowered his voice to a mere whisper. "It's Rhiannon. He actually believes this ceremony will bring her back from the dead."

Rhys gave another snort of disgust. "I've never understood the king's attitude toward women. The way he carried on about the queen's death—why doesn't he just find another comely bitch to warm his bed? They all have the same thing between their legs. Sometimes I wonder if his mind isn't as addled as his enemies say."

"That's why it's our duty to protect him. We must prevent the ceremony. We simply can't allow it to take place."

"How do you mean to stop it?"

Although they were clearly alone, Balyn leaned even closer and lowered his voice. "Most of the other princes of Gwynedd are Christian. They would be as appalled by Maelgwn's plans as we are. I intend to summon them here for a council meeting. After they arrive, Maelgwn will be forced to abandon his plans."

Rhys's eyes bulged in surprise. "You would do this— thwart the king's will?"

"It's for his own good. I'm trying to protect him!"

"And when the other chieftains arrive, what do you mean to tell them? How will you explain the summons?"

"I don't know. Perhaps we could say Maelgwn called a council meeting to discuss the alliance with the Brigantes. Perhaps even form a delegation to visit the north and meet with their new king."

Rhys made a sour face. "There's no love lost between the other Cymry princes and the Brigantes. Maelgwn used the northern warriors to subdue these men. Why should they care who the Brigantes name as king?"

"It's the best idea I could come up with," Balyn said defensively. "I'm not sure it matters what we tell the other chieftains, as long as this blasphemous ceremony does not take place."

"I don't share your faith," Rhys said grimly. "Maelgwn could dance naked in the chapel and fuck on the very altar for all I care. But I agree this ceremony is a mistake. It makes the king look like a half-wit. Believing that his wife will return from the dead—what nonsense!"

"You'll help then? You'll compose the message to the other chieftains and deliver it?"

Rhys's dark eyes narrowed. "Aye," he answered after a moment. "I'll do it, and Maelgwn be damned. If he decides to banish me, there are plenty of other chieftains to take me in. The only men who can read and write these days are churchmen. I can make a fair living as a courier in any part of Britain."

"Don't talk as if we're betraying Maelgwn," Balyn said in an anguished voice. "We're trying to help him."

"Aye. But it's help he hasn't asked for, that he may never appreciate. Consider this carefully, Balyn. Do you do this for Maelgwn, or the Christian god?"

"Both," Balyn answered resolutely. "I do it for both of them."

"It's beautiful, Rhiannon." Arianhrodd smiled with delight as she looked down at her new gown. The fine wool cloth was a deep saffron shade with bands of crimson at the hem of the skirt and the long loose sleeves. "Truly a garment fit for a queen."

"Nay." Rhiannon shook her head. "Not a queen, a priestess."

"Very well then, a priestess. I'll look forward to wearing it at the ceremony at Degannwy."

Rhiannon's face clouded. "Are you sure this ceremony

is wise? Maelgwn's people believe I'm dead. My appearance will likely frighten them."

"Not if you play the part of the Goddess's daughter, the maiden of spring. They will remember the old magic, the old legends. Like Persephone, you disappeared into the world of the dead during the winter and are returning in the spring. They will greet your reappearance with awe and skepticism, but in the end they will accept you. Besides, you must make yourself known sometime. Even if you never return to Degannwy as Maelgwn's queen, rumors and whispers will inevitably reach his people that you're alive. This way we use your reappearance to glorify the Goddess. What could be more fitting?"

Rhiannon chewed her bottom lip uneasily but did not argue. Everything Arianhrodd said made sense, but she felt unsettled and uneasy about the plans for the ceremony. Maelgwn would be there. He would be watching her. What was to say he would not try to carry her back to Degannwy by force and hold her prisoner? The thought terrified her. Never to wander the beach again, never to go off to the woods by herself—she would die if she were trapped within the four square walls of Degannwy.

Surely Maelgwn would not do that to her. He was not an utterly selfish man. He wanted her to be happy. He cared that much for her. A stab of longing went through her, and she wondered again if she could continue to defy her husband's wishes. He was so strong, so compelling. When he confronted her in the hut, it had been a terrible struggle not to give in to him. She loved him so desperately, so passionately. If only she could have him, and keep her own soul as well.

She looked up. Arianhrodd was watching her with a look of compassion. "You're still troubled. Is it because of Maelgwn?"

Rhiannon nodded.

"He's very special. It's rare for the Lady to reveal herself to a man."

Arianhrodd met Rhiannon's startled gaze with a knowing look. "It's true. He experienced Her power when he was with you in the cave. I said the drug would give him visions, and it did. He journeyed very far for someone untrained."

Rhiannon took a deep, steadying breath. "I thought he behaved rather oddly. Never said a word, merely dragged me away to the cave and began to make love to me. His passion was even fiercer than usual, but I thought . . ." She blushed. "I thought it was because he was so glad to see me."

"Oh, there was that, too, I'm sure. But the Goddess was with him. He saw Her, felt Her. For a time, he believed he mated with the Lady Herself."

"But that's unfair!" Rhiannon put a hand to her mouth, shocked by her outburst. "I didn't mean that . . . it's only . . ."

Arianhrodd's dark brows rose. "You're jealous of Maelgwn's knowledge of the Goddess? Why?"

Rhiannon turned away, clenching her jaw. She had imagined she had some special relationship with the Goddess, but even in that Maelgwn outdid her. As a man and a king, he had great power—why should he receive the Goddess's gifts as well? "It's stupid of me to think such things," she said.

"Feelings are not stupid, Rhiannon. They must be accepted and understood."

"I don't understand any of it. I love Maelgwn so much, but I resent him as well. I think a part of me wants to hurt him, just as he did me."

Arianhrodd nodded. "That is only natural. He caused you great distress, even physical harm. You must express your anger about what he did, then let go of it."

"But how can I know he won't hurt me again?"

"You can't know that. All love is a risk."

Rhiannon was silent. She could feel the anger and bitterness welling up inside her, twisting her insides into an aching knot.

"If you think on it, you will realize Maelgwn has risked a great deal for you," Arianhrodd said. "He has agreed to put aside his anger at his sister. He imperiled his life when he took the drug and went to the spirit world to look for you."

"I want to take it," Rhiannon said abruptly. "I want to take the drug myself. I want to go to the other side."

"That would not be wise."

"Why?"

Arianhrodd's face was sorrowful, tender. "Besides the fact of your small physical size and delicacy and the damage the drug might do to your body, I don't think your spirit is ready to visit the spirit world."

"You had no such doubts of Maelgwn."

"Maelgwn had already confronted the darkness in his heart. There was nothing in him he had not faced before. But you—Rhiannon, there are so many things that weigh down your spirit and confuse you. I don't think you are ready for them to be revealed."

"And so, you make that choice for me. Like Maelgwn, you seek to protect me, to cage me in this world!" Rhiannon gave a sigh of frustration and stretched her arms out in a gesture of longing. "I want to know the magic. To make the journey to the other side. If I do not do it, I will never be free."

Arianhrodd nodded slowly. Her eyes were brooding, velvety dark. She looked as if she might weep. "Do what you must, Rhiannon. But I can't aid you. If you seek the other side, you must find the way there yourself."

Chapter 29

"Cynan's at the gate."

Maelgwn looked up with surprise. "What's he doing here?"

Eleri shrugged. "He said he had a summons from you."

Maelgwn rose quickly and left the council room, trying to recall any message he had sent to the chieftain who guarded the far southeastern coast of Gwynedd. He had been busy with plans for the ceremony, and all the fortress had been in turmoil since Gwenaseth's desertion, but surely he would remember sending out a summons.

"Maelgwn!" Cynan greeted him heartily. The chieftain's bony, hawklike face was amiable, but a hint of worry glinted in his eyes. "It's not the Irish, is it? We've had several raids ourselves, but nothing to call out a war troop for."

"Nay, the problem is under control here." Maelgwn saw the questioning look in Cynan's amber eyes and inwardly cringed. Blessed Jesu, what was he to do? It seemed discourteous to tell the man he had sent no message.

Cynan's gaze probed a little longer, then softened. "Rhys reached me three days ago. Can't say I mind making the journey. After sitting around my own hearth all winter, this is exactly what I need. The weather's fine, too."

Maelgwn was silent. He would welcome Cynan into the hall, and offer him some of the food prepared for the feast. He could explain later—when he thought of something to say.

He had barely sent a slave for some water for Cynan to wash with when another shout came from the gate. The old mountain warrior, Drun, came traipsing in, accompanied by a small escort of men as fierce and gnarled-looking as the craggy highlands themselves.

"Damn you, Maelgwn, this summons had best be important. The sheep are lambing up in the hills. If the weather weren't so mild, we'd never dare leave the flocks."

Despite Drun's harsh words, he wore a smile, and Maelgwn moved to meet him with a feeling of genuine warmth. He could hardly ask for a more solid ally than Drun. The mountain man had fought beside Cadwallon in the old days and never wavered in his loyalty since.

Maelgwn greeted each man in Drun's escort in turn, then led them into the hall. He whispered a few words in Eleri's ear, and the sentry dashed off to the kitchen to see that their guests were brought food and drink. Servants soon filed in with platters of fresh bread with honey, chunks of garlic-flavored cheese, and a large pot of dried apples boiled with spices. It was hardly an extravagant repast, but the visitors eyed the food with obvious pleasure.

Maelgwn's stomach was too convulsed with anxiety for him to even think of eating. These men had come a considerable distance; he must somehow make their journey worthwhile. He thought of using the ceremony as a reason for the summons, then discarded the idea. Drun would be insulted at being asked to leave his precious sheep for a religious festival, and any plan to honor one of the old gods would upset the devoutly Christian Cynan. He had to think of something else, some serious political crisis to explain why he called them to Degannwy.

The food was served, and Eleri came in with the announcement of another arrival. Maelgwn went out to discover Rhodderi and three of his sons waiting sullenly inside the fortress gate. The hair on Maelgwn's neck stood on end as he approached them. Rhodderi was the last person he wanted to see. Good God, had Rhys carried a message to every chieftain in Gwynedd inviting them to Degannwy?

As the day wore on, it appeared that Rhys had done exactly that. Every little while, there was a new arrival. Arwystl, Caw, Hyel, even ancient Cuneglassus—they wandered in on horseback, on foot, some accompanied by escorts, others alone. Elwyn was the last to arrive. He met Maelgwn's gaze uncertainly as he rode through the gate, then dismounted and embraced him. Maelgwn felt his eyes dampen. He wanted to tell Elwyn that Rhiannon was not dead, and ask if he and Gwenaseth would consider returning to Degannwy. There was no time. A hall full of chieftains waited.

The constant commotion at least served the purpose of delaying his need to explain the summons. By now, the visiting chieftains assumed he intended to announce his plans to them as a group. If he pretended that all summoned had not yet arrived, he could hold off his announcement until the morrow. Tonight he would distract them with the wine.

His mind worked furiously during the evening meal and the entertainments afterwards. Several of the chieftains pulled him aside and tried to get an inkling of his intentions, but he put them off firmly. They would all know when the others did, he insisted.

He was grateful he had so many musicians available to keep up the festive atmosphere; they were as great a boon as the wine. As the night wore on, most of the visitors appeared to have forgotten the serious purpose of the gathering. They ate and drank heartily, obviously enjoying themselves.

Maelgwn waited until his guests were well into their cups, then left the hall. He had a serious problem to solve, and he planned to begin by confronting the man he suspected was responsible for the whole mess.

He found Balyn outside the stables. Maelgwn's first officer gave him an uneasy look. "I was just seeing to our guests' horses," he said.

Maelgwn resisted the urge to slam Balyn into the rough wood of the stable wall. For hours, he had racked his brain, trying to figure out who was behind the summons. Rhodderi's appearance had put him off track, making him wonder for a time if his reluctant ally had contrived this false message to embarrass him. But Rhodderi's manner was as curious and puzzled as that of the other chieftains. Maelgwn did not think even the Old Wolf could feign innocence so convincingly.

That left only a troublemaker from within the fortress, and Rhys would never come up with such a plan alone.

"Someone has sent a message to all the Cymry chieftains asking them to assemble at Degannwy," he told Balyn tersely. "What do you know of it?"

Balyn blinked once, then set his mouth in a stubborn line.

"Lludd's name, Balyn, I'm too old to beat the truth out of you! No one but Rhys knows how to make my mark, but he couldn't have done this thing alone. It had to be you who sent the message. I want to know why!"

Balyn's mouth worked. "I . . . I couldn't let you go through with it . . . I couldn't let you do such a despicable thing!"

"What?" Maelgwn barked.

"The ceremony, the filthy rite honoring the Goddess."

"You did this to stop the ceremony?"

"Aye."

"But why? You know this is my only chance to win back Rhiannon."

"Rhiannon is dead!"

"But she isn't, I tell you. I saw her, I held her in my arms. I spoke to her."

Balyn shook his head. "It was a dream, a wicked vision meant to turn you away from the true God. Rhiannon is dead. Until she walks into the fortress and I see her for myself, I will believe that."

"So, you sent for all the Cymry princes, hoping that with them here, I would delay the ceremony?"

"Not delay, give up the idea altogether."

"I see. And now that they are gathered, what do you mean to tell them?"

"I don't know."

"You don't know!" Maelgwn could hardly contain his rage. "You fool! If we don't think up some good reason for summoning them, I'll be the laughingstock of Britain. If you care anything at all for the country we've built up together, you'd best help me quickly think of a plan."

"I will, I will." Balyn nodded rapidly.

Maelgwn felt his anger drain away, replaced by despair. Balyn had betrayed him. The one man he had always counted on had embroiled him in a wretched muddle that might cost him both his newly won power and the woman he loved. He numbly shook his head. "Why did you do this to me?"

"I told you . . ."

". . . a bunch of inane and superstitious horse dung. I want to know why you oppose this ceremony so much. I accept that you don't believe in the Goddess, that you think I am wasting my time trying to win Rhiannon back. But this deliberate, vicious meddling—what horrifies you so much that you would betray the trust and friendship of a lifetime?"

Balyn was near to breaking down. Maelgwn could see the quiver of his jaw, the sheen of tears in his great brown eyes.

"You were planning to honor an ancient vile faith," Balyn whispered. "The very thought of it makes my skin crawl."

"You despise the Goddess that much?"

Balyn nodded convulsively. "She represents the darkness of the past. She controls the waves that drown men, the rain that floods the valleys and washes away our homes and crops. She shrivels the grain so we starve. She is Life, but She is also Death. I believe in a God who has conquered Death, has transcended it. Christ offers us something beyond this life, beyond the suffering and hopelessness."

Maelgwn sighed. How did anyone understand another man's beliefs? The Christian faith had failed to heal him or to hold his heart, but Balyn seemed obsessed by it.

"I can accept your beliefs, but not that you have imposed them on me," Maelgwn said bitterly. "It was not the ceremony itself which mattered, but the chance to win Rhiannon back. Now, I may have lost her forever."

"You're giving up the idea of the ceremony?"

"I must. The wine is half gone. The fortress filled with men who would be as repulsed by the ceremony as you are. I will have a feast tomorrow. I will feed my people and provide entertainment, but there will be no calling down of the Goddess." He sighed again.

"Why does having Rhiannon back matter so much?" Balyn asked. "What good did she ever do you? She lost the only babe she ever conceived. She brought the ugliness of Esylt's betrayal back into your life. You're better off without her."

"She made me happy, Balyn. She brought me peace. Haven't you ever loved a woman?"

"I guess not. At least I've never known one whose interests I would put completely above my own."

Maelgwn turned away. He felt empty, lost. He should stay with Balyn and try to figure out some way to explain things to his guests, but he had no heart for it. His kingdom would have to take care of itself for tonight. Rhiannon—she was what mattered.

He slipped into the stables and saddled Cynraith, then left the fortress and took the now-familiar eastern road. It was a heartbreakingly lovely night, radiant with moonlight and warmed with a soft wind that whispered of springtime. The very loveliness of it increased Maelgwn's agony. If all had gone as planned, he might soon be enjoying Rhiannon's beauty by the moon's silver enchantment.

He put the despair from his mind. He would not grieve before it was necessary. By the time he reached the lonely stretch of beach where Arianhrodd's hut stood, he felt a vague sense of hope. Rhiannon was alive, and she had not refused to see him. That, in itself, was something.

He dismounted and stood staring at the small daub and wattle structure. Around the edges of the hide door, he could see the glow of the firelight. He pushed the door aside and leaned down to look in. Arianhrodd and the swarthy fishermen were in bed. They sat up and stared at him as he peered in the doorway. There was no sign of Rhiannon.

Maelgwn motioned to Arianhrodd, indicating that she should come out to speak to him. Then he extricated himself from the tiny doorway. In a moment, Arianhrodd appeared. She wore only a short tunic, and the breeze whipped her unbound hair.

"I've come to tell you," Maelgwn said. "There is no way the ceremony can take place."

Arianhrodd raised an eyebrow questioningly.

"It's not my choice," Maelgwn continued. "There are others involved. I can't make them participate in something they don't believe in."

Arianhrodd said nothing.

"Tell me where Rhiannon is."

"She's gone away. She plans to journey to the other side."

"What? Where is she going?"

"You have made the journey yourself. You must know what I mean."

Maelgwn's eyes widened, and his body tensed. Some men—and women—trained for years to learn how to leave their body and visit the other realm. Others used powerful and dangerous drugs, such as he had taken when he made his own journey in search of Rhiannon. But the easiest, and most accessible pathway to the other side was to experience death, or near death.

"You fear for her?"

Arianhrodd nodded. "I warned her against it, but she would not listen. She is determined to do this thing. She feels angry, trapped in a life she does not believe she has chosen."

"Did I . . . did I do this thing to her?"

Arianhrodd shook her head. "Your betrayal flung her onto this pathway, but the fault is not yours to bear alone. She feels trapped by the lies that have shaped her life. She does not understand that her freedom cannot be taken away by others. She does not know she has choices."

"What can I do? Where shall I look for her?"

"I can't tell you that."

Maelgwn stared at Arianhrodd, recalling the cozy image of the priestess in bed with her lover. "Why didn't you follow her or try to change her mind? How can you pretend all is well when Rhiannon's life is in danger?"

"There are worse things than death, King Maelgwn. Don't you know that yet?"

Maelgwn shivered as he took leave of Arianhrodd, although the night was unseasonably warm. No matter how he tried to tell himself that Arianhrodd was right, that death was not the end, his heart protested. He loved Rhiannon. He needed her in this world.

He glanced back at the fisherman's hut. He had forgotten to tell Arianhrodd the reason he sought Rhiannon this night. He had decided to accept Rhiannon on her terms. No longer would he claim Rhiannon as his wife or seek to have her return to Degannwy. He would meet with her whenever or wherever Rhiannon wished, but he would not pursue her against her will. If he gave Rhiannon her freedom, perhaps she would accept some part of his love.

A sob wrenched through him. If only his decision had not come too late!

Arianhrodd was right, Rhiannon thought wearily as she walked along the moonlit beach. She had not faced the darkness that dwelled inside her. It was there, a choking, overwhelming rage that threatened to drown her. All the lies, the betrayals, the disappointments of her life. She was angry at everyone. Not only Ferdic and Narana for failing to love her, and Llewenon for hurting her. But even Esylt, who loved her but perversely bound her to Maelgwn. And Gwenaseth, who protected her and comforted her but could not accept that she could not be a queen. And especially Maelgwn, who cherished her and brought her deep pleasure—and fought unceasingly to possess her soul.

A part of her hated them for chaining her spirit to this world, for preventing her from pursuing the knowledge she sought. Even Arianhrodd failed her. The priestess had suggested she was not ready, that she was too weak and vulnerable to undertake the journey. It was a galling thought, especially knowing that Arianhrodd had aided Maelgwn in his quest.

Rhiannon shook her head. She must let go of the anger,

she must be open and searching, or the Goddess would not come to her.

She looked around the moonlit beach. She had almost died here, along the coast near Degannwy. Instead, the Goddess sent her back among the living. What did it mean? What was her purpose? She glanced up at the moon, the Mother's face—peaceful, benevolent, changeless. Stretching her arms upwards, she felt the longing, the hunger humming through her. She wanted to know, to understand.

With quick impatient fingers, she undid her long braids and combed through her streaming hair. It fell heavy upon her back and shoulders as she stared again at the sky, basking in the moonlight. There was nothing between her and the Goddess now. Nothing except the thin fabric of her worn gown. She stripped it off and gloried for a moment in the gleam of her bare, white skin. Now, she was free.

The sand of the beach was soft and yielding beneath her feet. The moonlight danced on the waves before her, making sparkling patterns. She could hear music in the sea tonight. Above the pulsing beat of the surf, was another sound, a wild keening melody. It sought her out and pulled her nearer. There, down beneath the thrashing waves, the spirits called her to another realm. She remembered the first time she had walked into the sea and felt the enticing rhythm of the tide sucking her down. The ocean was the Mother's womb, safe, lulling, promising endless contentment.

If she dared, she could journey down to the very bottom of the sea itself, the place where the spirits lived . She had been very close before, once, twice. This time she would not fail. She would not turn back until she had gone to the very center of the bright light that awaited her on the other side.

The water was cold, numbingly so. Rhiannon took deep breaths, and walked further into the waves. The water felt dark and heavy, as if the gleaming moonlight only touched the surface. The reality beneath was deep, inexorable, grinding power. The Goddess was very strong, Rhiannon thought, to rule this massive, formless force that was the sea.

The sand shifted beneath her feet, and Rhiannon nearly lost her footing. She righted herself and whispered the Goddess's name, calling upon the Great Mother to protect her. Everywhere was the scent of the sea, the raw salty odor of blood and birth. The waves rose higher. They were almost to Rhiannon's neck now. There was nothing behind her, nothing she wanted more than this. She let herself float. Soon she would reach the bottom; the magic place, the sacred place, the source of life itself.

Cynraith's hooves made a soft thudding sound on the muddy trackway as Maelgwn headed towards the cliffs above the beach at Degannwy. The night was cloudless, and the moon lit the hills as bright as day. The air was even wetter than usual, a curtain of dampness the wind dangled in his face. Maelgwn reined Cynraith to a stop, then closed his eyes and listened to the rumble of the waves echoing in the distance.

He had sought Rhiannon unsuccessfully in the woods and along the coast near Arianhrodd's hut. As the night passed, he realized he had little hope of finding her. By now she would have found refuge in some hidden place. He prayed she was asleep, safe, lost in her dreams. He should be sleeping too, but he could not bear to return to Degannwy. To go home was to admit defeat.

He dismounted and let the horse wander off to graze. Walking to a place where the cliffs jutted off into empty space, he stared down at the moonlit beach. He felt the urge to jump, to know the thrill of hurtling through the air like a bird. The landing would bring brutal pain, but for those few moments he would be free. If Rhiannon had gone to the other side, he could join her there.

He turned away from the cliff. He would not give up hope. Once before, he had thought Rhiannon lost, then found her again. He would rest a moment, then renew his search.

His limbs shook with fatigue as he sat down on the damp grass. Wearily, he took off his cloak and spread it beneath him. He lay down, spread-eagle. He would lie here a moment, only a moment. Then he would continue his search.

He dreamed.

He was late to the ceremony. People were already gathered on the cliffs, chanting, drinking, dancing around the fires. He could hear the vague thunder of drums, the eerie melody of the pipes. He wandered to the center of the crowd. The people swirled around him, laughing, embracing. He watched them solemnly, feeling very far away.

He heard cries and shouts and turned to see people backing away from a dazzling light. It seemed as if a star had fallen to earth in their midst. Maelgwn watched as a small figure leaped out of the brightness. It was a woman, a woman whose skin was silver, shimmering with the brightness of the sea beneath the moonlight. Her hair was long and dark, and it whirled around her as she danced, barely covering her nakedness. The glow of her skin emphasized every sinuous line of her body. He admired her small, up-tilted breasts—the nipples black against the silver of her skin—her long, narrow back, her delicate legs. His loins tightened with desire.

She drew nearer, and he saw that her face was painted, her lips blood red, her eyes dark with kohl. She gave him a bold, mocking glance that thrilled him. He wanted her, this wild goddess, but he also feared her. He felt the power in her, the blazing energy she gave off in the misty night air.

Her dance changed, becoming slower and more seductive. She circled him, her small body twisting and swaying, casting rays of light into the air around them. With her mask of kohl and rouge and her wild hair, she reminded him of an animal, a mountain cat, stalking him. Her fingers grazed his body. She lingered her hands over his arms, his chest and then moved close, still swaying, to caress his back, his shoulders, his buttocks.

He trembled, afraid of the power he sensed in her, but drawn to the small enticing creature who swayed so near him. He could smell her, the warm, eager scent of a female in heat.

She touched his shaft, her dainty hands surprisingly strong and demanding. With thoughtless hunger, he reached out and lifted her up to straddle him. Her legs spread wide as he impaled her, then she wrapped them around his waist, clutching tightly.

He gasped from the pressure, the maddening sensation of her body sheathing him. He tried to move within her, but could not. She held him tightly; her hands dug into his arms. Throwing her head back, she exposed her slender neck, her small, perfect face.

He slumped to his knees, lowering her to the ground, driving into her. Her body took him in, swallowed him. The earth below them began to shake and quiver. The cliff gave way. He was falling.

He landed in water, not the ocean, but a fast-flowing river. The water foamed white, boiling over the rocks. He remembered the dream with the baby and the river and knew he must find Rhiannon. Soon it would be too late; she would be gone forever.

He took a deep breath and dived. The sun shone through the water, making everything so dazzling bright he could not see. He closed his eyes and searched the river bottom by feel. The rocks tore at his hands; his lungs ached from lack of air. There was no more time. He must go up to breathe, or die himself.

He woke gasping. His chest felt squeezed and tight. It took awhile for him to get his breath back and realize where he was. Someone was leaning over him, calling his name. His eyes struggled to focus. At first, he did not believe what he saw. He had been thrashing in the water, searching desperately for Rhiannon. Now he woke to find her mere inches away.

He reached up for her and pulled her down to lie on his chest. She was naked, trembling, and her hair was damp and cold. She pressed herself against him, weeping. He felt her fear, and a chill went through him.

"Oh, Maelgwn," she murmured. "I'm so glad you are safe."

He said nothing. His throat felt tight, and tears burned at the corners of his eyes.

She lifted her head, and he saw the wondering, far-away look on her face. "I tried to go to the other side, Maelgwn. I wanted to see Esylt . . . to ask her why . . . I wanted to see . . . our baby." Her throat convulsed. "I did not find them. When I was very far into the other realm, the mist thinned and I saw a woman . . . a woman I had never seen before. She was very beautiful, with dark hair and strange features. She carried a baby in her arms. When she saw me, she spoke your name."

Maelgwn gasped and sat up, pulling Rhiannon onto his lap. "Aurora," he whispered. "You saw Aurora."

Rhiannon nodded. "She told me to return to you. She said . . . you needed me."

Maelgwn closed his eyes against the emotions swelling his throat. Rhiannon had gone very far, to the very depths of the spirit world. It was a miracle that she lived, that she had returned to him. "How did you find me?" he asked in a wondering voice.

Rhiannon settled herself more comfortably against him.

Her voice remained awed. "When I came to awareness again, I found myself lying on the beach, soaking wet. I knew I had to find you. Somehow I was drawn here, to these cliffs, to the place where I first felt my spirit touch yours."

Maelgwn swallowed. "Oh, my sweet Rhiannon. I am so glad to have you back. Aurora spoke the truth," he whispered raggedly. "Without you, I am lost."

Rhiannon nuzzled his neck, and he felt the pressure of her soft breasts against his chest. The sensation aroused him, and he remembered his own dream. "And I dreamt you were the Goddess," he said. "You danced naked in the moonlight, and I knew your power." He took Rhiannon's hand and pressed it against his swelling erection. "You have held me in thrall since the beginning. Since you first knelt between my thighs and took me into your sweet, soft mouth. My soul was yours then, as it is now. You *are* the Goddess, Rhiannon, at least as She appears to me."

Rhiannon took her hand away to stroke his face. "I have wondered for months why the Goddess saved me. Now I know it is so I will love you, and bear your sons."

"Oh, aye, Rhiannon." Maelgwn's voice trembled. "Tonight, I will fill your womb with my seed. You will bear my children, and suckle them and love them."

He lifted her face, cupping her chin in his hand so he could look at her. There was mystery in her expression, the haunting, wild beauty that drew him. He felt the beating of her heart, the blood flowing through her limbs. He let himself be swallowed in the depths of her enigmatic eyes. His spirit merged with hers, floating in a velvety darkness.

"My beautiful Rhiannon. You do have power. You utterly ensorcel me."

She smiled faintly. His hand lingered upon her back and touched her soft bottom. "I want to mate with you," he whispered. "Get up so I can undress."

Rhiannon left the warmth of his embrace and stood.

Despite her nakedness, she did not feel the cool evening air. There was a fire inside her, heating her. With Maelgwn watching her, she felt beautiful, absolutely desirable.

She swung her hair back so he could see her body. Turning, she lifted her arms, flaunting herself. Across the few feet that separated them, she sensed the quickening of his pulse, the bubbling heat of his blood.

His hunger intoxicated her. She began to dance to the silent music the sea and the moonlight made together. The rhythm made her twirl wildly. Never had she felt so free. Her body was light, transparent. The bonds holding her to the earth loosened, and she felt as she had at the ceremony in the forest. She floated on a cool wind, flying in the darkness.

Maelgwn stopped her mad dance with his body hard against hers. He was naked, huge. But she did not fear him. He was a mere man, and she—she was a woman. He lifted her, and she opened herself to him, eagerly, triumphantly.

They were joined. The fire burned and seared between them. She gasped as he went to his knees, then pressed her down upon the ground. He kissed her as he loved her, hard, demanding kisses that sucked her soul from her body. She gave it willingly, knowing that he would return it to her, knowing that she possessed his as well.

A sea of sensation crashed over them, and they were lost in the waves of passion, throbbing, incessant, timeless. The splendor turned to vivid light, then darkness, and they found themselves mere flesh and blood creatures again, lying exhausted on the grassy cliff.

Chapter 30

In the distant east, dawn crept into the sky. Rhiannon shivered against her lover, then nestled closer. She sighed. "How do we return to the world after this?"

Maelgwn sat up. In the gathering light, she saw the lines of weariness on his face. His tanned cheeks were darkened by a day's whiskers, his beautiful blue eyes smudged with shadows.

"Jupiter be damned!" he whispered.

"What? What is it?"

"My fortress is crammed to bursting with my allies. They expect me to make some important pronouncement."

Rhiannon stood up and watched him, wondering. She would not be afraid; she would not.

He turned to look at her. His eyes blazed with determination. "I mean to take you back with me, Rhiannon. I will make you the reason for my summons. Will you go?"

This was it, the moment she had once dreaded. The moment when he asked her to come back, to leave her own life behind and become his queen again. The prospect no longer dismayed her. She knew now that she was meant to walk beside him. It was not a denial of who she was, but an affirmation.

She nodded slowly, and he stood and reached to caress her face. "It will not be easy," he said. "Many of them are wary of the old ways and the things you represent. It will take all your strength and courage to face them, but I know you will do it. You are my queen, my mate, my consort. We have overcome so much together—hate, despair, anger, even death. We will survive this as well."

Rhiannon dressed in Maelgwn's undertunic, then looked down at herself. Barelegged, barefoot, her hair thoroughly disheveled—she hardly looked like a queen. More like a grubby peasant girl, a wild fairy child at best.

Then Maelgwn came to her and kissed her, open-mouthed and hot. "You are beautiful," he said. "My blood turns to fire just looking at you."

She smiled back at him. When he said things like that and looked at her with his glowing blue eyes, she felt like a queen indeed.

Maelgwn went to find Cynraith, who was grazing some distance away. He returned with the stallion and lifted her up onto his back, then mounted himself. Rhiannon leaned back, feeling her husband's strong arms around her as he guided the horse. It was bliss to be near Maelgwn, to listen to the sound of his breathing, to feel his warm breath against her skin. There was peace between them, a deep peace bought by all they had gone through together. She wondered if there was anything strong enough to shatter her sense of contentment this morn. Even returning to Degannwy did not daunt her. With Maelgwn beside her, things would be as they should.

Cynraith's steady trot ate up the distance rapidly, and within moments they could see Degannwy, perched on the hill above the coast. The fortress looked much less threatening than Rhiannon remembered. It did not seem like a prison now, but merely a solid, sprawling hill-fort.

She had once been filled with awe at the size and grandeur of the place—and fear at the thought of the great king who commanded it. Now she returned, cradled in the arms of that king. She knew now that he was merely a man, a man who wept and worried and struggled. He needed her.

The gate was open, the courtyard crowded with people. Rhiannon could not remember ever seeing so many gathered there. Her stomach lurched suddenly, and she lifted her head and straightened her shoulders. She was a queen, after all.

At first, they went unnoticed in the confusion of the courtyard. Gradually, people began to recognize the king, then her. Faces went white, and some pointed or whispered. Rhiannon felt Maelgwn's arm tighten around her. She could sense his tension—not fear, but readiness for combat. The reminder that he was willing to fight for her made a lump form in her throat. She forced herself to smile and look calmly into the startled faces around her. The Goddess—she pleaded silently. *Be with me. Make me strong.*

They had almost reached the great hall when Rhun came running up, his eyes wide in amazement.

"Rhiannon! You're back!"

Maelgwn released her, and Rhiannon slid off the horse. Rhun had grown while she was gone. It seemed as if they looked at each other nearly eye to eye.

"I've missed you," she said with a smile. "I have come back to be with you and your father."

Rhun's embrace was exuberant, his words half-choked by tears. "How we have missed you, Rhiannon! Papa especially. I'm so glad you've returned."

Tears formed in Rhiannon's eyes, but she did not yield to them. This was the warmest welcome she would receive. She must be prepared to face the others—those who would think her a witch, an enchantress. Those who resented Maelgwn's love for her.

Rhun's greeting seemed to reassure the people standing nearby, and Rhiannon felt a lessening of the fear her appearance had roused at first. Maelgwn moved quickly. After hugging Rhun, he sent his son on his way, then turned and led the crowd into the hall.

Maelgwn went to the fire, taking her with him. He took his place at a table near the hearth and pulled her down to sit beside him. The others gathered around them, some sitting at the trestle tables, others standing. Rhiannon saw many unfamiliar faces; she guessed they were the other chieftains of Gwynedd. Their eyes showed surprise, curiosity . . . and frank hostility.

When the assemblage quieted, Maelgwn turned to Rhiannon and kissed her. The kiss held little of Maelgwn's usual passion. It was not a show of affection, but a proclamation, a challenge. The men's reactions varied widely, from amusement to anger. Rhiannon was relieved to see satisfied grins on the faces of most of Maelgwn's officers. Except Balyn—he wore a look that could best be described as terrified. Rhiannon was puzzled; Balyn had always been so easygoing.

Maelgwn cleared his throat and spoke in his deep, rumbling voice. "All of you have heard the tale of my wife's disappearance this past winter. As you can see, thanks to the Goddess, she has been restored to me. I called you here to join in celebrating my queen's return." He paused for a moment, then again spoke in a challenging tone. "If any of you have doubts about the events of this winter or Rhiannon's fitness to stand at my side, speak now, for I will never raise the matter before you again."

Rhiannon's heart lurched as a tall man whose auburn hair was going gray stepped forward.

"Is this another trick of the clever Dragon? Did you conjure her up out of the mist with the aid of the Goddess, Maelgwn? I think not."

Rhiannon held her breath. This man was Maelgwn's

enemy, Rhodderi, she was certain of it. He meant to make his stand here, before all of Maelgwn's allies. He would use her to make her husband look the fool, to weaken Maelgwn's influence over the other Cymry chieftains. She had to say something in her husband's defense.

Before she could gather her thoughts and speak, another voice broke in sharply. The man's rough wolf-skin cloak marked him as being from one of the mountain tribes, and his weathered, toothless visage suggested he was as ancient as the peaks of Eryri themselves.

"Your words are disrespectful, Rhodderi. Maelgwn has met with us in good faith. We owe him a chance to explain. I would hear the full story ere I judge."

Although the old warrior's words were reasonable, they aroused Rhiannon's apprehension even more. What could Maelgwn possibly say? The truth was too strange and incredible to satisfy these hardened men. She glanced at Maelgwn and saw him frown. He, too, realized that the facts as they knew them would not be accepted here. Before she could lose her nerve, Rhiannon stood. "I would like to speak," she said.

There were startled looks among the men, and the pressure of Maelgwn's hand on her shoulder was hard and swift. Rhiannon shook her head at his warning and continued. "It is my place to explain, for I am the cause of this . . . this confusion."

"'Tis not your fault, Rhiannon," Maelgwn murmured, leaning toward her.

She turned to him, begging him with her eyes. *I must do this, Maelgwn,* she said silently. *I must.*

He nodded. Rhiannon turned back to the others. Her hands trembled; her heart thundered in her chest. She had never spoken before a group of men before. If she had attempted such a thing with Ferdic's council, she would have been laughed at and sent away. And these men were not Brigante warriors indulging a princess they had known from babyhood; they were grim, suspicious men. Some of them already seemed to hate her.

She took a deep breath to steady her voice. "It all began some weeks ago, slightly before the snow moon. I quarreled with my husband, and when we could not reconcile, I left the fortress. I went down to the beach to be alone. While I was there, I weakened and grew insensible from the cold. I collapsed and would have died there, except a kind fisherman found me and took me to his home." She paused for a breath, surprised at how self-assured and calm she sounded. "He and his wife revived me and cared for me. I meant to return to Maelgwn, truly I did. But I was afraid he was still angry at me. I put off returning until the days stretched into weeks."

She paused and looked around at the solemn faces of the men. They were listening at least, and she could sense some of them were sympathetic to her tale.

"I should not have grieved my husband so," she continued. "It was wrong to worry him. But I was sore afraid. It took me a long time to convince myself that I dared let my husband know I lived. By then, Maelgwn had heard I was living with the fisherfolk. He came looking for me. He found me, and we were . . . reconciled."

No one spoke for a moment, then Maelgwn's cavalry chief, Gareth, cleared his throat loudly. "There you have it. No witchcraft or magic, merely an errant wife who defied her husband and was afraid she would be punished for it. I say Maelgwn should beat her soundly, then take her back." He cast a sly glance at the king. "Of course, knowing Maelgwn, I doubt beating is what he has in mind."

There were murmurs and slight smiles among the group, but Rhiannon sensed that the confrontation was far from over.

"Lady Rhiannon's story is incomplete." A startlingly handsome young chieftain spoke up. From his glossy dark hair and piercing gray eyes, Rhiannon guessed he was

Arwystyl, one of Maelgwn's coastal allies. She remembered Gwenaseth describing his striking looks. "What of the strange rumors we have heard this winter? Lady Rhiannon calls the conflict with her husband a quarrel, but surely it must have been more than that. It was reported that Maelgwn stabbed his wife before she left the fortress. Few men draw their knife upon their wives." Arwystyl glanced at Rhiannon suspiciously, then searched Maelgwn's face with a steady gaze. "I would like to know what Lady Rhiannon did to make you want to murder her."

Maelgwn made no response, and Rhiannon felt her own throat close up. She doubted these men would understand the truth of who her mother was.

"Perhaps Maelgwn is afraid to tell us the nature of the quarrel." Rhodderi broke the silence with a voice thick with malevolence. "Perhaps he thinks we would not like to know the reason he attacked his wife."

Everyone turned wary eyes toward Rhoderri, and Rhiannon's blood went chill. What did this man know that made him smile in such a mocking, self-assured way?

Rhodderi licked his lips slowly, looking exactly like a hungry wolf preparing to feast. "The truth is, Maelgwn stabbed his wife because he finally discovered who she was." His smile broadened. "Tell me, Maelgwn, which repels you most—the fact that Rhiannon is your niece as well as your wife, or that she is Esylt's daughter?"

Rhodderi's words struck like a stone thrown into a still pool. The ripples fanned outward as the implications struck one man after another. Faces went pale and shocked. Some made the ancient sign against evil; others, like Balyn, crossed themselves. Only Maelgwn retained control. He put his hand upon Rhiannon's shoulder, his touch firm and insistent. Although she could not see him, she guessed his gaze met each man in the room, warning them, commanding their silence without a word.

"What Rhodderi says is true," he announced in a calm,

even voice. "I have since reconciled myself to the facts of Rhiannon's birth. I intend to keep her as my wife anyway. That is the end of it."

Cynan, a southern chieftain whom Rhiannon recalled visiting Degannwy in the fall, responded in an equally reasonable tone. "With all due respect, Maelgwn, this is a serious thing Rhodderi has brought before us. If Rhiannon is Esylt's daughter . . ." He shook his head. "It seems very close to incest."

"Still, there is a tradition for it." Old Caw, the overlord of the rich island of Mona, spoke up. Rhiannon vaguely remembered his craggy face and thick mane of white hair from the night of her wedding feast. He was an old ally of Maelgwn's, a man who had backed her husband since the early days of his kingship. "It has long been a practice to mingle royal blood with royal blood," Caw noted. "We knew Ferdic and Maelgwn were kin of sorts when the wedding was contracted, and that seemed only to enhance the alliance. As long as they are not father and daughter, or brother and sister, I have no worries about the closeness of their kinship."

"The blood tie between the two is not as close as you think," the old chieftain garbed in wolfskins announced suddenly. "Few men know this, but Esylt was only a half-sister to Maelgwn."

"What?" Maelgwn's gasp of surprise was echoed by murmurs from the other men. Everyone stared at the old high-lander, waiting for him to explain. He grinned toothlessly. "It was before your time, all you young ones. Only Caw and I . . ." He gestured to the white-haired chieftain. "We're the only ones old enough to remember. You see, Queen Rhiannon—that is, not this Rhiannon, but the one that would have been her grandmother—the queen hated her husband. While he lived, she did not dare plot against him, but neither was she faithful. Maelgwn's sister, Esylt, was sired by a man other than Cadwallon."

"A convenient lie," Rhodderi sneered. "How could anyone know who bedded whom so many years ago? Old Drun is making this up, trying to save Maelgwn from disgrace."

Drun bristled, his mouth working as he sought to control his anger. "Damn fool! I was fighting beside Cadwallon when you were only a babe at your mother's teat! There is no one living to back me in this, but at one time it was well known among Cadwallon's men that his queen strayed from his bed." His voice softened, and his eyes went distant at the memory. "In truth, I heard of Esylt's parentage from her real father. The man didn't brag of it either; he told me because he was disgusted with himself for betraying his king. 'All this guilt,' he said, 'And all I have to show for it is a bad-tempered, haughty lass.' He was disappointed that his seed had begot a female while Cadwallon had sired five lusty sons off the same woman."

The room was silent for a moment, then Cynan spoke, his voice as cool and temperate as ever. "I would like to believe your story. But considering the strong resemblance between Maelgwn and Esylt, it's hard to imagine they had different fathers."

Drun shrugged. "They both took after Rhiannon. In fact, of all the babes Rhiannon bore, only Maelgrith favored the king. Just as well, too. Cadwallon was an ugly bastard, while the queen . . ." He bestowed a toothless leer upon Rhiannon. "She was well nigh as fair as her granddaughter."

For a time, no one spoke. It seemed as if everyone felt they had learned too much too fast. One astounding disclosure led immediately to another.

"Enough of this." Gareth interrupted the silence impatiently. "The king and his wife are not horses. It's unseemly for us to debate their bloodlines as if they were no more than breeding stock."

"Well, I, for one, am not satisfied!" Rhodderi thundered. "Whether or not Esylt and Maelgwn shared a father, the fact is, Esylt was a wicked, treacherous woman, and Rhiannon is her daughter. How do we know that Esylt's evil will not be passed on to Maelgwn's heirs?"

There were murmurs around the room, and Rhiannon felt a new weight of grief. She had known Esylt was reviled among Maelgwn's people; she had not guessed the extent of the Cymry's hatred for her mother.

Maelgwn sighed wearily. "I have agonized on this very thing ever since I discovered the truth. If Rhiannon bears me a child, will we unleash the curse, the ungodly lust for power that tore my family apart and nearly destroyed Gwynedd?" He sighed again, and the sadness of his face made Rhiannon want to weep. "I can't help but think that evil is not a thing carried in the blood, but something learned," he continued. "Esylt was evil, aye, but she learned it. My mother taught her to scheme and plot from the time she was a little girl."

His glance met Rhiannon's, and she saw the determination there. His gaze moved slowly around the room, his eyes meeting each man's in turn. "This I vow—if any of my sons by Rhiannon ever appears to have inherited my sister's evil, I will see to it that he gains no share of my kingdom."

Rhiannon's heart twisted in her chest at Maelgwn's words. For her sake, Maelgwn was ready to repudiate his son's heritage. For a man like Maelgwn, whose very soul was one with his kingdom, it was an incomparable expression of love. Yet, even as she recognized Maelgwn's sacrifice, the thought of what he promised worried her. His son would be her son, and she was not sure she was willing to barter away her unborn child's future so easily.

Maelgwn's words were accepted with nods and quiet sounds of agreement. Only Rhodderi appeared unpacified. His jaw clenched with anger, and when he spoke, his voice was harsh. "Once again, Maelgwn's fine words, his dedication to Gwynedd, have won you over. But you are fools,

all of you. Maelgwn is a weak king, a man ruled by his cock
and his heart rather than his mind and sword arm. I will
not swear my allegiance to such as him!''

They all watched in silence as Rhodderi stalked out,
followed by three young men. Rhiannon guessed that they
were his sons.

Caw spoke. ''Well, that's no surprise. Rhodderi's always
been a troublemaker. I'm amazed he's been loyal this
long.''

''Aye, you are right,'' Cynan said. ''He will honor no
king but himself.''

''The rest of you . . .?'' Maelgwn asked. ''You are satisfied? You will keep your agreements with me?''

''Aye.'' ''Aye.'' ''Aye.'' ''And aye for me as well.'' The
other Cymry chieftains nodded in turn to Maelgwn, reaf-
firming their loyalty. Rhiannon breathed a sigh of relief.
She had not destroyed the allegiance of the other Cymry
princes to Maelgwn. For now, Gwynedd was safe.

Drun gathered his wolfskin around his shoulders and
sent another leer in Rhiannon's direction. ''It's time we
made ourselves scarce until the feasting. We must let
Maelgwn and his wife reconcile properly.''

Maelgwn stopped the old chieftain with a raised hand.
''Stay, Drun. Please. There are questions only you can
answer. You and Balyn.'' He gave his first officer a hard
look. ''I would speak with you *both* alone.''

Some of the men looked surprised, but Rhiannon was
not. Too many secrets had been casually revealed this day.
Maelgwn would want to know who had betrayed the secret
of her parentage, as well as the truth of his own mother's
indiscretions.

Maelgwn's eyes met hers. She went to him and leaned
her face against his chest. It did not seem fair he must
endure these new trials. She would do anything to spare
him, but it was not possible. The truth must be brought
out into the open.

"I will wait for you," she whispered. He nodded, his eyes bright with love, and she left him.

"Balyn swears he told no one about you and Esylt," Maelgwn said wearily. "I'm inclined to believe him."

Rhiannon nodded. She found it difficult to think of Balyn betraying Maelgwn. They had been together so long, and Balyn was not the sort for secrets and intrigue.

"How could Rhodderi possibly have known the truth? Surely he couldn't have guessed."

Rhiannon reached up to smooth the worry lines from her husband's brow. They were in their bedchamber, having left the feasting as soon as it was possible to do so politely. After their own private reunion on the cliffs, the merrymaking in the great hall seemed anticlimactic. The main surprise was that Arianhrodd had come to the feasting. After greeting Rhiannon with a warm hug, she teased Maelgwn about his remaining obligation to the Goddess. It made Rhiannon feel good to see her former protector and know the priestess believed Rhiannon's true place was beside her husband.

It was also a relief to converse with someone who did not have endless questions to ask her. Rhiannon had explained her rescue by Ceinwen to a dozen women, as well as an anxious Elwyn. He would be departing in the morning to bring Gwenaseth and their boys back to Degannwy. It seemed Elwyn's wife, for all her complaining, sorely missed overseeing Maelgwn's fortress. Rhiannon was very pleased at the thought of having Gwenaseth at her side again. Part of her understanding with Maelgwn was that she would not be forced to supervise the operations of Degannwy. She would be free to ply her needle and cast her pots—when she was not seeing to her husband's needs.

Rhiannon moved her hand down to stroke Maelgwn's

broad chest. Despite her soothing touch, Maelgwn's troubled look remained.

"Rhodderi was asking odd questions when I saw him last winter," he said. "I wonder if he knew even then. But how could he? How could anyone chance upon such an ironic twist of circumstance without some sort of hint?" Maelgwn's eyes rested on Rhiannon's features appraisingly. "You do bear a vague resemblance to my mother. It's a matter of your small size and the delicate cast of your features. Nothing that a man who has only seen the other Rhiannon once or twice in his life could ever guess."

"If it troubles you so much, why don't you ask Rhodderi how he knew the truth?"

Maelgwn's expression contorted with disgust. "He'd only taunt me and refuse to say." He patted Rhiannon's cheek. "Don't you understand, *cariad*? If Rhodderi knows such secrets about us, it means there's a spy at Degannwy."

"One of the servants?"

"What of Taffee? Do you mistrust her?"

"Nay, for all her impertinence, Taffee is too impressed with her role as my body servant to betray me. Did you see her greet me? She's always said such bold, rude things; I never thought she'd cry with pleasure to have me back."

"You hold yourself too cheap, Rhian. It wasn't only Rhun and Taffee who wept with joy to see you again. I swear, there was hardly a woman in the hall whose eyes weren't misty."

"They were all envying me the look on your face, my love." Rhiannon rolled over to press herself against Maelgwn's outstretched body. "It's not every husband who dares defy the Church and half his allies to welcome back his errant wife."

Maelgwn grinned like a boy, the worry lines on his face vanishing. "Who cares what they think? So, they believe I am ruled by my cock and my heart. What man isn't, if he be honest?"

"Are you sure your talk of my powers wasn't merely cheap flattery?" Rhiannon purred. She moved her fingers down her lover's body and entwined them in the drawstring to his trousers. "I vow I mean to test my hold over you— tonight and every night."

"Mmmmmm." Maelgwn mumbled against her hair. "Tempt me then, *cariad*. I vow I shall fail each and every time."

Sometime later they lay naked and content. Maelgwn reached out to idly pat Rhiannon's narrow belly. "If I haven't planted a babe yet, it's not for want of trying."

"I'm curious, Maelgwn. When I miscarried, you said you didn't care if I ever bore you a child. What changed your mind?"

Maelgwn shrugged. "Perhaps after coming so close to losing you, I'm satisfied the Goddess doesn't plan to take you from me in childbed. I never had the chance to know Rhun when he was small. I have a deep need to discover what fatherhood is like from the beginning. I can scarce imagine what it feels like," he added wistfully. "To have a mother and father who love each other and their children as well."

"Does the news of your mother's unfaithfulness grieve you?"

"I'd be a fool to let it. I knew exactly what my mother was, before I was Rhun's age."

Rhiannon touched his cheek softly. Despite Maelgwn's harsh words, she was sure Drun's revelation had hurt her husband. "I love you enough to make up for a dozen mothers," she assured him. "Truly, I do."

Chapter 31

Rhiannon lifted her face to the warm sun streaming down through the budding birch trees, expecting the beauty of woods in springtime to banish the lingering anxiety that nagged at her. When the tension inside her did not ease, she sighed and continued down the forest pathway.

She could not forget Maelgwn's worry that there was a spy at Degannwy—someone who had discovered the truth of her relationship to Esylt and shared the news with the traitorous Rhodderi. Despite Maelgwn's doubts, she sensed no treachery at Degannwy. Was it possible that someone at Catraith had overheard Ferdic's deathbed confession and carried the secret south?

Rhiannon shook her head. She did not want to dwell on the unpleasantness of the past. She would think of the good things instead. Her mind turned to Maelgwn, and her gloomy mood lifted. Nothing had ever felt so right, so natural as to wake up beside her dark, massive husband each morning. She could scarcely wait for him to open his glorious blue eyes so she could see the love there, the contentment. He filled her soul with his body, his voice, his scent. Even now, she carried a part of him within her.

She reached down and touched her belly tenderly. It was too soon to be sure, but her senses told her that a child grew inside her. Maelgwn's baby. A faint sadness drifted across her mind as she thought of the other child she had lost. Nay, she would not grieve for it. The dead babe's spirit was free to find another body in which to return to the living.

Breaking her reverie, she walked faster. A plover sprang up from the forest floor with a frantic cry and a flutter of feathers, startling her. She shook her head at the foolishness of her quickened breath and pounding heart. Here in the king's forest, she was safe; even Maelgwn admitted it. He had said she might walk alone here if she promised not to be gone from Degannwy too long. He meant to allow her her freedom, he said. Her spirit could not endure to be trapped inside the walls of a fortress. But, then, neither could his. He often came walking or riding with her, enjoying the peace and freedom of the woods or the beach as much as she did.

But this day, Maelgwn had left early to visit Cynan's holdings. It was time, he said, to begin making the rounds of his allies. He would often be gone throughout the sun season. Rhiannon would go with him sometimes, but she must also learn to do without him for a week or more at a time. Rhiannon smiled ruefully at the thought that even though she had won her husband's heart, she must share his soul with Gwynedd.

She touched her midsection again. If her instincts were true, she would likely be too busy this summer with the travails of carrying Maelgwn's child to miss him grievously. Already she experienced nausea in the morning and a slight lightheadedness when she got up suddenly. If the fine weather held, she meant to visit Arianhrodd and ask

her advice on foods and potions she might take to assure
the babe thrived.

Thinking of healing herbs, Rhiannon spied some May
lilies growing beneath a bush. She unhooked her knife
from her belt and bent to cut some of tiny, white flowers.
They made an excellent treatment for nervous disorders,
headaches and gout, and could only be found in early
summer. She filled the pouch at her waist with the fragrant
blooms before refastening the small curved knife and continuing on. It pleased her to be able to provide remedies
and potions for Maelgwn's people. Their acceptance of
her return to Degannwy had surprised her. They had not
blamed her for Maelgwn's grief over the winter, and they
seemed genuinely happy to have her back.

A relieved Gwenaseth had returned to the fortress and
resumed her former duties. She still grumbled about being
overworked, and the servants avoided her sharp tongue,
but underneath her brusqueness, Gwenaseth also seemed
content.

Rhiannon considered Gwenaseth's delight when she
told her of the babe. She had seemed almost as excited
as Rhiannon was. She hoped it was a girl, Gwenaseth said.
Having herself borne four future warriors for Maelgwn's
army, it seemed only fair that the queen's first child be a
daughter. Rhiannon had laughed and told Gwenaseth she
did not care in the least whether the babe be male or
female.

There was a scuffling sound in the bushes, and Rhiannon's carefree mood faded. A stifling dread wrapped itself
around her heart. Although the sunlight still trickled down
through the budding branches, and the sweet scents of
blooming flowers and growing things drifted on the
breeze, underneath the tranquil atmosphere, Rhiannon
sensed danger.

She took a cautious step, listening. There was no sound
except the trill of birds and the music of the wind. Even

so, her skin prickled, and her muscles tensed. She had the feeling she was being watched by eyes other than those of the forest creatures. Slowly, she turned, scanning the dappled, shadowy woods with the alertness of a doe. Her body jerked as a voice came from behind her.

"I see you have lost your forest ways, Rhiannon. There was a time when I could no more surprise you than I could a roe deer."

Rhiannon's eyes widened as she recognized the voice and then the man to which it belonged. "Llewenon," she whispered.

He stepped forward, grinning. He looked little different than when she had last seen him. His greasy brown hair and beard were threaded lightly with silver now, the lines etched more deeply in his tanned face, but his gray eyes were the same. Closed, opaque, almost guileless, they failed utterly to reveal his thoughts. It was one of his greatest tricks; Rhiannon had never known anyone who could lie as smoothly and convincingly as this man.

"You are surprised to see me. Did you think me dead?"

Rhiannon shook her head. "What are you doing here?" Her voice sounded strangled.

"I thought I might pay a visit to the great King Maelgwn. Perhaps he needs a bard to brighten his evenings with a tale or two."

"Maelgwn has a bard," Rhiannon responded. The terror inside her deepened, clenching her guts. "In fact, he has two. Taliesin and Aneurin are renowned throughout Britain for their melodious voices and clever stories."

Llewenon shrugged. "Mayhaps he tires of them. I'm sure Maelgwn has not heard any of the tales I tell. I would entertain him well."

Rhiannon suppressed a rising wave of nausea. "Maelgwn won't welcome you," she warned.

Llewenon's eyes were all startled innocence. "Why not? Have you told him the truth? Does he know his bride was sullied ere he took her maidenhead? Did you tell him how I put my hands upon you, how I defiled your scrawny body?''

Llewenon took two steps closer. His eyes glittered, the mask of guilelessness lifted. ''I doubt he will want you once he knows. What man would wish to pleasure himself on your tainted flesh, knowing what you are?''

Rhiannon shook her head. She would not listen. His words were evil. Maelgwn knew she was not a maiden when she came to their marriage bed. He would not care. He loved her.

''Ah.'' Llewenon smiled. ''I see you have not dared to tell your husband about me. You were afraid of what he would think. Now I am here to refute your claim that I ravished you, to tell him how you reveled in my touch. He will always have doubts.''

Llewenon's voice was silky, and he moved even closer. He reached out, as if to stroke her cheek. Rhiannon froze. She could not seem to control her body. She watched in horror as his brown fingers touched her arm.

Why had she not told Maelgwn the truth of Llewenon's attack long ago? Was it all revulsion at the memory? Was there not also a grain of fear inside her that Maelgwn would be disgusted? She had been so stupid to trust Llewenon, to go off alone with him. Maelgwn would see that. He would know what a detestable fool she was.

''There now.'' Llewenon pretended to soothe her. ''I'll protect your secret. Perhaps I won't go to your husband's fortress after all. You're the reason I've come here, not Maelgwn.''

Llewenon's other hand tightened around Rhiannon's wrist, and she gasped in fear. ''What is it? What do you want from me?''

''The same thing I've always wanted.'' Llewenon's eyes, so close, mesmerized her like a snake's.

''What do you mean to do?''

Llewenon smiled his soft, innocent smile. "You remember, don't you, the feel of me inside you?"

Her stomach roiled. Her vision faded to dark spots. "And if I refuse?" she managed to ask.

Llewenon's fingers tightened brutally around her wrist. "Then Maelgwn will pay. Your beloved husband will die."

Rhiannon closed her eyes. This could not be happening. The Goddess would not save her from death only to suffer again. There must be some way out of this trap.

Her eyes flared open. "If I do what you wish, will you leave Maelgwn be?"

Llewenon shrugged. "Who knows? It is Rhodderi who plots Maelgwn's death." Llewenon's lips curled into a sly, repulsive smirk. "If you please me well, I might be persuaded to forget Rhodderi's plan."

"And what is his plan?"

Rhodderi shook his head. "You've changed, Rhiannon. Now you ask questions. You probe my mind as if you have a right to know my thoughts. But I am much stronger than you. You cannot best me in a battle of wits."

Rhiannon's heart sank. Llewenon was right. She was no match for his skill in sensing weakness. He was a master at it.

Another thought came to her then, startling her from her despair. "How do you know Rhodderi?" she asked. "Did you travel to his court as a bard?"

"Of course. He was pleased to welcome me. Unlike others, he is discerning enough to appreciate my gifts."

Rhiannon's mind worked frantically. She must discover the connection between Rhodderi and Llewenon. Llewenon, by himself, could not hope to harm Maelgwn, but in league with the treacherous Rhodderi, he presented a real danger to her husband. She forced her voice to calm. "How long have you been at Rhodderi's court?"

Llewenon smiled. "Long enough to gain his confidence,

to arrange things so he is in my debt. He does not give orders to me. No man does.''

Llewenon's voice lowered to a hiss, and the sound affected Rhiannon like the deadly warning of a serpent. Again, she froze. Her limbs became utterly rigid, her body so paralyzed she could scarcely breathe. Llewenon's hand climbed her arm. He moved closer so she could smell his sour breath. "I know all your secrets, Rhiannon. Long ago, I overheard Esylt and Ferdic talking, arguing about your future. Knowing who you were, I did not think Ferdic would care if I shamed you.''

His fingers continued crawling upwards. They stopped on her shoulder and cruelly squeezed. "I never guessed Esylt would succeed in forcing Ferdic to punish me. What an evil bitch your mother was." Rhiannon felt Llewenon's spittle spray her face. He was inches away, his weathered features contorted with hatred. "Because of you, Ferdic banished me. Me—the finest bard who ever graced his court—banished because I dallied with a skinny red-haired whore, a slave's bastard!''

Rhiannon closed her eyes. She wanted to faint, to escape into unconsciousness, even death. But she could not leave Maelgwn to be entrapped in this creature's foul schemes. She must not swoon. She must find the strength to fight Llewenon.

She took a deep breath and forced her eyes open. "You told Rhodderi that Esylt was my mother, didn't you?''

"Aye. He was very pleased. He believed he could use the knowledge to ruin Maelgwn. How furious he was when his plan failed. Still, his honor demands he defeat Maelgwn. But he hasn't the men to succeed, unless he uses treachery.''

Llewenon's bitter mood seemed to vanish, and he smiled a wicked, thoughtful smile. "Rhodderi hopes to use you to lure Maelgwn into a trap. It is said your husband loves you. It would be amusing to see if he loves you enough to follow you to his death.''

Rhiannon's heart went cold. She did not doubt that Maelgwn would try to rescue her. The thought that he might die because of her was unbearable. She must keep Llewenon talking. Appeal to his pride.

"This plan of Rhodderi's—you mean to go through with it?" she asked. "You will let him tell you what to do?" Llewenon's smile faded, and Rhiannon continued on, disregarding the pounding of her heart. "You said yourself, it's me you want, not Maelgwn. Are you Rhodderi's servant then, that you follow his instructions even if it ill serves your needs?"

"I'm no man's servant," Llewenon ground out. "I don't need Rhodderi. It's he who needs me. Without me, there is no hope he will defeat Maelgwn."

"And if I give you what you want, will you leave Maelgwn alone?"

The wild look in Llewenon's eyes faded. His expression went cold and dead. "You're in no position to bargain." His hand moved down to cup Rhiannon's breast. "What I want from you, I will take. I mean to make you pay for what Ferdic did to me."

He squeezed her breast until tears formed in Rhiannon's eyes and she bowed her head in misery. It was terrifying to be so close to Llewenon's malevolence. His intentions were clear; he meant to rape her even more brutally than before. This time he might kill her. Or the babe . . .

The thought flashed through Rhiannon's mind, stunning her with its implications. Somehow she must not only protect Maelgwn, but his child. She would not let this babe die.

A wave of anger and determination swept through her. She ignored the pain of Llewenon's cruel caress and spoke. "It would be unwise for you to take me here. My husband warned me not to be gone too long. If I don't return to Degannwy soon, he'll send soldiers after me."

"You seek to protect me from your husband's men? How very touching." Llewenon sneered. "I need no protection. My powers are great. Do you think I can't elude Maelgwn's bumbling warriors?"

Rhiannon shook her head, trying to clear it. There must be some way to distract Llewenon from his violent intentions. "Why do you want me?" she whispered, deliberately making her voice as meek and frightened as possible. "You've had me before, and you said I was too thin and pale to satisfy you. Why do you want me now?"

Llewenon's voice softened to a velvety whisper. "Long ago, you said you wanted to learn sex magic. Now, we will learn together."

"I have no power. I gave up my dreams of magic long ago."

"You lie! All of Gwynedd says you have bewitched your husband—that he scarce strays from your side." Llewenon's fingers slid to her neck and tightened. "You have some of your mother's skill. She also bent proud men to her will. It was sex magic she used. You will teach me what she taught you; you will share your skill!"

Rhiannon struggled to breathe. Until now, she had not been able to follow Llewenon's twisted thoughts well enough to devise a plan against him. She had always thought he hated her because she was weak. Now he spoke as if he were jealous. Could he really have hurt her because he envied her?

"I will teach you." She nodded confidently. "But not here."

"Where?"

Rhiannon straightened, silently calling upon the Goddess to aid her. To her surprise, Llewenon's talonlike hands slid away as she summoned the energy, the weightlessness she felt in the sacred circle. She was light, transparent, her soul set free, connected to her body by only a gossamer strand.

She returned to her body and glanced at Llewenon. There was a look of awe on his face. "What god do you call on?" he demanded. "What is the source of your power?"

"The Great Mother of us all, the Goddess."

Llewenon's eyes widened even further. "The Goddess! You worship a female deity?"

"From whence else would a woman learn sex magic?"

"I don't believe it."

Rhiannon smiled. "Did you ever hear Esylt call down her gods? Do you know for sure whom she worshiped?"

Llewenon's eyes narrowed. "You will share Her power with me, a man? Is it possible?"

Rhiannon's smile deepened. "When the moon is full, as it is tonight."

Llewenon stared at her. She could feel his doubt. It was proof how much she had changed that she could even begin to convince him. It was not all the Goddess's power, she thought. Something inside her was different. She was not afraid anymore.

Llewenon's arm jerked hard around her waist, and she knew he remembered she was only a small, helpless woman. "Until tonight, you will remain with me," he warned. "You will not leave my sight."

Maelgwn squinted into the sun, frowning. Clear days were rare in Gwynedd, so rare they almost made him uneasy. He kept waiting for a storm to rise up. His eyes scanned the sky above the barely greening hills. He saw nothing to worry him, but the vague discontent continued to gnaw in his belly. He must get used to leaving Rhiannon. After all, it was not as if she would not be there when he returned. She was well-guarded, completely safe. He was a fool to worry so.

"What fine weather we have for our journey," Gareth announced emphatically beside him. Maelgwn turned and gave his officer a vague smile. Inside, the familiar wound ached with grief. Balyn had always accompanied him on diplomatic journeys. But he could not trust him now. Even if Balyn had kept the secret about Rhiannon, he had also defied Maelgwn and manipulated him. Things would never be the same between them.

"It is well the trackway is clear and dry." Maelgwn answered. "We started late, and we have many miles to go today."

Gareth nodded cheerfully, and Maelgwn returned to his own thoughts. If it were Balyn riding next to him, they would be discussing Cynan, assessing his committment to Maelgwn, determining how best to deal with him. Gareth did not have the subtlety for that sort of planning. Maelgwn's eyes scanned the other men riding beside him. He felt homesick already. Mayhap if Elwyn had come, he would be more content. But Gwenaseth liked to keep her husband close to her side, and Maelgwn would need Elwyn with him later in the summer when he visited northwestern Gwynedd, where Elwyn knew the chieftains well.

Maelgwn's hand tightened on the reins in unconscious frustration, making Cynraith snort and toss his head. Maelgwn soothed the stallion with soft words and tried to relax. He could not escape the feeling that something was amiss. He again perused the sky, searching for a hint of bad weather to blame for the tightness in his guts. The sky was clear, serene, and only a slight breeze teased the strands of hair around his face. The ominous dread he felt had another source.

It was not something he could explain, but Maelgwn knew when to obey his inner sense. He pulled Cynraith to a halt and gestured to his men.

"We're returning to Degannwy. I have a feeling we are needed there."

The men gaped at him for a moment, their eyes puzzled. Then they wordlessly eased their horses around and followed Maelgwn down the trackway the way they had come.

"Do you mean to lead me near Rhodderi's holdings? Then, when Maelgwn follows, Rhodderi and his men will attack?"

Llewenon's eyes glittered gleefully at Rhiannon's words, but he made no response. It had been the same all day. Llewenon refused to answer any of Rhiannon's questions about his plans. He was willing to talk of the past, but too canny to risk revealing the trap set for Maelgwn.

It did not matter, Rhiannon thought wearily. Her worries were undoubtedly true. They had walked all day, and even with the sun's path obscured by the boughs overhead, she knew they were moving west, toward Rhodderi's lands. Llewenon had made no attempt to cover their tracks. It was obvious he expected them to be followed. How long did she have? How long before she was missed at Degannwy, and a messenger sent after Maelgwn to warn him she had been abducted?

It might take days for Maelgwn to piece together the facts of her disappearance and come after her. Or, perhaps he would not bother. Perhaps he would decide she had left him of her own accord. Rhiannon's insides clenched at the thought, but she realized such fears might be used to undermine Llewenon.

"Maelgwn may not follow me, you know," she told her captor boldly. "I disappeared once before, and it took him some weeks for him to search me out. By then the trail will be cold, and Rhodderi's men will have tired of waiting in ambush."

"Oh, he will come after you—of that I have no doubt. I have no worries for Rhodderi's men. If they fail in their mission, it will not matter to me. I will still have you."

Llewenon's hand tightened on her arm, and Rhiannon's stomach heaved suddenly. Besides the dread Llewenon's words aroused in her, she was tired, thirsty and near faint with hunger. They had walked constantly for the last few hours, and she was not certain how much further she could drag herself. Did she dare reveal her misery to Llewenon? If he realized how weak and ill she was, he might guess about the babe. Then he would have a new weapon to use against her.

Another wave of sickness assailed her, and Rhiannon realized she had no choice but to ask Llewenon to stop. She ceased walking, and Llewenon jerked to a halt beside her. "If you do not let me rest soon, I will have no energy to perform the ceremony for the Goddess," she said. "You always slept the day before you called upon your magic. How can you expect me, a woman, to have the strength to exert my powers if you do not let me rest?"

Llewenon frowned but did not urge her on. As his eyes perused her, Rhiannon forced herself to stand straight and tall, but she could not hide the sweat that trickled down her forehead or the pallor of her face. She could only hope he attributed her distress to her fear of him.

Slowly, Llewenon nodded. "We will walk until we find a clearing where the moon can shine down upon us. There we will remain until tonight."

Chapter 32

"By the true God, Maelgwn, how did you know we had visitors?"

Maelgwn ignored the awestruck look on Gareth's face and gestured for the men behind them to come to a halt. Together they watched the small party of mounted men traveling toward them down the coast road. A crimson and green pennant flapped above the lead man, indicating the travelers were of the Brigante tribe.

Maelgwn frowned. He had received no word from his northern allies all winter. Had they heard some rumor of Rhiannon's disappearance or, worse yet, the scandal of her parentage? Either way, the alliance was threatened. Could this be the reason for his forboding?

Beside him, Gareth let out a sigh of relief. "It's a fair sign that Gavran leads them. He's a good man. I can't think he'd get himself too tangled up in this nonsense over Rhiannon and Esylt."

Maelgwn gave his officer a sharp look, then turned back to watch the approaching envoy. The Brigantes spotted them and increased their speed. When he was a few paces away, Gavran let out a shout and rode his horse straight at Maelgwn. Maelgwn hesitated, unsure whether to draw his sword to defend himself or wait.

He did nothing, and at the last minute Gavran swerved. As he pulled the lathered horse to a stop, the Brigante warrior let out a hoot of laughter. "Ho, Maelgwn, you unlikely bastard! Do you have the sight? We sent no word of our arrival, and yet here you are, waiting to meet us. It's uncanny!"

Maelgwn felt a smile of relief creep across his face. "Gavran," he said heartily. "It's good to see you. What brings you to visit?"

"What? You don't know?" Gavran asked, his eyebrows raised in mock surprise. "I thought surely by now you'd have searched your scrying bowl and learned the events of the winter." Gavran puffed out his chest and smiled broadly. "By rights, you ought to bow your head in homage to me. Behold, my lord, you speak to the new king of the Brigantes."

"You?" Maelgwn could not keep the shock from his voice. Fortunately, the Brigante man appeared to take no offense. Gavran chuckled and shook his head. "I should challenge you for the insult, but I dare say I was as surprised as you to find myself king." He gestured toward the fortress on the hill above them. "Welcome us to your hearth, and I will gladly tell you the whole tale."

Llewenon paused in an oak grove. Rhiannon came up behind him, panting and holding her belly. They had stopped once to drink from a stream, but not a bite of food had passed her lips since morn. She was weak and dizzy, from fear as well as hunger.

Collapsing on the ground, she heaved a sigh of relief. When she looked up, Llewenon stood above her. He watched her with narrowed eyes. "The Goddess must be a weak deity indeed to choose such a pitiful vessel for her power. I begin to question whether you possess any real magic. Perhaps your hold over your husband is merely the love spell of a comely woman over a feeble-minded man."

Rhiannon regarded Llewenon warily, but did not answer. It might serve her purposes to have Llewenon doubt her power. In any case, she did not have a scrap of energy to argue with him.

Llewenon pulled his eyes from her and gazed at the sky. It was barely past twilight, and the moon was still faint. Rhiannon saw him clench his hands into fists and she sensed the tension which throbbed through her captor's body. It was little wonder true power had eluded Llewenon, she decided. In her experience, the gods did not reward impatience.

It seemed they had rested only a few moments when Llewenon turned to Rhiannon again and announced, "It's time. You'd best get up and prepare yourself."

Rhiannon rose. Prepare she would, she thought grimly.

She shook off her weariness and forced herself to stand tall, then stretched her arms upward to the sky. The position made her back ache and her head swim with dizziness. She willed the discomfort away and concentrated. She was so untried at this, so new to the power.

Sweat trickled down her face and neck as she strained to clear her mind of distracting thoughts. Memories flashed into her mind. Another moonlit grove, Llewenon grabbing her from behind and pushing her down to the ground. The pain, the blood seeping down her legs.

This time, she reminded herself, the blood would not be her own but from the babe inside her. Rage engulfed her, filling her with strength. She would not let Llewenon kill Maelgwn's child! This time the Goddess would come to her as Morrigan, the goddess of vengeance and war. Llewenon would suffer!

Rhiannon's mind emptied and the power filled her. The

weightless energy made her limbs tremble and her blood thunder through her veins. She opened her eyes. Llewenon was watching her. She turned deliberately away from him and lifted her head up, seeking the moonlight on her face. As she did so, her right hand reached slowly for the knife in the pouch at her waist. It was a small knife, the blade short and curved. If she were careful, she could conceal it in her hand.

"Enough!" Llewenon's voice seethed with impatience. "Remove your clothes now. I want to see your body bared."

Rhiannon took a deep breath. The thought of being naked and vulnerable before this man terrified her. She clutched the knife more tightly.

She turned to face him and slid the knife into the folds of her skirt. "You must be naked as well," she said. Her eyes met his defiantly. "You said you wanted me to teach you my secrets. This is one of them."

Llewenon hesitated, then his hand went to the drawstring of his trousers. He jerked them down, exposing himself. Rhiannon looked away. "What do you wait for?" Llewenon snarled.

Rhiannon pulled her gown over head, revealing the shift of fine white linen beneath. She looked at Llewenon, her eyes focused firmly on his face. "Your tunic," she prompted.

His mouth twitched. "You first."

Rhiannon pulled off the shift and gazed at Llewenon. His expression was gleeful. "Ah, Rhiannon," he taunted. "You are no longer the unappealing little rack of bones you once were. The Goddess has made you into a woman. I could almost think to get some pleasure of you. Almost."

Rhiannon gritted her teeth and held the knife more tightly as Llewenon approached. His smile gleamed in the moonlight, then the shadow of his body loomed over her. He was so close, she could smell his stale, unwashed scent. "Your tunic," she said. "Take it off now."

Grinning, Llewenon grabbed the edge of the long dirty russet garment and lifted. For a moment his chest and neck were exposed as he struggled to pull the tunic over his head. As if of its own accord, Rhiannon's hand jerked forward, and the knife slipped silkily through the curve of Llewenon's bare neck.

The tunic tumbled to the ground. Llewenon went still, staring at her. Rhiannon held her breath. Had she truly slashed his throat or merely imagined it? She saw the river of red seeping across Llewenon's throat. His eyes widened and he clutched his neck.

Rhiannon watched him. Nothing could stem the flow of his life's blood. Already he was strangling in his body's fluid, slowly choking to death. She expected to feel pity or horror, but she did not. The Goddess's power still hummed in her veins, filling her with a sense of triumph. Justice was served by what she had done. Llewenon was at last stripped of whatever meager power he had possessed, his twisted cruelty banished at last.

Llewenon fell to the ground, still clutching his throat. On hands and knees, he writhed and made ugly gurgling sounds. Rhiannon went to him and spoke. Her voice rang out with the metallic coldness of the deity. "You have failed, Llewenon. It is time to return to the spirit world. Perhaps there you will find the knowledge which has eluded you in this life. Remember these words, if you can. The power cannot be taken by force. You must surrender your soul to possess it."

Llewenon's body went still. Rhiannon knelt and reached out a trembling hand to touch him. When he did not move, she heaved the body over so Llewenon lay on his back. His eyes stared blindly at her. She waited, expecting his spirit to leave his body and confront her. There was no sound except the soft sigh of wind through the grass.

The sense of power vanished, and Rhiannon shivered in the cool night air. Wave after wave of dizziness assaulted her. She retched, vomiting up the bitter dregs of her belly. When the worst had passed, she crawled to where her shift lay and pulled it over her. Her senses were thick with the smell of blood and death. Cold moonlight seeped into her thoughts. She welcomed it.

It was morning when Rhiannon opened her eyes. Rhodderi was leaning over her, his eyes staring with dread. He backed away as she sat up.

"You," he whispered. "You killed him!"

Rhiannon sat up and took in the bloody scene that horrified Rhodderi. Llewenon lay a few feet away from her. Black blood stained the ground between them, and her bare body was smeared crimson from where she had crawled through the grass. Her eyes met Rhodderi's.

"I did not kill him," she said. "This was the work of the Goddess. She sent Llewenon back to the spirit world to learn some humility and compassion."

Rhodderi backed further away from her, crossing himself in the Christian fashion. When he made a movement as if to leave the clearing, Rhiannon held her hand up and spoke commandingly. "Stay. I have something to say to you."

Rhiannon stood and retrieved her gown. She pulled it on quickly, then turned to Rhodderi. He had not moved, but his face was pale and sweat ran in rivulets down his temples.

Rhiannon took a deep breath. The Goddess was not with her now, but perhaps she could feign a semblance of Her power. "In the past you have doubted me, Rhodderi, doubted that I had the right to be Maelgwn's consort. You have plotted against my husband and me. As you can see, I am under the protection of the Great Goddess, and She will avenge any wrongs done to me or mine. If you try

again to trick or murder Maelgwn or any one I love, I will
call down the Lady's vengeance in all its fury."

She gestured toward Llewenon's gruesome corpse. "Her
hand against Llewenon was gentle, for She knew he was a
weak man, his mind poisoned by old jealousies and hatreds.
But you," Rhiannon faced Rhodderi threateningly. "You
know exactly what you plot. For your greed and selfish
lust for power, the Goddess would punish you even more
horribly."

Rhodderi's mouth worked. "I don't believe in the Goddess," he said, "but I would be a fool to brush aside your
threats completely. You are Esylt's daughter." He smiled
faintly, and Rhiannon sensed some of his tension ease. "I
knew your mother in the old days, even before Maelgwn
thought to claim the kingship. Quite a woman she was,
too, with her remarkable height, that black hair and white
skin. She pulled more men into her sticky web than I care
to count. I always said, if she'd had a pair of balls between
her legs, she'd have ruled all of Britain."

Rhodderi paused. Rhiannon continued to watch him
warily. Her eyes caught movement in the low bushes and
scrub behind him. Her heart sank as she saw the sun glint
off weapons and mail among the green foliage. Rhodderi
had brought his war party. He did indeed plan to ambush
Maelgwn.

Rhodderi's eyes moved over her in a way that showed
both admiration and revulsion. "I never knew Esylt to kill
in cold blood. You must get your ruthlessness from Ferdic.
Tell me, how did you trick Llewenon?"

Rhiannon tried to calm the pounding of her heart. At
least Rhodderi did not know who her true sire was. That
was a secret best kept between her and her husband. "Llewenon knew the Goddess worked through me," she
answered. "He wanted a share of my power. He was too
much of a fool to realize it only comes to women."

Rhodderi walked over to Llewenon's body and stared at

the corpse a moment, then shook his head. He lifted his eyes to meet Rhiannon's. "I've misjudged you, Lady Rhiannon, princess of the Brigantes. I've thought Maelgwn a simpleton for insisting that you remain his queen. Now, I see he has known all along exactly what he possesses."

The gray-bearded warrior lifted his hand in a kind of salute. He turned and began to walk away. When he was halfway to his war band, he called out over his shoulder. "Go back to your husband, Lady Rhiannon, and breed up sons endowed with your courage and your husband's might. In the future, Britain will need such men." He turned and a wolfish grin flashed in his beard. "And if you have a daughter, send me word at once. I have five sons, and I would not mind allying my house to one that possesses your unearthly powers."

Rhodderi reached the underbrush and signaled his men to disperse. Rhiannon waited until the final glint of weapons and armor vanished, and only the gentle breeze stirred the bushes. Her head whirled with amazement at what she had done. She had faced down Maelgwn's greatest enemy, and without the Goddess's power behind her. She—little Rhiannon—had dared to send a warrior away.

The awe of it made her dizzy. Or was it the lack of food and water which made the ground reel underneath her feet? The past hours had taken their toll. Her body felt as if it had been pounded from head to foot. Her tongue was thick and swollen in her mouth, her head ached, and her stomach roiled with queasiness. It would be a wonder if she could walk back to Degannwy. Certainly she could not do so unless she had some water.

She searched her mind, trying to remember when she had last seen a spring or a stream. The landscape around her was completely unfamiliar. She could only guess which way Degannwy lay, and hope she would encounter some source of water on her journey.

Rhiannon began to walk. The slight breeze brought her

the sweet scent of blooming hawthorn from a distance. She inhaled deeply and asked the Goddess to refresh her weary body—just as She restored the forest's splendor each spring. Sighing, Rhiannon thought again how wonderful it was to be alive, to hear the music of the birds in the trees, to feel the moist air caress her skin. Deep in her body, safe from the trauma she had endured, the babe slept, rocking gently in its water cradle as she walked.

She made good progress for several hours. The thick, silver clouds overhead made it difficult to determine the passage of sun in the sky, but she guessed it was about midday when she finally encountered a bubbling stream and drank her fill of the cool, refreshing water. After that she walked faster, renewed by the Goddess's life fluid.

The day wore on, and Rhiannon's strength began to fade. Each step was an effort, and she wrapped her arms around her belly to quell the agonizing hunger burning there. The landscape around her still looked unfamiliar, and she had the sinking feeling she was no longer headed in the right direction. Rhiannon shook off her doubts and kept walking. The Goddess had protected her this long; she must keep her faith and believe She would continue to help her.

As the forest shadows lengthened, Rhiannon heard sounds in the distance. She cocked her head and listened. Several horses at least—her heart leapt for joy. Maelgwn's men had come for her! There could be no other reason for mounted men to travel in this way.

Sinking down on the ground, Rhiannon decided to wait where she was. She did not think she could take another step anyway.

The mounted party grew nearer. Worried that they might run her over, Rhiannon staggered to her feet.

"There she is!"

The riders drew to a stunned halt. For a moment Rhiannon and her husband merely stared at each other. Then

Maelgwn flung himself from his horse and came rushing toward her.

"Who did this to you?" he gasped as he neared her.

Rhiannon shook her head mutely. She was so relieved to see Maelgwn, she could hardly respond. Then she realized Maelgwn thought the blood smearing her clothes was hers.

"I'm not hurt," she reassured him. "Only exhausted."

He enfolded her in his strong arms. She resisted the urge to collapse completely as Maelgwn touched her face with soothing tenderness. "Dear God, Rhiannon," he said. "Tell me what has happened."

Rhiannon closed her eyes, her body brimming with contentment at the sound of her husband's voice. "Why are you here?" she said. "I thought you'd gone to visit Cynan."

"It doesn't matter. Nothing matters but that you are safe."

She sagged against him, letting his strength fill her. "Llewenon kidnapped me," she said. "He made me follow him west to Rhodderi's lands. It was a trap. Rhodderi planned to ambush you when you came looking for me."

"Llewenon!" The shock in her husband's voice made Rhiannon open her eyes. Maelgwn's face was filled with a cold fury that made her flinch.

"Llewenon," he demanded. "Where is he?"

Rhiannon paused, suddenly afraid again. Would Maelgwn condemn her for murdering a bard? All her life, she had been taught that bards were special, revered. She had not thought of it before, but perhaps she had done wrong in killing such a man.

Nay, she had done no wrong. She had obeyed the Goddess. It was not evil to choose her own life over a man's, even one who was a bard. She lifted her head so that her eyes met Maelgwn's. "I killed him," she said. "He was going to hurt me again, so I cut his throat."

Maelgwn stared at her so long and hard, Rhiannon grew uneasy. Finally, he heaved a deep sigh and pulled her close. "My lovely wife, how I underestimate you, even now. You appear so small and fragile, but underneath there is a core of iron."

Rhiannon leaned into her husband's chest and sighed with relief. It was only the sound of a familiar northern accent which roused her from her exhausted reverie.

"Your wife—she is well? She was not kidnapped?"

Rhiannon looked up to see Gavran watching her and Maelgwn with a puzzled expression. His bewilderment only increased when Maelgwn responded. "Aye, my wife is well. But she was indeed kidnapped. It seems that your old bard, Llewenon, teamed up with Rhodderi and tried to use Rhiannon to get at me."

"Llewenon and Rhodderi—now that's a foul alliance." Gavran's eyes settled on Rhiannon with a look of interest. "What happened, Rhiannon? How did you escape?"

Bracing herself for her countryman's shock and disapproval, Rhiannon answered. "I killed Llewenon. He meant to hurt me and use me to hurt Maelgwn. I could not let that happen."

Gavran's eyes rounded with shock exactly as Maelgwn's had. Then he laughed heartily. "By Lludd's silver hand! It's true what they say, a magician can only be killed by one whose powers are greater." His gaze shifted to Maelgwn, and he shook his head in exaggerated dismay. "I warned you, didn't I, that your wife was a sorceress? You'd best sleep with a sprig of witchbane under your pillow, Maelgwn, lest you wake up some morning to find yourself transformed into a bat or a toad."

"Nay, his namesake, a dragon," Rhiannon interjected, her face radiant with relief. "I think he would make a very handsome dragon. One with sleek green skin and eyes like great glowing rubies."

"This dragon ..." Maelgwn murmured, leaning over to speak close to her ear, "... wants nothing more than to carry off his mate to his den in the hills and keep her to himself forever."

Chapter 33

safe and secure in Maelgwn's arms, Rhiannon dozed as
they made their way back to Degannwy. Despite the jostling
caused by Cynraith's fast pace over rough terrain and the
shouts of the men, she could no longer resist the lure of
sleep.

It seemed only moments had passed when she felt herself
being lifted down from Maelgwn's arms. She opened her
eyes and realized that Balyn held her as Maelgwn dismounted. The big man's deep brown eyes gazed down on
her tenderly.

"My lady, I am glad you are well, truly I am."

Rhiannon smiled up at him and even dared to brush
her hand across his brown cheek. "Thank you, Balyn. I'm
pleased to know you joined the search party to look for
me."

"What else could I do? Maelgwn cannot live without
you, and I would give my life to make him happy."

"Enough," Maelgwn pronounced gruffly. He took Rhiannon from Balyn's arms and cradled her in his own. "Any

more whispering, and I will suspect the two of you are
conspiring to retire me into my dotage."

Rhiannon leaned against Maelgwn's broad chest and
smiled. The strain between Balyn and Maelgwn was still
there, but in time it might vanish altogether. Maelgwn was
too fair and reasonable a man to condemn his friend for
one mistake in a lifetime of service.

Maelgwn carried Rhiannon to the bedchamber and laid
her on the bed. Taffee came rushing in after them. "You'd
best learn to look after your wife better," she chided
Maelgwn. "This is the second time you've near lost her."

"Your duty is to see to your lady's comfort," Maelgwn
growled. "Even a slattern such as you should see she is in
grave need of a hot bath. Be off and see to having some
water brought." Sitting down on the bed beside Rhiannon,
Maelgwn shook his head after the slave woman's departing
form. "I don't know how you endure her. She has a dis-
gracefully impertinent tongue."

"She is loyal, though," Rhiannon said. "And efficient.
Not only will she see to my bath, she will also think to
bring me some food, and I'm utterly famished. This babe
must be a boy; I vow I could eat for a sennight and never
be satisfied."

"Babe?" Maelgwn's eyes jerked back to her face.

Rhiannon gave him a shy smile. "I waited to tell you
until I was certain its spirit had taken hold in this world."
She sighed contently. "Now I am sure. The whole time I
was with Llewenon, I could feel the baby inside me, willing
me to live, to fight."

"Do you mean to tell what happened?" Maelgwn asked.

"You mean . . . with Llewenon?"

Maelgwn nodded. "Not only this time, but before. What
did he do to you?"

Rhiannon sighed again. "It's a long story, but perhaps
you have guessed some of it." She leaned back against the
bed and spoke in a low soft voice. "Years ago, when I was

girl, Llewenon came to my father's hearth and sang a
song of magic . . ."

Maelgwn listened silently. When she reached the part
about the rape, his eyes darkened and his hands clenched
into fists, but he did not interrupt.

The return of Taffee and two servant boys carrying huge,
steaming buckets of water over their shoulders halted Rhiannon's narrative. The servants quickly filled the large
wooden tub another servant carried in, and then Taffee
ordered everyone from the room. When she turned to
Maelgwn and gave him an expectant look, he exploded.
"If you have any sense, woman, you will absent yourself
from my presence immediately!"

Taffee's bearing was haughty as she sauntered toward
the door. She paused there and faced the king. "If I leave,
who will bathe your lady?" she asked him boldly.

"I will!" was his outraged response.

Despite her fatigue, Rhiannon could not help giggling
at Maelgwn's anger. When Taffee left, and he turned his
stern, forbidding countenance to Rhiannon, she laughed
even harder. "Poor darling. You know Taffee is right."

"I will bathe you."

Rhiannon's eyes sought Maelgwn's and she caught her
breath at the look of tenderness she saw there. He leaned
forward and pulled a strand of matted hair away from her
face. Rhiannon closed her eyes as he kissed her, then let
her body go limp as he pulled off her soiled gown and
lifted her from the bed.

The bath was hot, gloriously so, and Maelgwn's big hands
were gentle on her sore, battered skin. She lay back and
let him tend to her, half in a daze of fatigue and delicious
satisfaction. It took a long time to wash the blood and dirt
from her skin and hair, and as he bathed her, Maelgwn
asked not a word more about the kidnapping. It was only
after he had wrapped her in large warm cloth and brought
her back to the bed that he urged her to finish her story.

She began again, speaking slowly and without emotion. Looking back, it seemed almost impossible that she had outwitted Llewenon and killed him with her own hands. A sense of awe went through her as she described the Goddess's power entering her body, the anger and feeling of vengeance which had driven her.

"I truly thought," she said, her voice shaking suddenly, "I thought that I was acting on behalf of the Goddess. The power was there, and I did not doubt it. In a way, I almost pitied Llewenon, for I had the thing he had always sought but would never have a chance to find himself."

"Pity?" Maelgwn's voice was hard. "How can you pity a man who hurt you so badly? Llewenon deserved to die— and in a manner far more cruel than having his throat cut."

Rhiannon shook her head. "He was twisted inside. He could not really help what he was." Her eyes met Maelgwn's. "All the more reason to send him back to the spirit world. Perhaps next time he will find what he needs and his spirit will know peace. Most men have more good in them than Llewenon did. Rhodderi, for example, he is not all the villain that I had thought."

"Aye, tell me of Rhodderi," Maelgwn prompted.

Maelgwn listened in amazed silence as Rhiannon told of finding Rhodderi leaning over her, and how she had threatened him and then somehow managed to convince him to leave her alone. "It was very odd," she finished. "I have the feeling he will not oppose you in the future, that there might be a chance he will honor you as overking after all."

"Astounding." Maelgwn shook his head, then leaned down to smooth a tendril of damp hair away from her cheek. "The dream was true. You were meant to be my consort, Rhiannon. With you at my side, Gwynedd is safe. The Goddess's magic is within you, and no man will deny it now."

"I can't help thinking, though, that the Goddess's days are ending," Rhiannon said in a troubled voice. "More and more people are accepting the Christ God. I fear the magic will be lost. People will forget that all of us are born from the sea and the earth."

Maelgwn stood and went to a narrow opening in the timber wall. Now that the weather had turned warm, some of the wall coverings had been removed to let in light and air through the small high windows in the bedchamber. "How can they forget?" he asked. "The Goddess is all around us, everywhere. In these hills the spirits whisper on the wind. They speak in every ripple of water and gleaming green leaf."

Rhiannon shook her head, not answering. A chill ran through her as she recalled things she had seen on her journey to the other side. She had dreamed of great fortresses of silver and glass. The people who lived there did not look up at the sky or gaze down at the vacant fields where no grass grew. The Goddess had left them, and they were lost.

Maelgwn crossed back to the bed and sat down beside her. Before he could speak, there was a knock at the door.

"Taffee," Rhiannon said. "No doubt she is finally bringing me some food."

But it was not Taffee who stood in the doorway when Maelgwn called out a welcome, but Gavran. "I don't mean to disturb you," he said. "But I would like to convey my concern for Rhiannon."

"Of course." Maelgwn motioned him in. Gavran came to the bed and bowed to Rhiannon. "How fare you, my lady?"

"Well enough," Rhiannon answered with a smile. "My bruises and scrapes will heal quickly."

"I'm pleased to hear it." Gavran's eyes flickered hesitantly to Maelgwn. "Perhaps she is well enough to consider my proposal. What do you think?"

"Tell Rhiannon the story from the beginning. She has not yet heard the news that you are king of the Brigantes."

"King?" Rhiannon gasped.

Gavran's characteristic smile broke free. "Nay, do not apologize for your surprise, Rhiannon. I must say I was amazed myself."

"How—how did this come about?"

Gavran's grin widened with honest amusement. "As you know, your father's other children were hardly of an age to lead a group of warriors, and Ferdic's brothers had left the tribe so long ago, no one was sure of their fitness, either. In the end, it came down to a contest of battle prowess among the warriors . . . and I won."

"I suspect it also had something to do with your reputation as a fair man and a good leader," Rhiannon suggested with a smile. "Your men have always respected you. I'm sure offering you the kingship came naturally to them."

"Ah, warm words from a lovely lady." Gavran's eyes again strayed to meet Maelgwn's. "But do you think her fondness for me extends as far as the other matter?"

Maelgwn shrugged. "Ask her."

Garvan slid gracefully down upon one knee and took Rhiannon's hand in his. "Obviously, I am pleased to find myself king, but it still troubles me that the line of Ferdic and his father, Cunedag, will not continue to lead the Brigantes. It came to me that I should form some bond with you, a princess of their blood." Garvan's eyes twinkled with self-depreciating humor. "I asked Ferdic for your hand once, you know, but he refused me. It was clear he had much bigger plans for you. Indeed, now I see the wisdom of his wedding you to Maelgwn."

Gavran cleared his throat, and his face grew uncharacteristically solemn. "But my desire for an alliance between your blood and mine remains strong. I have three fine sons, and I would like to propose that if you bear Maelgwn a daughter, she be betrothed to whichever of my sons she chooses."

Rhiannon looked quickly at Maelgwn, trying to read his wishes in this surprising request. His impassive face suggested the decision was hers to make. "I have yet to bear a living child," she answered. "Do we dare tempt the Goddess by arranging the betrothal of a babe still unborn? I might well have all sons."

"You cannot tell me, Lady Rhiannon, that you have no inkling of the future. By killing Llewenon, you obtained what power he had, along with the gifts you undoubtedly inherited from your true mother, Esylt. It is clear to me you must have some sort of sight." Gavran reached out quickly and captured Rhiannon's other hand. Holding them tightly within his, he faced her with a look of earnest entreaty. "Search your mind, Rhiannon, and tell us what the future holds. And if it seems that you will bear a daughter, consider my offer and give me some hope of allying my blood to yours."

Rhiannon gave Maelgwn a bewildered look, then turned back to Gavran. He was a handsome man, his coloring and build much like Ferdic's but without the smug cleverness which had made Ferdic such a hard man to like. No doubt Gavran's sons would also be well-favored, she thought. Certainly she could search long and hard to find a potential father-in-law as honest and generous as Gavran. Still, his request frightened her. If she bore a daughter, should the girl not have the right to choose her own husband rather than being bartered away for a political alliance as Rhiannon had been?

As if reading her thoughts, Gavran spoke. "I promise it would be the maiden's choice, and if she found all three of my sons lacking, I would not to force the matter. All I'm asking for is a promise that you would consider such a marriage before any other."

Seeing Gavran's pleading face so close to hers confused

Rhiannon's thoughts. She closed her eyes and listened for the voice inside her which had always guided her wisest decisions. This time, there was no voice, but she did see images. When she had been in the ocean that night she had dreamed of more than misty visions of buildings and empty fields. She had also seen children playing in the king's forest. They were all blue-eyed and lithe. Some with dark hair and some with red. And there was not just one girl among them, but three.

Rhiannon's eyes sprang open, and she heaved a sigh. "Must it be my eldest daughter, Gavran? Would you not be satisfied with a younger one if she suited better?"

Gavran laughed heartily, then released Rhiannon's hands and stood up. Turning to Maelgwn, he gave him a look of exaggerated sympathy. "I don't know how you endure it, Maelgwn. The thought of being married to a woman who sees the future makes my skin crawl. No wonder you always act the devoted husband. If you ever strayed, Rhiannon would surely know it and take you to task."

"But I don't seek to know the future, Gavran," Rhiannon protested. "It comes to me only in glimpses, like fragments of dreams. I can't even be sure it will all come to pass." She moved her fingers down to splay across her belly. "I must first carry this child nine moon cycles and suffer through his birth before I can plan for another one."

"So it is a boy then?" Maelgwn's deep voice rumbled across the room.

Rhiannon frowned and nodded slowly. "I think so. I can't be sure, but it seems to me that the tallest child I saw in my dream was a boy."

"And does he favor me or you?"

Rhiannon looked up and saw the teasing smile on Maelgwn's face. "For shame," she scolded. "To ask me such a thing. Some things should be surprises, even for the father."

"And I should leave Lady Rhiannon to rest." Gavran bowed again, then headed toward the door. He paused there to wink at Rhiannon, then let himself out.

Rhiannon lay back and exhaled a weary breath. "I don't know, Maelgwn. I think we should have told Gavran the truth about Ferdic. It really is unfair of us to offer him our daughter when in fact, none our children will possess a drop of Ferdic's blood."

"What's the harm of it? Let him think he has allied himself with Cunedag's dynasty. You know as well as I that royal blood doesn't matter as much as he thinks." Maelgwn approached the bed, his eyes a soft, misty blue. "Since I learned who he was, I have often thought it was your Irish slave father who bequeathed to you your gentleness and kind heart. The royal families of Britain could do with an infusion of your sweet nature."

"Sweet nature?" Rhiannon twirled a lock of her hair and regarded Maelgwn with a look of queenly disdain. "If you do not bring me some food soon, I fear you shall be greatly disappointed in your assessment of my disposition. I swear I am hungry enough to cause a scene to rival even your fiery temper."

Maelgwn gave her a stricken look and hurried toward the door. "Damn me, but I completely forgot! Some ladies' maid I am. You and the babe would starve to death under my care."

A contented, lazy smile adorned Rhiannon's face as she watched her husband tear from the room. Not a full turn of the seasons had passed since she had wed the formidable Cymry king. She could not help being amused by how much he had changed.

Even more striking was how much *she* had grown and gained in confidence. A year ago, she would have hidden in the shadows while Gavran talked to Maelgwn. Today, the Brigante king came on bended knee and solicited her approval. It was not merely the Goddess's power, Rhiannon decided. She was a queen in her own right. For all Esylt's faults and failures, she had judged her daughter correctly. As long as there was a breath in her body, she would strive to rule at Maelgwn's side strongly and well.

Chapter 34

She needed to see Maelgwn. The thought came to Rhiannon as she crossed the courtyard. She wasted no time in heeding it, but walked quickly toward the gate.

Outside the fortress, she paused to catch her breath before attempting the journey down the trackway. For someone who had always been small and slender, being heavy with child was a cumbersome trial. At least this winter she did not suffer from the cold. Even in a light cloak, she would not be chilled as she walked to the practice field. The babe inside her warmed her body even as the thought of it warmed her heart.

The short distance to the frozen meadow where Maelgwn and his men practiced their fighting skills seemed very far this day. Each step made Rhiannon's hips and back ache. She wondered if even following her inner voice was worth this torment.

As she reached the practice field, her doubts were resolved. In the unseasonably warm weather, most of the men and boys had stripped off their tunics. The sight of so much sleek, sweaty male flesh exhilarated Rhiannon. If her visions were true, someday this boy babe she carried would train on this very field, and his dark hair and lithe body would shine with sweat as he fought to earn his place among Maelgwn's warriors.

Smiling, Rhiannon found her eyes drawn to a corner of the field where Gareth instructed the younger men and boys on the techniques of fighting on horseback. Maelgwn was among those men who watched, his broad bare back gleaming in the pale winter sunlight as he leaned on his sword.

At the sight of her husband, a surge of longing passed through Rhiannon, so intense she felt it ripple all the way to her womb. The babe kicked emphatically, as if protesting its father's hold on her flesh. Rhiannon laughed out loud with pleasure. Then a sharp pain tore through her belly, and she gritted her teeth instead. For a moment, she wondered if it was the beginning of her labor, then dismissed the thought. By her reckoning, it was still early for the babe to be born.

She walked along the edge of the practice area. The sight of her husband was enthralling her senses. Never would she grow tired of watching the sleek, animal-like grace with which he moved. The supple elegance of his form made ripples of desire uncoil in her lower belly.

He turned to talk to the man next to him, and Rhiannon caught a glimpse of her husband's handsome profile. Maelgwn had grown his beard for the winter, and the fringe of dark hair on his chin emphasized his proud features and piercing blue eyes. She moved closer, intent on admiring her husband from a more advantageous angle. Despite the other men on the field, it seemed as if there was no one there but her and Maelgwn.

She edged close enough to watch the individual muscles in Maelgwn's back flex as he demonstrated a particular sword thrust. His sweat-streaked hair coiled into dark ringlets trailing over his shoulders. He threw back his head and gave a hearty, triumphant laugh. Rhiannon's breath caught. Maelgwn had seen thirty-four winters pass, but the years had not dimmed his magnificence. He was still a man at the very height of his physical power.

Another pain ripped through Rhiannon's midsection, startling her. She tried to breathe slowly and evenly until the spasm passed, but a twinge of doubt stirred in her mind. Perhaps it was the babe, come a fortnight too early. The child seemed to have an impatient spirit, always twisting and turning in her womb with a dissatisfied rhythm. Probably a boy, she thought wryly. Only a foolish male would be eager to leave his lulling shelter and enter the bright, cold, uncomfortable world of the living.

Maelgwn turned suddenly. His eyes caught hers, and Rhiannon felt the powerful energy flowing between them. She stared at her husband, entranced. This was her mate. Till the stars burned to nothing and the seas boiled dry, she would love him.

He approached her, a smile on his face, his movements, languid and relaxed. She watched him as if seeing him for the first time, marveling that this beautiful man belonged to her. Then the pain caught at her again. She clenched her teeth. Maelgwn saw and was beside her in seconds.

"Rhiannon, what is it?"

"I'm not sure."

Maelgwn's eyes widened, and a look of alarm crossed his face. "It's time? The babe means to be born?"

Rhiannon hesitated, then nodded.

"Is that why you sought me out?"

She suppressed a smile. What would her husband think if she knew she had really come to admire him at swordplay?

Maelgwn scooped her up in his arms and began walking toward the fortress.

"We should ride," she suggested, concerned that he meant to carry her all the way back to Degannwy. "I'm not as light as I once was. You're likely to strain something."

Maelgwn gave her an insulted look, and Rhiannon knew further protest would be useless. His back and shoulders would ache later, and she would be too busy with the babe to tend him. Then he would regret his impulsive exertions. For now, there would be no swaying him.

Another pain rippled through her. Rhiannon forgot everything but the urgent warning that her time was near. She closed her eyes and concentrated. Her body had begun its struggle to open the birth passage so the babe could journey to the world of the living. She willed herself to relax, to let go and accept what was to come.

Sweat trickled down his brow as Maelgwn entered the courtyard carrying Rhiannon, but it was not the effort of the journey which made his heart race alarmingly. He had avoided thinking of Rhiannon's labor for months. Now the babe was on its way. He could no longer deny the sick dread coursing through him.

There were so many things that could go wrong during childbearing. If the babe was too big or positioned wrongly, days of labor might result in a stillborn child. Even if the babe survived, the mother risked bleeding to death or succumbing to childbed fever.

Maelgwn struggled to force his foreboding away as he entered the bedchamber and crossed the room to lay Rhiannon down on the bed. He leaned over and gazed at her intently. Her eyes were closed, her features still and peaceful. For a moment, he thought she dozed, then he saw her bite down upon her lips as another spasm racked her body.

The dread intensified around him like a noose. Rhiannon was so small, so frail-looking. It did not seem possible she could survive the pain and exhaustion of giving birth. Never should he have risked getting her with child again.

"Maelgwn." Her eyes fluttered open. She watched him

with a distant, almost dazed expression. "Have you sent for Arianhrodd?"

"Not yet. Balyn is fetching Gwenaseth and Bleddryn. I can send someone for Arianhrodd, if you wish it."

She smiled faintly. "Of course I wish it. Not only is she skilled at midwifery, she played a vital part in this child's conception. If it were not for Arianhrodd, I might never have survived to return to you."

Maelgwn leaned closer and kissed Rhiannon's forehead. "Are you scared, *cariad*?"

She shook her head. "The pain frightens me a little, but I'm certain I can bear it."

What of dying?—Maelgwn thought silently. Was Rhiannon's faith in the Goddess so great she could enter this life-threatening ordeal without doubts? He repressed a shudder, wondering why his own faith was so lacking.

Rhiannon took a sharp breath as the next contraction came, and Maelgwn's heart seemed to leap into his throat. His wife must have sensed him tense, for she looked up at him, her eyes puzzled.

"You're afraid?" she asked.

Maelgwn shook his head. He did not want Rhiannon to guess the awful, choking terror he felt. "Nay, merely excited that the babe finally means to be born. I've waited so long for this day."

"You must not be too impatient. Most first babes take their time arriving. I might be in labor 'til morn."

The thought of a long labor intensified his torment. Maelgwn straightened and turned away from the bed, sure he could not hide his fear from Rhiannon if she watched his face. "I will see about sending an escort for Arianhrodd," he said.

Taffee came rushing in as he reached the door. Her plain face glowed with excitement. "My lady, is it true?" she asked. "Has your water broken? Are the pains close together?"

Maelgwn grimaced. He did not wait for Rhiannon's answers, but hurried out the door, almost running into Gwenaseth. She was as annoying as Taffee, plaguing him with questions until he brusquely took his leave and strode rapidly to the gate. He sent Mabon after Arianhrodd, then stood panting in the wan winter sunshine. A breeze blew from the sea, chilling his bare torso. He was still half-naked and sweaty from the practice field. Striding to the well, he began to sluice water from the nearby trough over his face and chest. The cool dampness revived him, but did nothing to ease the cramping dread in his belly.

Belatedly, he considered that he should have gone after Arianhrodd himself. It was too late now; he dared not leave Rhiannon. What if she were to call for him and he was not there?

He glanced toward his bedchamber for the dozenth time and sighed. He despised this helplessness. There was nothing he could do to aid Rhiannon. Childbearing was a woman's trial. Even other women could do no more than offer sympathy and encouragement. The thing was in God's hands—or more likely the Goddess's. After saving Rhiannon from death three times, surely the Great Mother would not desert her now.

The thought heartened him. He remembered Rhiannon's look of contentment and peace, and knew he must strive for the same. Perhaps if he saw her again, he would feel better.

He began toward his bedchamber, then paused. Could he endure watching Rhiannon suffer, knowing there was nothing he could do? His body went rigid at the thought. When Balyn called his name, he jerked as if from a blow.

"Jesu, Maelgwn, you twitch like a maddened dog. What is it? Do you fear for Rhiannon?"

Maelgwn nodded. Balyn met his apprehensive look with a wide smile. "Sewan assures me all is well. She said Rhiannon's labor is progressing normally—and right quickly, too. She suggested you might have another heir before nightfall.''

"First babes are seldom born quickly," Maelgwn scoffed. "Rhiannon said as much, and I know it to be true.''

"Sewan has had five herself, and she thinks this one means to surprise us all with its hurry to be born.''

Maelgwn shot a glance toward his bedchamber. The suffocating fear returned. If the babe came too quickly, Rhiannon might tear inside and bleed to death. These next few hours could be her last among the living. He would not lose these precious moments with her simply because he was coward. He dashed toward the bedchamber, pushing his way through the crowd of women in the anteroom outside.

Pausing inside the doorway of the dimly lit bedchamber, he fought to control his panic. He could not allow Rhiannon to see the dread in his eyes. He must compose himself.

Gwenaseth, Bleddryn and Taffee were arrayed around the bed, blocking his view of Rhiannon. Sewan and Melangel stood in a corner, talking softly. For a moment no one noticed him, then Sewan looked his way. "My lord," she gasped. "It's not fitting for you to be here!''

Gwenaseth whirled around at Sewan's words. Seeing Maelgwn, her expression hardened. "Wait outside, Maelgwn," she ordered. "We'll send for you when the babe has come.''

Maelgwn shook his head. His fear for Rhiannon overwhelmed him. All these woman and Bleddryn hovering around his wife—it reminded him of a deathwatch. Was he too late? Was Rhiannon dying?

Advancing toward the bed, he pushed Taffee aside. Rhiannon was half sitting up, with a pile of sheepskins wedged behind her shoulders. Her eyes were closed; her face tense with concentration. Damp strands of hair curled around her face, and her chest rose and fell rapidly. She wore only her shift, and it clung to the mound of her belly. One small, slender hand clutched so tightly at the bedcovers her knuckles were white.

His eyes focused on the streaks of crimson staining the damp shift in the hollow between Rhiannon's legs. Shocked and horrified, Maelgwn fell to his knees. He pressed his face against Rhiannon's hand.

"Sweet Rhian, what have I done to you," he whispered.

She did not answer. Another contraction made her body shudder.

Maelgwn took a breath like a sob. He felt someone trying to pull him away from the bed. Gwenaseth's voice was hoarse in his ear. "You fool! Do you mean to destroy her mastery of the pain? Get out. The babe comes even now."

Maelgwn stood up. "Nay, I will not leave her." He glared at the others in the room, then motioned toward the door. "All but Bleddryn—be gone with you."

Taffee made a sound of disgust. She grabbed his arm. "Have you no decency, my lord? Men do not attend their wives in labor." Her eyes flicked contemptuously to Bleddryn. "Take this butcher with you. My lady does not need him."

Bleddryn started to protest, and one of the women stepped forward to gainsay him. They began to argue. Something inside Maelgwn snapped. He pulled out the sword slung at his side and brandished it at the crowded room. "You will heed my will in this matter—and promptly!"

His voice shook with anguish, but it was still fierce enough to frighten the women and Bleddryn. They moved toward the door. Gwenaseth was the last to leave. As she reached the doorway, she turned, her eyes imploring. "Please, Maelgwn. Let me stay. This is a time when a woman needs other women at her side."

Maelgwn glanced toward the bed. Rhiannon was breathing strangely. Her face contorted in a grimace of pain. Stark panic swept through him. He wanted to be with

Rhiannon, but in truth he had no idea what to do, how to aid her.

"Aye, you may stay," he answered, his eyes still focused on Rhiannon. "But only you, and only if you quit your demand that I leave my wife."

Gwenaseth hurried to the bed. She lifted up Rhiannon's shift and examined Rhiannon gently. Maelgwn swallowed as he saw the bloody bedcovers at the juncture of Rhiannon's legs. The memory of Aurora hemorrhaging to death in childbed filled his thoughts.

He shuddered. "She bleeds. This is the end, isn't it?"

"Aye. It will not be long now. I can see the babe's head."

Maelgwn swayed on his feet, and his throat filled with grief. How could Gwenaseth be so calm? Rhiannon was dying and all Gwenaseth thought of was the babe. He could not bear it. How was he to live without Rhiannon? She was not merely his love, his wife—she was part of his soul.

He knelt down by the bed again, his face near Rhiannon's. He reached out and stroked her damp brow, and her eyes opened. "It's time," she said softly. "I'm ready to push." A slight smile touched her lips. "Your son is being born."

Maelgwn tried to nod. His vision swam with tears. How brave she was. Like Gwenaseth, she thought only of the child. But he, he was selfish. If this child cost him Rhiannon, he would never love it.

Rhiannon's features tightened with pain. She gasped. Maelgwn stood up abruptly. He untangled Rhiannon's hand from the bedcovers and clasped it in his own. "Hold on to me," he whispered. "I will not let you go."

Rhiannon cried out, once, twice. Then she began to pant heavily. From the end of the bed, Gwenaseth spoke words of encouragement. Seconds passed. Maelgwn felt the beating of his own heart, then the pulse in Rhiannon's wrist. The two rhythms seemed to merge. Maelgwn willed his strength to flow into Rhiannon, his blood to replace that which she lost. Another spasm racked Rhiannon. For a moment, Maelgwn had the sensation of urgent pressure mingled with pain. He found himself breathing in time to Rhiannon.

Five, six times, the wave of pain rose and fell. Another cry, almost a shout, issued from Rhiannon's lips. Maelgwn watched her in awe. Rhiannon no longer looked like his gentle, delicate wife. Her features were grim, her eyes slitted with intensity. The muscles in her neck and shoulders stood out like ropes, while her hair burned in a wild flame around her face. She looked savage, powerful. He watched her take a deep breath and let out a blood-chilling scream.

The sound seemed to make his heart stop, and the room darkened. Maelgwn fought for control. He gripped Rhiannon's hand more tightly and leaned over her, calling her name. She fell back against the sheepskins. Her eyes closed; her face was pale with exhaustion.

"Rhiannon," he begged. "Rhiannon, don't leave me."

His desperate plea was interrupted by a harsh, squeezing cry from the other end of the bed. Maelgwn turned at the strangeness of the sound. He saw that Gwenaseth held something very red and squashed-looking. It did not seem possible the thing could be alive, but it flailed its tiny arms and legs with obvious energy and a kind of frustrated fury. That was the sound it made—of anger, and impatience.

"It's a boy," Gwenaseth exulted. "You have a son!"

Maelgwn shook his head. All that mattered was Rhiannon. He turned back to her, appalled that he had forgotten his wife for even a second.

To his surprise, her eyes were open, her face weary but no longer so sickly looking. She watched Gwenaseth and the baby with a dazed, tender expression. Her parched lips moved. "A son, Maelgwn. We have a son."

* * *

His body felt liquid, melting into the chair beneath him. The sight of his son suckling at his wife's milk-engorged breast sent tremors of rapture through every inch of Maelgwn's body. Was ever there a vision as beautiful as this? Rhiannon had never looked so exquisite. Her eyes shone a misty purple in the flickering rushlight, and her skin gleamed translucent, as pale as the creamy milk that trickled down her breast.

The babe turned from the nipple and gave a soft, contented sigh. Maelgwn felt his breath catch at the sight, and he knew tears glittered in his eyes. He shook his head. His son was making him act a fool, and he had been enough of one already. What a dolt he had been to think Rhiannon was dying. In his panic, he had confused Rhiannon's exhaustion for impending death, the normal birth fluids for a life-threatening flow of blood. Thank the Christian saints, Gwenaseth had ascribed his strange behavior to awe and amazement rather than the stark terror it really was. If she guessed what really had gone through his mind, the acceptance of men in the birthing chamber would have been set back at least a hundred years.

The fire crackled and hissed in the hearth behind him. Arianhrodd moved silently, tending it. She had arrived a short time after the babe was born. Unlike the other women, she showed no shock at finding him in the birth chamber. It was well and fitting, she said, that he witness his wife's travail first-hand. Now he would never doubt that a woman's strength and courage could be as great as a man's.

Nay, Maelgwn decided, he would certainly never doubt such a thing.

"He sleeps." Rhiannon's voice interrupted his thoughts. "It might be a good time to introduce Rhun to his new brother." A smile touched her lips. "Now—when Bridei is not howling loud enough to deafen everyone in the room."

"He's certainly a noisy one." Maelgwn rose and walked toward the door. "For all his smallness, there is nothing amiss with my son's lungs."

Most of Degannwy was waiting in the hall when Maelgwn entered. They gave a rousing cheer as they saw him and gathered around eagerly.

He gestured for silence. "The queen has been safely delivered of a healthy son," he announced. "We have named him Bridei."

The cheers erupted again. Maelgwn savored them briefly, then his eyes searched the crowd for the golden sheen of Rhun's hair. He spied the boy next to Sewan and Balyn. For a moment, Balyn's eyes caught his, and the old affection flowed between them, unspoiled and strong as ever.

Maelgwn gestured for Rhun to come forward. Rhun's small face was jubilant. His expression of pleasure deepened as he approached his father.

Laying his hand on Rhun's shoulder, Maelgwn again gestured for silence. "Rhun has a brother now, but that does not diminish his place in my heart." He gazed at the boy fondly, then continued. "I mean to raise my sons as friends and companions. Someday when I am gone, I vow they will rule my kingdom side by side." There was another chorus of cheers, and the men pounded on the heavy oaken tables. Maelgwn let a smile break free before turning and leading Rhun from the hall.

"Lady Gwenaseth told me that he will sleep and eat all the time at first. I must not be disappointed he can't play with me. I must be very quiet and gentle and hold him as I would a small and helpless puppy. But if I am patient, she said, someday he will grow up and play with me and look up to me as his big brother. I think I will like that part the best. I've always wanted a brother. Dogs are nice, but they don't talk to you. A brother will talk to me, maybe someday he can share my pallet, and we can sleep together in the barracks. . ."

Rhun prattled on, making Maelgwn smile so hard his jaw ached. His chest ached, too, filled with the same exhilarating sweetness that settled there the first time he held Bridei in his arms.

"Hush now," he told Rhun as they entered the antechamber. "We don't want to wake your brother. I'll warn you, he can make a fearsome racket."

Rhun nodded and clamped his mouth shut.

The room was quiet as they entered. They neared the bed, and Maelgwn saw Rhiannon gazing silently down at the baby in her arms. Rhun hesitated. Maelgwn grasped the boy's shoulder and pulled him forward.

Rhiannon watched her husband and stepson approach the bed. She was tired and sore everywhere, but her physical discomfort seemed a paltry thing compared to the joy that filled her. Her soul soared as if it flew with the eagles above Degannwy.

"Come, Rhun," she coaxed. "Say hello to your brother." The boy stepped forward. His lower lip caught in his teeth in an expression of uncertainty. He reached out a slim hand, grimy and scarred from the adventures of boyhood. Gingerly, he took the baby's tiny fingers in his own.

"Gwenaseth was right," he said. "He's very small. I think even Belga's puppies were born bigger."

Rhun looked up. His blue eyes, shot with wonder, reminded Rhiannon immediately of her husband. She laughed and sought Maelgwn's gaze, drowning herself in the compelling blue.

"This is a dream come true," Maelgwn said, moving closer. "I have waited all my life for this."

Rhiannon shook her head. Tears made her vision blur. "Oh, Maelgwn—the dream has only begun."

Dear Readers,

The writer of a romance based on historical characters must find a balance between the pitiless facts and the reader's need for a happy ending. While *Dragon of the Island,* the first book in the Dragon trilogy, evokes the historical Maelgwn the Great's ruthless reputation and military successes, it does not deal with the other aspects of his life recorded by the chroniclers of his time, and I realized that my sequel must weave some of those more awkward details into my story.

Most challenging was a need to explain why, at the height of his power, Maelgwn the Great chose to renounce his kingdom and retreat to a monastery for several years. (He later changed his mind and returned to being a formidable warlord.) What, I wondered, could make a man such as I had created, do such a thing? Sadly, I realized the only explanation I could write. Aurora, the beloved heroine of my first book, must die. Only the terrible grief her death would cause him could explain Maelgwn's utter defeat and despair.

It is not easy to kill a character of your own creation, let alone one who is as appealing and moving as Aurora. In a sense, I did not kill her. She dies between books, thus sparing me the trauma of having to write her death scene. Yet my grief for Aurora is real, and it fuels Maelgwn's bone-deep anguish and loss.

The Celts believed that death was only another dimension of life and not to be feared, and I have explored that philosophy in depth in this story. Aurora continues to touch the lives of those who knew her and to reach out, even to Rhiannon, the woman who takes her place in Maelgwn's life. Aurora lives on, immortal to those who loved her, as we all are.

As Maelgwn comes to realize that Aurora's death is not the end, I hope readers will too. Rhiannon's story is as important as Aurora's was, and in a sense, a more inspiring one. Rhiannon must triumph over not only misunderstanding, jealousy and treachery, but the soul-scarring effects of abuse and degradation. Although not a traditional one, she is a *true* heroine as she grows from a victimized child-woman to a powerful, dynamic woman-goddess who chooses her own destiny.

If you are still disturbed by Aurora's death, I apologize. Her death is simply that aspect of reality that I cannot deny, even when writing a romance. My life journey has convinced me that the Celts were right—death is a part of life, and we can take comfort in the knowledge that *love* transcends death, time and all realities.

Happy reading,

Mary Gillgannon

P.S. I always enjoy hearing from readers. Please write me at:

P.O Box 2052
Cheyenne, WY 82001

A S.A.S.E. is appreciated.

If you liked this book, be sure to look for others in the *Denise Little Presents* line:

PUT SOME FANTASY IN YOUR LIFE—
FANTASTIC ROMANCES FROM PINNACLE

TIME STORM (728, $4.99)

by Rosalyn Alsobrook

Modern-day Pennsylvanian physician JoAnn Griffin only believed what she could feel with her five senses. But when, during a freak storm, a blinding flash of lightning sent her back in time to 1889, JoAnn realized she had somehow crossed the threshold into another century and was now gazing into the smoldering eyes of a startlingly handsome stranger. JoAnn had stumbled through a rip in time . . . and into a love affair so intense, it carried her to a point of no return!

SEA TREASURE (790, $4.50)

by Johanna Hailey

When Michael, a dashing sea captain, is rescued from drowning by a beautiful sea siren—he does not know yet that she's actually a mermaid. But her breathtaking beauty stirred irresistible yearnings in Michael. And soon fate would drive them across the treacherous Caribbean, tossing them on surging tides of passion that transcended two worlds!

ONCE UPON FOREVER (883, $4.99)

by Becky Lee Weyrich

A moonstone necklace and a mysterious diary written over a century ago were Clair Summerland's only clued to her true identity. Two men loved her— one, a dashing civil war hero . . . the other, a daring jet pilot. Now Clair must risk her past and future for a passion that spans two worlds—and a love that is stronger than time itself.

SHADOWS IN TIME (892, $4.50)

by Cherlyn Jac

Driving through the sultry New Orleans night, one moment Tori's car spins our of control; the next she is in a horse-drawn carriage with the handsomest man she has ever seen—who calls her wife—but whose eyes blaze with fury. Sent back in time one hundred years, Tori is falling in love with the man she is apparently trying to kill. Now she must race against time to change the tragic past and claim her future with the man she will love through all eternity!

Available wherever paperbacks are sold, or order direct from the Publisher. Send cover price plus 50¢ per copy for mailing and handling to Penguin USA, P.O. Box 999, c/o Dept. 17109, Bergenfield, NJ 07621. Residents of New York and Tennessee must include sales tax. DO NOT SEND CASH.